Time Benders and the Chase Through Time

Time Benders and the Chase Through Time

Book IV

JB Yanni

JB Yanni Press

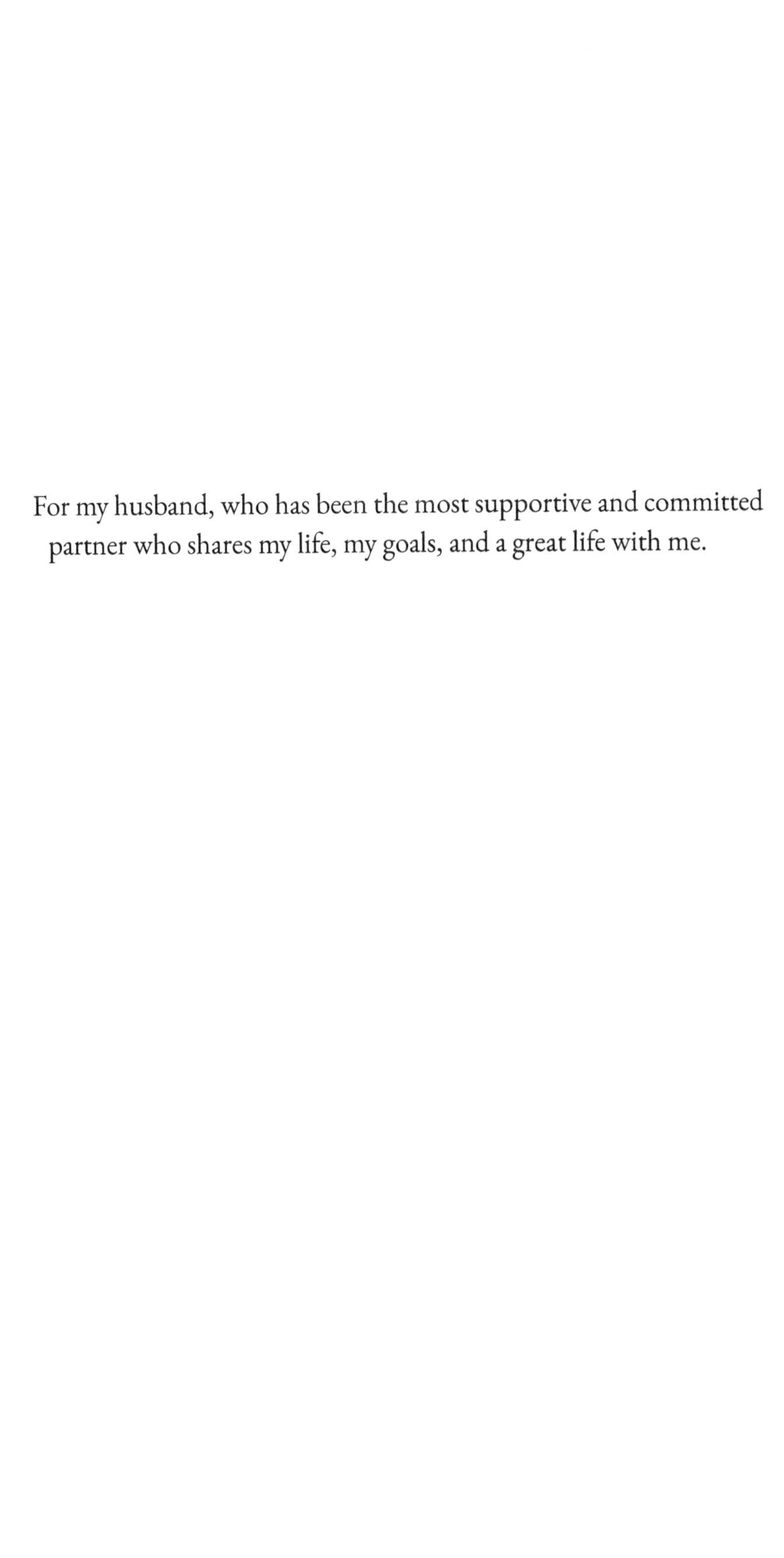

For my husband, who has been the most supportive and committed partner who shares my life, my goals, and a great life with me.

Ken sat in shock for a moment. "What do you mean, the machine is gone, Mr. Brewster?"

"I went into the barn and the machine was gone. So are some notes and folders that Joe left on the shelf by the machine. It appears someone took it all."

"Do you think someone moved it physically or started the machine up and went away with it?"

"I'm not certain. That's why I think it's important you all get here as soon as you can."

"I don't even know what to say about this. Let me think a minute." Ken closed his eyes and was quiet for a minute, then he said, "I will contact Joe immediately to see what he left there. Then I will contact Deb and everyone and we will do our best to get there as soon as we can."

"I will keep looking around the barn and please let me know as soon as you've checked with everyone and when I can expect you to be here."

"Sounds good. Talk to you soon, Mr. Brewster."

Ken immediately dialed Joe and got him on the phone as he was working away at MIT. He explained what was going on, although the information was brief. Joe said he would let his research buddies know he was taking off for a visit with his family and not reveal anything. He hung up and called Becky, who was at home for the summer. He packed up a few things and headed out to pick her up and get to Mr. Brewster's as soon as possible. While that was going on, Ken called Mary back and told her what was going on. She was a little shaken up, but they decided she would stay at home while Ken went to Mr. Brewster's. She and her mother had planned to do some dress shopping for their wedding, but asked that Ken keep in touch with her. Then he called Deb and told her what was going on. She was set to fly home from an archeological dig on a summer internship with a professor for a brief break, but not for a week. Ken woke her up as it was the middle of the night in the middle east. She said she would see if she could change her flight and get there sooner and asked that Ken call Ryan for her.

"Hello," Ryan replied as he answered the phone at his parents' house in New York.

"Hey Ryan, it's Ken. Hope I didn't disturb you, but I have some bad news."

"Is Deb ok?"

"It's not Deb, sorry, I didn't mean to worry you. No, Mr. Brewster called me a few minutes ago and apparently the machine and lots of the papers that Joe had are missing from the barn."

"Oh, my gosh! Do you think it was stolen?"

"It looks that way. We are all getting organized to go over there. Joe was on his way to grab Becky, and I talked to Deb. She asked me to call you. She's trying to re-arrange her flight right now."

"I was planning to pick her up on Sunday when she arrived. Do you know what she's doing?"

"She's trying to catch an earlier flight, like tomorrow. She said she would call you as soon as she finished with the travel agent."

"Ok. I'll wait for her call and be there to get her, and then we can head out of the city and get there as soon as we can."

"That's the plan, Deb, and I talked about it, too. Just let me know what the fight she ends up on."

"Should I call you at work or what?"

"No, call Mr. Brewster when you know something. I'm leaving work as soon as we're done and packing up some things and heading out my-self. I will call to make some hotel reservations for all of us and then I'm heading out."

"Are you picking Mary up too?"

"No, she's staying her. She and her mother have appointments for dress shopping this weekend and I told her to go ahead with that until we know more."

"Ok, so I will call Mr. Brewster when I hear from Deb. See you soon."

"Yeah, bye."

Ryan waited by the phone and told his parents he was heading out to meet up with old classmates after he picked up Deb. She called about twenty minutes later.

"Hello," Ryan answered.

"Hey Ryan, did you talk to Ken?"

"Yep, I did. Was waiting for your call. Sorry you had to be woken up over there."

"It's ok. I don't sleep too great here. They say they have air conditioning in this boarding house, but it sure doesn't feel like it."

"Maybe it's the weeks out in the desert that have you just really warmed up."

"Probably has something to do with it. Anyway, I got my flight changed and I am packing up now. I have to head to the airport soon as they got me moved to a four in the morning flight. Have a short fueling layover in London, then on to LaGuardia."

"Ok, so what is the flight information so I can be sure to be there for you, baby?"

"It's American flight 2109. It leaves here at four ten and arrives in New York at nine-forty-eight."

"What time is it there right now? I forget the difference."

"It's just after one in the morning here."

"Oh, yeah. How are you getting to the airport?"

"Professor Reinhardt called me a car service when I told him I had a family emergency."

"Good, I don't want you trying to hail a cab in the middle of the night."

"Oh, aren't you the worrier!"

"You're kind of important to me. I don't want anything to happen to you."

"Love you too."

"See you soon, baby."

Deb hung up and finished packing everything up. She went downstairs and got the car service to the airport. While all that was going on, Ken was packing at the New York apartment, thankful he didn't have to explain this to Aunt Alicia and Darrick. They were away for a long weekend that had extended into a week or more. He finished packing, made hotel reservations, talked to Joe one more time and left. Joe, meanwhile, had packed, left MIT, and called Ken while he waited for Becky to finish packing. They had contrived a story about Ken wanting to get everyone together to do the wedding planning, and visiting with old classmates for Becky's parents. They left for their much shorter drive to Mr. Brewster's house.

Kim, now a junior in high school, did not know what was going on, when she needed a bit of help on the latest science material for finals, which were next week. She packed it all up in her bag after finishing her other homework and walked across campus to Mr. Brewster's house. Knocking on his front door and when he answered, she started with an apology.

"Mr. Brewster, I'm really sorry to just come over, but I was hoping you could help me with some of my science work. I know you're not my teacher this semester, but I kind of need help to understand this chemistry."

"Kim, I would be glad to help you. Did you know everyone is on their way here?"

"Really? Why are they all coming here? You meant Ken and Joe and Deb? I thought Deb was still on the archeological dig."

"She was intending to start her way home at some point in the next few days, according to Ken, for a two-week visit with all of you. Since you have only one week left."

"That's what I was needing help with. I really can't get through some of this studying for the final next week. Thankfully, it's my first test, but since it's the first, I'm all stressed over it. Why are they coming over here now?"

"Well, I went into the barn today after my classes ended to finish tinkering with that car. It was going to be a gift for you, my dear."

Kim grinned at him. "For me? What for?"

"Your birthday that's coming up. You're going to be driving soon and I know how you loved that old mustang and I wanted to give it to you."

"You have been such a prominent part of our family since we arrived here! That really is too much though, Mr. Brewster."

"Well, you all brought such light into my life and I think of you all as dear members of my family. And I remember a year ago when you were really struggling over not having anything special to claim yet. I thought this might help you see you were reaching the point where you could do all the things your siblings were doing."

"So, what happened in the barn? I didn't mean to interrupt you."

"The machine is gone, and so are many of Joe's papers. I called Ken and they are all on their way, so we can try to figure this all out. However, they aren't due for at least an hour. How about we sit at the kitchen table and look over your notes and study issues?"

"The machine is gone? What do you think happened? Did someone take off in it or just take it, do you think?"

"Well, given the mess strewn all over the barn, I think it was activated and taken somewhere."

"That's going to really mess things up. Remember the mess we made when we went back to Philadelphia before the Civil War? We changed everything about the Civil War, and the civil rights history doing that. Imagine what someone could do that doesn't care about this?"

"Exactly. That's why I called Ken and sounded the alarm. Let's sit down and see if we can use this time for your studies before they arrive and we all gather to discuss this?"

Kim agreed, and they went to his kitchen table and went over chemistry notes and the book she brought. They were deep into it when the doorbell rang again. Joe and Becky had arrived.

"It's so good to see you both!" Mr. Brewster said as he opened the door.

Joe and Becky said together, "It's good to see you too, Mr. Brewster!"

They went into the kitchen, where Joe and Becky greeted Kim. Mr. Brewster asked if they had eaten dinner yet, and when Becky responded they hadn't, he began rummaging through the kitchen to prepare some food.

"When is Ken due to arrive?" Joe asked.

"He called just before he left New York almost two hours ago," Mr. Brewster replied.

"Can I help you with anything?" Becky asked.

"That would be wonderful. Can you peel and cut up these potatoes while I prepare this chicken?" Mr. Brewster said.

The two of them worked to prepare dinner and Joe sat down at the table with Kim. "What are you working on?" Joe asked as he sat down.

"Studying for Chemistry final," Kim groaned.

"Well, you are sitting in the science teacher's house. That ought to be a big help!"

"That's why I'm here. I came over for some help, and Mr. Brewster told me what was going on and that you and Ken were on your way."

"Need more help?"

"Yes, I can't figure this reaction theory out!"

"Let me see the book for a minute."

Kim slid the book across the table to Joe and then she slumped down in her chair, crossing her arms. Joe grinned at her frustrated stance as he looked over the book's explanations. A few minutes later, he set the book down and moved to a chair closer to Kim. He pulled out a piece of paper from her folder and grabbed the pencil. As Becky and Mr. Brewster finished preparing dinner, Joe drew and went over details with Kim to help her grasp the concepts of chemical reactions. By the time the chicken and mashed potatoes were ready, Kim finally understood the reaction theory section. Joe cleared up her papers and books and set them in the living room while Kim set the table. The four of them set down and enjoyed a nice meal, catching up on all the doings that spring with classes and Choate activities. Toward the end of the meal, Joe and Mr. Brewster discussed the issue at hand. As that discussion began, the doorbell rang, and Mr. Brewster welcomed Ken. They returned to the kitchen, where Joe asked, "How was the drive? Hope you ate, cause we seemed to have finished all of Mr. Brewster's fine chicken and potatoes."

"I ate. Before I left the apartment, I grabbed a sandwich and a Pepsi. I'm good. It's good to see you all!"

Ken went around and hugged everyone and told Kim she had to have grown more than a few inches since Easter. The girls offered to clean up the kitchen, suggesting that Mr. Brewster, Ken, and Joe head to the barn. They agreed. With the kitchen cleaned up, the two girls joined them in the barn.

"Did you find anything?" Kim asked as they entered the barn.

Ken looked up from behind a shelving unit where he was picking up papers that had flown all over the barn. "Nothing but the mess left by what we now know was the machine leaving the barn."

"How can you be sure?" Becky asked.

"There are some notes scratched on a small scrap of paper that Ken found that show coordinates that none of us recognize from the trips already made," Mr. Brewster replied.

"If you give them to me, I can go now to the library and look them up, since I have to get back to the dorm now. I can come over here after class tomorrow if you want," Kim said, taking the scrap of paper that Mr. Brewster held out.

"That would be great! How about I come over around your lunch time and grab whatever you learned though?" Ken said as he approached the big work table with another pile of papers.

"Sure, I get done around eleven with class. Can you meet me outside the math and science building?"

"Sure. Do you need me to walk you down to the library?"

"Kenny, I know you think I'm your baby sister, but honestly, I am a junior in high school, remember!"

"Sorry, I'm trying not to treat you like a baby, but you know, you'll always be my baby sister!" Ken said as he picked Kim up and swung her around.

"Does that mean he doesn't know about your prom date?" Becky asked, laughing.

"What prom date?" Ken said as he set Kim down.

"I went to prom, ok. Becky came over and took me shopping since Deb's gone and Aunt Alicia was busy. But we went to the store Aunt Alicia had arranged for us and we had so much fun trying on dresses!" Kim explained.

"Great about the dress, but darling Kimberly, who was your date?" Ken asked as sternly as he could, while smiling at her.

"His name is Jake, and we have been seeing each other for about two months now. And, furthermore, Kenneth, I told you about him when he first asked me to walk into town for ice cream. This shouldn't be a surprise. I told Aunt Alicia about him and Uncle Darrick has met him," Kim answered with her hands on her hips.

"Ok, ok, I know you went to prom. I felt terrible I couldn't get out here to take pictures and all, but I know Uncle Darrick was here and that Becky helped you. I'm just razing you a little bit. It's hard to imagine my little sister going to prom, that's all."

"Hey, I found something!" Joe yelled from behind a stack of boxes and several tools.

"What?" Becky said, as she walked toward the sound of his voice, since he had not yet materialized.

By the time Becky got there, Joe emerged from the dark corner. He was holding two things in his hand. When he got to the table and into the light, they could see it was an old picture and a small notebook. Inside the notebook were several other pictures and papers folded into the pages. Joe looked at the first picture and then put it down on the table in front of the others, saying, "I don't think I recognize the little boy or the older guy in this picture."

The others looked and agreed until Kim picked the picture up. "Hey, Joe, isn't this that kid on your dorm floor here that was always giving you trouble? Wasn't he always picking on you and didn't he really try to make it difficult when you went to do that very first presentation on your computer?" She asked.

Just as Joe picked up the notebook, one picture fell out, and it was a picture of the dorm floor of boys standing outside the dorm the year Joe was a sophomore. Kim came around to Joe's side of the table and put the two pictures next to each other on the table. She pointed to the kid in the picture of all the boys and said, "That's him. Wasn't his name Tom Thorton?"

They all looked and agreed. The small boy in the picture was a younger Tom Thorton. At that point, Kim said she had to go. She thanked Mr. Brewster for his help and dinner, and he walked her inside to get her books. When he returned, Ken, Joe and Becky were combing through the small notebook.

"Did you find anything?" Mr. Brewster asked as he approached the table.

"Yeah, it looks like this guy was obsessed with Joe. He has all kinds of newspaper clippings in here about the computer, and pictures of Joe around campus when they were attending here," Ken replied.

"It's creepy to think of him following us around. He has pictures of Joe and I when we were heading over here for the trip to Philadelphia," Becky said, with a sick look on her face.

"Do you think he followed you and saw the machine? Maybe that's why he took it?" Ken postured.

"Wow, look at this!" Joe said as he had turned to the last few pages of the notebook. On it were scrawled repeatedly, eight or nine pages of 'I hate you, Joe Fitzgerald!' When Becky turned the page as she was counting, they discovered the last ten pages were scrawled with 'I will get you, Joe Fitzgerald!' The four of them sat for a moment, each contemplating the anger and intensity of Tom's feelings expressed on the pages of this small notebook. With the deep scrawled letters, spelling out his hate.

"So, I guess we can assume that Tom figured out what the machine was about and took it to get back at you, Joe," Becky finally broke the silence by saying.

"Do you think the coordinates that Kim has might be where he's gone?" Ken asked.

"There are some other notes in this notebook and I found a bunch of torn up parts of pages that might have some clues," Joe pondered. "We should probably go through this notebook and try to piece together the pages that he probably tore up to see if we have any clues about what he might be up to."

"Good idea. I'll go get some tape from inside. Why don't you three try to piece the torn paper together on the table?" Mr. Brewster said as he got off the bench and headed to the barn door.

The four of them spent another hour piecing together the scraps of paper. They had three pages taped together when Mr. Brewster announced he might need to be done for the night. They agreed to meet the next morning at the barn while Mr. Brewster was teaching classes and try to finish piecing pages together and see what they could learn. Ken, Joe and Becky left for the hotel, but no one got any rest contemplating what Tom might be doing. Joe and Ken talked late into the night and Becky tossed and turned, thinking about all the times that Tom must have been following them and how creepy it was to think about being watched.

The next morning, Joe called Becky's room and found her already dressed and ready to go. They got some breakfast at the hotel restaurant and then headed over to Mr. Brewster's house. When they had sat down at that now familiar work table, Joe set the notebook down on the table and looked at both of them as he said, "Tom appears to have written in this notebook the fall we all arrived here at Choate. His hatred of me is palpable from the very beginning. I guess he was good friends with Dave, who ended up being my best friend here. We're still in touch, in fact. That was the start for Tom. Then it got to what I'd call the obsessive state when Aunt Alicia and Uncle Darrick showed up the second year with us. He talks for pages about the car Ken was driving and the limousine. It hit a crescendo the year the computers came out."

"Did you have any sense of this when we were students here?" Becky asked.

"Not really. I mean there were times when he was very aggressive in field games, and he always seemed to have a foul look on his face, he bugged me a lot at the dorm by moving things and trying to take papers and stuff from my room under the guise of trying to stay friends with Dave. That's what Kim referred to as his bugging me. But it never escalated to the point of a fistfight or anything, and he never said or did anything to me other than that."

"I remember he spent most of the year of physics trying to one up you. It usually backfired on him, but I remember him raising his hand to answer questions, and then when called on he did not know or totally didn't answer correctly," Becky remembered.

"Ok, so this guy spent the last six years hating you. What made him snap now, Joe?" Ken asked.

"I'm not sure. There's an article here about the project at MIT this spring that's drawing some news attention. But where that clipping is in the notebook, all he talks about is that he's going to get me and all the Fitzgerald's for what we did to him. There doesn't seem to be any real connection," Joe replied.

"What did you do to him?" Becky asked, knowing full well there wasn't anything.

"Aside from developing that friendship with Dave, I don't know."

"I don't even remember him. It was strange looking at that picture you all took of your floor the year you started rooming with Dave. He looks downright sinister in this picture," Ken added.

"Yeah, like maybe I or we didn't do anything to him, he might have just associated us with something that was eating away at him and eventually made us and me the target," Joe thought out loud.

"Maybe we should start focusing on trying to figure out what he's up to. I mean, he's been gone for over twenty-four hours for sure, and we have no idea where and when he went," Becky said, trying to focus them on a solution.

"He rambles in this notebook about his great grandfather having some invention that he's certain our family stole, and how he wants all the money he's sure we have. I think we should start there," Joe offered.

"I think that's the best place. So do we know who his great grandfather is?" Ken asked.

"On the back of this picture are some faint names. I wonder if we can figure it out from this picture. It must be Tom here in the picture, so this must be the great grandfather he's referring to," Becky said as she peered at the back of the picture.

Ken got up from the table and rummaged on a shelf. He came back carrying a magnifying glass. After wiping it with a towel he found on the shelf with it, he handed it to Becky. She looked at the writing for a minute and then got up with the picture and magnifying glass and went toward the open door of the barn. She called them after a minute, "I think it says grandpa Reggie. One of you come look, please."

Joe came over and agreed. Becky suggested she go down to the library and see what she could find on a Reginald Thorton. Ken then thought out loud, "How can we use what we find on this guy and, hopefully, the coordinates to trace back where he is? Joe," he looked up, "Is there any way we can use that spectrograph or whatever we used when you went to Philadelphia to see anything?"

Joe came back to the table and said, "Well, I'm not sure, but I think something we were working on with the project at MIT might kind of apply here. It that might allow us to trace something. Becky, head to the library and Ken and I will ponder this."

2 |

A week ago, as Tom sat in his little shed behind his mother's house contemplating how to get Joe and all the Fitzgerald's, he remembered something and started tearing through all his notes of the all wrongs they had done him. He smiled when he found it. It was a small note from their senior year at Choate. He had followed Becky as she went into town and went to a costume store and then he followed her as she met Joe, looking all smug. They went across campus to Mr. Brewster's, that awful science teacher, house. They went into the barn. Tom tried to get close to the window, but he was afraid they would see him, so he just left, meaning to go back and see what they had been up to.

As Tom sat there, he wondered if whatever they had been doing was still in that barn. Come to think of it, he always saw those Fitzgerald's going toward that place. He was going to go check it out. Even though Joe was no longer at Choate, there might be some clue how he could get them.

The next day, he drove from his mother's house in the less wealthy end of Boston to Choate. As he drove, he thought about all the wrongs done to him. How his father used to drink and hit him and his mother. How he walked out when Tom was eleven years old, never to return. Tom went to Choate, but he went on a scholarship from his mother's church. Not like the Fitzgerald's that had all kinds of money. No, Tom had to claw his way to that elite school. Those Fitzgerald just walked up, in the middle of a term ad took over. They probably got all kinds of money from their parent's dying. In fact, Tom was sure they probably have been stealing business for generations. They probably were part of the effort to take Grandpa Reggie's invention! Why wouldn't that be the case? Tom thought.

When Tom got to Mr. Brewster's house, he parked down the street and then crept up to the barn. He knew that Mr. Brewster was teaching a class, but he needed to make sure there was no one else around. When he was fairly certain there was no one, he opened the barn door and quickly went inside and closed it behind him. He turned from closing the door and saw the thing in the middle of the barn. Walking around a big wooden table with stools around it, he approached the large metal thing that had a door, like one found on a navy ship. Peering into the round portal window in the door, he saw the seats and what appeared to be controls. He tried the handle, and the door opened. He went inside and determined there were four chairs with cross body harness or belts on them to hold someone in, and the console had screens and some lights and knobs and some sort of dial to enter numbers. Nothing he saw gave him any idea what Mr. Brewster was up to, or if Joe was involved in this. He stepped out of the machine and started looking around on the shelves that were on the side of the machine. Excitedly, he found a binder with Joe's handwriting on the cover. He took it over to the table and started reading. He looked up a few minutes later and said out loud, "There's no way he created a time machine!" After a minute more, he looked up and smiled, an evil kind of smile.

Tom kept reading and then he took the binder into the machine and started playing with the screens and knobs and turned it on. He saw the entry was for coordinates, like longitude and latitude. He turned things off and then he took the binder and left to go home. On the drive home, Tom smiled at the idea that had come to him. He would get those Fitzgerald's and all their friends. With a plan forming, he was going to use this machine to right the terrible wrong in his life and make sure he had the money, and not them. He was going to go back and help Grandpa Reggie. Then, after he had all the money he would ever need, he was going to come back here and make sure Joe Fitzgerald was the laughingstock of all the news and media. He had been the darling and now Tom could change that. Tom would be the one that would invent the computer. All he had to do was use that time machine to go to where Joe was figuring out the computer and steal all of his notes. Then he, Tom, would go back in the time machine a year before Joe presented his ideas and Tom would present it all before Joe could. Tom would get all the money and recognition, and all the bad things that had ever happened to him would fade away. No more would he be teased and harassed because he was a scholarship kid. He wouldn't be that lanky kid on the playground, or have to hide bruises on his arms and legs from the beatings his father gave him.

The next day in his shed, Tom started to plan. He would have to get a lot of money first. Grandpa Reggie said that if he had more money, he could have fought Henry Ford and he would have won the patent fight and he would be rich. Where would Tom get that kind of money? He started rummaging through the books he had checked out of the library that morning when one caught his eye. It was a history book from the turn of the century through the great depression. Tom started reading about the stock market crash, and it was then that he knew he had a solution. He would go back to New York a week before the crash and make all kinds of money because he knew exactly what was going to happen over that three-day period. Quickly pulling out a new notebook, he started jotting notes of the events of the week of the crash and the week leading up to it. He would go back to that time in Joe's silly machine and get all the money he needed. Then he would go further back and give all the money to Grandpa Reggie and help him beat Henry Ford. Then he would come back to Choate, before Joe even showed up and he would invent that silly computer and he would be on the news and get all kinds of offers from colleges. He wouldn't have to worry about not being able to pay for college anymore. They would come to him with scholarships and offers. He would leave Joe in the dust.

Tom went inside at the end of the day and asked his mother where the old family photo albums were. She asked why he wanted them and he said he had been thinking about Grandpa Reggie and just wanted to look at them. As she went and got them, she complained the whole time about Tom not having a job yet, and spending all day in the shed. She turned before she went to her bedroom and said, "You're turning out just like your father!"

He looked up at her as she turned to open her door and he smirked. He would show her too. Tom didn't care. Truthfully, what his mother said hurt. After all the times he got between her and his dad and prevented her from getting beat up, he knew he was about to change everything. He also decided he wouldn't share any of his good fortune with either his father or his mother. He stomped back to his shed and went over the pictures. As he finished up that night, he lay in bed thinking about how it had to be the Fitzgerald's and all their goody two shoe boyfriends and girlfriends that made his life so terrible. He would have his revenge. Joe's little barn surprises would give him the way.

A few days later, Tom was ready. He had the old coins his Grandpa Reggie had given him, and he had figured out coordinates for where he was going. Knowing he couldn't just land this machine in time square, he had to find a better place. But he also knew the train from White Plains, New York, had been in place since before the crash. He told his mother he was leaving for a few days to find a job in Virginia. After he drove to the barn and set everything up on the machine, he decided not to take his notebook, but on the off chance that Joe showed up, he didn't want him finding out what he was up to. He tore out several pages and ripped them into pieces, then he hid the notebook behind some car parts on the shelves. This was easy, he thought. Why would Joe just show up here, anyway? He got into the machine and started it up. He wondered what the costumes were for as he heard the noise starting. At the last minute, he sat down and tried to get the straps on. He got thrown across the inside of the machine and hit his head. When he opened his eyes, the machine had powered down and he peaked out the window. He was hidden in some wooded area, as he hoped he would be. He stepped outside the machine and walked out of the woods. When he got to the road, he saw a carriage go by. The people were dressed funny. That's when he realized why Becky needed costumes. He hurried along the road to the first shop he came to and bought a new suit with the money he had. Then he bought a ticket on the train from White Plains to New York city. The problem for him, he realized too late, was that he didn't have a large amount of money. He would have to do a little trading right away to have the funds to live while he really made his fortune here. He counted out what he had left and made his plans.

When he arrived in New York city, he exited the train station and headed toward Wall Street. He found a savings and loan building across the street from the early stock market and he went inside. A man approached him and asked if he could be of assistance. Tom explained he had just come to town from upstate New York, and he needed to put the money he had on deposit. Adding that he needed some credit to do some shopping and open a trading account. The man sat Tom down and opened an account, extended him credit and referred him to a building two doors down to open the trading account. Joe went down the street and met with the man at that office and opened a trading account. He was ready. He asked about a hotel nearby and the man at the brokerage house referred him to the Waldorf. Tom went to the address he had been given and checked into the hotel. He asked for assistance getting some clothing and they made him an appointment the next morning at the men's store across the street from the hotel. This was too easy! Tom thought all these trusting people from the nineteen twenties were easy to fool. He didn't need to spend hardly any of the money he brought. He liked this. People just assumed he was rich. That's how he wanted to be seen. This was going to be fun, he decided.

During the first few days, Tom made considerable amounts of money. Thrilled with how things were going, he also met all kinds of people. New wealthy people and some old money families. He got invited to parties and had lunch. This was how he was supposed to be living. Finally, he was in a better position than those Fitzgerald's.

3

Becky was busy looking at material on the combustion engine when Kim walked up and tapped her on the shoulder.

"Hey you, what are you doing back in our library?"

"I'm trying to figure out who Tom's great grandfather was. He wrote about how the Fitzgerald's messed his family up and I'm trying to find a connection. What are you doing here?"

"I've got a free hour before my next class and I needed to look up those coordinates. I got down here last night just as the library was closing, and promised Ken, so here I am."

"I wondered if you'd make it before the library closed, last night."

"Did you find anything?"

"I did in fact. What I found is that Tom's great grandfather might have invented a combustion engine before Henry Ford, and there might have been a little corporate espionage going on. But I can't find a connection to your family."

"Where was all this going on?"

"In Ohio, but there's also a reference to Tom's great grandfather being from a family with some wealth and influence from Rochester, New York."

"Why both places?" Kim asked.

"Well, I think some of the patent fight was centered in Ohio. See there was this organization formed to collect the fee for every combustion engine put in a car because of the patents. I think the patent battle started where this organization is, but I think Tom's great grandfather was in Rochester."

"Both my parent's families were in Massachusetts as far back as I can remember grandma telling me about. I don't see how any of my relatives would have been involved in the automobile inventions. And none of them were from either Ohio or Rochester."

"That's what I was thinking. Joe has told me that your father's family has a long history of pastors and farmers, so it can't be those guys. I didn't know your mom's family was from that same area."

"Mostly newspaper people and teachers in her family. During the Civil War there were some surgeons and doctors, but nothing related to innovations until Dad."

"Ok, well I'll wrap up these notes anyway, while you look up your coordinates."

"What are Joe and Ken up to?"

"They're trying to figure out a way to trace the energy signature or the residue of the energy the machine uses, I think."

"Necessity is the mother of all invention, isn't it? Isn't this somewhat close to the project Joe is working on at MIT this spring?"

"I think so, and Joe was kind of agreeing there might be a way to use what they're doing at MIT for this, when I left to come up here. I'll wait for you and walk to your meeting spot with Ken, if that's ok."

"Sure."

When Kim came back, she was joined by a young man Becky had never seen. Kim introduced Jake to Becky.

"It's nice to meet you," he said as Becky greeted him.

"I've heard some things about you, Jake, but Kim failed to mention how tall you are," Becky said laughing as she looked up, way up to Jake's face.

Jake smiled down at Kim as he laughed too, "Well, we hardly notice it so I guess we figured no one else would."

"Yeah, it's barely noticeable, really!" Becky said, laughing at how much taller Jake was than Kim.

They walked out of the library together with Becky quizzing Jake on everything she could think of, knowing Ken and Joe were curious. They found Ken and Joe standing by Ken's car at the appointed spot by the road to the cafeteria. Becky again did some introductions. Jake complemented Ken's car, and Ken smiled. They chatted for a few minutes about football, and basketball, which Jake had revealed he played. Kim handed Ken a piece of paper and said she and Jake were heading to the cafeteria but she would find them all later at Mr. Brewster's. As they walked off, Joe said, "He seems nice. What did you think Becky? It seems you had more time to find out about him."

"I did. He's funny and he really likes Kim, I can tell. I think he's ok."

"Well, we'll see," Ken said, watching them walk down the road.

"Relax, big brother, I'm sure you'll have some time this summer to interrogate him. I think he's coming out for her birthday celebration!"

"Great," he said shaking his head. Sometimes the burden of being the head of their little tribe of siblings and friends was hard. He always felt he had to watch out for them. Now that Joe was doing so well at MIT, Ken had concentrated his watchfulness on Deb traveling so far away and Kim. She was his youngest sister and the one he felt the most paternal for all his life.

"We came to see if you were done. We thought we'd head into town and get a burger or something," Joe said as he grabbed Becky's hand.

"Sounds good. Then we can go over what I learned," Becky said as she got into the car.

They got to the burger place, ordered and sat down. While they were waiting for the food, Becky told Joe and Ken about Reginald Thorton, who had invented a combustion engine that looked eerily like the one that Henry Ford said he invented. There was a patent court battle, that Henry Ford won on an appeal, and then Reginald disappears into obscurity. The food arrived and while they ate, they talked about the possibility that Tom just associated the Fitzgerald's with Fords and that in his obsessed state, replaced the two. No one could come up with a way the two families would have crossed paths. They looked at the coordinates and notes from Kim and then finished eating and headed back to the barn.

Becky laughed as she entered the barn as the big chalk board was pushed up to the table and there were all kinds of formula, figures and equations on the board. She asked what they had found and Joe suggested they figure out where on the map the coordinates were, as they seemed to be outside or what would have been historically outside, New York city.

"It looks like this is kind of in White Plains, New York," Becky said as she checked the map hanging near the old car that Mr. Brewster had almost fixed completely.

"Can we try to find the exact place of those coordinates?" Ken asked.

"If we have a globe with the longitude and latitude on it," Joe answered from the blackboard.

"I think there's one in the library, should I go there, and see?" Becky asked.

"Yeah, can you do that?" Ken asked.

"Sure, I will go check it out and come right back."

Becky left, and the two concentrated on the theory that Joe had come up with to trace the energy signature of the machine. About an hour later, Becky came back into the barn, but she had both Kim and Mr. Brewster in toe.

"Any progress?" Mr. Brewster asked.

"Well, I think we can use the spectrometer and this other device that I think we can build and attach it here to trace the energy of the machine. Plus, I have this idea about putting that data into the computer. I was thinking last night that there might be a way with the exit energy data and the coordinates to figure out the when part of the path of the machine," Joe detailed.

"I found Becky at the library and we looked up the coordinates in a few maps and found that it is a very large waste management plant now. I don't think the machine could land there without either notice or getting trashed," Kim said.

"Do you know when that management place came into existence, Kim?" Ken asked.

"It looks like it opened in nineteen sixty-five," Becky replied.

"So, we know he went to an earlier time than that," Mr. Brewster said.

"I was wondering, and couldn't find anything in the library to support this, but as concentrated as the notebook was on the issues with his grandfather, he has to be going somewhere to change that, right?" Becky asked the group.

"But wasn't his grandfather in Ohio?" Kim asked.

"Well, he might have been there for meetings and things, but that was where the association was located that billed each car manufacturer for the parts they used. I think all of the combustion engine work Reginald did was done near his family? I found some references that his fighting the patent battle estranged him from his family. That would mean the engine work happened near Rochester."

"How about some drinks and a snack before we ponder this more?" Mr. Brewster asked.

"Sounds good, I'm starving. Also, I need to check in with Mary, but I can help you get things ready Mr. Brewster," Ken said laughing.

The two left the barn and went to the house to make the call and gather some snacks. Joe detailed his theory for the program and spectrometer to Becky and Kim looked over the notebook. When they returned, Deb and Ryan were with them. After all the greetings, hugs and asking about the flight and dig, they sat down for the lemonade and cupcakes.

"What first? The notebook, the coordinates, the theories or the plans to track them?" Joe asked.

"How about we start with some logistics first to be sure we're all good? And Kim, isn't it just about your finals week? What can we do to help you or keep you on track while we do all this? Then, what about Becky's parents, our aunt and uncle and everyone we need to check in with? And finally, where's Mary?" Deb rattled off.

"I'll start, Mary stayed at home as she has appointments tomorrow for dress stuff. Uncle Darrick and Aunt Alicia are away until next weekend when you were originally expected back," Ken put out there.

"My parents think I'm with Joe out on Long Island. That was the plan when he was to finish up this week and I called them this morning and said Joe picked me up, so I'm good for two weeks," Becky added.

"I'm ready for all my finals but I need to finish a paper and go over chemistry this weekend. My tests are all Tuesday and Wednesday," Kim chimed in.

"Ok, so where are you three staying?"

"We are at the hotel, Deb, you're going to room with Becky and Ryan will be with Joe and I," Ken replied.

"Ok, you guys have everything covered. Now, someone get Deb and I up to speed," Ryan said, as he gave Deb an 'I told you so' look. She frowned at him. He knew she liked to plan and organize, that's why she was so good at the research.

Joe went in detail about all they learned since those first calls day before yesterday. Mr. Brewster asked him to go into more detail on the theory to track the energy and Ken asked about the program plan. Ryan and Deb looked through the notebook and Kim announced she was going to go to the library to finish her paper and she would join them for dinner and was bringing Jake. Deb grabbed a bulletin board that was leaning against the wall and asked if Mr. Brewster had any note cards. He told her where they were in his office in the house and Ryan went and got them. Deb and Becky used the cards to note all the details they knew about Tom, his family, the dates and things Becky found, the coordinates and anything else they could think of to come up with the why part of the search.

The girls finished and then attentively listened to the discussion on how to adjust the spectrometer to track the energy signature of the machine, when Deb slapped the table and yelled, "I know why he went to New York and that area of White Plains!"

The discussion stopped and Ken said, "Well?"

"In the notebook, he talked about how his family was sure that if they had more money, they would have been able to fight Henry Ford and retain the patent for the engine. He went to White Plains to be close enough to New York and on a train route to the city to be there when the market crashed in 1929. I remember the history teacher here talking about how you could have made a fortune if you knew ahead of time and bought and sold at the right time. Tom went there to play the market, make a fortune Then he must be planning to get to where his grandfather invented the engine!"

"That makes perfect sense, Deb. Then his family would have had a lot of money and he would have something on the Fitzgerald family," Becky said triumphantly.

"I still think you should finish your adjustments to the spectrometer and do the programming, Joe. That way we can be sure and if we miss him, it will allow us to track him to the next place he goes with it," Deb said, looking at Joe.

"I agree, we should complete this work, but once we confirm, then what should we be doing?" Ryan asked.

"We need to go after him. First, we need to get the machine back, but we know what happens when we go back and try to change things. The ripple effect through history could be disastrous. Not just for the stock market crash, because I'm certain there would be a notation in history about the young man that beat the odds and made millions and then disappeared, but if he succeeds and changes the history of the automobile, that would have a monumental impact on all kinds of other things," Ken said ominously and vehemently.

"So, Joe, your theory seems sound. We need to start work on the spectrometer, but we should also, to Ken's point start work on another machine. Thankfully, that theory is already proven and we have the other parts of the machine we used on the last trip to pre-Civil War Philadelphia," Mr. Brewster added.

"Do you still have that other engine?" Joe asked.

"Yes, I ended up putting it all in a few boxes back there," as he pointed to the back corner of the barn. "It's a good thing too, since Tom seemed to rummage through the papers and files on the shelves, but left the boxes alone."

"Ok, Ryan, how about you help me build another machine to put that engine on, and Joe, you and Mr. Brewster can work on the spectrometer? Becky and Deb, we need some review of history of nineteen twenty-nine and the market crash and what led up to it to pin-point when we think he went and what we need to prepare for to go there," Ken directed the group.

"It's so like you, boss man to supervise all of this!" Joe said, punching Ken in the shoulder.

"Sorry, just trying to organize."

"Leadership is so hard, isn't it Kenny!" Deb added, laughing.

"Back on track now, what do the two teams here need?" Becky asked.

"I need a few things, I think I can find what I need at the hardware store and maybe RadioShack," Joe said, "I can either go or make a list."

"We'll need some materials to build the new machine, but first, we might want to determine who all are going and any other particulars to be sure we build it to fit our needs," Ken added.

"Joe, how about you make a list and Becky and I can do your shopping before we go pick up Kim and Jake for dinner. That way you four can work on dimensions and whatever for the machine, is that ok?" Deb said.

"Sounds like a plan," Joe replied.

"Take my car, baby," Ryan said as he handed Deb his keys.

Joe finished his list, handing it to Deb and the two girls left to do a little shopping. The guys started doing some drawings of the new machine and discussed who all would go on these trips. They decided that since they had no way of knowing what they were going to encounter, they would build the machine to support at least six people. There would always be someone that stayed behind, but they expected Mary and Kim to want to be part of this. By the time the girls returned,

Ken and Mr. Brewster had left to get some parts for this new machine. They all helped with the unloading of the truck when they returned and invited Mr. Brewster to have dinner with them. He declined, saying that he had some grading to finish up, and he wanted to go ahead and get that done so he would be available to help Joe over the weekend. Becky, Joe, Deb and Ryan all went back to the hotel to get cleaned up for dinner. Ken went to pick up Kim and Jake.

They all met up at what had been their dinner place, the Italian restaurant, but it had changed hands and was now a steak place. Now called, Grimaldi's Steak and Seafood, they decided to try it anyway. The hostess sat this sizeable group of seven in the corner at a large round table. They had decided not to discuss plans at dinner, as no one knew if Jake knew what they were up to. They kept their conversations about Deb's dig, summer plans, and various interests of the group. When dinner was over, Deb and Ryan took Kim and Jake back to Choate and then met the others in the hotel lobby.

"Do you have everything you need to start on the machine?" Deb asked when they sat down.

"No, but Mr. Brewster called our room while we were out, and I called him back just now. He has a friend that can get us the rest of the metal we need to skin the machine and we're going to pick that up first thing tomorrow morning," Ken answered.

"Does Mr. Brewster still have that truck you guys used today?" Deb asked.

"Yes. He told me the friend he borrowed that from said he could use it for the rest of the week," Ken replied.

"Ok, what are you going to do Joe?" Becky asked.

"I'm going to the barn when Ken goes with Mr. Brewster, to work on the spectrometer. Then I'll be starting on the program."

"Ryan, are you going with Ken in the morning?" Deb asked.

"I can, if you need help, Ken."

"That would be great. I don't know what shape this metal is going to be in, and I don't want Mr. Brewster to get hurt."

"Then, that's my plan for tomorrow too!"

"How about, Becky, you and I go to the public library here in town and do some research?"

"Sounds good, but you'll have to lead this research. That's not really my thing."

"Sure," Deb replied, smiling.

"Don't you need to get Kim for that?" Joe asked.

"No, I asked her what her plans were for tomorrow on the ride back to Choate and she said she was studying with some friends most of the day and then Jake was taking her out tomorrow night. I said that was fine cause you boys would be messing on some machines with Mr. Brewster and us girls would be shopping. That was my cover since Jake was there. I will call her in the morning and explain what's really going on. I told her I would call," Deb replied.

"Do you think there's any risk that he's already done something that has trickled down? I mean, what if we don't know what he did, given we aren't on the trip? Will we remember how it should be?" Ryan postured.

"I think because we are aware he went and we have a good idea what he might be up to, we can monitor it. I was going to check out some books on the market crash and copy some pages as a basis for us," Deb responded first to the question.

"I just finished the roaring twenties in one of my history classes this spring. I can write down everything I can remember. That might help us have a reference," Becky added.

"We're going to need to plan for a trip, too. We'll need clothes and money and things ready for whichever of us decides to go soon. I don't want to lose the urgency we have here to get this guy and the machine back," Ken exerted.

"I, for one, want us all to go. We don't know what's going to happen and I think it would help to have all our different expertise when we do this," Joe offered.

"We need someone to stay back, don't we?" Becky asked.

"Yes, but we have to be conscious of the time lapse issues. We can't have all of us gone for weeks, especially Kim, who has finals this week," Joe replied.

"Let's discuss the who is going and such once we have the machine ready and we're sure about when and where we're going. I don't want to wait until the end of next week to go after this guy, but, you're right Joe, we can't mess up Kim's test schedule to do this," Ken pronounced.

They all went up to their rooms at this point and agreed to meet in the restaurant at the hotel for breakfast in the morning.

4

On Saturday, Joe spent the morning building his attachment to the spectrometer. Ken, Ryan and Mr. Brewster returned at lunchtime with burgers, drinks and a lot of metal. The four of them ate, and then Mr. Brewster helped Joe complete his attachment. Then they tested it in the barn for the signature of the machine that was taken and it compiled data, just as Joe said it would. While that was going on, Ryan and Ken got out the machine parts from the boxes and began to weld and assemble the frame for the new machine. By the time Deb and Becky arrived, late in the afternoon, the machine was completely framed, and Joe was inside at the computer he had given to Mr. Brewster, working on coding, while Mr. Brewster was now helping Ryan and Ken cut the metal for the sheathing of the machine. Becky suggested they get pizza and everyone agreed. When Deb and Becky returned with the pizza, they all stopped for the day and sat at Mr. Brewster's table for dinner.

"How are Thomas and Brittany, Mr. Brewster?" Deb asked as they sat down.

"He's doing wonderfully. He's at Johns Hopkins working on cutting-edge cancer research. It's amazing how much they've learned in a brief time. Brittany is doing wonderfully, too. She's made associate partner at her firm and, I don't think I've told any of you, they are expecting their first child."

"Wow, you're going to be a grandfather, Mr. Brewster!" Joe said, holding up his glass of soda.

"Yes, I am and I can't wait to teach this young child so many things!"

"That's so exciting! Can they consider us all aunts and uncles?" Deb asked, laughing.

"You know, Thomas asked about you all just last week, and said he hoped to see you all soon. He said to tell you and suggest that you would all be drafted for that very job as aunts and uncles!"

"Have they picked out names yet?" Becky inquired.

"Not that I'm aware. But moving on, how are the wedding plans coming for you and Mary?" Mr. Brewster asked, looking at Ken.

"Great. We picked out the venue last week, and today, Mary's out with her mother looking at dresses. We have lots more to do, and it's turning into a circus, I think."

"A circus? How?" Mr. Brewster asked.

"Well, Mary's mother wants three of Mary's cousins to be in the wedding. She wants three of her friends, so there is either a big compromise coming, or we will have six bridesmaids and six groomsmen, because apparently you have to have a groomsman for every bridesmaid. Then there is the fact that Aunt Alicia wants to invite most of New York and some of Paris."

"You only get married once, I guess," Mr. Brewster added, shaking his head in agreement with the circus evaluation.

"Tell us about the dig, Deb. I can't imagine being in the middle of a dessert and finding treasures like you do," Becky prompted.

"Treasures for sure got found this spring, but not in the sense of gemstones. We found all kinds of artifacts from where Jesus did his ministry and where the apostles were from. It's incredible to see the evidence of Jesus really living and teaching!"

"What exactly did you find on your dig?" Mr. Brewster asked.

"We found a byzantine home chapel that had engravings referencing Simon's home and then we found some Samaritan settlements that had bits of papyrus referencing Jesus of Nazareth."

"How exactly do you identify the things you find? And how do you know you have bits of papyrus?" Joe asked.

"Once we get to the right time period in the digging, we stop using big shovels and start using tiny trowels and brushes. That way, we don't miss anything."

"Yeah, but how do you know what's good and what isn't?" Becky asked.

"We pull anything that even looks like it might be something. If you're holding something that seems solid but covered in dirt, you try to crumble it a little. If it crumbles in your hand, it's dirt. If not, you put it in the box."

"Then what?" Mr. Brewster asked.

"Well, we need to clean the items first, carefully, then we work to compare them to other items of different periods of time. We compare it to other items found at that depth and if there's writing at all, we can identify the when by the language, and sometimes by the writing style if there's enough of it."

"How far down do you dig?" Becky asked.

"In this case, we have to go down like six feet or so. There is a wind scrub that goes on in the middle east that keeps the earth from building up too far as the ages progress. But you determine the age based on the type of soil you find, and the noted moments that would impact the soil, like a volcano."

"Is the professor doing this a religious man?" Mr. Brewster asked.

"He is not a pastor or anything, but his specialty is Jewish and early Christian history."

"Is this what you want to do for a living?" Joe offered.

"I'm not totally sure I want to spend my life digging, but I really like learning about history and writing about it. I'm contemplating a few things for next year, though."

"What does all this mean for you, Ryan?" Ken asked Ryan quietly as he was sitting next to him.

"I'm trying to persuade her toward professorship or something, but I don't know, really. The fact is, I can't practice investment management from the sandy back area of the middle east, so who knows. I was hoping to have a lot of conversations with her to figure this out this summer. Then this came up, so who knows?" he answered a bit forlorn.

"You can still be together even if you have very different career interests, you know. When were you planning to propose?" Ken leaned in to say this quietly.

"Are you asking as a big brother slash family leader or as a friend?"

"Well, both maybe."

"Well, head of the family, I want to ask permission from the family leadership before I do this, and I was hoping to seek that permission later this summer, so I could plan this big moment for some point in the next year."

"You don't have to ask, you have permission. I can't imagine a better person to take care of my sister than you."

"Thanks, but I still feel like I need to have a conversation with you, Joe, and your uncle. Maybe you could help me put that together?"

"Sure."

"What are you two whispering about over there?" Becky asked.

"Nothing too important," Ken answered quickly.

Changing the subject, Ryan asked, "Mr. Brewster, is it ok if we come over tomorrow afternoon and work on the machine some more? Or would that be an imposition on your Sunday?"

"Nonsense. I think that's a great idea."

"I'd like to work on the programming tomorrow too, if that's ok," Joe asked.

"Of course," Mr. Brewster said, smiling at Joe.

"What are we going to do?" Becky asked Deb.

"Well, I want to take Kim out for lunch and then I want to finish the research if we can. Did you want to have lunch with us?"

"Sure, that sounds great."

"Should we all go to church on campus tomorrow?" Ken asked.

"That sounds good," Deb answered.

Mr. Brewster then asked Deb all kinds of questions about the digging, the cleaning, and identifying process. He asked about the tools used, the method of cleaning and if they had to engage other experts in their identifying process. Deb details all of that while the others listened and ate. When they finished, they decided they would head back to the hotel. Joe headed up to the guy's room to go over his code and the others stayed in the lobby and went over the research the girls had done.

The next day, after church, the girls went back to the dorm with Kim and went to lunch and guys went back to Mr. Brewster's. Later, the girls were at the library for several hours, while Ken, Ryan and Mr. Brewster worked on the machine and Joe coded. When Deb and Becky had completed their research and rechecked the market crash information to be sure Tom had done nothing yet, they went to the barn. By that time, the machine was completely sheathed and the engine parts were being put on the top. It was at least twice the size of the original machine. Deb asked if that would impact the energy requirements and Mr. Brewster replied he didn't think so, but they would have to run some tests before they made any final plans. Joe, they found, was a little frustrated with his coding effort and didn't want to be disturbed. At Mr. Brewster's suggestion, the other four left Ryan's car for Joe so he could continue to work. Mr. Brewster said he had some test preparations to complete and he would use the kitchen table while Joe continued to code. When Becky asked if he would stop for dinner, Joe grunted, so Mr. Brewster said he would be sure to feed Joe.

The next day, Becky and Deb headed out on a shopping trip to various vintage clothing and costume stores to gather the clothing they might need for a trip to the nineteen twenties and the early part of the century. Ryan and Ken and Joe headed back to the barn, where Ken and Ryan completed the engine setup on the machine and installed the seats and the console for the controls they would need to run the machine. Joe kept coding. They stopped around noon to go get a burger, but were back at it by one in the afternoon. The work continued until Mr. Brewster came home from classes at four-thirty. By then, the seats were in, the various compartments were done, including several drawers for storing things, and they framed the console area out. Joe had managed to get past the issues he'd been having for the past day and was making progress on his program, which he thought he would have completed the next day. The girls had successfully outfitted all of them for the trip and they had even got some older money from a community bank that was in one of the small towns as they were making their way back. They stopped at Choate to see Kim before her tests started and to wish her luck. Kim told them she intended to tell Jake about the time traveling, but not until after tests were done. She understood if she needed to stay behind on this first trip, both because of tests and her plans to have Jake spend time with her at the Long Island house right after classes were over.

Becky called Mr. Brewster when they got back to the hotel and he told them the guys were cleaning up to head to the hotel and would be there soon. They ate in the hotel restaurant and everyone went to bed early. It had been a busy day.

If Monday was busy, Tuesday was even more busy. The girls helped get the rest of the machine ready, and Joe finished the programming and ran a test with the data they had gathered from the spectrometer. The data showed exactly what Joe was hoping for and it pinpointed the timeframe the machine went to as late nineteen twenty-eight to mid-nineteen twenty-nine. Given what they had learned about the stock market crash and the events leading up to it, they figured it was early nineteen twenty-nine so that Tom could make money from the highs that occurred during this timeframe. They were just about ready to plan a trip, but needed to run some tests on the new machine. They set Wednesday for test day.

The tests went so smoothly that Ryan said he was worried. Mr. Brewster was really the reassuring factor that afternoon by reminding them they had more than a little experience with the machine and time travel at this point. They sat at the table in the barn to do their final planning on Thursday and finished early enough so they could relax that evening. Mr. Brewster joined them for dinner, but then went right home, while the others went bowling. They called Kim and wished her luck on her last test the next morning and she agreed to come to the barn after the test to plan with them before she had to pack up.

As they gathered at the barn table yet again to plan a trip in the time machine, they all contemplated the coming interaction with Tom and hoped it would go smoothly.

"Ok, first let's go over a checklist of things we need. Deb, you and Becky got this," Ken started.

Deb and Becky went through the clothing they had acquired, the need for older money so it would not stand out, and the books and various things they should plan on bringing.

"Why do we need toothpaste and shampoo?" Joe asked.

"Because we don't know what we're going to find, and I distinctly remember you complaining about the use of baking soda to clean your teeth in Philadelphia," Becky answered in a patronizing manner.

"Yeah, but shampoo?" he asked again.

"Because I've spent the last three months not getting to wash my hair every day, and I want to make sure I can. We don't know how long we're going to be there, and I still think I have sand in my hair," Deb answered.

"I suggest we also take some tools. I doubt we'll have to do anything to our machine, but we might need tools for the other machine if he's done something to it," Joe added.

"Can I ask about that?" Becky tentatively interjected.

"What?" Mr. Brewster replied, hoping to reassure her there was always room for questions.

"Well, say we find Tom. What are we going to do?"

"We're going to try to talk some sense into him, put him in the original machine with me and all of us get out of there before something bad happens," Ken stated somewhat strongly.

"Have you seen this notebook?" Deb asked, holding the little insight into Tom's thoughts up in front of her.

"Yeah, but if we show up where he is, I'm just thinking it might shock him into some sort of sensible place."

"What if that isn't what happens?" Joe asked.

"Then we force him into the machine, and get him back here. We destroy both machines and all the reference to it in documentation, so if he goes to the press or something, we can verify we don't know what he's talking about and that will be it."

"How are we going to force him?" Joe asked, looking mainly at Ken and Ryan.

"Ken, what if we get there, try to talk to him, and he sneaks away and goes somewhere else in the original machine?" Ryan asked.

"I think that means we have to strap the computer into our machine somehow so we can track him if he leaves. You might be right, we don't want to risk coming back here if we think he's gone somewhere else," Joe added.

"And some rope maybe, if you think you have to force him," Ryan concluded.

"Taking the spectrometer and the computer might be a good idea, Joe," Mr. Brewster thought out loud.

"Alright, we better strap that into the machine today. Do we have the power in there to run it?" Ken inquired, as he looked at Joe and Mr. Brewster.

"We could change the wiring for the power cord and get several batteries to power it, since we won't have electricity where we're going," Joe considered.

"No, there's electricity in the cities in nineteen twenty-nine, just probably not steady electricity that your computer relies on," Deb disagreed.

"What do you mean?" Becky asked.

"It's early in the use of electricity and the current isn't very stable. It might not go well if you try to plug in a computer or something like it from our time," Deb explained. "It might work, but I don't know."

"So, we still have some work to do before we can leave. Do you have a plan, Deb?" Ken asked.

"And some packing still to do," Joe added.

"Here's what we came up with. There was a period where the market rebounded in June of twenty-nine. The prices on many stocks surged up quite a bit. I think Tom probably went in May, bought stock and was planning to sit on it for the month and then sell out when the demand was high and prices were climbing," Deb explained.

"Ok, so do you have a date and coordinate picked out?" Joe asked.

"I think we should go the first of June of twenty-nine, pick a coordinate close to the one Tom used and make our way into the city on the train. I discovered that back in the twenties, the coordinates he used were the ruined farmland of a man who signed the constitution. He was George Winston, the representative from New York. He was the one that fought the reference to free men. He owned slaves. Even though he was famous, the house and land were just abandoned. It looks like, from the map we found, that Tom probably landed in or near a barn on the property. There were some woods at the farthest end of the property that I think we can try to land in or near enough to camouflage the machine," Deb explained.

"Oh, don't forget that two of the books we found in the public library had been checked out by Tom!" Becky said excitedly.

"Which ones?" Ken asked.

"The ones on the market crash and the events leading up to it, and one about Winston's farm," Becky answered.

"Good work, girls!" Ken said.

"Do you have coordinates on this farm already?" Joe asked.

"Yes, we have them here in our notes," Becky replied.

"Ok, let's gather tools, rope and the spectrometer and get them stored in the machine. Joe and Mr. Brewster and Becky, can you work on the computer and Ryan and I can determine where in the machine we're going to put that computer? Deb, where are all these clothes? Do we need to pack them in the machine, too?"

"They're in the trunk of Ryan's car right now, and yes, I think we need to all change before we leave and pack the other clothes. There're three or four changes of clothes for each of us," Deb explained.

"That is a question we haven't answered. Who all are going?" Joe asked.

"Are we planning to leave tomorrow?" Becky asked.

"I think we should. We've been monitoring things, but if we don't get there to stop him from selling, it might change history," Deb suggested.

"I think that means we have to have Kim stay here," Joe said, looking around. "I'm not sure she's going to like that."

"Actually, she told Becky and I last night that she wanted to stay here for this trip because she had plans with Jake and she was going to fill him in all of this. I think that's a good idea. Plus, we might want to put a call into Aunt Alicia tomorrow before we leave so we can clear a way to be gone. We don't know how long this will take," Deb explained.

"Good idea. Does everybody have coverage to be away?" Ken asked.

"My parents think Joe picked me up and we are going out to Long Island for a few weeks. They're out of town for the entire month, so I'm clear," Becky said.

"Aunt Alicia thinks I'm bringing Becky out this weekend. We're going to need a plan," Joe continued.

"I need a plan too. Ryan was planning to pick me up on Friday and take me out to Long Island," Deb said.

"Maybe I can help with Joe and Becky. You can say you're coming to visit me and work on some project with me," Mr. Brewster finally spoke up. Although he didn't approve of the lying, he wanted to help them as much as he could.

"That sounds great. That would give us a week anyway," Joe replied.

"Yes, and we probably shouldn't have the same story," Deb added.

"How about if we say we're going ahead with the plans we were thinking about a few weeks ago?" Ryan offered.

"That's a great idea!" Deb said, hugging him.

"What were those plans?" Ken asked.

"We had been asked to join some of my hockey buddies and their girlfriends down in Savannah for a couple of weeks. I think Deb even mentioned it to her aunt but, did you ever confirm with her?" Ryan explained.

"No, she and I haven't talked about those plans since you first asked me, so she doesn't know what we decided."

"Ok, that means both Joe and Deb need to call Aunt Alicia tomorrow before we get into the machine. Let's get busy!" Ken said as he got up and walked toward the machine.

Kim arrived just then and Becky sat down with her and explained the plan. She helped Deb get the clothes organized and into the machine and marveled at the bigger, fancier machine they had built in a few days. Deb asked her about her tests. Saying she was only glad they were over, she left to go meet Jake for their evening and to pack. She said she would stick with the plan where Deb came home early and came over to see her before they left for Savannah. And she would prepare Jake to not reveal he's already met Joe, Ken and Becky.

They got the computer wired to take batteries, while Deb and Becky went to get these batteries and some fried chicken for dinner. After they ate, they installed the computer into the machine and headed back to the hotel for some rest.

The next morning, Joe called Aunt Alicia and told her of his change of plans for the next week to help Mr. Brewster. He said depending on how long it took, he would still bring Becky out to the house. She was fine with change of plans, as she had found out she would be busy and asked if he was leaving that day, and if so to let Kim know Michael would be there mid-morning on Friday. He said he would try to get there in time to tell her. When Deb called, she was again agreeable to the confirmation of the plans she and Deb had discussed earlier. She was a little disappointed about not being able to see her Friday evening, but as it happened, she had a party that now she could go to. Deb told her she was going over to see Kim Friday morning as they were leaving, even if it was out of the way. Aunt Alicia asked Deb to relay the message about Michael, and Deb said she would.

With the cover calls all made, Deb called the dorm and found Kim just getting back from breakfast. She said Jake had a last test that morning and she was planning to head over to the barn after more packing. Deb confirmed when they would all be arriving. The four at the hotel went down for breakfast and then drove over to the barn.

5

At the barn, they got everything packed up, checked the computer to make sure it turned on and worked, checked the spectrometer and went over the checklist one more time. They all changed clothes and hugged Kim and Mr. Brewster. They climbed into the machine and started it up. The wind kicked up in the barn, swirled anything that was loose and then the bright light and they were gone.

"When do you think we'll hear from them?" Kim asked as she bent down to pick up some papers from the floor.

"I don't know. Joe did some calculations from the formula you and Becky came up with Philadelphia and he said he thinks if they go no farther than nineteen hundred, they can be gone for fifteen days until it messes Deb's return to the middle east and all the cover stories they've put out," Mr. Brewster responded.

"I'm worried. Are you worried?"

"Yes. I don't like that we cannot communicate with them and have no way of knowing what they're dealing with. This is different than any other trip you've made since now you are chasing someone through time."

"Deb gave me a list of the books they were monitoring to be sure things didn't change and copies of everything Becky copied showing the present understanding of history. I'm going to go check them out for the summer from the school library so I can monitor."

"That's a good idea."

"What are you doing this summer, Mr. Brewster? That is until this happened. I mean, if we can't catch Tom on this trip, who knows what's going to happen."

"I was planning on finishing and delivering a car to Long Island. Then visiting with Thomas and Brittany."

Kim smiled and looked over at the nearly finished car in the corner. "What do you have left to do?"

"I have a little wiring to finish, because I know the new owner will want the radio working, then I have to install the muffler. I have to replace the headliner and then get it to the body shop for a new paint job."

"That seems like a lot, and expensive. I hope you're not doing this alone."

"First of all, the only real expense is the painting, and that won't be much, as the owner of the shop is a friend of mine. Second, it's doing this work, and doing all this with you and your siblings, that keeps me young."

"I'm sorry. I wasn't trying to say you're old."

"I know. Well, I have some tests to grade. How about you?"

"I have to pack and meet Jake. Mr. Brewster can I ask you something? How did you tell Thomas about all this? I'm telling Jake about this and I just don't know the right way to tell him."

"I didn't really have to start the conversation with Thomas, remember? He walked in on us. I know when Deb told Ryan, she started with how you all felt coming to Choate. Maybe that's where to start."

"I really like Jake, Mr. Brewster, so I don't want to keep it from him, but what if he's not the guy for me, I mean, what if it doesn't work out and we break up, then he knows this big secret of ours."

"If you feel compelled to tell him, I think it would be fine. He seems like a very nice gentleman."

"He is, and we have such a wonderful friendship. We've been talking for a year now. We started having classes together last spring and we've done things together and I went to his basketball games and it just seemed like we were meant to be."

"Then I think telling him would be a good idea."

"Thanks, I'm feeling ready. I guess now that you've told me you think he's so good."

"You should probably head back to campus and get packed up, since Michael was coming to get you tomorrow. Enjoy your evening with Jake."

"Ok. I will call you every day, though, if that's ok, once I get out to Long Island."

"Of course, and I have that number. If something happens and your siblings come back here, one of us will call you."

"Thanks Mr. Brewster."

"Of course, I'm always here for you and all your siblings. I expect to see you again this summer, as we try to sort this out."

"I expect to see you too!"

Kim left then and returned to the dorm. She chatted with the floor mates and talked about summer plans as she packed up all of her clothing into the suitcases to be ready. She was so excited to do this as she and Aunt Alicia had gone shopping at Easter and Christmas and she had a wonderful wardrobe. Everyone was so jealous of her clothes and she was thrilled with all the clothing. Now that she was older and could wear all the things Aunt Alicia made and sold in her boutique, it was wonderful to be all dressed in the latest fashion and have all the frilly girl things. It was getting time for Jake to come over, so she stopped packing and got dressed to go out to dinner with him. Just as she was finishing doing her blonde hair into the updo with curls all over, someone came running up the stairs and told her Jake was waiting in the lobby.

As she walked up to him, he smiled down at her and said, "Wow, you look great, Kim!"

"Thanks."

"I've got to say this. You are the most beautiful girl I've ever known and I'm so lucky to be with you."

"Oh, Jake, you're so nice. I'm lucky to have you, too."

"Let's go. I'm ready to show you off to wherever we go!"

Kim laughed as he took her hand and walked her out to his car. He opened the door for her, and then went around and got in. They went to a new dinner place that had opened in town a week ago. They had a big menu and both of them had a great dinner. Afterward, they went back to campus and Jake suggested they go for a walk. Kim agreed, and instead of getting out of the car, he drove her to the park. They got out and walked out to the dock area of the lake that had benches on it. They sat down and just sat quietly, holding hands for a few minutes.

"You seem like you're deep in thought. Want to share?" Jake said to Kim.

"You know me so well, Jake. Yes, I'm thinking about things and I need to tell you something."

"Well, tell me. I have to say first, though, I hope this isn't a breakup talk."

"No, I'm sorry. I'm not here to break up with you. I want to share something with you. I need you so much in my life. But I just have some family things you should probably know about."

Kim sat for a moment and then went into the long speech she had planned, starting with their arrival at Choate and Joe being so unhappy, and the trip to the closed building and all their findings. Jake listened to her and when she finished, he said, "Wow."

"Yeah, right?"

"You went back to nineteen sixty-three, and eighteen fifty-three?"

"Yes. We went to nineteen fifty-eight too."

"Ok, I get why you went to help the underground railroad, and why you went to help Mr. Brewster, but why go to nineteen sixty-three?"

"We went there to stop President Kennedy from being shot in a parade. We did that because that event is what brought our father to his partner. We figured if we stopped that event, we might stop that partnership."

"They shot President Kennedy in his car in Houston, not Dallas, honey. You didn't stop it?"

"No, originally, he was shot in Dallas. You wouldn't remember that though, cause you neither went on the trip nor knew about it. That is the only way that anyone can remember the old history and new history if we change something, and even then, sometimes we lose the memories after a few days."

"So, someone stole the machine and went somewhere?"

"Yes. We figured out who and probably when he went to. We're trying to figure out where he might be, though."

"I don't think I get that?"

"Well, we know Tom had a great grandfather, and he had invented an engine that was what patented and there was this organization that charged car manufacturers for using the patented parts. Henry Ford didn't want to pay and he had advanced that combustion engine so he fought Tom's great grandfather in court over it. Anyway, Tom's great grandfather couldn't fight that big money and he lost the patent on it and lost everything. Tom seemed to focus all the family anger on Joe because of Joe's accomplishments and that's how we figured it out."

"That was quick. How did you focus on him?"

"He left a notebook in Mr. Brewster's barn."

"Oh. So, they all left yesterday to try to catch Tom?"

"Yeah. The tough part is we have no way of knowing what's going on. So, we have to sit and wait."

"Gosh, Kim, I had no idea I was dating such a smart girl!"

"Oh, come on Jake, you're in most of my classes this year," she said, blushing and looking down.

"I know that, but to come up with all this and help plan for trips through time, my gosh, that's both cool and very scary."

"Well, we all kind of agreed with that two years ago. We all decided together to not use the machine anymore. See, we messed up a lot of history, not just ours, but lots of other people too. When we went to Dallas, we saved the President, but it ended up we also almost got Mrs.

Kennedy killed, and the civil rights movement was delayed by about ten years, hurting all kinds of people. Then when we went to Philadelphia, we really messed up history because Joe was in jail with one conspirator of Lincoln's assassination. He basically talked him out of support for the South and that guy stopped the assassinations and caused an even bigger mess for the freed slaves."

"But Lincoln was assassinated."

"Yeah, but only because Ken and Ryan showed up to stop Joe from getting arrested!"

"You mean they came back, and met you and fixed everything?"

"Yeah."

"How did they get to you if you had the time machine?"

"They built a new engine for the machine, but they didn't go back to meet us actually until after we had come back so the machine was back in the barn."

"Wow."

"When we got done with all that mess, and a mess we made trying to help Uncle Darrick, we all decided it was way too risky. Plus, we decided we really couldn't have done all the things we did without going to Choate, and that only happened when our parents died. It's really weird when you think about it. Some great things have happened to all of us, but it was only possible because our parents died. And, we are really close, I mean super close, and I know that wouldn't have been the case either, if what happened hadn't happened."

"It's like going down a rabbit hole when you think about it, huh?"

"Yes. If you change one thing in the past, it changes everything from that point on in a ripple effect. You don't know how things will turn out and where you might end up."

"That makes what Tom is doing terrible, doesn't it?"

"Yes, that's why we're all here, working on this."

"Can I help?"

Kim smiled and leaned over, wrapping her arm around Jake's shoulder. She kissed his cheek, saying, "You're really great, you know that!"

Jake returned the hug and kissed her. Then he said, "I know, my girlfriend keeps telling me! You're pretty remarkable yourself."

They sat for a few more minutes, making their plans to leave campus tomorrow. His parents were coming to get his things and then they were going with Michael to Long Island to the house there and spending a couple of weeks. Then, they walked back to Jake's car and returned to the girls' dorm. Kim said goodbye and went inside.

While that monumental conversation was going on, Ken, Deb, Ryan, Joe and Becky, having arrived at the newly abandoned property just inside one barn on the property, covered up the machine with things they found in the barn. Then they pulled out the luggage with their changes of clothing and money and notes. They walked two miles into town and bought tickets to New York city. By late afternoon, they had arrived in the city and, after marveling at the differences between nineteen twenty-nine and nineteen eighty; they made their way to a hotel that Deb had found that they knew was opened at this time. It was brand new, but they could get rooms for them all. After checking in, they put their luggage away and returned to the lobby. Becky went to the desk and inquired about a restaurant. Receiving the recommendation, they went out and made their way near Times Square to have dinner and discuss how they were going to locate Tom.

After they had determined that food was very different in the nineteen twenties, they ordered what they hoped was steak and potatoes. Perhaps the names for food were the only thing that was different, Ryan thought as they sat at the table. Anxiously waiting for their food to arrive, Joe said, "How are we going to find one guy that has no record of being in this city, with only us here?"

"I know the city is much smaller than we expected, but I don't know," Ryan replied, as he looked around the room at the other diners and noticed the men were all in tuxedos, "Did we bring the wrong clothes here or what?"

"I'm feeling a little uncomfortable as well," Deb acknowledged.

Just then, a middle-aged man walked up and addressed Ken, "My good man, are you just off the boat?"

Ken stood to shake his hand as he said, "No, Sir, we only just arrived and of course, the hotel laundress was out sick today. No way to press our any of our clothing. Can you believe the absurdity of that? We have to spend all day in our traveling clothing!"

"I say, are you staying at the Waldorf?"

"No, the Stafford, actually."

"I've never heard of such deplorable service! How can I be of service? My name is Benjamin Worthington, of the North Hampton Worthington's."

"Happy to make your acquaintance, Mr. Worthington. My name is Kenneth Fitzgerald, of the Cambridge Massachusetts Fitzgerald's. And may I present my brother Joseph and sister Deborah?"

Both Joe and Deb stood up and greeted Mr. Worthington. He then looked at Ryan and Becky with his eyebrows raised and then looked back at Ken.

"My apologies, good man. May I also present Mr. Ryan McDonnell, of the Charleston McDonnell's. He is my sister's fiancé. And this is Rebecca Simmons, Joseph's girlfriend. We just arrived today on some personal business."

"It's a pleasure to meet you all. What business are you in town for?"

"Well, Mr. Worthington, we are trying to locate a long-lost relative of ours. His name is Thomas Thorton. I don't suppose you might have heard of him?"

"No, I have not. What are his circumstances, may I ask?"

"Well, he recently came into some cash and we fear he is here, falling prey to one of those investment brokers that swindle unsuspecting country folks into poor deals. We've tried to help Thomas, and we really want to stave off disaster."

"How generous of you all. Might I suggest, if you believe he is here to invest, that you start with the reputable establishments on Broad Street? Hopefully, he has stopped in and they can direct you."

"Why, thank you so much, Mr. Worthington!" Deb exclaimed, "We've been so worried about Thomas!"

"Of course, Mademoiselle. I am always ready to assist a lovely lady such as yourself. May I extend an invitation also? I am hosting a little gathering at my home on West 45th tomorrow evening. You must all come and meet some of the best people in the city."

"We'd be delighted, Mr. Worthington. Thank you so much for the hospitality," Ken said, holding out his hand to shake his again.

As Mr. Worthington shook his hand, he said, "Please, we no longer stand on formality. Please call me Benjamin. I will send information to you at the Stafford. And do call tomorrow if their laundress is still out and I shall send over someone to assist you."

In unison, they all said thank you and wished him well.

"Well, that was a little scary and a little good fortune," Becky said after Mr. Worthington had gotten out of earshot.

"I'll say. I thought we were goners there. Nice thinking Ken!" Ryan replied.

"I'd like to say that was good planning, but honestly I was just think-ing, what would Gatsby say?" Ken said, laughing as he finally sat down.

"Now we have a new problem, though, Ken. We have to find tuxedos and dresses by tomorrow night. And we are here to get some-thing done," Deb said, a little worried about how they were going to pull this off.

"We have plenty of money. We'll get what we need. I, for one, am glad about this as now we have some ideas where to start. Ryan and I can go out in the morning and see the banks and investment firms that Benjamin suggested, and then we can meet you for lunch and get the clothing we need. Girls, you go out in the morning and find dresses and then we can get the tux's we need after lunch," Ken said in that I'm in charge voice.

"I'll go with the girls, to chaperone, in the morning and find a place for us to get our clothing later," Joe said and then went on, "I can get to know the concierge in the morning and get all the good scoop on shops that can cater to last-minute shoppers like us. Plus, if you two happen on a place where Tom is, I think I shouldn't be there."

"Good idea. We don't want him to know we know about him until we're sure, and we have a plan," Ryan said, giving Joe the thumbs up.

With that, they finished eating and returned to the hotel. The next morning, they all met for breakfast in the hotel, Joe having already charmed the concierge, and procuring appointments for the girls at the best dress shop and the three gentlemen would be taken care of in the afternoon by the best tailor in town. They all left for their various assignments.

The girls thoroughly enjoyed their shopping spree. They each bought two rather extravagant dresses, new shoes and the all essentials for a night out. The shopkeeper said they would send the clothing and accessories over to the Stafford by three that afternoon. They bought some items for the guys on their way back to the hotel and met Ryan and Ken in the lobby. They left the hotel and returned to Times Square to eat lunch and discuss the morning events.

"Did you find dresses?" Ryan asked as they sat down.

"Yes, we did, and was it fun! I love shopping here and now," Deb answered, beaming at him.

"It was so much fun!" Becky gushed, "We got waited on and the dresses were so beautiful! I'm rather excited to be wearing them."

"Tell me what happened to you guys this morning," Joe interrupted as he was eager to hear what they found out.

"Well, we found a guy at the Bank of New York that recognized the name and said that Tom had exchanged some old coins for money and said he was investing with a firm, but the bank man was not entirely sure which one as he had given him several suggestions. We got him to write them all down, so we'll have to go tomorrow to find out which one he's at and if they know where he is," Ken replied.

"Don't you have to list an address when you open a bank account?" Becky asked.

"Not in nineteen twenty-nine, you don't. The bank didn't have his address," Ryan said, shaking his head at the trusting nature of the world. "Who knew you could be this anonymous? You can't do that where we're from."

"Ok, well, we have a list now, don't we?" Deb asked.

"Yes, one is right near the shop we're going to, so maybe we can ask them after the appointment to get the tuxedos today. But the others are back near the banks," Ken added.

They finished lunch, and girls walked the block back to the Stafford while the guys went in a different direction, toward 5th Avenue for their appointment. The guys returned a few hours later, just as the girl's purchases were arriving at the hotel. They sent a bellhop up with the tuxedos and the girl's things and they went directly to the girl's rooms.

After the bellhop left the girl's room, Ken said, "We found him! He's using this investment firm that is not a big place. They were thrilled with him and were more than a little hesitant when we gave him our story about being a long-lost family."

"They didn't want to give us his location and didn't want to say when he expected to see him next, but he seemed a little scared about that part of it. I think he might show up there soon," Ryan added.

"Maybe you should go back tomorrow and say that you were so impressed with him you wanted to invest too, then maybe he will be more open with you, just an idea," Deb said as she unwrapped her new dress.

"That's a great idea, Deb," Ken said, as he walked over and admired her new white and silver sparkled gown.

"Did we get the invitation from Mr. Worthington?" Becky asked as she unwrapped her dress.

"Yes. We have a car picking us up at seven tonight," Ken said.

"Are we supposed to eat before this thing?" Joe asked, "Cause I'm hungry."

"You're always hungry!" Becky said as she sat down on the sofa he was sitting on and grabbed his hand.

"I want to wash some of the road grime off me before I put on a dress," Deb said in reply to the hunger joke.

"How about we go downstairs and see what we can scare up in the bar to eat while the girls get ready? Then we can all get into our dapper clothing and sit down in the lobby awaiting our car," Ken suggested as he got up and walked toward the door.

Joe needed no encouragement and jumped up too, stopped, turned back and bent down and kissed Becky and then went back to the door, laughing. Ryan hugged and kissed Deb and did the same. The girls laughed about all of this for a few minutes before they gushed over their dresses and shoes and things. When they had primped and curled and gotten dressed, they joined the guys down in the lobby.

"Wow, you sure clean up nice!" Becky said to Joe, as she leaned down to him in the chair he was sitting in and kissed his cheek.

"You look ravishing, my dear," Ryan said as he rose from his chair and took Deb by the hand. He offered the seat he had been in to Deb, and she sat down. Then he looked at Joe and said, "This is how it's done, my young friend."

Ken laughed and added, "I guess he isn't the gentleman now!" He then got up and offered Becky his seat.

They sat and talked about what they had seen that day from shopping until a man in a black suit came over to them. "Excuse me, are you the Fitzgerald's?" the man in the black suit asked.

"Yes, we are," Ken answered.

"Right this way, the car is waiting," he said as he gestured them with his arm toward the doors of the hotel.

They all followed him out to the car, and Joe said, "Wow."

"What a nice vehicle you have," Ryan added.

"Thank you, Sir," the man said as he opened the back door to the very long, very sleek, grey Rolls Royce limousine.

"Ladies first," Ken said, as he helped Deb and Becky enter the back seat and slide in.

Then the boys entered and slide left to the seats that faced the girls. They looked around at all the appointments of this vehicle and commented about the glass decanter and the plush seating. Before they were done admiring the interior, the vehicle came to a stop and the black-suited man opened the back door, and held out his hand to assist the ladies out of the vehicle. Once they were all out of the vehicle, the man in the black suit got back into the front seat of the car and drove away. Ken was the first to speak as they all stared at the large estate they were standing in front of.

"Ok, remember, we're supposed to be from the very wealthy Fitzgerald's in Boston. We are railroad money from over fifty years ago," Ken said, reminding them of their cover story. "Ryan, you are Deb's fiancé, and Becky, you are the woman Joe is courting right now," He added.

"Got it," Ryan said, smiling at Deb. He had purchased a ring that day that was a ruby surrounded by diamonds. It wasn't large, but it was very classic. He had given it to Deb for their dating anniversary, but they had decided they would place it on her left hand, ring finger, to show their engagement for the stories here. Or so that was the story Ryan gave Deb when he gave her the ring that afternoon.

They walked up to the steps and began to climb them to the entryway of the large, gothic revival architectural home of Mr. Worthington. They entered with some trepidation, but were greeted by Mr. Worthington as he turned from a group he was talking with just inside the ballroom to the right of the entryway.

"There you are! It is so nice to see you all tonight," he said, as he walked over to them and shook Ken's hand.

"Thank you so much for the invitation, Mr. Worthington. And, might I add, you have a wonderful home," Deb said, stepping forward and offering her hand to him. He took her hand and brought it to his lips and lightly touched Deb's white-gloved hand and then released it. He then looked at Ryan and said, "What I lovely fiancé you have, Sir."

"Why thank you, Mr. Worthington, I rather think so," Ryan said as he took Deb's left arm and wrapped it in his arm to escort her. He added, "Please, call me Ryan, Mr. Worthington."

"My pleasure to all of you and please, you and Kenneth may call me Benjamin, as I stated yesterday," Mr. Worthington replied.

Mr. Worthington began talking with Ken about the people that were present and who he should introduce him to so he could begin to grow his business in New York. Ken engaged him as they walked and tried to circle the conversation around to Tom. Ryan and Deb were right behind them and when the conversation stalled a bit, Deb pulled Ryan around so they were standing next to Mr. Worthington and she asked, "Mr. Worthington, did you happen to see our distant relative, Mr. Thomas Thorton?"

"I do not recall if he was on the invitation list, but perhaps he is here with his financial advisor," he replied. "Do you have his name? I will seek him out to discover if that is true and then bring him to you all."

"His name is Michael Salinger," Ken said.

"Oh, well, certainly he is on the invitation list. He's a distant cousin of my wife, so of course, he receives an invitation to all of our functions. However," Mr. Worthington put his hand in front of his mouth and leaned in toward Ken as he continued, "only because of his relation to us. He has some rather shady clients at that brokerage firm."

"If you could point him out to us, or make contact with him tonight, so that we might speak with him, we would so appreciate it," Ryan added.

Mr. Worthington had directed them to the refreshment table and when they arrived, introduced them all to all the guests standing nearby, which included Andrew Mellon. Joe was beside himself to make the acquaintance of these business innovators. He became animated asking them about their initial ideas and how they made them grow. While all that excitement was going on, Deb was scanning the crowd. She thought she glimpsed Tom near the patio and she pulled on Ryan's arm to have him walk with her toward the patio. He whispered to her to ask what was going on and she stopped long enough to whisper back of her sighting. When they arrived at the patio, they searched around and didn't see him, but then Ryan pointed out to the distance of the property, where he saw a man sneaking through the trees. They weren't sure, but they saw him look back and see Deb, and then he shot through the trees.

"It might have been him," Ryan said, as he looked again to see if he got back into the property somewhere else.

"I'm almost sure it was him. When he looked over to where we were standing near the refreshments, he saw me, and I looked cause I could feel someone watching me. We looked at each other for a moment and he seemed to remember who I was. Then he bolted out of the patio doors," Deb said, explaining what happened.

Deb and Ryan returned to where Joe was still talking with the business tycoons and reached for Ken. She whispered what had happened and Ken was about to turn to go see if he could find Tom outside when Mr. Worthington walked up to them.

"My oh my, Joseph is really one of those business tycoons, isn't he?" He asked as he approached Ken and Deb.

"Yes, he is, Benjamin. He is soon to be a business leader, I believe," Ken replied.

"Oh, say, I just saw the financial advisor, Mr. Michael Salinger, and he said that Thomas was with him here, but he said he had to leave because of an issue. He departed just a few minutes ago. I requested Thomas' address and Mr. Salinger wrote it down for me," Mr. Worthington said as he handed Ken a small piece of paper.

"Thank you so much, Benjamin. This is just what we need. We will contact Thomas tomorrow to be sure he is alright. How fortuitous that we found you!" Ken said as he took the paper, folded it, and put in his pocket.

"Well, my new friends, you are always welcome," Mr. Worthington replied as the group Joe was talking with broke up and he walked over. Mr. Worthington turned to him and said, "I must say, Joseph, I am so impressed with your business knowledge and interest in everyone in the financial world. You will have to make arrangements to meet me next week at my bank to discuss some investment money for your business plans."

"Why, Benjamin, I would be delighted!" Joe replied and held out his hand.

"Here's my card, then," Mr. Worthington said as he handed Joe the card and then shook his hand, then he added, "my apologies, but I must attend my other guests now."

He walked away, and they circled around Ken as he pulled the paper out and looked at the address. Not recognizing the address, but at Ryan's suggestion, they were going to ask the concierge at the hotel when they returned. They enjoyed the food and marveled at the people they met there. They returned to the hotel around midnight. The concierge was not on duty, so they vowed to get up early to see if they could find Tom.

Tom charged through the brush surrounding the property and circled back to the front drive. He couldn't believe it. How had those darn Fitzgerald's found him? He was so angry, he almost charged back into the building and brandished either the knife he carried or the pistol he had bought yesterday. He couldn't believe he finally was treated as he felt he deserved, and those Fitzgerald busy bodies needed to show up and ruin it. Well, they wouldn't ruin it. He would make sure he got the money he needed. He was planning to wait for a few more days, but he had already made so much money, he could afford to sell out and leave. Those Fitzgerald's may have figured out where he was, but they had no way to know where he was headed.

As he walked back to the Waldorf, he wondered how they had figured it out. And how did they get another time machine? There was only one machine in that barn. How did they hide another one, and where did they hide it?

He stormed through the lobby and totally ignored the clerk that inquired about his night. He went to his room and poured a glass of water from the pitcher that was on the table. How had they found him?

Tom slumped down on the plush sofa and thought about his plan. He didn't think Joe and his cohorts knew where he was staying. They could have shown up at that party because they met someone. Now that he thought that through, though, that really made sense. They figured out he was in New York, but they had only got in with the people they knew. The wealthy people that had finally accepted Tom. It must be something all rich people know, how to find other rich people. How else could they just push their way into the group he had found? He was a somebody here. He rather liked it here. Why did they have to ruin everything?

As he closed his eyes to further plan the demise of Joe Fitzgerald and all his family, he realized they must have found his notebook. Sitting up, he cursed himself for leaving it. He shouldn't have left it. He was too rushed, and now he had to evade them. He was smarter than those Fitzgerald's, he would show them.

He stood and went to the desk in his suite and returned to the sofa with the papers that Mr. Salinger had given him. It showed the current holdings in his trading account. He was poised to make well over two million dollars if he did this correctly. He leaned back and went over the plan he had set to determine where he might make adjustments.

He stayed up most of the night, going back and forth on whether or not to wait one more day. Finally, he decided in the wee hours of the morning to go ahead and get out of New York today. He walked down to the desk and asked to send a messenger to deliver a note. The front desk clerk thought it a bit odd, but he did as he was asked and called for a messenger to come and get the note.

Tom went back upstairs and packed his things. He planned to catch the first train out of the city as soon as he met with Mr. Salinger. As he left the hotel, he smiled as he remembered what he had written in his notes about Grandpa Reggie. Of course, they would figure he was always in Ohio. Little did those stupid Fitzgerald's know that Grandpa Reggie started out at his family home in Rochester, New York. They would search all over Ohio for him and he wouldn't be there. He had already won. He knew it!

7

The next morning, Joe, Ryan and Ken rose early and dressed in their suits and went downstairs to have breakfast. After they ate, they went to the concierge desk and asked about the address. The concierge said the address was the Waldorf Hotel. When Ken asked if it was walkable, he said it was, but he called for a taxi out front and sent the boys on their way.

The taxi pulled up outside the hotel and Joe, Ryan and Ken paid him and got out. They went to the desk and asked for Thomas Thorton. The desk clerk informed them that Mr. Thorton had checked out of the hotel that morning.

"How long ago?" Ken asked the clerk.

"Approximately thirty minutes ago, Sir," the clerk responded.

"Can you get us a taxi, please?" Ryan asked.

"Certainly, Sir. Where do you wish to go?" the clerk asked as he raised his hand to signal the doorman.

"Downtown to Broad Street, if you please," Ryan replied.

"Very good, Sir. Your taxi will be waiting for you through those doors," the clerk said, motioning them to the front entry door.

The three of them rushed out the door to the waiting cab. Ryan leaned toward the driver of the old-time model automobile and said, "Six, one, two north broad street, and go as fast as you can!" He then smiled and looked at Joe and then Ken as he said, "I've always wanted to do that!"

The car raced through traffic that in nineteen twenty-nine still included some horse-drawn carts. It was a perilous trip that took longer than all three of them suspected, but finally they arrived, paid the driver and went inside, asking the front desk receptionist for Mr. Salinger. The rather tall woman left through a door beside the front area of the office and came back in a few minutes, holding the door and looking at Ken, saying, "Mr. Salinger is free. You can follow me."

The three of them filed into an office that was rather large and a man stood up from behind the desk and, coming around, held out his hand to shake theirs. He introduced himself and Ken, Joe and Ryan in turn introduced themselves. Mr. Salinger motioned for the men to sit down and when they were all settled, Ken said, "Mr. Salinger, thank you so much for seeing us without an appointment. We don't mean to interrupt your day, but, we are desperate to find a gentleman. He's a lost relative of ours, that frankly we thought we lost in the great war. We've only recently discovered that he might be alive. As you might imagine, we have been frantically searching. We learned only a night ago that you might help him with some financial matters."

"Of whom do you speak of? I do have many clients," Mr. Salinger replied.

"Mr. Thomas Thorton," Ken answered.

"Ah, I remember the note left me by one of the receptionists. Yes, he is a client of mine, well was. I did not realize you feel you might have lost him in the great war. The note I received just said you were looking for a lost family member. I am sorry, though. You just missed him. He was here moments ago to collect his funds."

"Excuse me, Mr. Salinger, but do you mean he liquidated his interests today?" Ryan asked.

"Yes. It's rather strange, actually. He contacted me through messenger this morning at my home and said he needed to leave town today to assist his grandfather in Ohio. Are we talking about the same man?"

"Oh, this could be a miracle. You see, Mr. Salinger, we determined he came back with a severe head injury and likely had amnesia. If what you're saying is true, perhaps his memory has returned!" Joe said, excitedly.

"That would be wonderful news," Mr. Salinger said, smiling, "then I suppose you know where he is headed and can find him with this man he refers to as his grandfather."

"Our uncle, Sir, and we know right where he is headed," Joe said as he stood up.

They all stood when Joe stood up and thanked Mr. Salinger, saying goodbye. As the three exited the building, Ken said, "Why didn't you let us question him some more, Joe? We might have gotten a city or address or something."

"No need," Joe said as he hailed another taxi. "I know right where his grandfather is, and I know exactly when Tom is going there."

As they rode in the taxi at a more reasonable pace, Ryan added that if they hurried, they might be on the same train as Tom to get to the machines and they could intercept him there. Ken thought that was a fabulous idea, so when they entered the hotel, he sent Joe and Ryan up to get the girls packed and their things packed while he went to the desk to check them out of the hotel.

The girls understood the urgency and basically threw their things into the suitcases and got downstairs in record time. The concierge got them a car to the train station, and they just made the train before it left the station. They elected Ryan to search the train for Tom, since they believed he was the least familiar to Tom. Not finding him, they all anxiously sat and willed the train to go faster to the White Plains station. It was agreed by the time they arrived the guys would find a way to travel to the farm as quickly as possible, where they expected Tom's machine was hidden, while the girls planned to have a younger boy take them and all the luggage in a cart to meet the guys at the driveway to the farm on the other side of the barn their machine was hidden in.

As soon as Ken, Ryan and Joe got the girls situated with a cart, they took off down the road toward the farm they expected Tom to be at. As they ran down the road, Ryan said, "We searched the barn and the sheds for the other machine. Where do you think we should search when we get there?"

"I'm thinking he might have hidden it in behind that grain silo or in the brush behind that. I know he isn't experienced with the machine, like we are, but I don't think he's careless enough not to hide it," Joe replied.

"Let's split up a little when we get there. There's also that chicken coop shed we didn't check when we arrived," Ken said, as they approached the drive leading to the farm. Joe and Ryan headed for the silo, and Ken went in the opposite direction toward the chicken coop.

Ken circled the chicken coop quickly, realizing the machine could not be inside, and then he dashed off to where Joe and Ryan were about to reach the silo. When the three of them arrived, they saw the machine was not behind, nor in the silo. They all turned together toward the brush and headed in. The three of them fanned out a bit and then suddenly Joe, trying not to alert Tom, said, "Over here!"

Ryan and Ken rushed to where Joe was, and seeing the machine a short distance away, Ken started toward it. Ryan pulled on his arm to stop him, saying, "Wait, Ken. We can't just rush up to it. If he's started the thing up, it will catch us in the force preparation and throw us, hard."

"Is that what happened to you?" Ken asked.

"Yeah, and it wasn't pretty."

"Let's approach it slowly and low and maybe we can assess what's going on in there," Joe suggested.

They crept up closer to the machine, and Ken heard Tom inside cussing about something. At that, he rushed toward the door and tried to open it. Tom, hearing the door being rustled, turned and approached the window. He saw Ken and his eyes got big and he ducked away from the door. Ken looked in and saw him working the settings into the console to the left of the door. He tried to force the door open, but it wouldn't budge. Tom turned to Ken and gave him a snide look as he sat down and buckled himself into the seat. Ryan saw that too and pulled

Ken back from the door. Ken tried to resist being pulled away, but when he heard the noise of the systems starting up, he allowed Ryan to pull him back.

The machine roared to life, and then it was gone. Joe stood there with his head down for a few minutes. Ryan and Ken were also lost in thought for a few minutes when Ryan said softly, "Did you see his face?"

"What?" Joe asked.

"Tom looked over at us in the door window and had the meanest grin on his face," Ken said, looking at Joe, "We have to figure out where he's gone and stop him."

"Let's back to the girls. I know where he's gone and probably when. His ancestor invented a combustion engine and fought with Henry Ford for the patent. We know this. Tom has taken the money to help this great, great, whatever fight Henry Ford," Joe said.

They took off at a slow run to where the girls were waiting in the next farm driveway on the other side of the woods.

The girls were sitting on the luggage when the guys came running up. Deb stood and reached out for Ryan, who got to her and gave her a hug. Becky asked, "What happened?"

"We found him and got there just as the machine was starting its process. We couldn't get close enough to stop it before it took off," Joe said as he, too, hugged his girlfriend.

"After what happened to me when we went to stop Joe that trip, I stopped Ken from running right at the machine when we found him. It wouldn't do for one of us to have an injury at this point," Ryan added.

"But we know where he's headed, I'm certain of it," Joe replied.

"Me too," Deb asked.

"Remember we found his notebook, and he talked about his great grandfather's engine that Tom's whole family believed Henry Ford stole? I'm sure he's going with all that money, whatever he made, to correct what he thinks is the source of his problems," Joe said.

"What are we waiting for, then? Let's get all our suitcases in the machine and get out of here!" Ken said, as he picked up three of the cases and turned toward the wooded area.

While they walked, Becky said, "So, what's the plan?"

"I think we should go to where we expect him to be and grab him. I will take him back in the machine he stole, and you three will go back in our machine. Quick and painless," Ken said rather emphatically.

"But we don't know the exact location. He will take that other machine, do we? How can we catch him if we don't know the exact day he's going or where he's going?" Becky asked.

"We'll use the tracking system we made. It will see the trace energy discharge elements and we can estimate his trajectory. That will help us find a close measure of the coordinates. Then all we have to do is figure out the dates," Joe answered.

When they got to the machine, Ryan and Joe set up the tracing computer and sensors. Ryan took the sensors toward where they found Tom's machine. He put one in a low-hanging branch of a tree and the other an old fence post. When he got back to where the others were, Joe had the system up and running. Deb had the map spread out on the suitcases they piled up to make a table. Ken had a notebook, ready to jot down anything they found. Becky was looking through Tom's notebook for clues about the dates he might pick.

Joe called out the trajectory data from the sensors, and Ken wrote them down. After Joe had powered down the system and Ryan was storing it back in the machine, Joe and Ken worked out the calculations, and they determined where Tom had probably gone. While Joe and Ken were working on the coordinates, Deb and Becky were going through the notebook and their notes to determine the when part of the equation.

Deb excitedly yelled, "I've got it!" She looked around at the others expectantly as she said, "He had to have gone to right after his great-grandfather's case went into appeal by Henry Ford. That's when the money would have done the most good, to fight back after they won the first case, but it got appealed."

"That's as good an answer as any, I think," Joe answered, "And, that makes these calculations easier because there is a barn structure behind their family home that was his workshop, but there is this other smaller building next to it. I think that's probably where Tom is taking the machine."

"What day are we using?" Ryan asked.

"I don't think we should go on the date they filed the appeal. It gets filed in New York city and then likely a notice goes out to him in Rochester. He won't even know there is an appeal for a few days," Becky said.

"What if we go three days after the appeal file date?" Joe asked.

"I don't want to miss him again, so I'd rather find a hotel and monitor him than miss him again," Ken said, a bit emphatically.

"Why don't we just go on the filing date then and find a place near him to stay and wait it out?" Ryan asked.

They decided that was a plan and after they confirmed all the settings; they strapped into the seats and left nineteen twenty-nine behind.

8

Deb and Becky entered the hotel they were staying at in Rochester, New York, just as Ken and Ryan returned from their investigation of the Thorton house and grounds in the grove neighborhood of Rochester.

"What did you find?" Deb asked as Ryan took her hand, walking through the lobby to the stairs.

"Well, he's there. We saw him walking from the barn to the house with an older guy that looks a lot like Tom. I'm pretty sure it was his great-grandfather. We couldn't search around much for the machine, but he's there," Ken said.

"What do you have there?" Ryan said, as he took the bags from Deb and Ken took the bags from Becky to go up the stairs.

"Clothes mostly and some extras we might need. The clothes for men aren't much different, even though we've gone back twenty years, but for women, it's a little more complicated," Deb explained.

"Complicated how?" Ken asked, smiling at his sister as he unlocked the suite door.

"Complicated because the skirts are different and in nineteen eleven women still wear bustles and things. It's just complicated, ok? We were able to get most of what we needed at the costume store back home, but we needed a few things," Deb said, sticking out her tongue at her brother when he laughed at her.

They all sat down in the sitting area of the suite as Becky asked, "What's the plan?"

"I want to go back there tonight and see if we can find the machine," Ken said.

"I think we should monitor the house, the coming and going of Tom and his great-grandfather, to see if we can find a pattern of behavior," Becky said, speculatively.

"That way, we can find a time when we can snatch Tom and get out of here," Ryan added, smiling.

"I really think we need to think this through some more. I mean, he's already talked to his great-grandfather. Maybe he's even shown him the machine. We can't simply snatch him off the street and disappear. That will cause questions, maybe even a search, and it might impact history. Remember, the goal here is to keep history from being messed up while we get the machine back," Deb said as she looked around at each of them.

"Why don't we just locate the other machine and get us out of here and leave Tom here?" Ken asked.

"Ken, that's the definition of messing up history. It would strand Tom here, and there is a possibility he would be born before this version of himself dies. I mean, remember, there was that picture of him with this great-grandfather, that you just saw him walking with, looking much younger. That would cause an enormous problem. When Deb and I tried to do that for a few minutes, we both felt like our insides were coming out," Joe replied.

"Ok, I get it. We're too close in time to when he would be born in the sixties, so we can't just leave him here. He'd end up meeting himself. But could we force his hand to come to us somehow? Like maybe locate his machine and move it, or maybe send some of us back in it and then Tom would be forced to find us. I mean, he knows we're chasing him. He saw me at the window of the machine," Ken said, trying to sort out a solution that would end this quickly.

"I still think watching him for a day or so would be best. We don't know exactly what he has planned, so until we do, should we risk it?" Deb asked.

"Ok, but I still want to know where that machine is tonight. So, girls, you take up some watch. There is a park across the street from the front of the house. Ryan, Joe and I will watch the workshop and I will follow him if he leaves the house," Ken said, setting out a plan for tomorrow.

"Let's get changed into the new clothes and go get something to eat. I'm starving. Then we can set up to watch. Joe and I can go between the back and front to communicate with the girls, let's say every half hour," Ryan said, standing up.

"After dinner tonight, I'm going over to see if the machine is in that shed. One of you should stay with the girls, and one can come with me," Ken said as he stood.

"Ok, the bags over there are for you guys. Different style ties and shoes, but your suits and shirts should be ok," Becky said, "Deb and I have a little more changing to do, though."

The girls took several of the bags into their room and closed the door. Twenty minutes later, they emerged wearing new skirts with their day shirts. "How do we look?" Becky asked as she spun around.

"Not that different," Joe said, laughing.

"Took you long enough to not change that much. Now I'm really starving!" Ryan said as he watched Deb turn around in front of them.

"Nice, Ryan, no compliments for my sister!" Ken added as he reached for Deb to give her a hug. "You look great, my younger sister."

"Thanks," Deb said, smiling at Ryan.

They had lunch and then took up their places for surveillance of Tom and his family's home. With nothing new to report except a gathering of people to the front entrance of the family home, Deb and Becky left their front door watch and found the guys. When they reported it appeared a dinner party of some sort was picking up steam, they left their watches and returned to the hotel. The girls cleaned up from their afternoon in the park while Ken and Ryan made friends with the concierge in this new hotel in order to get good information should they need it. The five of them went to the recommended restaurant and ate, returning to the hotel around eight that night. As soon as the girls were situated, Ken suggested Joe and Ryan accompany him to snoop around the barn and shed at the Thorton property while the dinner party was going on. He said as long as the girls stayed in the hotel, the three of them could probably cover more ground. They agreed.

Finding the barn door facing the back road of the property locked, the three made their way around to the side that was both hidden from the street and the house. Joe found an open window and Ken hoisted him up to it so he could climb in. Ken and Ryan waited, and soon a side door was opened, with Joe appearing around the door. He motioned for them to come and the three entered the barn. Luckily, there was enough moonlight and windows to illuminate the barn enough they could search around. Joe concentrated on a table in the middle of the room with drawings and designs all over it, in no real order.

"Look at this!" Joe exclaimed as he moved a large drawing and found several forms underneath.

Ken and Ryan came to the table and looked over Joe's shoulder. Ken said, "What did you find?"

"It's the original patent form and drawings for the engine that Tom's great-grandfather submitted back in eighteen ninety-seven. But here's a form. It looks like he's about to submit with updated drawings," Joe replied, pointing to a form on the table.

"What do you think he's up to?" Ryan asked.

Ken looked at the original and the updated drawings for a minute and then the form and then he said, "It looks like he's incorporating some updates to the engine that might be from Tom. See, the original has a combustion engine, but it only had one cylinder. Tom's great-grandfather had a patent that predated the more advanced engines, but it had the workings of all engines at the time. That was how he got royalty payments from the manufacturers. But because he never went into production with any vehicle, and he showed no real advancement in the design, Ford won the appeal. These newer drawings and the updated filing are going to put that appeal into question. I think."

"So, do you think that's Tom's plan? Get his great-grandfather in a better position to win the appeal and then they will have royalty payments for many more years?" Ryan asked.

"Maybe. But they'll still need some skilled lawyers to make this case, since he's going to be filing these updates after the first case," Ken added.

Joe put the papers back to the way they found them and they made their way over to a door that looked like it might go into that shed that was against the barn. The door did lead to the shed, but with no windows, there was no light at all. Joe returned to the workroom and located a lantern. He returned and lit it once he was in the shed so as not to draw attention from the house. The light showed shelves and shelves of parts and in the center, an engine on a table. No machine. Ken turned to Joe and said, "Darn it, I really thought it would be in here. I really wanted to force his hand and get this over with."

"I know you did, but maybe he will go check it out tomorrow and we can follow him," Joe said, as he walked back to the door separating the barn from the shed and distinguished the lantern. The three of them left the barn and made their way back to the hotel.

When they entered the suite, Deb and Becky were going over notes. Deb looked up and said, "What did you find?"

"Drawings and a filing to update the patent information on the engine, but no machine," Ryan said as he sat down next to Deb.

"What do you think Tom is up to?" Becky asked.

"We think he might have helped his great-grandfather update the engine design documents to put him in a better position for the patent and hearing," Ken said as he too sat down.

They all sat for a minute in their own thoughts when Ken asked, "How much time do you think has gone by back at home?"

"I've been keeping track using the formula we refined on our trip to Philadelphia, and I'm pretty certain three days have gone by back at home. That would make it Monday afternoon there," Becky replied.

"Is everyone still covered with their stories?" Deb asked.

They all agreed they would be ok for a few more elapsed days before they needed to go back and get new cover stories started. With that, they all went to bed.

For the next two days they watched the Thorton house, the barn in back, and Ken and Ryan followed Tom whenever he left the house, which wasn't very often. Unfortunately, each time he was with someone from his family. The first time, he went with his great-grandfather to Thorton Trucking Company and spent the day talking with people. That afternoon, he and his great-grandfather went to a law office downtown. The next day, he went walking with a pretty young woman in the park where Deb and Becky were watching from. They were careful not to be right in his way as he walked, but wandered behind him so they could listen to what they said.

That night, over dinner, Deb and Becky recounted what they had heard in the park. Deb said, "We think we've pieced together what he's been up to. He arrived here two days before we did. He claimed to be a nephew of what really is his great-grandfather, by a brother that left the area to go west just before nineteen hundred. At least that's what he told the wider family."

"Tom told Abigail, who is his actual aunt, that he won't be in town for much longer. He said he was helping his uncle and then had to get back to his family in Minnesota," Becky added.

"We better get our hands on him tomorrow then, cause it doesn't sound like he has too much left to do. They went to the lawyer's office yesterday afternoon and a clerk from that office delivered some papers today," Ryan postured.

"We haven't seen him do anything with any money. Could he have dealt with that the day he arrived before we found him?" Joe asked no one in particular.

"I'm pretty sure they dealt with the updated patent filing at the meeting with the lawyer yesterday and likely what was delivered today was a copy of that filing that is being submitted. I overheard the clerk telling Tom's great-grandfather that he was leaving for the city that afternoon to take care of it," Ken said, then added, "If I were Tom, I would wait to give the money right before I left. That way, the least amount of people know about it."

"But you're not Tom. He's done some quirky things," Joe said, shaking his head.

"Maybe not quirky, Joe. Maybe he's doing the things he's doing because he doesn't know what we know about time travel. He hasn't learned about what happens when you change history and he doesn't know what his being here can do," Becky said as she put her hand on his arm.

"Should we try to draw him out tomorrow? Show ourselves and get him to come after us somehow?" Ryan offered.

"If the opportunity presents itself, I think it's time we stopped just watching him," Ken said, as he looked at each of them.

The next morning, just after the girls were positioned in the park and Joe, Ryan and Ken were positioned in back near the workshop barn, Tom and his great-grandfather came out the front door of the house in suits and got into a carriage and left. Becky went around to tell the guys what was going on and Deb watched the carriage. Ken hailed a carriage for hire, and they picked Deb up just as the carriage with Tom inside turned a corner toward downtown.

Tom and his great-grandfather exited their carriage in front of a bank building. Ken organized their efforts, which began with directing Deb and Ryan to go into the bank. Deb and Ryan searched around the bank lobby but couldn't see either Tom or his great-grandfather. Then Ryan pulled Deb's hand toward an office in the rear of the lobby. There, behind a window, sat Tom and his great-grandfather.

"Let's sit over there. It's right next to the office and maybe we can hear what they're saying," Ryan said as he pointed to some seating. As they sat, they heard Tom say, "This should be more than enough for you to win the case, Grandfather, and then you and our family will be set for years to come."

No one said anything for a few minutes and then the bank manager re-entered the office. He did not sit down, but looked somewhat agitated as he looked at Tom and his great-grandfather. Then he said, "Well, this is most unusual. I'm at a loss about how to address this. You, Mr. Thorton, with your father, the founder of this bank. What can you be about? What is this money you brought me to make this deposit?"

"I don't understand what you mean," the older Mr. Thorton replied.

Tom looked around a bit and seemed very nervous as the bank manager continued, "Well, perhaps we should just start with this. Just where did you get this money?"

"I gave my grandfather this money," Tom said, unable to look the bank manager in the eye.

"And where did you get it?" The bank manager said, leaning over his desk toward Tom.

"From my father, out in Minnesota where I'm from," Tom answered him quietly so that Ryan and Deb could barely hear him.

At this point, Tom's great-grandfather stood up. He pointed his finger at that bank manager as he said, "Just what are you accusing my nephew of? In my family's bank, I might add."

"Mr. Thorton, you grandson has presented this bank with one-hundred-dollar bills that have all the markings of US currency, but are not in the form, with the correct format and layout and pictures, I might add, of currently circulating currency. The printing day, in fact, is a date in the future. I can only presume that these are forgeries," the bank manager said, squaring off with the older Mr. Thorton.

"What do you mean?" Mr. Thorton asked.

At that, the bank manager laid one of the hundred-dollar bills Tom had brought next to a one-hundred-dollar bill that the bank manager had brought. Ryan stood up and nonchalantly turned so that he could glance at the money laying on the desk. They were different, very different. Tom looked down at the two bills and closed his eyes. Ryan smiled a bit as he turned away from the window. He knew what Tom had probably only just figured out. When you travel through time, you have to check the details of where and when you're going to be sure you don't mess things like this up. He whispered to Deb what was happening.

"These bills were obtained from a bank in Alexandria, Minnesota, founded by my brother. It is very near a new minting facility. Perhaps you just don't have the newest currency here in Rochester, New York!" Mr. Thorton thundered, "And how dare you accuse my nephew of counterfeiting money!"

"While that might be true, Mr. Thorton, none of that explains the future print date," the Bank Manager said, standing firm on his position.

At that moment, another bank employee entered the office carrying a brown briefcase. He placed the briefcase on the desk and left quietly. The entire time he was doing this, Mr. Thorton stared at the bank manager, and the bank manager stood his ground.

"We cannot take this deposit. Perhaps you should contact the bank you received these bills from and ask them to write you a bank check. That we will deposit for you," the bank manager said as he placed the one bill from the desk on top of the briefcase and pushed it across the desk to Mr. Thorton. Without saying a word, Mr. Thorton picked up the bill and the briefcase, touched Tom's shoulder to get his attention and turned and walked out of the office. Before they had taken a few steps, the bank manager said, from the doorway of his office, "I will have to report this, as you know. Expect the authorities at your door tomorrow."

Both Tom and his great-grandfather turned to look at the bank manager and when Tom turned, he looked straight at Deb. Recognition dawned on him as he looked back at Deb after turning and walking toward the door.

A few seconds after they left, Deb and Ryan made their way to where Ken, Becky, and Joe were waiting. They saw the carriage Tom was in make its way back toward their house as Deb and Ryan approached.

"What happened?" Joe asked. "They were in a big hurry to get out of there."

"They tried to deposit all the money Tom got from trading in nineteen twenty-nine and the bank manager wouldn't take it. Said it was counterfeit cause it didn't look like current money," Ryan explained.

"They got angry at each other, with Tom's great-grandfather accusing the bank manager and the bank manager accusing them," Deb added.

"The best part is, the bank manager said he was going to report them to some authorities and told Tom and his great-grandfather to be expecting a visit tomorrow," Ryan said.

"But I'm sure he recognized me," Deb said, looking down the street.

"We should get back to that barn quick. This is going to mess up their plans and I'm sure Tom's going to try something," Ken said, as he approached a coach that sitting in front of the bank. He motioned for the others to join him.

"I think I should not be sitting in front of their house today. He recognized me and we don't know what he'll do," Deb said.

"Why don't we go back to the hotel and have some lunch and wait for the guys," Becky said.

"Ok, we'll go watch the barn. You two stay at the hotel," Ken said as he closed the door to coach.

The girls walked the two blocks back to the hotel and Deb recounted all the details of the conversation they overheard in the bank. They went into the hotel lobby and asked if the restaurant was still serving lunch. Luckily it was, and the two girls sat in the sunny room and ate. Just as they finished their meal, Tom barged into the dining room and placed both of his hands on the center of the table in front of Deb and Becky and leaned over them. "You might have stopped me today, but I'm going to get you Fitzgerald's!"

"Tom, we did nothing to stop you today. You aren't thinking about what your actions are doing. Time traveling is a risky business. You have to think through so many things. Today, you didn't get stopped by us. You got stopped because you brought nineteen twenty-nine money to a bank in nineteen eleven," Deb said, trying to settle him down.

"I saw you at the bank. You probably said something to the bank manager!"

"No, Tom we didn't. We did nothing. You are the one that has done all of this. You're the one that stole the machine. You're the one trying to change your family's history," Becky said, standing up.

"I know that's how you got all your money and how Joe got to do that computer and how you're all so popular and have everything! Joe probably stole Dave that way too!"

"No, Joe, we didn't use the machine to gain wealth or opportunity or anything like that. We tried to stop our parents from being in a plane accident, we tried to help Mr. Brewster, and we tried to help others. That's all. And you know what we found? We found that whenever you get into that machine, you change something and the consequences can be huge," Deb said, also standing up.

"How did you get here? There was only one machine in that barn! And how did you find me?"

"How about you tell us where you're hiding the machine? Then we can all get back to where we belong," Deb said, completely dismissing his question.

"So you can win again? You Fitzgerald's are the worst! You think you get everything. I will show you all!"

With that, Tom stood upright and turned and left the dining room. After a minute, Deb thought it best to follow him. She directed Becky to bill the meal to their room and come out front and she walked out of the hotel. She searched left and right and didn't see a trace of Tom. Then she caught sight of him rounding a corner down the street. She turned to see if Becky was coming as she appeared out the front of the hotel. They hailed a carriage and Becky paid for the taxi service, while Deb directed the driver which way to go. As they got around the corner, Deb saw Tom turn onto, just in time for Becky to spot him turning down a street two blocks ahead. They directed the driver to turn two blocks up and waited. As they rounded that next street, Deb and Becky scanned for him up and down the street and saw nothing. They asked the driver to stop for a moment and Deb got out to look around. After some time, they realized they had lost Tom and had the driver return them to the hotel.

Just as they were stepping out of the carriage at the hotel, Joe and Ken walked up. Ken asked where they had been and Deb said, "Let's go up to our suite and discuss this."

"Where's Ryan?" she asked as they entered the suite.

"We left him to wait since we saw Tom walking back and entering the back of the workshop," Ken replied. "Where have you been?"

"Well, we were just finishing lunch when Tom walked up to our table and accused us of messing things up for him at the bank. Then he blamed us for all the bad things he's dealt with, including losing Dave as a friend, and said we used the time machine to make all our family money and all our opportunities," Deb explained as she sat on the sofa in the sitting area of their suite.

The others joined her. "How did he find out where we're staying?" Joe asked.

"I don't know, but he ended his little tirade with the declaration that he was going to get us all," Deb said as she leaned back and closed her eyes.

"We asked where his machine was and he wouldn't tell us, of course. He asked us how we found him and how we got here, but we didn't share that with him. Oh, and he asked where the other machine was. He basically admitted to being in the barn and stealing the machine," Becky added.

"I'm heading back to Ryan. Joe, stay here with the girls since Tom knows where we're staying. I don't want him showing up here with only the girls here again. As agitated as he is, I don't trust that he won't try something terrible if one of us isn't here. And don't hesitate to get physical with him if he shows up here and tries to threaten them again," Ken said as he headed for the door.

"Be careful, and tell Ryan I said to be careful too!" Deb said as Ken left the room.

"Now what do we do?" Deb asked to no one in particular.

"I think we should get everyone packed up. I feel like Tom's going to make a run for it tonight and I think we should be ready," Becky said as she stood up.

Deb and Joe agreed they might need to be ready, and it helped that they had something to do. By late afternoon, they had heard nothing from Ryan and Ken, and Joe was hungry. He suggested they go across the street to the restaurant that was there and eat an early dinner. After leaving a message with the front desk for Ken and Ryan in case they returned, they went and had some Italian food at the restaurant.

After they finished their dinner and returned to the hotel. They waited in the suite. But that became rather excruciating as the hours passed. By late that evening, Becky had fallen asleep on the sofa leaning on Joe, who was getting drowsy. Deb was pacing the suite, back and forth, when suddenly Ken burst into the room with Ryan leaning on him for support. Deb rushed to them and helped Ryan into a chair. She turned to Ken with an expectant look on her face as he said, "Ryan had snuck into the back room of the barn and was listening to what Tom and his great grandfather were talking about. He came out and said that Tom's great grandfather told him he needed to get us where we live and to get the heck out of there before the authorities showed up. With that, Tom took off. We followed him, but he got to some woods and we lost him."

Deb was peeling the coat, shirt, and tie off of Ryan as Ken retold the events of the night. Ken continued, "Ryan and I split up in the woods to locate him, and we figured the machine was there somewhere. I went left and Ryan went right. While I was making my way back toward where Ryan was searching I heard him scream. I ran through the brush and found him lying on the ground. He said that Tom had a box cutter style knife and cut him when Ryan and he were fighting. I saw the lights from the machine as I was trying to lift Ryan off the ground. He got away."

"It's ok, we need to take care of Ryan," Becky said as she returned from her room with bandages and towels and Joe followed with a bowl of water.

Deb cleaned the wound, and it was then they saw the cut was long and deep. It was seeping blood badly. Joe took a towel and put some pressure on the wound as Ryan winced from the pain of it.

"We have to stop this bleeding or this is going to get really bad, fast," Becky said.

"First, we need to clean it out. We don't know what Tom used that knife on before he cut Ryan," Deb said, with tears in her eyes.

"We don't have anything in this room but soap," Joe said as he put his arm around Deb.

"I'll go downstairs and buy a bottle of whiskey. We can use that to clean the wound," Ken said as he dashed out the door.

While Ken was gone, they checked, and the wound was still seeping blood. Deb asked Ryan how much it hurt and he said it burned and it really hurt when they put pressure on it. He also said he felt very queasy, so Joe got a garbage can and brought it close to where Ryan was half laying on a chair.

"We need to move him to lay him flat, I think," Deb said, "and we're going to need to stitch that wound up somehow or he's going to lose too much blood."

"I have a sewing kit in my bags!" Becky exclaimed as she ran to her room to get it.

Just then, Ken returned with a bottle of whiskey. He helped get Ryan to a bed after Becky and Deb had put towels on the bed under him. Then Ken told Ryan to take a big drink of the whiskey before they poured it on the wound.

"I don't drink," Ryan said with his face all scrunched up.

"I know, but you're going to need something to help knock you out, cause pouring whiskey on this is going to hurt," Ken said as he handed the glass he had poured to Ryan.

Ryan drank the whole thing and then seemed to choke on it. He lay back and Ken and Deb worked to open the wound and gently poured some of the whiskey on it. Ryan yelled and then fainted. They finished cleaning it and then they looked at each other as Deb asked who was going to stitch Ryan's skin together. They all hesitated, so Deb took the needle and thread from Becky and kneeled down next to the bed and began to stitch Ryan's skin together.

"This is so grouse!" Deb whispered as she made the first stitch.

"You're going to have to pull the stitches tight to get his skin to pinch together, Deb," Ken added as he watched her trying to be gentle.

Deb pulled tight and kept doing this with close stitches to be sure his skin was pinched tightly and there was no place it could open up. When she was about halfway done, Becky exclaimed, "I have some antibiotic ointment in my bag!"

"What from?" Joe asked.

"I cut my finger a couple of weeks ago at my grandmother's house, helping her cut vegetables. She gave it to me to be sure the cut didn't get infected. Let me get it. We can put some on the skin once it's stitched up to keep germs from getting in there."

When Deb was all done stitching Ryan's left side back together. She put the ointment on it and then Becky helped her bandage him up. At Ken's suggestion, they also wrapped Ryan all the way around his torso to be sure his movements didn't open it back up.

"Should we be worried? He still hasn't woken up?" Joe asked as Deb pulled the towels out from under him and covered him up.

"I think between the pain and the whiskey, he's probably better off to stay this way. Let's go out here and talk about what to do now," Ken said as he headed back into the sitting room.

Deb went and washed her hands and cleaned up before coming to sit in the chair that Ryan sat in when they came in tonight. She looked at Ken, sitting in the other chair as she said, "Did you or Ryan hear anything else from Tom to help us figure out where he went?"

"He didn't say much. Just that they were talking about what to do now for the engine invention and then the bit about how Tom should get us where we live," Ken replied.

"We might have to wait until Ryan wakes up," Joe added.

"You're sure that Tom left in the machine?" Becky asked.

"Yes, after I saw the lights, Ryan told me to go look. He'd left," Ken said as he closed his eyes.

"Well, if he's gone and we're not sure where, we need to wait for Ryan. I'm going in to lie next to him in case he wakes up," Deb said as she got up and went to Ryan. The others decided some rest would help, and they all went to get some sleep.

Some hours later, as the sun was starting to peek around the curtains at the window, Deb woke up to find Ryan's head turned toward her, his eyes open and him looking at her.

"Hi," she said smiling, "how are you feeling?"

"Better, with you here. Have you been here all night?" he answered.

"Yes, but that's not what I meant," she said as she rolled over to face him.

"I haven't moved yet, so I'm not sure, but it's not burning like it was last night. Or whenever the night was that I tangled with Tom," he said, turning his head to look at the ceiling.

Deb got up and came around to Ryan's side of the bed and checked his bandage wrap. As she did this, she said, "It was only last night."

"I was a little afraid I might not get back to you."

"I was afraid you would not make it last night."

"What happened?"

"Since you got back here last night, you mean? Well, we poured whiskey on your side, and then I stitched your skin back together, and then we put some antibiotic cream Becky had in her bag on you, wrapped you and let you sleep. You probably needed it," she said as she brushed his hair off of his eyes.

"You stitched my skin back together? With what?" he asked, raising his eyebrows and smiling at her.

"Becky has a great bag. It had a sewing kit in it. I didn't know what else to do. You were bleeding pretty badly, and we needed to close it up and stop it before you lost too much blood."

"Thanks for saving me, sweetheart."

"I kind of like having you around, so I guess I had to. Plus, nobody wanted to put a needle and thread through your skin, so I had to save you. Now, your turn."

"My turn for what? Saving you?"

"No, telling me what happened last night."

"Oh, that. Ken and I saw Tom go into the barn and I could hear them talking but couldn't make out what they were saying so I went to the side door and snuck into the room just outside the big work area where Tom and his great grandfather were talking. I could hear from there."

Ryan tried to sit up and then fell back on his back. Deb told him to try to first turn onto his side so he was facing the edge of the bed and then she would help him try to sit up. They did this. It was a struggle, but then he was sitting up.

"How does that feel?" Deb asked him.

"Ok. It hurts some, but it's ok."

"Then finish your story."

"Wow, you're a task master, huh? Not a great bedside manner, doctor!"

"I'm not trying to be that way; I just want to hear what you heard them talking about."

"Ok, so, first they talked about what to do now that the money would not be accepted and Tom's great grandfather was telling him he should leave town before the bank manager has the police come and find him. Tom talked about how mad he was that he couldn't help make this fight over the patent easier, and his great grandfather told him it wasn't his fault. Then he asked Tom about the people he said he recognized at the bank. I guess they talked about it after they left the bank this morning. Tom said that he knew us from Ohio. I guess that's his story.

Oh, and his great grandfather thinks Tom is really his grandson from a son that left home years ago and never returned, even though they were both calling Tom his nephew. Anyway, Tom complained about us, how we took business from him, took friends from him and made his life miserable in Ohio. That's when his great grandfather said he should get us where we live. Tom asked what he meant, and his great grandfather told him to take what we had, steal our business and friends, and do something that would hurt us. Maybe something that was important to us, but not to other people. Make it worse or take it away. Tom said he knew just how to do that, and he said he would get ready to leave. His great grandfather then pulled a bag out from under the table and said he already got him packed so he wouldn't have to go back to the house and explain his departure. That's when Tom started for where I was, so I hid inside a cabinet and then snuck out to get Ken after I heard the door shut. Ken and I followed him, and when we got to the woods, we split up. I spotted Tom making his way along a stream and I crossed it on a log and crept up along with him until I saw another way across. When I got to that spot, I jumped off this log and pulled him to the ground. We wrestled for a minute and then I got up, thinking I could punch him better standing up. He scrambled up and reached into his pocket and pulled out that knife. I tried to lock his arm up to get him to release the knife, but he was able to yank free of my hold and when he did that, he swiped down my left side with the knife and I knew he cut me. I felt weak suddenly, and I fell. He took off. I must have yelled cause Ken came tearing through the brush to me. I got out that he should follow Tom, which he did for a minute, then he came back."

"I wish you hadn't taken such a chance, Ryan, you could have really been hurt."

"Worse than this? How bad was the cut?"

"It was deep and about five of six inches long."

"Yikes!" Ryan responded to this news.

"Yeah, it was about an inch deep at the deepest point, but he didn't hit anything, just muscle and skin. You're probably very lucky to still be here."

"Why am I all wrapped up? Did I break a rib or something?"

"No, we just didn't want you to turn in your sleep or do anything that would open the cut back up. So, we totally wrapped you up."

Just then, Ken and Joe entered the room. Ken smiled and said, "Well, look at you, sitting up and everything! Thank goodness."

"Yeah, don't let me fool you. This hurts, and I mean really hurts, just sitting here," Ryan said.

"Maybe it will be better if you stand up," Joe said as he and Ken reached the bed where Ryan was sitting.

"Sitting on the bed isn't giving you much support, so if standing doesn't help, sitting in a chair might be better," Deb said.

Ken and Joe helped Ryan stand up and walked beside him into the sitting room. Becky was there, giving some money to the busboy who had brought them breakfast on a cart. Deb prepared a plate for Ryan and brought it to him. Then she got some food for herself and sat in the chair near him. The others got food and sat down. Ken asked Ryan how he was and what he heard from Tom before he came out of the barn. Ryan retold the story, and they all pondered what Tom might be planning.

"I think we should go back. I think it will be easier to figure this out with the technology of the nineteen eighties and it will help us make sure nothing big got changed from these trips," Joe said when he finished his food and was returning his plate to the cart.

"I agree," Becky added, "and we're all nearly packed."

"We need to check Ryan's stitches and then I'd like to take a bath and change clothes," Deb said.

"I think we could all use a bath," Becky replied, laughing.

"Becky, why don't you go ahead first while I check on Ryan's stitches," Deb said as she helped Ryan stand up and walk back into the room and lay down.

"You go first, Joe, and I'll help Deb," Ken said as he followed Deb into the bedroom.

When Ken and Deb got Ryan unwrapped, he laid down and Deb carefully pulled the bandages off his wound. There was some blood that had dried near a few of the stitches, but otherwise, it looked good. Ken commented as such, then he said, "You did good, Deb."

"I don't think it looks infected. It isn't red or swollen or anything," she added.

"My own personal Florence Nightingale," Ryan said as he tried to sit up to see the stitches.

"You're lucky, my friend. We're in nineteen eleven for starters, but we have someone with us who thought to carry a sewing kit with her, and Deb was brave enough to put that needle through your skin. You were bleeding the entire way back here, and you lost a lot of blood," Ken said, as he helped Deb re-apply the bandage wrapping after she put more antibiotic ointment on the stitches.

"We should probably find a way to get you some antibiotic pills or something when we get back to make sure you don't get an infection," Deb mentioned as she bandaged Ryan's side back up.

"I think my mother keeps some of that in her medicine cabinet. I'll try to grab some," Ryan said as Ken helped him stand up again.

After they all bathed, with Ken assisting Ryan to clean up around his bandage, they packed up and checked out of the hotel. They made their way to where their machine was waiting and set the system up to return them to Mr. Brewster's barn.

9

Tom exited his machine in the shed. He covered it with tarps and blankets and stomped around the small workbench table in the middle of the shed. He alternated between utter happiness that he had really cut Ryan McDonnell, and angry that the stupid Fitzgeralds had stopped him from turning his life around by getting his great-grandfather established. If he had only had enough money and had thought about what Deb Fitzgerald, the darn brainiac, had said. She said his mistake was taking nineteen twenty-nine money to nineteen eleven. It couldn't have really been just that simple, could it? No, it had to be something she said to the bank manager. Those darn Fitzgerald's ruined everything!

He went into the house, and up to his room to change clothes. His mother wasn't home yet from work, so he had time to get out of his suit. He contemplated taking the money he made in the stock market and going to a bank and trying to get it converted. He would be wealthy and he could do what his great-grandfather said and get those Fitzgerald's where they lived, if he could just get the money converted.

Tom went out to the shed and shut himself in for some thinking. He probably should go to the bank and ask about money he got from an old trunk in his great-grandfather's house, and not just take it all in there. That would be the smart thing to do. He would go there tomorrow.

That problem solved, now to decide how to get those Fitzgerald's and all their friends. He was deep into a destruction plan for each of his enemies when he heard his mother open the back door and go inside the house. He left the shed and went in after her.

"Hey Mom," he said.

"Oh, you're back, are you?"

"Yeah, I'm back."

"Did you get that job in Virginia?"

"Not really. I did some work and got paid. I have to go to the bank tomorrow and take care of cashing the check."

"So, again, nothing permanent. I swear you couldn't hold down a job for more than a few weeks. After everything I did for you."

"Really? Everything you did for me? Let's see what that is, shall we, Mom? You got me beat up by my dad for, oh, about ten years. Then you barely kept food on the table for the next ten years. You harp on me all the time because I didn't go to college and get a good job, but I ask you, how was I to pay for college?"

"I did my best to protect you from your father. I was the one that kicked him out of here, remember? And I do my best with two jobs to provide a place for you to sleep and eat. I was the one that asked the church to help you go to Choate. That was supposed to be a pathway to a better future. You are a hateful young man that just wants things handed to him."

She turned and went to her room to change. She said no more. Tom stormed out the back door, down the steps, and back into the shed. He didn't bother to see what she made for dinner. It couldn't possibly compare to the meals he had enjoyed while time traveling to New York and Rochester. If the Fitzgerald's hadn't had another machine hiding somewhere, if he had found it, and destroyed it, everything would be different today. He would be living in the lap of luxury. He would be the inventor of the personal computer and he would have a house on Long Island.

After several hours of scratching out his rage in a new notebook, he realized what he had to do to get the Fitzgeralds. Why, it was so simple. Deb handed him the solution at the nice hotel restaurant. They cared about history. She was all about warning him not to mess up history. Not sure what for. It was history, after all. Becky cautioned him, too. That entire clan of do-gooders probably all cared about history. It was the answer, and he knew how to get them. He would use the time machine and go back and mess all kinds of events up. That would make them all nuts and they would spend years trying to figure out what he did. Maybe they would even feel the need to fix it and that would distract them. While they were all busy doing that, he would swoop in and take over the businesses they were neglecting here. It was a perfect plan. He smiled because he knew he was smarter than all those Fitzgerald's and their friends combined.

Tomorrow he would go to the bank, and then to the library to start picking the events he was going to go to and mess up all that the Fitzgerald's loved.

The next day, he walked to the bank. He had no car, he couldn't afford one, yet. He waited to talk to a person sitting at a desk. When he explained his situation, the thing the woman wanted to focus on was how much money was he talking about. She kept trying to explain rules about older currency having to be documented and he was getting really mad at her. He finally asked if it was just a small amount. Could he bring it in? She said, "Of course, Mr. Thorton, if you're really describing a small amount, say, under twenty-five hundred dollars, we can easily take that and convert it for you."

"If I just want to convert and deposit it, is that still the case?" he asked.

"Well, if you're planning to put it on deposit, we can take five thousand."

"Thank you."

Tom got up to leave and then turned and asked, "Is this a banking industry rule or just this bank's rule?"

"Why, it is a federal regulation, in fact," she replied.

Tom left and went to the library. He pondered on his walk to the library how this was going to mess him up because he wanted to get back to hurting the Fitzgeralds, but if he had to wait until he could trickle that money, it was going to take some time.

While he was reading and taking notes, he smiled. He had events picked out quickly, and he decided how he would solve this banking issue. He would go tomorrow to several branch office and deposit five thousand each time. Then he would go back the next day to several different branches and just cash out twenty-five hundred at each. That should be fine and then when he got back, he would do the same with the rest of the money and he would have more than enough to plan his next step to take over the Fitzgerald's world.

10

It was early evening when they got out of the machine in Mr. Brewster's barn. They all changed back into their regular clothes and took all the bags and things out of the machine. Deb went and knocked on Mr. Brewster's door while the others finished cleaning up.

"My goodness, you're back!" Mr. Brewster exclaimed when he opened the door and found Deb standing there.

"We just got back," Deb said, smiling at him.

"The others?"

"In the barn, cleaning up."

"Well, let's go see what they're up to," he said as he came outside and closed the front door.

The two of them walked back to the barn and when they came inside, the table was all cleaned up and tracker parts were on the table.

"Tell me, what happened?" Mr. Brewster said as he sat down at the table.

Ryan was having trouble getting onto the stools at the table, which Mr. Brewster noticed, and he asked, "What happened to you?"

"I had a little run in with Tom last night," Ryan replied as he stood next to Deb at the table, having given up on trying to climb onto the stool.

"Do we need to get you to the doctor?" Mr. Brewster asked.

"I think that might lead to too many questions, given our medical care of him," Joc said.

"Whatever do you mean?" Mr. Brewster asked.

"You see, Tom had a box cutter style knife, and he cut a five- or six-inch slice into Ryan's left side last night when Ryan tackled him and tried to stop him from getting into the machine he stole," Ken said.

"What medical care was available?"

"Deb," both Joe and Becky said at the same time.

"What exactly did you do, Deb?" He asked, looking over at her.

"Well, we poured whiskey into it, then I stitched it up with Becky's thread and needle from her sewing kit," Deb replied, putting her arm around Ryan's shoulder.

"Maybe you better start at the beginning, and tell me the entire tale," Mr. Brewster said, shaking his head, "that is, if you're ok standing there and really don't need me to take you to the emergency room."

"I'm fine. It hurts the least when I'm standing up, actually," Ryan said.

"Ok, I'll start with the explanation," Joe said, looking around to see if anyone would object. When they didn't, he began, "We got our machine hidden and made our way from White Plains to New York City. We met a wealthy man who invited us to a big elite party, where we were introduced to a lot of wealthy people, and we also found out who Tom had been dealing with to trade. He admitted to knowing Tom and said he was investing. He might have seen Deb at that party. We went to that guy's office the next morning and just missed Tom. Then, we missed him, barely at his machine back in White Plains, and so went to nineteen eleven to his great grandfather's, the inventor of an early combustion engine. We followed him for a few days and then caught him trying to deposit all that money he made investing in nineteen twenty-nine at a bank. When he couldn't because it was from eighteen years in the future, he got angry and confronted Deb and Becky and then tried to sneak out under cover of darkness before the police came calling from all that counterfeit money. That's when Ryan and Ken followed him and tried to stop him from getting into the stolen machine again. Ryan jumped him but, in the scuffle, Tom pulled that knife and sliced Ryan open. We came back here to figure out what his next move might be, and to be sure Ryan was ok, and to cover our stories for the next trip."

"Well, you've had some adventures. What do you mean, counterfeit money? How did he find Becky and Deb? And, more importantly, what ideas do you have about what Tom might be up to next?" Mr. Brewster said, shaking his head a bit.

"It wasn't really counterfeit money. The bank manager in nineteen eleven thought it was because it had odd information on it," Deb explained.

"Yeah, like a printing date that was in the future," Ken said, rubbing his temples.

"I overheard him talking with his great grandfather, that engine inventor, about getting us where we live, taking something important from us," Ryan said.

"Well, I talked to Kim earlier today, and she said everything was fine out on Long Island. I don't think he's done anything to them, anyway," Mr. Brewster pondered, rubbing his chin like he always did when he was thinking.

"We should probably call her," Deb said.

"That's a good idea. Why don't you do the honors, Deb," Ken said.

"Use the phone in my kitchen, dear," Mr. Brewster said.

After Deb left the barn, Mr. Brewster said they should probably look at Ryan's injury to be sure nothing else needed to be done. He sent Becky inside to get more bandages and some hydrogen peroxide to clean it up with. Ryan leaned his back against the table and took off his shirt. Ken and Joe unwrapped his bandage, and Ryan carefully pulled the inner bandage off his wound. By this time, Becky was back, reporting that Kim and Deb were still talking.

"The skin in pinched together nicely. And the stitches are closed so it won't open up anywhere. Your nurse did a good job," Mr. Brewster announced after inspecting the six-inch-long line of stitches.

"It looks pretty good," Becky added.

"Yes, we just need to keep this line clean and covered for a few days, I think. In about three days, though, the stitches are going to need to be pulled out. If you don't, the skin will grow around this thread and it will probably cause an infection," Mr. Brewster said as he dabbed at the stitch line with a pad wet with hydrogen peroxide.

Flinching back, Ryan said, "That's cold, and it stings pretty bad!"

"We can't waste all the effort to get it clean and stitch you up by getting an infection. I thought you were a strong hockey player, Ryan," Mr. Brewster said, chuckling.

"I don't play anymore," Ryan said, sulking.

"We poured whiskey in there, and then Deb stitched him up right away, Mr. Brewster. Should we be worried about infection down in there now that it's closed up?" Ken asked.

"It was like an old black and white western when a guy gets shot and they douse it with whiskey," Joe said, laughing.

"Was it clear whiskey or brown in color?" Mr. Brewster asked.

"It was clear," Ken replied.

"Why does that matter?" Becky asked.

"The coloring would indicate other substances in the whiskey than just the alcohol. What you did was pour alcohol on and into his wound, which should ensure no infection," Mr. Brewster explained, "and yes, it was used in the old west, and in wartime as a disinfectant."

Becky handed Mr. Brewster the antibiotic cream when he finished with the hydrogen peroxide.

"Where did you get this?" he asked her.

"I got it from my grandmother a couple of weeks ago when I was helping her and cut my finger. I had it with me when we left in the machine."

"Oh, I was wondering how you found that on your time travels. I didn't think this ointment was available in the early nineteen hundreds," Mr. Brewster said, smiling. "Did you put this on the wound?"

"Yes, after the stitches were done, Deb put it all over the stitches and the line of the skin," Ken answered.

"That's good. That will probably ensure he doesn't get an infection. But, Ryan, if you start to feel warm or get the chills, meaning you have a fever, or you see any red streaks leading from these stitches in the next few days, go to the emergency room right away. Just tell them you were camping and got cut and your friend stitched you up because you couldn't get back quick enough from the wilderness," Mr. Brewster explained.

"Maybe we should use that story and go today, anyway?" Becky asked.

"No, I think it's going to be ok. I've been cut pretty bad on the ice in a battle and stitches and antibiotic ointment was all we used then." Ryan tried to coax them not to go to the hospital.

"This was a little deeper than a cut on the ice from a fistfight," Joe said, putting his hand on Ryan's shoulder.

"Was it a clean cut in there or all jagged or torn looking?" Mr. Brewster asked.

"It was a clean slice," Ken said.

"Then the outside stitches and the alcohol and ointment should be fine. The muscle tissue and skin tissue are resilient and can heal themselves pretty efficiently if you seal them up, keep them clean, and don't get infection," Mr. Brewster explained as he put fresh bandages on Ryan's injury.

Just then, Deb returned to the barn. She smiled at Ryan and all of them gathered around him, saying, "It looks like our stories are all good, and no questions are being asked. This is probably the best way to deal with Tom right now. Get our plans in place and then move forward."

"What's up with Aunt Alicia and Uncle Darrick?" Joe asked.

"They expect us back to the Long Island house tomorrow afternoon," Deb answered, "And, since Ryan was with me and some friends, and Becky was with Joe and then going to Long Island, we're good. Except for you, Ken. Kim said that Mary was anxious and was calling her every day. You should probably go call her."

Ken jumped down from his stool and headed toward the door as he said, "You're right, I better call her." He stopped and turned back. "Mr. Brewster, is it ok if I go in and call her?"

"Of course."

"I think, if we're to arrive tomorrow, we should just stay in town tonight," Becky postured to everyone at the table.

"That's a good idea," Joe answered, "then we can get a decent meal! The food is very weird in historical time."

"Really?" Mr. Brewster asked.

"Yeah, they serve duck and lamb and all kinds of sausage and everything is smothered in sauces. And they eat steak in the morning. It's really weird," he replied.

"You and your stomach, Joe. You're always hungry!" Deb said, as they all laughed.

"Hey, Joe, I was just thinking. Is there any way to use the new spectrometer devise to figure out where and when Tom has gone?" Mr. Brewster asked, interrupting their banter about Joe being hungry.

"The problem is, we don't know where he has the machine located. We aren't where it was anymore. We were too worried about nursing Ryan to go back to the woods to do the search. Now we would need to know where he has the stolen machine to scan for where he went, I think," Joe replied.

"Well, if find out where he is, then maybe that's an option," Mr. Brewster pondered.

Ken returned, saying that he had talked to Mary, and she was glad they were all back and safe. She was going to take the day off tomorrow and drive out to Long Island for the weekend. Joe reported their plan to stay in town tonight and get some food, and Ken agreed that would be a good idea. They thanked Mr. Brewster and Joe said he would call Saturday to let him know what they were up to.

They got checked into the hotel in town, where they had stayed many times in the past, and all went to dinner at Grimaldi's. The food was good, especially for Joe, but Ryan was uncomfortable, so Deb took him back right away after they finished eating. The others said they were going to walk through town.

The next morning, after breakfast and checking Ryan's wound, which still looked pretty good, they all piled into Ryan's and Ken's cars and headed to New York and Long Island.

11

While the others were traveling to the early part of the century, Kim and Jake arrived at the house on Long Island after finals were over to find Uncle Darrick waiting on the front steps. He hugged Kim as she and Jake came up. Jake held out his hand to shake, "It's a pleasure to see you again, Sir."

"No need for those kinds of formality here. Just call me Darrick," Uncle Darrick said as he shook Jake's hand.

"How about Mr. Reynolds? My mother always told me to respect parents of my friends," Jake replied.

"Well, I guess, but that always makes me want to look around for my father. Anyway, it's a pleasure to see you again," Uncle Darrick continued.

"Thanks, and thanks for letting me come out here and stay and spend time with Kim."

They turned and walked inside the house. Uncle Darrick indicated to Michael where to put Jake's things and then he said, "So, how were finals and the end of the year?"

"Good," Kim replied, "But we're starving."

Uncle Darrick laughed as he said, "I think we can do something about that."

Kim took Jake into the kitchen and the cook made them some sandwiches and got them some lemonade to drink. They ate out on the terrace and talked to Uncle Darrick. He told Jake about his job and then quizzed Jake on his family, plans, and school.

While Kim was unpacking and putting away all her school things and clothing, Jake sat in the family room and watched television. Just after Kim finished and joined him, Aunt Alicia returned home. Jake greeted her, and then she and Uncle Darrick went to the study for a bit.

They ate dinner and then Kim took Jake down to the beach.

"Wow, this is cool. The beach at night is so different!" Jake exclaimed as they stood near the water's edge.

"Yeah, I love it here."

"Your aunt and uncle are nice. Their house is pretty huge, huh?"

"Thanks. Yeah. When we came here for the first time, it was like coming to an enormous mansion, almost a museum. It was weird that they had a butler and a cook. But I've gotten used to Michael and the cook."

"It is a mansion. That's why it seemed like that! Michael's cool. Do you mind that they're the ones you come home to? I mean, do you miss your parents?"

"You know, for the first year we were at Choate, I really missed them. It was all I thought about, basically. How we were in that strange place, how it was so different. I wished they could see me, and all of us. But now, it doesn't hurt so much, it just sometimes makes me sad."

"I can't even imagine what it would be like without my parents. I don't think I could do what you've done. You seem so strong and so happy. If I were in your shoes, I don't think I would recover like you have."

"Well, I have Ken, Deb and Joe. It's strange, but I feel like this is how my family is supposed to be now."

"Really?"

"Well, you know, the machine and the time travel and Mr. Brewster helped, but my sister and brothers are closer than we would have ever been if our parents hadn't died. Each of us would probably be doing our own thing and I would never see them or talk to them like I do now. I like how we are with each other now, and I wouldn't want to lose that."

"It's really cool the way you all talk and help each other. I don't really have that with my older sister or brother."

"That's what I mean. If we hadn't lost our parents, we would probably be like you and your siblings."

"Probably. I mean, you had to kind of fend for yourselves so you had to be close, right?"

"It sure felt that way when we first got to Choate."

"I never knew you were sad all the time. You hide it well, I guess."

"It's not like that. I still think about my parents, probably every day. You know, I think about what they might say about things I do. I think about how they would react to my plans and accomplishments. I guess there's something every day that I wish I could share with them. But I wouldn't trade what I have now. Not anymore."

"You're really strong, you know that, right?"

"Strong, no. You're just a little biased, I think!"

He hugged her, and then kept his arm around her as he said, "Yes, you are strong. You lost your parents when you were what, ten, and you still have had an art show in a gallery in Boston, and you get good grades. Plus, you still laugh and have fun. That takes strength when you lose your mom and dad."

"Maybe, but I still think you're biased."

"Probably, but it's pretty darn cool that you're my girlfriend!"

They stood looking out on the water for a few minutes, when Jake said, "Your uncle sure drilled me."

"Sorry about that. I'm sure he feels he has to protect me or something."

"Yeah, I get it. I was kind of expecting it. My mom coached me on the phone last week, you know. She told me I was supposed to answer every question a parent asked me when dating a girl."

"Really?"

"Yeah, and when I asked if I could ask questions, you know what she said? She said you can only ask one. When should I have your daughter home?"

"Well, you didn't have to do that at school, and you don't have to do it here!"

"Hopefully, I gave your uncle the answers he wanted."

"I'm sure you did. He's a pretty easy-going guy, and besides, I've told him how much I like you, so that should count for something."

"You told him that, did you?"

"Yeah, I did."

"Is it weird that he's your uncle and doing the things your father would have done?"

"I remember the day he came to Choate and asked us to have lunch with him and asked us if we were ok with us all becoming a family. We focused primarily on what we were going to call him. We all seemed a little preoccupied with that. But really, it's very natural now. We call him uncle, but he does everything a father would do."

He smiled at her and then kissed her. They stood there for a few more minutes, silently looking out at the water. Then Kim suggested they go in.

The next day, after they had breakfast, Kim called Mr. Brewster, who reported that he had not seen either machine come back yet, but hadn't expected it for a day, or so at least. Then Kim and Jake went to the beach. They took a picnic and played in the water and had fun. They ate alone that night since Aunt Alicia and Uncle Darrick had an event in town. The next day they went into town and walked around, window shopping and had ice cream. They rented bikes one day and pedaled around until they were too tired. One night, they saw a movie and then on Friday, Uncle Darrick took them out on the boat. Uncle Darrick let Jake steer the boat for a while, which he really loved, and they stopped at a little shack that had fish and chips for lunch.

Uncle Darrick returned to town for another fashion event with Aunt Alicia, so Kim and Jake got to spend the night by themselves. They ordered pizza and watched movies. While they lay on the couch with the movie on, Jake asked, "Any word from Mr. Brewster today?"

"I tried to call him just before we left on the boat, and I tried again when we got back and I didn't reach him. I'm getting worried. Deb has to get back to the dig, and we have a story that has them covered for a bit, but if they don't get back here soon, I'm going to have to come up with some story to cover Joe, and Deb. Ken might be ok, but I don't remember what his plans were."

"What about Becky?"

"I don't even know what they told Becky's parents, so I don't know if I need to cover for her. That has me worried, too."

"I'm sure they're ok. I mean, they have Ken and Ryan with them."

"I totally forgot about Ryan. I think he was supposed to go to his grandparents in North Carolina this next week. Or you know what, that was maybe the next week when Deb goes back to the dig."

"It will be ok. We can call Mr. Brewster tomorrow before my parents get here."

"I'm really worried. I think something bad happened. When Becky, Joe, and I went to Philadelphia, Joe ended up getting arrested and was in jail for a few days."

"Really?"

Kim retold the story of their trip to pre-Civil War Philadelphia and Joe's encounter with the fugitive slave act and several nights with David Herold. It amazed Jake at all their adventures and said he was still a bit stunned about all the trips they had made to different times.

They watched the movie for a while and then the phone range. Kim ran to the study to answer it. Jake could hear her talking animatedly, and he hoped it was good news.

Hello?" Kim said as she picked up the phone.

"Hi Kim, it's me, Deb," Deb answered.

"Oh, thank goodness. This means you made it back!"

"Yeah, we just got back, and I wanted to let you know right away."

"I'm so glad. I was so worried I would have to come up with a story to cover you all! Did you find Tom?"

"Well, we found him twice, but twice he got away."

"Oh, no! What happened?"

"You know what, Kim? I'm not trying to keep anything from you, but we're pretty wiped out and hungry. We're staying here in town tonight and will be out there tomorrow on schedule. Can I go through it all with you, then?"

"Yeah, that's fine. I'm just so happy you made it back."

"Is Jake still out there with you?"

"He is, but his parents come tomorrow to pick him up."

"Oh, I'm sorry to miss him. But I'll see you tomorrow early afternoon, ok?

"Sounds great. Tell everyone that I'm happy you're back and I'll see you all tomorrow."

"I will. I'll see you tomorrow."

"Bye."

"Bye little sis."

She came back to the family room and announced that her siblings had returned. She was smiling, and he jumped up and wrapped his arms around her. They got some snacks and returned to the movie. At some point, they both fell asleep on the couch. Waking up in the wee hours of the morning, Jake helped Kim, who was still practically asleep, get to her room. Later in the morning, they laughed about it while they ate breakfast and then they went to the beach one last time. Jake packed up his things and they waited for his parents to arrive.

Jake's parents arrived. He introduced Kim to his parents, and she handed them pictures from their prom since they could not be there. They thanked her and loaded Jake's things into their car while Jake and Kim said goodbye for a couple of weeks. Then Jake got into the car and they left. Kim was left feeling a little sad that he was gone and then she smiled, thinking this must be because she liked him so much. She turned then and danced back into the house.

Kim seemed to sense the imminent arrival of her siblings as later she was standing at the bottom of the stairs to the house when they pulled in. She jumped up and down when she saw them pull up and bounded up to the first car. Deb got out and Kim ran to her and hugged her. "I've missed you so much! What happened on the trip? Tell me all about nearly catching Tom?"

"I've missed you too, Kim. You've grown taller since I left! Let's talk more about the dig later. The trips were a mess, but the digging was just ok," Deb said laughing.

Kim reached for Joe next and hugged him. He laughed and hugged her back. "You'd think we've been gone years and not a few days!"

"I was so worried about what was going on. Unpack quick and tell me all about it before Aunt Alicia and Uncle Darrick get home!"

She ran around the car and hugged Becky and then reached for Ryan. He put his hand out to stop her. "You can't hug me today. I have a minor injury."

"What happened?" She exclaimed as she reached out and just side hugged him on what appeared to be the good side.

"Tom and I had a bit of a tussle and he pulled a knife. Your sister stitched me up."

Kim looked over at Deb and raised her eyebrows. Deb smiled. "I didn't have much of a choice. No one else wanted to use Becky's sewing kit on him."

Ken walked up to Kim then and swung her around. "You have grown up, my little sister! One more year and you graduate, huh?"

Kim laughed as he swung her around, hugged his neck and said, "I'm so glad you're all here and ok. Well, mostly ok. Where is Mary?"

"She's on her way."

They unloaded their cars and went inside. By this time, Michael had come out and helped them carry luggage into the house and to their rooms. They got unpacked, all the while listening to Kim as she went back and forth to their rooms asking questions. Joe finally stopped her and said they would have to wait until Mary was there, so they only had to tell the story one time. Kim relented and helped Deb unpack. Mary arrived just as they were sitting down in the kitchen with snacks all around. She greeted them all, but then hugged Ken and he said they would be right back and took Mary into the study. The others finished their snacks and walked out to the back terrace. As they did, Joe knocked on the study door and said if they wanted to discuss anything before Aunt Alicia got home, Ken would have to curtail his greeting with Mary. They all laughed and waited for them on the terrace.

"Let's go down to the beach. That way, we don't accidentally give anything away to the staff or Aunt Alicia," Ken said, as he walked out with his arm around Mary.

"Where's this young man of yours, Kim?" Mary asked.

"His name is Jake, and he was here, but his family took him on a vacation to see his grandmother in Michigan," Kim replied, turning a bit red.

"What did you do here for all these days, by the way?" Ken asked.

"I don't know what you mean," Kim said, speeding up so she would be ahead of them and he couldn't see her face.

"I mean, what did you and Jake do for the last week? You know, during the day, and during the evening," Ken said.

"Well, at night, Aunt Alicia and Uncle Darrick were here, so nothing happened. During the day we went to the beach, saw a movie, got ice cream and one day Uncle Darrick stayed here and took us out on his boat," Kim said as she kept walking in front of Ken and Mary.

"I don't think she appreciates this inquisition," Mary whispered to Ken as they followed Kim to the beach.

"I know, but I've got to look after her," Ken whispered back.

"Actually, I think that's Aunt Alicia and Uncle Darrick's job, isn't it?" Deb asked as she caught up to where Ken and Mary were, with Ryan chuckling next to her.

"As if! You know you're just as protective of Kim as he is," Ryan said to Deb, as he took her hand and pulled her just in front of Ken and Mary.

"Geeze, I'm glad we didn't have to go through that!" Becky said to Joe in the back of all this whispering.

"Me too!" Joe responded.

They got to the beach and Kim, who had been carrying the blanket, spread it out and sat down on one corner. She crossed her arms and looked at Ken first and then at Deb. "I'm not a little kid, you know. I took drivers ed and I can drive now!"

"I know, Kimmy, you're growing up and I should be more open to that idea. I didn't mean to pry, but you know, I care about what happens to you and you're all alone at Choate now, so I have to ask lots of questions," Ken said, trying to help her see his side, or justify his questioning.

"I know all about your questions. I've taken yours and Deb's calls each Sunday all year, remember?" Kim replied.

"Ok, I know I'm not usually the one that mediates, but Kim, remember, you're gonna always be Ken's little sister. So, how about we call a truce on the grounds that he does what he does because he cares, and you tolerate it because you care?" Joe offered as he sat down next to Kim.

"I'm sorry. I'm so insistent on knowing your business, Kim," Ken offered.

Kim smiled at him and lowered her arms. "Then let's get to the bigger issue here. Tell Mary and I what happened."

Joe began with a small explanation of the new tracking system and how it worked to capture the energy signature and light wave trail of the machine, and how it helped them deal with tracking Tom. Then, between Ken, Joe and Ryan, they went through the timeline of New York in nineteen twenty-nine and then in Rochester, in nineteen eleven. Deb jumped in when they talked about seeing Tom in the hotel restaurant, his cryptic vow to get them, and then Ryan's run in with Tom in the woods. Both Mary and Kim held their questions while this tale was being told.

"Now what?" Mary asked when they had finished.

"I don't know," Deb replied, lowering her head.

"We have to go back to his notebook and see if there's anything there, I think," Becky added. "Did anyone bring it along?"

"I've got it in my bag. I can bring it to you when we go back up to the house. The only problem I see is that it was his plan to fix his great grandfather's invention and make his family famous and we stopped that. I don't know if there'll be anything in the notebook about what he might do next," Joe answered Becky.

"Do you know if anything changed?" Kim asked, "Remember when we went to Philadelphia? We changed all kinds of things. It's been a day since you got back. We might not see if something changed."

"I checked at the public library when we got into town late yesterday. I don't see anything that changed on the engine invention. Henry Ford still wins the appeal and goes on to be the leader in the car industry," Becky replied.

"But we don't know if something small changed, do we?" Kim continued.

"No. He spent almost a week in New York city and then almost a week in Rochester interacting with his family, working with his great-grandfather. We think he cleaned out his account in nineteen twenty-nine, but we realized later that we didn't specifically ask his broker if he had done that," Ryan added.

"So, we're going to hope there's something in his notebook. If not, then what?" Mary asked.

"If that notebook doesn't give us answers, we're going to have to locate Tom and see what we can figure out," Ken said.

"Ok, so the plan is to read the notebook first. But will we all be together tomorrow?" Deb asked.

"I have to get back to work," Ken answered, running his hand through his hair, "And I have a fiancé that probably is mad at me for not helping with the wedding plans this past week."

"I'm not mad. I know you have to track him down. It's really just about how I don't like the risks you're all taking. I mean, Ryan got really hurt. What if something worse had happened?" Mary answered.

"I'm fine. But I have to say, we aren't going in the machine again without bandages, antiseptic and that sewing kit!" Ryan said, laughing, then grabbing his side when it started to hurt from the laughing.

"Let's get back to plans, can we?" Joe said.

"I think Ken and I both need to get back to the city soon. Why don't we stay and see your aunt and uncle before we do that?" Mary started.

"I have to get back home, too, but I think I can wait until tomorrow," Becky said.

"I need to check in with the project team at MIT, but I can do that from the city," Joe offered.

"We have plans with Aunt Alicia, Deb. She wants us to go with her to her studio on Tuesday and then go shopping," Kim added.

"Oh, I didn't know about this," Deb replied.

"How could you not know? I mean, really. All you were doing is time hopping through the early part of the century!" Kim said, laughing.

"So how about if the rest of us stay here tonight, then all go into the city tomorrow? I can go home. Becky can contact her parents and deal with her getting home. You and Kim would be close for Tuesday and Joe could call his project team," Ryan summed it up.

They all stood up. Deb helped Kim and Becky fold up the blanket as she said, "Sounds good. Joe, you get the notebook and Becky, Kim and I can pour through it my room tonight."

They walked back up to the house just as Aunt Alicia and Uncle Darrick were getting home. After all the hugs and greetings, they went inside and enjoyed a dinner of steak and lobster. Everyone talked about their various activities and plans, and it was a boisterous meal. Ken and Mary left, and the rest of them settled into the family room for a movie while Aunt Alicia and Uncle Darrick went up to their room.

Later that night, as the three girls sat on Deb's bed, the notebook between them, they took turns reading different sections and pages, hoping for a clue.

"Nothing. All he goes on and on about is how much he hates Joe and how he blames our whole family for his not having what he wants," Kim lamented as she fell back onto Deb's pillow.

"Yeah, except for his grand plan to take advantage of the stock market crash and then save his family's fortunes by giving his great grandfather the money to take back the automobile engine he designed," Becky said, looking up at the ceiling.

"I don't think we're going to find the answer in this notebook. We're going to have track him down again," Deb said, closing her eyes. "But how?"

"It's summer break and he should be home from college, right? I mean, that's what you guys are doing," Kim said as she sat back up.

"You're still so insightful!" Deb exclaimed, "but do we even know if he went to college?"

"Does anyone know where his parents live?" Becky asked.

"I don't, but I bet Joe's friend that used to be Tom's friend knows how to find him," Kim said excitedly.

"Good plan. We'll talk to Joe about this tomorrow," Becky said as she got up off of Deb's bed, "I'm tired, I'm going to bed."

12

The next morning, Michael drove them all into the city in the limousine. The girls filled Joe in, and he said he would work to track down Tom's home address after he checked in with the MIT team on the phone. When they got to the apartment in the city, Deb did a little more unpacking after she said goodbye to Ryan. Then she and Kim went into the park to walk around while Joe talked to the MIT team.

When they were just about finished up, and several of the team members had left the room they called from, Joe thought it might be a good idea to ask these guys about how to track Tom down.

"Hey, before we finish up, I was wondering if any of you would have any ideas on how I can track someone down," Joe said.

"Who're you trying to track down, Joe? On some secret mission or something?" Ron Whitehall said, laughing.

"No, just someone I went to school with. Nothing really secretive about it," Joe replied.

"Does he go to college?" Steve Rogers asked.

"Yeah, I think he goes to Penn State, but actually I don't know that for sure," Joe thought. That's where Tom talked about going to the dorm before they graduated, but he didn't really know for sure.

"Then let's use the database we tapped into of all the college students in any public college in the US. It should be no big deal to find him that way," Steve said.

"But does it give you his home address? And what if he doesn't go there or anywhere? I'm wanting to get in touch with this guy, not just verify which school he goes to," Joe said, with a bit of a sarcastic tone.

"Do you not remember that database? I mean, you set up the link this past winter. Are you ok? A week away and you're losing your mind?" Ron said, pressing Joe.

"I forgot, ok? Can you run the search for me and call me back with the details you find?" Joe said.

"What's this guy's name?" Steve asked.

"Tom, or maybe it might be listed with Thomas Thorton," Joe provided to him.

"Ok, I'll run it right after lunch and call you later today, ok?" Steve said.

"That's great, thanks," Joe replied.

"Ok, talk later," Ron said.

When the girls returned from the park, Joe told them about the plan to get Tom's home address later that day. They went get some lunch, but while they were putting shoes on, the phone rang.

"Hello?" Deb said.

"Hey baby, it's Ryan."

"Hi. Everything ok with your parents?"

"Sure. I was just thinking that we might need to do some prep work since we don't really know what Tom might be up to."

"What kind of prep work?"

"Well, I'm not sure, but is there a way we can get copies of or write out things so we can tell if he messes anything else up before we can find him? I mean, how are we going to know what he changes?"

"We can't write done all of history to compare it to, but I don't know."

"How are we going to know, then?"

"You know, Becky did something when they were doing their traveling with Kim to know what changed. I can't remember how she kept some books safe or not changed as history changed. We're going to have to ask her."

"Can you call her?"

"Yeah, we were just heading out to get some lunch. I'll call her when we get back."

"Ok, then call me, ok?"

"Sure. What are you doing today?"

"I'm seeing my dad, and then we're going to do some clothes shopping. I have to get ready for the internship I have this fall."

"Well, if you're going to be shopping, why don't you call me when you get home later? I'm sure I will have talked to Becky by then."

"Ok. Love you, baby."

"Love you too, bye."

Deb turned to see Joe standing in the office's doorway.

"Oh, love you too!" he said, laughing at Deb.

"Be quiet," Deb said as she came around the desk and walked to Joe, giving him a shove out of the doorway.

"What did Ryan want? I mean, you just saw him a couple of hours ago."

"He thought of something we hadn't talked about. How are we going to know if Tom changes something right now? Like if he gets back into the machine he stole, and does something, since we're not with him," Deb said as they got to the door where Kim was waiting.

"Didn't Becky write in a book or something and it kept it somehow as the original history?" Kim said as they got in the elevator to go down to the street.

"Yeah, she did. I don't remember what she wrote or how she stored the book, though," Joe said as they walked down the street to the restaurant.

"I'm going to call her when we get back from lunch and see. Ryan's right, we need to make sure he doesn't change something so we can try to fix it, if he does," Deb said as they sat down and started looking at the menu.

"It would also be a way for us to find him, if we kept track of things," Joe said as the waiter brought them drinks.

After they ordered burgers and onion rings, Kim said, "We'll have to check every day. That way we can track him down, but also so he doesn't alter too much."

"Yeah, I mean he had no sense of how he was interacting with people in historical times and what that might do," Deb added.

"He's going to have troubles. Maybe that's how we'll catch him," Joe said.

"What do you mean?" Kim asked.

"Well, remember when we prepared for the trip to Philadelphia? We got clothing and money and researched places to stay and everything. Tom didn't do any of that. That's why his plans got messed up, cause the bank caught him with money from twenty years in the future," Joe explained.

"Oh, I see what you mean. When he messes up, that might be a way to catch him. If we know what is needed and he doesn't," Kim said, smiling, as she added, "Joe, you've been hiding an investigator in there under all that computer skill?"

"Very funny!" Joe said, laughing. "Yeah, maybe if the computer thing doesn't pan out, I can be a private investigator!"

"Sure, not pan out. I would be worried about that if I were you!" Deb said, as she looked up to the ceiling, laughing.

They enjoyed their lunch and as they were walking back to the apartment, Kim said, "I miss these days, when we all spend time together."

"Oh, Kim, we'll always come back to this!" Joe said as he wrapped his arm around Kim's shoulder.

They laughed and reminisced for the block or two walk back and were laughing when they got into the apartment to the phone ringing. Deb ran to the office and called to Joe, "Joe, it's Steve, from MIT for you." She set the phone receiver down and walked toward the door, where Joe passed her on the way to the office.

"Hello," Joe said when he picked up the receiver.

"Hey, it's Steve."

"Yeah, I know."

"Got your info on that guy, Tom."

"Great, hold on a minute while I find a pen and paper."

"No problem. So, he wasn't in the college database, but we found him in an application database from Penn State. He never went there, but he applied and was accepted. I couldn't find a college he attended, though," Steve said.

"Really? Why wouldn't he go if he was accepted?" Joe asked.

"Don't know, but he got far enough in the process that all his paperwork was submitted, so we've got all the info you could want on this guy," Steve replied.

"Great, let's start with his home address," Joe said.

Joe searched the top drawer of the desk and found a pen and then pulled a notepad out of the other side drawer, digesting the information that Tom may not be going to any college, as he said, "Ok, give me the info."

"Ok, 3-4-1-1 Summerville Ave."

"Got it," Joe said as he wrote this information down.

"Medford, Mass."

"Ok. Got a home phone?" Joe asked.

"Yeah, 6-1-7-7-8-1-4-2-3-6."

"Thanks, Steve."

"Can I ask what this is really about? I mean, you're not just looking up an old friend, are you?"

"Well, not really."

"So, what gives?"

"He took something from me. Well, I'm pretty sure he took it, and I want it back."

"You mean like espionage or something? You think he stole one of your ideas?" Steve asked.

"No, well, it was a different idea and project I was working on, but it's not like it's something huge or anything. I mean, I'm just a guy with some ideas. I don't know why someone's got to steal from me," Joe said, feeling a weird about keeping things from Steve but not wanting to give too much away.

"Joe, I know you think you're just a regular guy, but man, you've been in the news, on T.V. and this guy is going to see you coming. If you're wanting to sneak up on him, you're going to need some help," Steve offered.

"I'm not sure I need any help, though."

"Listen, me and Ron can go over there, watch this house and see if this guy Tom is even there. Then if he's there, we can trail him for a day or so, and let you swoop in at the final hour and get whatever it is he took."

"That might be a good idea, Steve."

"You aren't going to tell me what he took, are you?"

"Is that required for you to take on this role of private eye?"

"Not really, but it would certainly help us if we knew what we're supposed to be looking for," Steve said, laughing.

"He took my notebooks on some research I was doing. And a machine Ken and I made when we were at Choate, that's all."

"Well, that could be important. I get it. Let me get Ron and we'll head over there and see if this guy is even there."

"Do you need a picture or anything?"

"No, man, the database has the school ID picture in a file. He must have gone through orientation at Penn State, 'cause he had an ID picture in the database. We've got it!"

"I'm going to have to take a better look at that database, I think!"

"Totally. I'll call you later tonight to let you know what we find."

"Thanks for doing this, Steve. It really is a great idea to send someone over to case the place that isn't me, so he doesn't get wind that I'm on to him and hide the notebooks and machine."

"No problem. What are friends for? I mean, you really helped me last semester, remember? I owe you."

"No, you don't, man. I was glad to help you with that guy."

"We can agree to disagree on that one. I'll call you later."

"Thanks, bye Steve."

Deb heard Joe hang up the phone, so she and Kim came into the office. He started to tell them what was going on when Deb held up her hand like a stop sign and said she wanted to call Becky first. Joe sat down on the love seat Kim was sitting in while Deb called Becky.

"Hello."

"May I speak with Becky, please?"

"This is Deb Fitzgerald."

A few minutes later, Becky came to the phone. "Hi Deb. Is everything and everybody ok?"

"Yes. Ryan called me early this afternoon, and he was thinking we might need to be careful and try to track anything that Tom was doing to change history. We remembered you did something to keep track, and I wanted to know what that was."

"I did. I don't know how it worked, but I wrote in two of my history books. See, I put notes on the pages and dated the notes. I also kept a set of books I didn't write in. I put the books I wrote in, in my cedar chest at the end of my bed, and I left the other books on my desk."

"Ok. Does it matter what kind of notes?"

"I don't think so. I put notes about events I remembered, questions I'd ask the people in chapters if I ever met them, that sort of thing. And I dated each note. I don't know if the storage method had anything to do with it. I think it has something to do with the notes I wrote the night before we left for Philadelphia."

"Ok. I'm going to do this. Do you think I need to write notes each day since we don't know when Tom's traveling?"

Kim, sitting on the other side of the desk on the loveseat, hopped up and said, "I think we better do that."

"I agree with Kim. I think you should write notes each day and date them until we either notice something different in the unmarked set of books or we track him down some other way," Becky said.

"Ok. Now I just have to track some books down."

Joe said, "I still have my history books from junior and senior year. Do you still have yours, Deb?"

"I think I do," Deb said, pulling the receiver away from her mouth so as not to yell at Becky.

"Did Joe figure out where Tom lives?" Becky asked Deb.

"Yes, but I don't know the details."

Joe stood up and came around the desk. He took the receiver from Deb and said hello to Becky. Then he said he was going to hold it out so she could hear and explain the plan.

"My friend Steve was able to connect to the public university database, and found Tom. He isn't attending any college, but they found him in the application data to Penn State and, more importantly, found Tom's home address. Steve and Ron are going over there today to see if Tom is there and monitor him. I told Steve Tom took my notebooks and a machine Ken and I worked on. I didn't go into too many other details so that they would look for anything. Anyway, he's going to call me later tonight to give me an update."

"They're on a stakeout, huh?" Kim said.

"Like Hawaii Five-O," Becky said from the phone.

They laughed and then Joe pulled to phone back to his ear and said goodbye to her. Deb went and grabbed her last two history books and Joe went to get his. They sat in the office and looked them over. Deb decided she would write in hers and keep them in the chest in her room. Joe would leave his on the desk in his room. Deb and Kim got pens, and each took a book and wrote some notes next to key events in US history.

"Don't forget to date them," Joe said.

Just as they were finishing, Ken arrived home from work and said he was changing and picking Mary up for dinner. He called Joe into his room to update him while he got out of his suit and into his jeans. He gave both Deb and Kim a high five when he emerged from his bedroom and congratulated them on the plan, and said he would be back later. A few minutes after he left, Uncle Darrick and Aunt Alicia got home and they all sat and enjoyed the dinner that Uncle Darrick had picked up from the Chinese restaurant. Deb regaled them with stories from the dig.

"We were near the border of Israel and Amman, Jordan. I was climbing down into this pit we were excavating and I turned and looked right into the eyes of scorpion!" she said excitedly.

"Oh my, I don't think I want you back there, Deb. You could be hurt. Does the professor keep venom kits?" Aunt Alicia said, looking very concerned.

"I'm pretty sure the nurse that is always with us on site has venom kits, but this thing was way more scared of me than I was of it. Well, after I screamed anyway," she laughed, "then it just scurried away into a crack in the wall of clay and sand that was behind the ladder."

"Did you find any treasure?" Kim asked.

"We found a lot of pottery shards, some small, smooth stones that were probably toys for some child, and few coins in that pit. But in one of the other dig sites, we found pieces of broken bricks that were dated to biblical times," Deb said, again animated over her passion for archeology.

"Do you think it was the walls of Jericho you found?" Joe asked.

"We've only been able to date the age of the brick. We haven't been able to connect it to any historical context," Deb answered. "That's the problem with archeology. It takes a really long time to connect the dots."

"It would be cool if you found the walls that came down, right?" Joe asked.

"Yes, and boy would Grandfather be proud you remember your bible stories!" Deb said, laughing.

The conversation turned to plans for the next few days once Deb had finished all the exciting stories of her summer in the middle east. She didn't tell them about the spider bite she got, or that one of her dorm mates ran off with one of the local workers. She didn't think it was important to share those details.

They went over the plans for the next day when Kim and Deb would go to Aunt Alicia's studio and see what was being made, have lunch, and do some shopping. Deb was excited that now Kim could join in this ritual as she was old enough for the designer clothing.

After dinner was cleaned up, and all the plans for the next few days arranged, they all went to the family room to watch some television. As they settled, the phone rang. Joe sprang up from the couch, since he expected it to be Steve. It wasn't, and he called Uncle Darrick to the office for the phone. When Uncle Darrick came back and settled in next to Aunt Alicia, the phone rang again, and again, Joe sprang up.

"Is he expecting a call from Becky or something?" Uncle Darrick asked to no one in particular.

"No, he and Becky talked earlier. He's expecting a call from one of the MIT team guys," Kim answered.

"Oh. Something big going on?" Uncle Darrick continued.

"Isn't there always something big going on with Joe and that team?" Kim asked.

"I suppose you're right," he laughed.

In the office, Joe answered the phone. "Hello."

"Hey, Joe, it's me, Steve."

"Hey, Steve. What did you find?"

"Well, he's here. I saw him when we first got here, going into a shed in the backyard. When it got dark, his mother called him and he left the shed. It's locked up with a heavy door that has a serious looking lock, but there was a window that had some paper on it that had fallen away a little so we could see in a little bit."

"What did you see?"

"Is the machine you're looking for the size of a phone booth? He's got something in there covered up with a huge tarp that is the size of a phone booth, but it has something pointing upward on its roof or whatever."

"Yeah, that's it."

"What the heck is it?"

"It's a time machine. What did you think it was?"

"Yeah, right? You don't have to tell me if you don't want to. I can take the hint. Anyway, there are some books on a workbench kind of thing and some notebooks. You think those might be yours?"

"Probably."

"Well, Ron has a friend that lives about two blocks from here. We're going to stay there tonight. We're going over now to get some food, and then Ron and I are going to stake the place out tonight."

"Ok, sounds good. Let me know if anything happens, or if you find a way into that shed."

"You got it, boss."

"Not really."

"Ok, how about sergeant? That's what we'll call you for code, huh?"

"Whatever, Steve. Don't get too carried away with this stake out, ok?"

"Are you kidding? This is way cooler than being stuck in the lab. It's like field work or something. We're loving this!"

"Ok, ok. Let's call you two detectives, then. Does that add to the field work idea?"

"Sure. I'll call you tomorrow unless something crazy happens. Listen, we might get the notebooks, but we don't have a way to heft that machine out of there. We're in my little Honda, not a moving truck. You might have to get up here to get that machine back. You better be thinking of a plan for that."

"I will. Thanks, Steve."

"Bye."

Joe returned to the family room, and Deb raised her eyebrows at him. He tried to motion something like "later" but she didn't get it and just put her head back into her book. An hour later, Ken returned. He greeted everyone and hugged Aunt Alicia as she got up and said she was going to get ready for bed. Uncle Darrick took Ken into the kitchen to get him something to drink and talk about some business opportunity. Uncle Darrick returned and told the other kids goodnight and left. Ken sat down, and Deb put the book down and said, "Ok, what were you trying to tell me?"

"I was trying to figure out a way to motion 'later'. Apparently, it didn't work. I wanted to wait until Ken got here to tell you all at once."

"Tell us all what?" Ken asked.

"Steve called. Tom is at home. He has the machine in a shed in his backyard and several books and notebooks on a workbench in that shed."

"Good work. Now, do we try to grab him there, or do we wait and see what happens?" Ken asked.

"I'm all for ending this as soon as we can. I've added a few days to my break, but I have to leave at the end of the week to go back and finish my internship," Deb said.

"Does Ryan know about this yet?" Ken asked.

"No, I was waiting to hear what Steve found out to call Ryan," Deb answered.

"Let's all go into the office and call him," Ken said as he got up from the chair and walked out into the hall.

They all followed, and Deb called Ryan. She held out the phone so he could hear the conversation.

"We can't grab him tomorrow. I have three really important meetings," Ken said as they started to talk about how they could confront Tom.

"We have to meet Aunt Alicia tomorrow, too," Kim added.

"Can we just keep an eye on him and grab him at the end of the week? That seems to work better for all of us and it will give us time to formulate a plan," Ryan said from the phone.

"As long as nothing changes before then, I think that's a good idea," Joe said.

"Will Steve let you know what's going on with Tom?" Kim asked.

"Yeah, he said he'd call tomorrow morning and check in regularly," Joe answered.

"Ok, let's all talk tomorrow early in the evening and come up with a plan. Everyone needs to contemplate anything they think is important for this confrontation Friday late afternoon. Joe, get Becky up to speed if she wants to join us, and I will update Mary," Ken summarized.

"I want to talk to Ryan some more, though," Deb said as she put the phone receiver back to her ear.

The rest of them left the office and went to their rooms. Deb finished explaining what she learned from Becky and what they were doing to keep track of anything Tom changed, but given that he was here, they agreed they didn't have to worry about that tonight. They said good-night and promised to talk tomorrow.

The next day, Ryan and Becky were joining them for dinner so they could have a small, pre-celebratory birthday for Kim. After dinner, they all went back to the apartment. Aunt Alicia and Uncle Darrick left the family room to the kids, and they used this as a chance to catch up and plan their confrontation with Tom.

Fortunately, Uncle Darrick and Aunt Alicia would be off at a business meeting starting on Thursday, to return Friday to see Deb off. Ken arranged his schedule at work to be off as of eleven in the morning on Friday, and the plan was for them all to drive up to Massachusetts that afternoon. Joe and Ken would get the machine back to the barn and everyone else would drive to Mr. Brewster's so they could dismantle the machines. Joe reported that Steve and Ron watched Tom meet some friends for lunch, stop at a bank and then go to the library, where he was all afternoon. All seemed good for them to get the machine back this week.

13

Deb prepared to leave late Friday night to return to the dig in the middle east. The rest of the family, including Becky, finalized their plans to confront Tom. Ryan was going with Uncle Darrick to take Deb to the airport, while Aunt Alicia was attending an event for preparations to host several aspects of the spring fashion show in New York the next year.

On Thursday, while Deb completed her packing and met Aunt Alicia for lunch, Joe was on the phone with the team from MIT and Kim was busy working on some new artwork. Becky knocked on their door. Kim went and answered it.

"Hi Becky! Aren't you supposed to be arriving later today?"

"I need to see Joe right away!"

"Come on in. He's in the office on the phone right now."

As Becky and Kim walked down the entry hall toward the office, Becky said, "I know he's on the phone. Steve called me when he couldn't reach Joe."

"Did something happen?" Kim asked as she stopped in front of the office door.

"Yes. Tom and the machine are gone!"

Kim knocked on the door, her mouth still hanging open, and opened it. She whispered to Joe, "You need to get off that call. Becky's here and something's happened!"

Joe motioned for them both to come in as he told the team on the phone that he needed to wrap things up. They finished the call, and he put down the receiver, turning to Becky, "What happened?"

"Steve called me. He tried to call you and kept getting a busy signal. They went over to Tom's house today and they could see that the machine was gone. They went to the door and asked for him and Tom's mother said he had gone to see friends. When Steve asked when he left, cause they were supposed to get together, Tom's mother said he had actually left sometime during the night and left her a note."

"I knew we should have just driven over there Tuesday when we got the confirmation Tom was there with the machine!" Joe said as he stood up and slammed both of his hands down on the desk. Then he picked up the phone and dialed Steve's hotel number.

"Hello," Steve said.

"Hey Steve, it's me, Joe."

"Joe, man, I've been trying to reach you for an hour or more. I had to call Becky."

"I know. She just got to our place in the city. I was on the call with the project team, sorry."

"Yeah, I didn't remember that was today, but Becky told me. Did she tell you what happened?"

"Yeah, she just did. Listen, I'm going to call my brother, Ken. I think we're going to be heading out there later today. I'll call you back when I have all this arranged."

"Ok. Do you want us to go over there and see what's left in that shed?"

"No. I think if we're going to break into the shed, we should do it under the cover of darkness. I'll talk to Ken and I'll call you back."

"Ok, I'm going to stay here, but I'm sending Ron over there now to keep an eye on things in case he comes back."

"Good idea. I'll talk to you soon."

"Bye, and hey, sorry about this, man."

"It's not your fault. He either just decided to jump or he caught on. Who knows?"

"Bye."

"Bye." Joe hung up the phone, but picked it back up right away. He called Ken and told him what had happened. Ken said he actually was free and was heading home as soon as he called Mary. Joe then sat down next to Becky in the office and closed his eyes as he leaned his head back on the sofa.

"What can we do?" Kim asked.

"Nothing until Ken gets here," Joe replied.

"I'm going to go make some sandwiches. You two want anything?" Kim asked as she stood up from the chair she had been sitting in.

"I'd love a sandwich. I'm starved," Joe answered, smiling.

"Me too. Need help?" Becky asked.

"No, I've got it. Come to the kitchen in a few minutes," Kim said as she walked out of the office.

"You, ok?" Becky asked Joe, who still had his eyes closed.

"Yeah, I'm ok. I'm just tired of chasing after him and I wish we could get ahead of this, finally," Joe answered as he lowered his head and opened his eyes.

He looked over at her and smiled, saying, "Your haircut looks nice."

"Thanks," Becky said, smiling as she leaned over and put her head on his shoulder.

"Did I tell you lately that you look great? Or that I love you?" Joe whispered as he put his arm behind her head and held her.

"Not today," she said, smiling.

"Well, you look beautiful and I love you."

"Thanks. Love you too," she answered.

They sat quietly together for a few minutes when Joe's stomach started growling. Becky laughed, and sat up, "We better get to the kitchen and feed you!"

Joe laughed, and they went to the kitchen to eat. While they ate, Kim asked, "Did you say the other day that there were books and notebooks on the table in Tom's shed?"

"Yeah, Steve and Ron said they saw all kinds of papers, books, and things on the table. Why?" Joe asked.

"Well, he had notebooks in the barn when he first took the machine. Maybe the notes and things Steve and Ron saw will give us a clue as to what he's up to now," Kim said as she got up to take her plate to the sink.

"Ah, I missed my insightful sister," Joe said, smiling as he got up, picked up Becky's plate, and took them to the sink.

When Ken arrived, Ryan was already over at the apartment. Deb had returned from her lunch with Aunt Alicia and they were all sitting in the family room waiting for Ken.

"Hey everybody," Ken said as he pulled off his jacket and undid his tie, and sat down in the chair.

"How was your day?" Deb asked.

"It was ok until Joe called. You?" Ken responded.

"Lunch was pleasant. But, yeah, it took a turn when I got back here."

"So, what's the plan?" Ryan asked as he got off the couch and came to sit on the arm of the chair Deb was sitting in across from Ken.

"I think some of us need to drive out there right now, and break into that shed and see what he left that will give us a clue to what he's up to. Kim had a great idea that all the papers, books, and notebooks Steve and Ron saw might give us that clue," Joe said.

"Yeah, I think that's a great idea. I was thinking the same thing as I was making my way home today. Give me a minute, I'll go get changed," Ken said as he stood up.

"Who all should go?" Kim asked.

"Well, I think it should be a guy's trip tonight, little sister. We'll get it all here, and you girls can begin your research," Ken said as he turned in the family's doorway room.

"I agree. I didn't ask Steve or Ron what the lay of the land is, but I'd rather us guys did this, so none of you girls get hurt," Joe said.

"Ok, us girls will stay here and make some dinner. That will distract Aunt Alicia and Uncle Darrick tonight," Deb said as rubbed Ryan's back.

Ken left and got changed. The rest of them went to the kitchen and while Deb and Kim hunted around to decide what to make for dinner, Ryan and Joe gathered up some flashlights, some gloves, and a couple of backpacks. When Ken came back to the kitchen, he was carrying a couple of screwdrivers and a bolt cutter.

"Where on earth did you find that?" Becky asked as Ken set the bolt cutters on the big island of the kitchen.

"I brought them in from my car from our last go round with this maniac. It was all in my closet," Ken said.

"I don't remember if Steve said he locked the shed with a padlock or not," Joe added.

"Well, I'm bringing it anyway," Ken said, as he put all his contributions and the flashlights into one backpack.

Joe, Ken and Ryan prepared to leave. Deb asked Ken what he told Mary as they were putting their boots on.

"I told her what Joe told me and that we were likely taking a drive tonight and wouldn't be back until late," Ken answered as he stood up from tying his boots.

"Be careful!" Becky said as she hugged Joe.

"You too," Deb said as she hugged Ryan.

"You especially!" Kim added as she reached up for Ken. He picked her up and hugged her and said they would do their best.

After they left, the girls returned to the kitchen and prepared dinner. When Uncle Darrick arrived, they told him the guys had left on a little field trip. He smiled, knowing something was up, but figured the kids would tell him when they were ready. He thought it had been a while since they acted this way, and he admitted to himself that he missed seeing this tight-knit group working on some project. Aunt Alicia came in just then, and they sat down and ate. After dinner, the girls went into the family room to watch a movie and Aunt Alicia requested Uncle Darrick review some reports with her, so they went into the office.

Later that evening, Uncle Darrick came to the family room to tell them he and their aunt were going to bed. He asked if they needed any help with anything and they said no. The girls were about to give up and get ready for bed when the door quietly opened announcing the arrival of Ken, Joe and Ryan. They went directly to the family room, where Ryan turned and shut the door after being the last to enter.

"What happened?" Deb asked as she rose to hug Ryan.

"How about something to drink or eat first?" Ken said as he sat down in the chair and set the backpack in front of him.

"I'll go," Deb said, as she got up and headed to the door.

"I'll go with you," Kim said as she first hugged Ken and left with Deb.

When they returned, they brought a tray with a bowl of fruit, some crackers and a plate of cheese and sliced salami. With it, Kim was carrying three cans of coke. Deb and Kim set the food on the table in front of the couch, and the three boys were quiet for a few minutes while they munched and drank.

Ken used a napkin to wipe off his face and then set back in the chair, as he said, "Ok. So, we met Steve at the place they were staying and then went over and parked the car a block from Tom's place. We found Ron and told the two of them to grab some food and we would meet them later. We snuck around Tom's house and into the backyard. His mother was knitting or something in the front of the house, so we figured we were safe. Anyway, we picked the lock on the shed. The shed's not a metal one, like from the hardware store. It was actually a fully built wood structure with a loft. It had a door with a lock on it. Ryan used I don't know what and picked the lock."

"Who knew you had these skills, Ryan?" Kim said, giggling.

"Yeah, but to be clear, this was my first picked lock," Ryan replied, smiling at Kim.

"Anyway, the machine is definitely gone. But, Kim, you were right. He had some books from the library, and a bunch of notes on paper and in a couple of notebooks, so we have those. I'm hoping they will give us a clue, but right now I'm beat and I have an eight o'clock meeting tomorrow, so I have to get some sleep. You all can stay up all night reading through this if you want. In fact, if you're up for it, it would be a good idea, so tomorrow we can make some plans to go after him," Ken said as he stood up.

"Thanks for the snacks, Deb and Kim," he added.

Becky stood up and took the snack tray and returned it to the kitchen and then came back to the family room. They had split up the papers and notebooks, and she picked up the pile that was in front of her place and sat down. After a few minutes, Joe laid back against the couch and looked up, saying, "All my papers have notes about the star-spangled banner. I don't know how that relates to any of this."

"My papers are all about the Civil War. Specifically, the battle of Gettysburg," Ryan said, putting his papers down.

"This notebook is a little more enlightening," Kim said as she looked up, "He seems to ramble in a page here about not being able to get his family back on track and since we stopped him, he would hit us where we live."

"This notebook says something similar. It says that he wants to distract us so he can come back here and take everything from us," Deb said.

"What do you think he means by hitting us where we live and distracting us?" Becky asked, putting her papers down.

"I don't know," Deb answered, closing her eyes.

"I think we all need some sleep. It's after one in the morning. Let's pack this all back into this backpack and try to sleep on this information. Maybe it will make sense after some sleep and some breakfast," Ryan said, picking up all the papers from the table and putting them into the backpack. Deb handed him both the notebooks, while she agreed with what he said.

Early the next morning, Ken looked into the family room and found that someone had packed everything back up. He was glad about that. He went on to the kitchen and was fixing something to eat when Kim came running in.

"I think I figured it out!" she said.

"Figured what out?" Ken asked.

"Last night, we found some notes that were a little cryptic. Tom talked about hitting us where we live and distracting us while he came back here to take everything from us," she replied as she climbed onto one stool at the kitchen island.

Ken sat down with his toast and hard-boiled egg and looked at her, asking, "Well, what have you figured out?"

"At any point when you were trying to track him down, did he figure out that we get time travel better than he does? I mean, did he actually mess something up or did any of you say something to him about messing up history?" she asked.

"He had issues depositing the cash he made during the stock market crash when he went to an earlier time to help his great-grandfather. And he talked to Deb and Becky that last day while they were sitting in the hotel restaurant," Ken said, after he finished chewing on the toast.

"I think Tom might have figured out that we care about history. That we know time travel has the power to mess up history," Kim said excitedly.

"Oh, Deb said that she said something about his not getting the impact when he confronted her and Becky at the restaurant. That's where the hit us where we live comes from, you mean?" Ken asked.

"Yes, and it would distract us, trying to fix things," Kim said, folding her arms in front of her.

"Ok. I think you should wake the others and talk this assessment over, Kim. We have to answer a few questions, though. Like, what history is he focusing on messing up, and how might he do that," Ken added, as he finished the toast and salted his hard-boiled egg.

"Oh, the notes tell us what history!" she exclaimed as she hopped down. She went to leave the kitchen and turned back to say, "I hope you have a good day. We should be ready to go after him by the time you get home!"

"I hope so. This guy is really starting to bug me," he said, smiling at Kim as he stood also to put his plate and cup in the sink.

Ken left for work and Kim showered and let the others have a bit more sleep. After her shower, she woke Deb and Becky. By this time, Uncle Darrick and Aunt Alicia had left for their workday. Becky woke up Joe while Deb was showering, and Joe woke up Ryan.

Deb and Kim made breakfast while the others got ready. Deb went to retrieve the backpack from her room and returned to find everyone seated around the island. They ate breakfast while Kim explained her reasoning about what she thought Tom was thinking.

"Kim, that's brilliant!" Deb exclaimed when she had finished explaining her thought process.

"He did ask us how we knew about the money and clothes when he confronted us in the hotel that day," Becky added.

"We even know what historical events he going to, don't we? From all those notes," Ryan added as he finished his eggs.

"What about the star-spangled banner would be historical?" Joe asked.

"The day the actual poem was written, or I should say night, Francis Scott Key was on a ship in the harbor where he had been trying to negotiate the release of prisoners from the British. I don't know any other details, but there has to be something in those events Tom could mess up, right?" Deb asked as she picked up plates to put in the sink.

"We need to read up on that battle to see what that might be," Becky said, as she turned to put the jelly jars back into the refrigerator.

"What's the other historical thing, the battle of Gettysburg I was reading about last night?" Ryan asked.

"It must be. We need to research that too, I think, to see what Tom might try to mess up there," Deb said as she sat back down at the island.

"You have leave tonight, Deb. Are you all ready?" Kim asked.

"Yeah, I'm all packed."

"When do you leave?" Joe asked.

"Uncle Darrick and Ryan are taking me to the airport. We planned to leave here around five tonight. My flight is at eight-thirty," Deb responded.

"Let's get all the notes back out and see if we can determine the thing Tom might plan to change," Ryan said as he got up.

"I'll bring the backpack to the dining room table," Deb said as she got up.

"Let's get some notebooks of our own and some pencils," Joe said as he headed to the office.

They gathered in the dining room and resumed looking through the papers and notebook. Around eleven, Ryan's stomach growled so loud everyone looked up and laughed.

"Maybe we should take a break," Deb said, as got up and wrapped her arm around Ryan's shoulders, "My guy here is pretty hungry."

"Should we bring any of this with us or pack it up?" Kim asked.

"I think it should be ok here. The cleaning service has already been here, and Uncle Darrick isn't due home until four today," Joe said.

The five of them left the apartment and walked across the park to a hamburger and deli place that faced the park. While they ate, they discussed what they learned from Tom's notes. They were pretty sure by the end of lunch that if Tom went to Gettysburg; he was trying to convince Richard Ewell to push forward instead of resting his soldiers when he got the notice from Robert E. Lee. That seemed to be a moment when the south could have defeated the north in the Civil War. Of the Francis Scott Key historical moment, they weren't quite sure what Tom would do.

When they returned home, Deb went and got her history book out and found some more information on the shelling of Fort McHenry in Baltimore harbor. After she read a page or two, she looked up and said, "here it is. A sniper shooter from land killed the British General,

Robert Ross. His death put the battalion of war ships in chaos, thereby changing what would have been a resounding victory for the British into a loss, and started the British on the path to defeat in the war."

"So, if Tom wants to hit us where we live, by changing history, and distract us, he will change the path of the war of eighteen twelve or change the course of the Civil War," Kim summarized.

"That sounds like his thought process," Ryan added.

"Now all we have to figure out is which one has he traveled to first," Joe said, as he slammed down the notes he had been holding in his hands.

"Wait a minute! I remember a note in the margin of one of his notebooks where he says something about shifting the whole history of America and if that didn't finish us off, he would shift the battle between the states, just for fun," Deb said as she reached for the notebook and turned to that page. She set the notebook down in front of the others.

"It's almost three-thirty. Deb, you need to get ready to go, and we probably should pick all this up so we don't have to explain it to Uncle Darrick," Kim said, standing and gathering up papers.

"We still have to make a plan," Joe said, "but we should wait for Ken."

"We can do that after Deb, Ryan and your uncle leave for the airport, don't you think?" Becky asked.

They agreed. Ryan loaded everything back into the backpack. Kim took it to her room. By the time she returned, Ryan and Deb had left for a short walk. Becky was in the office and Joe was on the phone.

"Who's he talking to?" Kim asked as she came in and sat down.

"Steve. He wanted to update him," Becky answered.

Just then, Ken came home. He called out for Joe, who answered as he hung up from talking to Steve. Ken came to the office and again, took off his suit coat and pulled at his tie.

"Where are Ryan and Deb?" Ken asked.

"They went for a walk," Kim answered.

"Any good news?" Ken followed up.

"Yeah, we figured out where he's going and we're pretty sure we know what he intends to do and where he's going first," Joe said, smiling.

"Well, you've had a successful day," Ken replied.

Kim ran through the details and all their ideas.

"So, when do we head to Mr. Brewster's to get into the machine again?" Ken asked.

Before anyone could answer, Ryan, Deb, and Uncle Darrick came in.

14

"I just wanted to say bye to you all. I'll see you in a few more weeks!" Deb said, as she looked around at all of them.

Kim came up and gave her a hug, saying, "Thanks for the birthday dinner and be safe."

"Yeah, Deb, don't fall in any holes!" Joe said, laughing.

Becky fake punched his shoulder, saying, "Nice brother you are!" Then she turned to Deb and said, "Have fun and find some wonderful treasures."

"Call someone when you land and when you arrive at the site, ok?" Ken asked.

"I will. You don't have to worry about me," Deb responded, smiling at Ken.

Ken hugged her, and then looked at Ryan. "You're going to be around this summer, right?"

"For a couple more weeks. My internship finished up a couple of weeks ago, but I'm going to spend a couple weeks with my grandparents in North Carolina, I think," Ryan answered. "I need to fill the time until Deb gets back!"

"Call me when you get home tonight, then," Ken said, and looked over at Joe while he said it.

"I'm sure I don't want to know what that's about, Ken and Joe, but I can bring Ryan back here if he wants," Uncle Darrick said, shaking his head.

"No thanks, Mr. Reynolds. I told my folks I would be home tonight," Ryan said. Then, looking at Ken, he added, "I'll call you later."

Deb, Ryan, and Uncle Darrick left the apartment. Ken again turned to Joe and the others and said, "Ok, so do we have a plan?"

"We think he will go to eighteen fourteen first. He has some kind of cryptic notes, but in one he said if he can't keep America from maintaining its freedom, he'll make the South win. We feel pretty sure he'll do that," Becky started.

"I think that's as good a theory as we can get," Ken said, sitting down.

"We're not sure what he intends to do, though. He mentions his hatred for the flag and the star-spangled banner, but he has a lot of notes about the British commander and how his death really is the reason the British don't win the war," Kim said, pulling out some papers from the table.

"Where does he get this theory about this commander?" Ken asked.

"There are several battle strategists and war historians that say that the chaos caused with the British fleet when this commander is shot trying to make land, and that the Americans latch on to the battle cry of the Defense of Fort McHenry, that's what the star-spangled banner was originally called, is what made the British lose the war," Becky relayed what they had researched earlier that day.

"How is he shot?" Ken asked.

"He and some of his troops attempt to make landfall south of the fort, and some American general guesses where this landing will take place from some intelligence and scouting. They determine this because it's where the British will land, because the water is shallow and it's a secluded inlet from the bay. It would allow a land attack on the fort that was weak on the land side. A sniper on some hill near the landing site shoots the commander. They captured the troops, the ships in the harbor get all confused, a few get wrecked and the rest sail out of the harbor in the next few days," Joe explains.

"You think Tom will try to stop this sniper, then?" Ken asks.

"That's our theory," Joe answers.

"Do you know the exact date of all this?" Ken keeping up his query.

"The bombardment is September thirteenth. The sniper shooting is two days later," Becky supplies.

"So, we go to this area on September eleventh, see if we can find him first, find the machine and just get out of there, or we track this landing and make sure the sniper does his job. How does that sound?" Ken summarizes.

"I think that would be a good idea," Becky says, pulling all the notes about Baltimore together.

"If we don't catch him there, do we go on to Gettysburg?" Joe asks.

"Yes, if that's where you think he will head to. If we can stop this first part and can't catch him, then we have to go directly to Gettysburg. Do you have all that part figured out?" Ken concludes and asks questions about this new topic.

"So, all the historians say that if General Richard Ewell had acted more aggressively, the South would have pushed the Union back from Gettysburg, and had a straight path to DC. There is a decisive moment on July first where Robert E. Lee sends a courier to Ewell telling him to continue pushing forward if he finds it practicable. Those were the words in the courier note. Ewell thinks this means only if he thinks it necessary, and he thinks they have it well in hand and can wait until his soldiers have rested. This gives the Union Army all night to get situated on Cemetery Hill and they just peck off the Confederate forces as they try to get close," Kim summarizes the notes and research.

"We figure Tom's going to find this Ewell or the courier and make sure that he pushes forward and takes that position on Cemetery Hill and the Confederates will win the war, probably. At least that's what the historians of the Civil War and battle strategy think," Joe added.

"If we don't stop him in Baltimore, we go to Gettysburg on June 28th or 29th and stop him there," Ken says, then adds, "I don't want to be doing this any longer, so we have to plan tonight and tomorrow to be sure we can catch this idiot!"

"I agree. It's taking a toll on all of us. I can't finish a project at MIT. Becky isn't working on her proposal for the grant for the research project. You aren't completing wedding plans. It's messing us all up!" Joe says, pounding his fists on the table in front of the couch.

"Kim, have you done your map magic yet?" Ken asks, turning to her.

"No. But we got copies of maps around the areas of the landing in Baltimore and Gettysburg. I will work on that now, or after dinner," she smiles.

"I'm going to change. Mary is on her way over here. How does Italian food sound to everyone? My treat," Ken said as he got up from the chair and headed down the hall.

"I'm going to have to go home tonight, but I can be here tomorrow," Becky puts out to Kim and Joe.

"When are we doing this trip?" Kim asks.

Ken came back into the room, changed into jeans and polo shirt, just as the doorbell rings, "Saturday, whoops, that'll be Mary. Hold this thought."

"Hey fiancé!" Ken exclaims as he opens the door and hugs Mary.

"You're such a goof!" Mary says as she kisses him. "The group busy planning?"

"Yes, and we're going out for dinner," Ken says as he wraps his arm around her and they walk back to the family room.

As they entered and Ken sat down in the chair with Mary on the arm of the chair, they heard Joe, Becky, and Kim talking.

"I'll have to come up with some other story than I'm spending time on Long Island, I think. I don't think my parents' care that I'm gone, I just think I might get some push back if I'm going back there," Becky was saying.

"How about you say you're with a girlfriend?" Kim offers.

"I don't know what to say about your parents not wanting you to spend time with me. I mean, what do they think? I will not keep you safe?" Joe laughingly interjects.

"Oh, Joe. It's not that. My parents really like you, and they know we're serious about each other. It's just that my dad said something when I got back suggesting that maybe my boyfriend should come spend time at his girlfriend's house every once in a while. That's all. I think they just want me around," Becky said, leaning into Joe and then planting a kiss on his cheek.

"Do you have a friend that your parents won't check up on? I think Kim's plan sounds good then," Mary asks.

"Yeah, there's a girl on my floor that I spent some time with last year. I can use her name with my parents," Becky said thoughtfully.

"I want to go on this trip," Kim said, looking at Ken.

"I don't think that's a good idea. I know we promised you. The last time we did this, Ryan got into a fight with Tom. I don't want my little sister around when we confront this guy. I don't really like Becky going, but we need someone around that can assist with planning and research. But Becky, if you want, I'll understand if you don't want to go along," Ken said, as he looked up at Mary.

"Is Mary going?" Kim asked.

"No, I can't go. I have an appointment to go with the bridesmaids to look at dresses. Didn't you remember? You're invited to that on Saturday, as is your aunt. So, you have to be here," Mary said, trying to make it seem important enough to make up for Ken's edict.

"Oh yeah, I forgot about that," Kim said, "I want to be there for the dress decisions, so I guess this is ok."

"But we still need you, Kim. We need you to help in reviewing the maps," Joe said, wrapping his arm around her and pulling her close.

"Let's go get some food. I'm starved!" Ken stood up and pulled Mary up.

They walked down a few blocks to Mama Leoni's for dinner and switched the conversation over to more fun topics, like the wedding, and what plans remained for everyone's summer. Becky took a cab to the train station and caught the train home, after dinner. The rest of them returned to the apartment and Kim, along with Joe, looked over the map and found several places where they thought they could hide the machine and where Tom might have his. Uncle Darrick returned just as they finished up with the maps.

"Hello everybody. How was your evening?" Uncle Darrick said as he came into the family room.

"Good. We had Italian food. Did you eat?" Joe responded.

"Yes. I took Ryan to a little place I've had lunch meetings at for dinner when we got back into town."

"Did Deb get off ok?" Kim asked.

"Yes, we sat with her and watched her plane take off. She's winging her way east right now," Uncle Darrick said.

"When is Aunt Alicia going to be home?" Kim followed up.

"In a few minutes, I suspect," Uncle Darrick said just as they heard the front door open. He went and greeted her and they walked back to the family room.

"Hi Aunt Alicia!" Kim said.

"Hi everyone. How were all of your days?" She asked them all.

"Good," they all answered together.

"Good. I don't mean to make this so short, but I've got to get some rest. I'm got an early breakfast meeting with a distributor," Aunt Alicia said as she looked up to the ceiling.

"You're still going with us to look at dresses later in the day, right?" Kim asked in a pleading voice.

"Yes, I wouldn't miss it for the world," Aunt Alicia smiled at her.

"Thank you, Mrs. Reynolds. I have all these girls that all want something different. I really need your help to make this not look like a giant fruit salad at the front of the church," Mary said as she and Ken came to the family room.

"Where did you two come from?" Uncle Darrick asked as he moved out of the doorway to let them in.

"We were in the office going over our list of wedding things to do," Ken answered.

"Isn't this wedding next spring?" Uncle Darrick chuckled.

"Yes, but apparently you have to do a bunch of tasks way in advance," Ken said, trying not to sound too pessimistic about it all.

"Now, I know it's hard for you guys to understand, but planning a wedding takes time and you have to keep to the schedule to be sure it all shows up on time," Mary said, as she pulled on Ken's arm, "But I have to get going. I have a story to finish for tomorrow."

Ken walked Mary to the door and said goodbye with a promise to call her tomorrow. Then he returned to the family room. Uncle Darrick and Aunt Alicia had left. He sat back down in the chair as he said, "Ok, let's talk some details now."

"Like when we need to get out to Mr. Brewster's and what we need?" Joe askcd.

"Yes," Ken said, pulling some papers toward him from the table.

"I think we should leave Saturday or Sunday," Joe said, "but we need to confirm map locations, get clothing, and probably gold again."

"I think we still have some clothing from the trip to eighteen fifty-three in the barn," Joe added. "I will do what I can to check tonight and then call Becky tomorrow, I'll have her see how different that is from nineteen twelve clothing, but it would work if we have to go to Gettysburg, I think."

"If not, what do we do?" Ken asked.

"I think Becky mentioned there is a costume place in town by Mr. Brewster's. I'll have her call tomorrow morning and see what they have," Joe said said.

"I'll deal with the maps and locations for you," Kim said.

"I'll get the gold tomorrow. I have to go to the bank anyway, so I'll take care of that part. How much should I get, though?" Ken asked.

"When we went to eighteen fifty-three, we had about twenty-five bars, but we might be gone longer, and in more than one place, which means we might end up needing more," Joe said, looking up at the ceiling like he was calculating some numbers.

"I'll get seventy-five. That should be enough, right?" Ken asked.

"Sure," Joe said.

"Ok, if we get the clothing situated and Kim does the maps tomorrow, I'll get the money and we'll head out tomorrow night. I want to be out of here before Saturday morning, so we don't get asked a whole lot of questions in the gathering for the dress adventure," Ken explained.

"We need to call Mr. Brewster, then to let him know," Joe added. "I can do that in the morning."

Just then, the phone rang, and Ken went to the office to answer it. It was Ryan, and Ken filled them in on the plan. Ryan said he would be ready to leave and go over to their apartment at ten tomorrow morning. Ken returned to the family room and told them when to expect Ryan, and then he said he was going to bed. Kim took the maps and said she was going to look them over in her room and left as well.

Joe went into the office and called Becky.

"Hey, did you miss me already?" She said, laughing when she came to the phone.

"Yeah, for sure," he replied. Then he asked about her cover with her parents.

She explained that she had received this invitation to go to a friend's house for a week or so and asked if that was alright. They said it was and then confirmed Joe was taking her to the friends tomorrow. Then Joe explained the issue with the clothing and Becky confirmed she would make the calls.

"I'm not sure I like you going along on this trip," Joe said as Becky finished her list of things to confirm.

"Why? Don't you think I'll be helpful?"

"It's totally not that. I know you'll be helpful to us. You always have such good ideas and you keep us all in line in terms of the time period we're in. It's just that Tom seems very desperate now. I don't know. Like it's not his goal to get money and fix his family fortune anymore. It seems like his goal is to hurt us. I don't like you being close, if that's what he's after, that's all," Joe said. Then he paused, hoping to get her reaction.

"Oh, well, here's a good point. In both times we're about to travel to, I will not be in a place with a lot of freedom for women. I won't be out unless one of you guys is with me. I won't be in a position where he can get me, right?"

"I hope so. You're way too important to me to risk your livelihood, and we already know he has no restraint. He cut Ryan, remember."

"I'm worried too, but I know I have you and Ken and Ryan to protect me. But I kinda like you being so worried about me. And, by the way, you're important to me, too."

They mulled the trip over a few more times to be sure they had a good packing and prep list. Then Becky said they should get some sleep. They hung up and Joe went to his room. Kim's light was still on.

15 ▊

The next morning, Joe gathered up all the notes he thought they would need, and some tools. He left his room to find food, but gave up. Ken had already left to go to the bank and Kim was not up yet. When he went back to shower, and then came back to the kitchen, Kim was up. She was in the kitchen eating some muffin and fruit when Joe walked in.

"Hey sleepy-head," Joe said in greeting.

"I was up late working on the maps and things," Kim said, smiling.

"And," Joe said as he pulled a muffin off the plate and ate, finally having something to eat.

"And, I have good locations for you to go to with the machine, places Tom might be, and I even have some inns and some good information on the layout of Baltimore when you'll be there, and for Gettysburg," she said, sitting up straighter on the stool, proudly.

"Good. I knew we could count on you to get our mapping ready. Where is it?" Joe said.

"In my room. I'll get it after I finish. Did you call Mr. Brewster yet?"

"No. I'm going to go do that now," he got up and left the kitchen.

Joe went to the office and called Mr. Brewster. He explained their plan and said they would be there that evening.

"Are you leaving in the machine tonight, then?" Mr. Brewster asked.

"I don't think we'll be ready. I'm not sure," Joe responded.

"Well, it seems you have some loose ends, but with this group of young people, nothing surprises me!" he answered.

"If something changes during the day today, I'll call you, but we will be there later today," Joe said.

They said their goodbyes just as Kim entered the office with papers in tow.

"Here's the maps and notes I made. And you're welcome for cleaning up your mess in the kitchen!" Kim said as she set the papers on the desk.

Joe looked them over after he grinned up at her. Just then, Becky called.

"Well, we can't use the clothes for either time we go to on this trip. The clothing is very different for both years from the stuff we used in Philadelphia. But I just called the costume store and they have what we need. I have suits reserved for you three guys and dresses for me," Becky detailed her calls.

"Ok," Joe said, "that's good."

"Hey, how late is that store opened?" Kim asked.

"Yes, they're open until six tonight. I think we can get out there in time, so long as Ken doesn't take too long at the bank."

"I'll call Ryan and see what he was planning to do this morning. Maybe you and Ryan and I can go earlier and Ken can drive out from work," Joe contemplated.

Joe then called Ryan. Ryan said he could be over to get Joe and Becky around eleven if that worked. Three more phone calls and everything was arranged. Joe had told Uncle Darrick that morning before he left, they were all going out to see Mr. Brewster that evening and then he was going to MIT for the next week to work on his project. Ken had left a note saying he was taking off with some college buddies for a week, Ryan said he was going with Ken and Becky laid her plans to be with her girlfriend, and said that Ryan and Joe were dropping her at this friend's house. Joe then packed up what he thought they would need. The notes from Kim and maps and all the notes and notebooks they took from Tom's shed.

Ken arrived and had the gold bars in an enormous duffel bag. He gathered up some more things. They decided to go ahead and take both Ken's and Ryan's car. Becky called and asked them to pick her up and Joe agreed. They waited only a few more minutes before Ryan arrived. When Ryan arrived, they said goodbye to Kim, then he prepared to leave in his car, while Joe, Ryan left to get Becky and head out toward Wallingford, Connecticut. Ken was going to call Mary and go over some wedding plans and then leave. They arrived in town around three in the afternoon and picked up all the clothing and then went to Mr. Brewster's, waiting for Ken. They got the coordinates loaded in the machine and got all the clothing ready to go in the compartments and barn. All the while, Joe updated Mr. Brewster on their plan.

Ken arrived around six. He came into the barn while the three of them and Mr. Brewster were talking about the latest news from Choate.

"Hey, everybody!" Ken said as he entered the barn carrying a backpack and a big bag.

"Hey Ken. How was your drive out here?" Mr. Brewster asked as he got up to help Ken with the heavy bag.

Ken refused his help, saying it was way too heavy. Then he looked at Ryan and said, "Did you hear from Deb before you headed out here?"

"Yes. She called right before I left to get Joe and Becky. She arrived at the dig site and was all unpacked. It was late at night there, so she was going to bed. I told her about the plan and she gave me the number for the professor that was at the actual dig site so I could call as soon as we got back. She said she would call Aunt Alicia and Mr. Brewster when she could," Ryan said.

"Get the clothing, ok?" Ken asked Becky.

"Yes, it's loaded already and what we need to change into before we leave is hanging over there," she said, pointing to an area of the barn that had a rod where she had hung the clothing.

"Kim got the mapping done last night and even has ideas where we can stay in Baltimore and Gettysburg and where Tom might hide his machine too," Joe said.

"Good. Seems like we're ready," Ken said as he sat down and slumped over.

"What's in the bag that's so heavy?" Mr. Brewster asked.

"Gold," Ken replied.

"I think it might be a good idea for us to wait and leave tomorrow morning. Ken, you look like you could use a little rest before we head off to do this," Ryan said, reaching over and patting him on the back.

"I would agree," Mr. Brewster added. "You'll all want to be in the best possible shape to face this troubled young man. Plus, I neglected to ask, Ryan, how is your wound?"

"It's healing pretty well. The stitches need to come out, but no infection. It bothers me a little when I twist and move, but I'm sure I'll be ok," Ryan said, rubbing his side.

"You're probably right about tomorrow, but man, do I want this over!" Ken said, looking up at everyone.

"I can take the stitches out tonight if you want, Ryan. Have you eaten at all today, Ken?" Becky asked.

"No," Ken replied, as his stomach growled as if to answer Becky's question.

"Let's get some food, go to the hotel, and rest and leave early tomorrow morning," Ryan said. "I already reserved us three rooms. Ken, you take one, Joe and I can take one and Becky can have one."

"Ok, you're probably right, dealing with that idiot Tom might need my full, rested attention," Ken said, getting up. "Sorry Mr. Brewster, I had wanted to visit with you a bit. We seem to only see you lately when there's some crisis."

"No worries. I know this is important. I feel badly that I left the barn at risk, thereby leaving the machine at risk. We'll need to talk about that once you get the machine back from Tom," Mr. Brewster said as he walked to Ken and put his hand on Ken's shoulder.

They left the barn and checked into the hotel. They ate, Becky took Ryan's stitches out, and then they all went to rest. The next morning early, they left the hotel and returned to the barn. Leaving both cars parked outside Mr. Brewster's house, they went into the barn and changed clothes. Joe went and got Mr. Brewster, and they returned to the barn. He helped them load their bags and then watched as the light flashed and the sound got loud and wind picked up inside the closed barn. Then they were gone.

Ryan looked out the window in the machine's door and saw only trees. He turned and said, "Man, Kim is the master at mapping! She has been spot-on with the perfect place to land this machine every single time!"

"That's only one of her special talents," Ken said, smiling. "We probably don't tell her enough."

"You're right. She's done so much for us, and she was so upset she couldn't go on this trip. We need to plan something for her and be sure to tell her about how great she is at mapping. Girl Scouts, that the ticket," Becky said, pulling the bags out of the compartments.

The four of them made their way north out of the wooded area, as Kim had instructed in her notes. They came to a road and could see a small community eastward down the road. They walked the mile to town and found an inn. Becky said as they walked up, they would have a common room and could buy some food and find out about ways to Baltimore and a bank. They went in and were greeted by a portly man with flour all over the apron he had covered his clothing. Ken introduced himself and said they had been walking a long way because of a wagon wheel that fell off and a horse that was too old to ride. The man said his name was John Holland, and they were welcome. Ken asked about food and Mr. Holland said he would bring them food right away.

They sat down and Becky whispered they needed to remember to be very careful about their conversations, because they were in a period where language was very formal. Ken thanked her as Mr. Holland returned carrying three mugs of coffee and asked if the miss would like tea. Becky smiled and said, "Thank you, Sir, yes, that would be lovely."

"Sir, would you happen to know of any conveyance that would take us on to Baltimore? We have family there and I need to see about Miss Simmons and my brother before my friend here, and I head back to repair the wagon and move it," Ken said to Mr. Holland when he returned with Becky's tea.

"Why, I believe Mr. Smith is taking a wagonload of goods to Baltimore this very afternoon. I am certain he would take you four along. After I bring your refreshments, I will walk down to ask him," Mr. Holland said as he turned to go get the food. He returned, placed four plates of what appeared to be beef and vegetables swimming in a dark gravy in front of each of them. He took off his apron and hung it on a hook by the kitchen entrance and walked out the front door.

"Well, the food's good," Joe said as he took several bites.

"Yeah, well, you can't really mess up beef and vegetables, right?" Ryan said, smiling as he took another bite.

"Yes, but how do I pay him?" Ken said.

"Hey, I forgot to mention, I had some really old colonial coins that my great-grandfather gave me. We can use those," Becky said, smiling and sitting up proudly.

"Imagine that! I have some too. I've had them since I was about ten. I found them at a garage sale when I was in North Carolina," Ryan said as he pulled eight or nine of the same kind of coins from his pocket.

"Wow, Becky and Ryan, that will really save us here, but I don't want you to give up something your great-grandfather gave you or something you've been collecting for years," Ken said.

"It's ok. I only have these four and I don't really collect coins. It's better use for them to help us here," Becky said and handed them to Ken just as Mr. Holland opened the door. Luckily, he was stomping his feet from the dust and was looking down, not at them. When he finished, he looked up and said, "Mr. Smith said he would be happy to take you on to Baltimore. When you finish, you can just walk down to the general store."

"Thank you for your assistance, Mr. Holland," Ken said.

They finished eating, and Ken stood. Joe stood and went to pull Becky's chair out and help her up. Ken turned and asked Mr. Holland how much for the meal. He hesitated, and Ken produced the four coins.

"My, oh my. Certainly, it was a filling meal, but not as fancified as all that!" Mr. Holland said.

"You have been very helpful, Mr. Holland. I insist you take it," Ken said, putting the coins on the bar in front of Mr. Holland. "Good day to you, Sir."

"Good day to you, as well, Mr. Fitzgerald," Mr. Holland said, grinning as he picked up the coins.

They walked out of the inn and down the street. Ken introduced them all to Mr. Smith, and they went out to the wagon that had two rows of seats. Joe assisted Becky onto the back seat, and then he and Ryan joined her. Ken handed Joe all their bags and Joe set them below the seat. Then Ken climbed onto the front seat with Mr. Smith. Mr. Smith entertained them with tales of his store and reports of the war going on mainly up north and down south by Washington. When they approached Baltimore, Mr. Smith asked where they were headed, and Ken informed him which street they wished to be left at. It was fortunately near the shop that Mr. Smith was headed to, so he stopped at the intersection of Beach and Harris and left the four of them. Ken asked if he would like payment for his service, but Mr. Smith said he was simply being charitable to weary travelers. Ken thanked him and they walked down Beach Street. The inn that Kim said should be there, was there, and there was a savings and loan a few doors down from the inn on the other side of the street. They entered the modest but sunny lobby of the inn, and Ken approached the desk.

"Excuse me, I need to procure three rooms for four nights please," Ken said to the gentlemen behind the counter.

"Certainly, Sir. What is the name on these rooms?" The man replied.

"Mr. Kenneth Fitzgerald," Ken answered.

"Very good, Mr. Fitzgerald. Do you need assistance with your luggage?" he asked.

"No, that will not be necessary," Ken replied.

"Very good. You will be on the second floor, rooms two-ten, two-eleven, and two-twelve. Up the stairs and to your left," the man said as she slid three keys across the counter toward Ken.

"Thank you. Do you serve meals in the morning or evening?" Ken asked.

"I am afraid we only serve a morning meal and afternoon tea service. There are several inns on Harris Avenue and on Second Street where you can obtain mid-day and evening meals," the man replied.

"Very good. Thank you," Ken said as he turned from the desk and walked to where Joe and Becky were sitting. They all silently picked up their bags and walked up the stairs. Becky put her arm on Joe's as she walked, and he carried both her and his bags. Opening the first door, Ken looked in and saw only one bed and he turned and said, "Becky, you take this room."

She went in and Joe put her bag on the bed. He turned and went to the next room, where Ken was putting his bag on one bed. Becky hung up her two dresses in the wardrobe and put the rest of her things at the bottom of it. Then she locked her door and went next door, where Joe and Ken were doing the same with their things. Ryan was in the third room, that also had only one bed. He returned shortly after Becky. As Becky sat down in one chair in the room, she said, "We're going to need some money to eat and to rent a carriage or something to get around."

"We should go to the bank and talk to the owner. We need to see about keeping the rest of the gold in their safe, I think," Joe said.

"But if we have to leave in a hurry, how will we get it?" Ryan asked.

"Ryan's right, Joe, we can't leave it in the bank like we did in Philadelphia. We have to keep it here," Becky said, putting her hand on his arm.

"Ok. I just don't like it," Joe said.

Ken put the bag with the gold bars on the bed and opened it. He said, "Well?"

"Did you ask what the rate was for the two rooms?" Becky asked.

"No. I completely forgot to ask," Ken said.

"It can't be much, and food here for breakfast, then lunch and dinner," Ryan added.

"Plus, the carriage. We need to get around for a few days," Joe said.

"Since we're not sure, let's see what five bars will get us. If it doesn't seem like enough, I can go back with a couple more," Ken surmised.

He put one each in his pants pockets and handed Ryan two to put in his pockets, and then the remaining one to Joe. They locked the room door after storing the bag under the bed and went down the stairs and walked out onto the wooden sidewalk. They crossed the street and walked to the bank.

The bank owner came from his office when Ken had asked to speak to him. Ken introduced himself and said he was from Virginia. He explained he needed to exchange some gold for currency to use here in Baltimore. The bank owner was happy to help him once he saw all the gold bars Ken had. He left with the gold bars and went behind his office to the vault. The bank manager returned a few minutes later carrying a small leather bag. He handed it to Ken and announced that he had exchanged the gold for three hundred dollars. Ken thanked him and they left the bank. Becky suggested they walk around a bit and they walked back to Harris Avenue and walked eastward. On Second Street, they saw several shops and inns and a general store. They walked further to the harbor, and they spent time looking out. They could see the British ships circling the fort at the front of the long harbor entrance.

"This gives me the shivers. Even though we read about it, and we know we're traveling to the past. It always gives me the shivers to actually be right in history," Ken whispered.

"Yeah. I know what you mean," Ryan said, looking at the ships.

"How are we going to locate Tom in this city? It seems too big for us to search," Becky said, focusing them back on the task that brought them here.

"I think we spend tomorrow trying to locate where he might have the machine. I don't see how we can find him in this big city. Also, he might not even be here yet," Joe pondered.

"Let's focus on the machine for tomorrow. We know where he's going to be on the twelfth. If we can find the machine, we can end this quickly by just moving the thing. Then Tom can't leave without coming to us," Ryan said, obviously wanting to end this chase.

"I think that's a great idea," Ken said.

"Remember, with the landing site fifteen miles from here, Tom might be at some inn in some village that way. His machine might be anywhere, really," Becky said, somewhat forlornly.

Ken turned with that note, and they followed. They walked back and found an inn that had a bar on the second floor and a restaurant of sorts on the first floor. They ordered some soup and bread and the owner brought cider for them to drink. When they had finished eating, Ken suggested he and Ryan go upstairs to see if there was any talk in the bar that might be some help to them. They left Joe and Becky at the table and went up the stairs to the bar area.

Ken found two stools in the middle of the bar, and they sat. He looked around at the people and saw a mix of aristocratic types and common folk. He noted that quietly to Ryan, saying it surprised him they all came to the same place. Then they listened for a while. There was talk of the war. Most people were supporting the effort or fighting for the fledgling America to preserve it. Someone mentioned the battle cry that was in the paper the day before and they all broke out in song. Although Ryan and Ken knew the words, they didn't know the tune it was being sung to, so they mouthed the words to act the part.

After a while, when there were clearly no details to be garnered, Ryan suggested they head out. They found Joe and Becky at the table. Ken paid the owner, and they left. Becky suggested they stop at the general store and pick up a few things, so they went there. Becky got a few things, like bandages, stockings and Ken bought two folding knives. They left the general store and returned to the inn.

Gathering in the middle room, the four of them looked over Kim's notes about the possible location of Tom's machine, they agreed to find a carriage to rent and check the sites out and scope out the location of the landing that would take place on the twelfth. Agreeing to meet the next morning at eight, they all went to their separate rooms and slept.

The next morning, they met in the hall outside the rooms, and Joe escorted Becky downstairs. They found a table in the dining room and a waiter came to the table with the breakfast menu. Ken said that was fine and to please bring three cups of coffee and a pot of tea. The menu included four courses of eggs, pastries, meats and fish. Before they had gotten to the end, they all decided they had enough. Ryan indicated as much to the waiter when he picked up the plates from the third course, because Ken had gone out to the desk to inquire about a rental carriage. The waiter seemed confused, but agreed to forgo the last course.

"Do we pay here in the dining room?" Ryan asked.

"Oh, no, Sir, we will add this to your room bill. What name is it under?" the waiter answered.

"Kenneth Fitzgerald," Joe responded.

"Very good, Sir. Have a wonderful day," the waiter said as he finished picking up plates and left the table.

The three of them went to the lobby to join Ken. There they heard the desk clerk saying, "Oh, No Sir, I will send a man to get the carriage and team and bring it here for you. It shouldn't take long at all."

"And how will I pay for this service?" Ken asked.

"We can collect the fee here and have it taken when you are ready to return the carriage to the barn, Sir," the desk clerk answered.

"Very good. We will be down shortly then," Ken concluded and turned from the desk.

The four of them went back upstairs. Becky donned gloves and a parasol and Ryan put the map and notes from Kim in his jacket front pocket. They left the rooms and went back to the lobby to wait for the carriage.

A young man came into the lobby and went directly to the desk. He reported that the carriage was in the back carriage area of the inn, as was requested. He then walked away. The desk clerk called for Ken and indicated the carriage was in back. He snapped his fingers for another young man to come forward and he took them out the door to the carriage area. They thanked the young man and Joe helped Becky into the carriage back seat, where he joined her and then Ken and Ryan sat on the front seat.

"Do you know how to do this?" Ryan leaned over and quietly asked Ken.

"Not really," Ken said, awkwardly holding the reins.

"Let me. I did this on my grandfather's farm years ago," Ryan said, reaching for the reins.

Ken gladly relinquished the reins to Ryan. Ryan then led the team out of the carriage area and onto Maple Street, then turned onto Beach Street and headed south. He reached into his pocket and pulled out the map and handed it to Ken, saying, "You get to navigate, then."

They rode out of town and checked several of the sites Kim had thought Tom might hide his machine. Having no luck, they turned again south and rode toward the landing site that would happen tomorrow night. They pulled off the road near the Patapsco River and Ken got out. He walked along the river for a bit.

"Should one of us go with him?" Ryan asked Joe.

"Probably, but I don't want to leave Becky here alone," Joe said.

"I'll go," Ryan said as he climbed down from the carriage and took off after Ken.

Seeing him, Ryan called out, "Hey, Ken, wait."

Ken turned and waited for Ryan to catch up with him. When he reached Ken, Ken said, "See up there? That's where I bet the sniper is going to be. There is great eyesight along this whole stretch of river. You come around that bend in the river from the bay there, and it will be like shooting ducks in a barrel."

"Yeah, I can see that. Where are we going to be waiting, then?" Ryan asked.

"There're some woods and shrubs leading up that rise. I think we hide out in there. It's also probably where Tom's going to come at the guy. Maybe stopping Tom will be easy this time," Ken said, pointing at the leading edge of the rise.

They turned and walked back to the carriage, climbing back in.

"See anything?" Joe asked.

"Yeah, I think I know where we'll be hiding out and where Tom's likely to be, too," Ken said as Ryan pulled the carriage back onto the road.

As he did, Becky said, "Hey look down the road, isn't that a village? We should go down there."

"Maybe there's an inn where we can eat," Joe added.

"Maybe that's where Tom is," Becky said, repeating what Joe said for emphasis.

"Yeah, let's go. I'm hungry too and we might get lucky," Ken said.

Ryan turned the carriage toward the village in the distance. They rode along for a bit without saying much. Then, Joe said, "Why, if we've done this so many times, and we're collectively so much smarter than Tom, can we not find him and put an end to this?"

"I was just thinking the same thing. What are we missing?" Ryan said.

"We aren't full of hate and rage. That must be it," Becky said, trying to be considerate of what Tom might be experiencing.

"I don't feel sorry for this guy at all. He's caused us all to have to do this now, three times, and he really hurt Ryan, and the havoc he might cause is immeasurable. I think he's messed up in the head," Ken said vehemently.

"I know he's got some issue, mentally. It's just that we don't under-stand what that feels like. Even you, Ken and Joe, that lost your parents, don't have the same issues Tom had. I remember now that they teased mercilessly him his first year at Choate because he was there on a scholarship. That was before you all came. But I think that's the reason he can evade us. He's driven by something we don't understand," Becky tried to explain her position.

At that, they arrived in town. They found an inn, and Ryan pulled the horses up to it and tied their reins off to the post. They went inside and Ken requested food for four and sat them down at a table. A young woman, who announced herself as May, the daughter of the owners, came to the table and asked what they wished to drink. Ken and Ryan asked for beer. Joe and Becky asked for cider. May left and returned quickly with the two mugs of beer. Then she left and returned with two more mugs filled with apple cider.

"What are you serving today, Miss May?" Ryan asked.

May smiled at Ryan as she said, "Sliced pork and carrots and potatoes."

"Thank you," Ryan replied.

There was an old man sitting at a table near theirs and a few men that clearly looked like they had come from a field standing by the bar. One of them turned to Ryan and asked, "Where are you from? Haven't seen you in here before, Sir."

"We are visiting from Virginia, Sir. We were out for a drive today and stopped. We're staying up in Baltimore," Ryan returned.

"We seem to be getting quite a bit of visitors lately," the man replied.

"Really? Why would that be with the British so close?" Ken asked.

"Maybe we have some Torries still here on our land. You wouldn't be siding with the British now, would you?" the man asked.

"No Sir. We love this country. Our grandfather fought for it," Joe said.

"Sir, we wonder, have you seen a young man, probably traveling alone? He is a cousin of ours and his family disowned him. He had some gambling issues, you see. We heard he might be around these parts, and, well, we have some news for him and would sure like to locate him," Ken asked.

"There was a guy in here the other day. Seemed kind of strange. His clothes were a bit off, if you know what I mean," the other man said, while rubbing his chin.

"Really. Do you know where he might be staying?" Ken asked as he stood up and walked toward the men with his beer mug.

"No, I only saw him the one day," the other man said.

"That is a shame, but we thank you for the information," Ken said as he walked back to the table.

May came back to the table to clean up. Ken left the money on the table and they left. As they pulled away from the inn, Ken said, "He's here. I know it. Where would he be staying, though?"

"I wonder, if after the whole money issue came up for him in nineteen eleven, did he maybe decide not to spend money on this trip?" Becky put out to the group.

"Wouldn't that mean he's camping out somewhere?" Ryan asked.

"Ah, now I get that note in his notebook! He mentioned needing traps, and it made little sense, but if he was living outdoors, he would need to trap animals for food, wouldn't he?" Joe said, punching one hand into the other.

"We're really going to have a hard time finding him, if that's what he's doing. There's entirely too much open land in eighteen fourteen," Ryan surmised.

"It's getting late, and we need to get back to Baltimore. We know where he's going to be tomorrow. We just have to be ready for that. Let's get back, have some dinner and get some rest," Ken said.

They rode the rest of the way nearly in silence, each contemplating what tomorrow would bring. They brought the carriage and team back to the inn, and Ken asked the young man who came out to rein the horses in if he could look after them and keep them in the barn at the inn. The young man said he would. They went through the lobby and out the front to walk to a place to have dinner. After dinner at a different, fancier inn, they returned and spent a few minutes planning their morning. Then all four of them fell into fitful sleep.

16

Ken rose early. In fact, he had slept very little. This constant chase after someone that didn't have their collective knowledge and understanding of time travel was really getting to him. How could they not reach this guy? Then, in the wee hours of the morning, he remembered his conversation with Mary. She postured that the reason they had trouble tracking Tom down was his rage-filled, somewhat evil side. His motivation was not something the Fitzgerald's and their friends understood, Mary said. Any attempt to judge him by their faithful, trusting, honest side was going to fail because they didn't look at the world the same way Tom did. When Ken thought about this, he realized Mary was right. If you don't know that rage, that displacement of blame or the understanding of right and wrong, you would look at every event, every person differently. Ken finally fell asleep with the warm understanding of how lucky they all were. The family they had built more by choice than chance was amazing, given their circumstances.

Ken got out of bed and got cleaned up and dressed without disturbing Joe. He left a note and went downstairs. No one was milling around the lobby at this early hour, so he went out the back door toward the stable. The young man that had been there yesterday came out when he heard Ken approach on the cobblestone drive, and asked, "Can I do something for you, Sir?"

"I would like to just saddle up one horse we have here for a morning ride, if you don't mind," Ken replied.

"Right away, Sir!" the young man said as he turned.

A few minutes later, the horse was led onto the cobblestone drive. Ken climbed into the saddle and rode out. He took the same route they had yesterday, but he stopped at what he believed the beginning of the rise over the river was located. He tied the horse's reins to a tree and crept up to the ridge. Someone had been there! There was trampled grass and a small wool blanket lay out between two large rocks. Ken remembered these rocks from yesterday. He figured that would be the best place to shoot at the arriving British soldiers. He was right. He looked around for a few minutes, wondering if Tom had already stored a gun somewhere nearby or if all of this was American soldiers preparing to knock off the British as they came ashore. When he couldn't find anything, he crept through the wooded area that led down to the road. Finding nothing that would indicate this was Tom's doing and not just an American soldier preparing, he spent a few minutes moving some brush around at the far end of the wooded area to make a hiding place for himself and Ryan. He was going to insist that Joe and Becky wait at the inn for this. He was worried about both of them getting hurt. Then Ken rode back into town. He stopped at a smith's shop and bought two guns and two leather bags of musket balls, powder and flint cloth.

When Ken returned to the hotel, he left the horse with the young man and went up to the room. Joe, Ryan and Becky were in his and Joe's room, waiting for him.

"Where did you go?" Joe asked when Ken walked into the room.

"I left a note. I went out for a ride to check out the place where we expect Tom to be," Ken replied.

"Find anything?" Ryan asked as he stood up.

"Yeah. Someone was at that spot we think is best for watching the river landing. There is a wool blanket on the ground and the rocks seem to have been moved a bit to provide cover," Ken responded as he went to the wardrobe that had his things and discreetly put the guns and leather bags into the bottom of it.

"We should get breakfast, I think," Becky said, standing.

"Sure, that sounds like a good idea," Ken said as he turned and walked back to the door. As he turned from locking the door, Ryan said in a quiet voice, "What did you put in your wardrobe?"

"I bought us some supplies for tonight," Ken answered as they walked a bit behind Joe and Becky down the stairs.

"Supplies to help us stop, Tom?" Ryan whispered.

"Yes."

They sat down in the dining room, and the same waiter brought coffee and tea to the table. He announced the breakfast menu and then began bringing plates of food to the table. As they were eating, Ryan asked, "When we're finished here, hopefully today, how are we going to get all the way back to our machine?"

"I was thinking about that today. We have plenty of money left. I think I'll see about buying this horse and team and we'll just leave it at Mr. Holland's," Ken said.

"What exactly is your plan tonight?" Becky asked.

"First, Joe, you and Becky are going to stay here. I think this guy is probably getting more and more desperate and I don't want either of you to get hurt. Ryan, I really don't want you there either, but I need some help," Ken started, "So, Ryan and I will ride out there early enough so we can see what we're doing. Then we will hide in the place I've prepared and wait. When we see Tom, we'll overpower him, find out where he has the machine, and go from there."

"I don't think it's a good idea that just you and Ryan go," Joe protested, "the best thing is for one of us to right away take him back in the machine, and the other two come back here and get Becky and then tomorrow morning, leave town for the other machine. That should be the plan."

"Becky can't be here by herself. It isn't safe for her without a male escort of some kind. Plus, we have no way to communicate once we leave here, so if something happens, Joe, you need to be here to take care of Becky," Ken reasoned.

"Ken's right, Joe. Stay here with Becky. We can handle that little pain in the neck. If we catch him, and get to the machine he took, Ken can stay with him and guard him, and we can get that machine ready to go and I can send them on their way, then I can come back here and get the two of you," Ryan added.

"The three of us couldn't stop him before. What makes you think the two of you can stop him now?" Joe asked, expressing all the frustration he felt.

"Well, for starters, we have this guy by more than a few inches and a few pounds. Second, we know exactly what he's here for and where he's going to be at a set time so we're not reacting, we're proactively waiting for him to come to us," Ken said, "I know you want to help, Joe, but I think without Deb, we have to have you here to keep Becky safe."

"I get it. I just don't want anything happening to you two. Also, I feel pretty responsible for all of this. I mean, I'm the one he started out being mad at. If I'd noticed it at all, maybe I could have prevented all of this," Joe said, looking down.

"No one blames you, Joe," Becky said, reaching out and putting a hand on his arm.

"Let's not discuss this anymore in the dining room, ok? We're getting some strange looks," Ryan said.

Ken looked around, and then he stood up because they were now done with breakfast. He led them out of the dining room and back up the stairs to his and Joe's room. When they were all inside, Ken shut the door and turned back to them all.

"I'm not trying to be autocratic or anything here, but my mind's made up about this," Ken said, then shook his head and ran his hands through his hair. "Ok, I guess I am kind of being autocratic. I'm sorry, Joe, but I think this is the way we have to play this out."

"Ok. I don't like it, but I want Becky safe so, I'm agreeing, but under some duress," Joe conceded.

"We aren't going to sit in here all day, are we? I feel rather cooped up," Becky said, in an attempt to change the subject.

"What would you like to do?" Joe asked her.

"How about a walk around town? Can we do that?" she asked.

"Sure. Do either of you want to join us?" Joe asked, turning and looking at Ryan and Ken.

"I want to go over some things with Ryan. How about if we meet you by the harbor in thirty or forty minutes?" Ken proposed.

"Sure. It's sunny out there, Becky. You might need your umbrella," Joe said, standing up.

"I need my gloves too. That's proper dress for a girl in these times. I'll have to get them from next door." She stood and walked toward the door. She turned just before she reached it, and said, "and it's a parasol, not an umbrella."

Joe laughed as she opened the door and went next door. While she was gone, Joe asked, "What did you put in the wardrobe, Ken?"

"Did everybody see me? I was trying to be a little discrete," He answered, again running his hand through his hair.

"I don't think Becky saw," Joe said, laughing.

"I bought two pistols today," Ken admitted.

"You what?! You can't kill Tom here. That would more than create a ripple effect in time," Joe said, as he rushed to where Ken was standing.

"I'm not going to kill him unless he comes at us again, like he did to Ryan last time. I might hit him with the handle, or point it at him. Remember, he's here to stop a sniper. He probably has a gun on him," Ken said, somewhat sheepishly.

"Didn't Ryan bring some huge pocket knives? Why do we need guns?" Joe asked again.

"I'm not letting this guy get away, Joe. I'm not, and Ryan will not do anything foolish," Ken said, trying to calm Joe down.

Just then, Becky came back to the room. Seeing Ken and Joe kind of squared off, she asked, "What is going on here?"

"Nothing, we're just going over details, and like Ken is worried about us, I'm worried about him," Joe answered her, as he took her arm and started for the door. "Are you ready?"

"Yes. We'll see you soon," she said, smiling at Ryan and Ken.

When Becky and Joe had left, Ken walked over to the wardrobe and took out the pistols, the supplies, and the leather bags. He laid them out on the bed and unwrapped them in the paper covering the shopkeeper had wrapped them in. Ryan unwrapped one, and Ken unwrapped the other. Ken opened the box and began taking out the small flasks of powder and the flint cloth. While he did this, Ryan said, "So, how do we load and shoot these? I've shot a pistol, but a nineteen seventy-five pistol, not a colonial pistol."

"The shopkeeper showed me. You open this little flask, load powder down the barrel, then a musket ball, then you put this little flint cloth here by the hammer and stuff it in this hole a bit. You cock the hammer and when you pull the trigger, it slams into this flint cloth, it ignites the powder and shoots the musket ball out. It's good for about sixty yards, the shopkeeper said," Ken explained.

"This is going to be hard. We have to load after each shot, right?" Ryan asked as he looked over the parts and repeated the process without actually loading anything.

"Yeah. I figure we take it all out in a saddlebag. Then we prep for one shot each in the brush while we wait for Tom," Ken suggested.

"This will work as long as he hasn't brought a modern gun with him," Ryan said.

"I was also thinking we needed some water, and maybe some food. Do you think we can ask for that downstairs?" Ken wondered out loud.

"They serve nothing but breakfast. I think we'll have to get it at that inn we ate lunch or dinner at. But will they have some way to carry the water?" Ryan said, thinking the effort through.

"The general store had leather flasks, that, I think, should hold water. We should go there and check those out. We can get some food then too, and two bags for all this," Ken said as he packed away the fling cloth, musket balls, and powder in the boxes.

Ryan helped him wrap the guns back up and put them in the wardrobe, and then they prepared to leave. At the general store, they bought two water flasks, and two saddlebags. They also found some smoked meat slices, a loaf of bread, and peppermints. Ken suggested this instead of a meal from the inn. Ryan agreed, but picked up some oyster crackers as well. They put all their purchases in the two saddlebags and slung the bags over their shoulders and went to meet Joe and Becky.

Ryan saw Joe and Becky sitting on a bench in the park near the harbor. He pointed that out to Ken and the two headed over to meet them.

"You two have been busy, haven't you?" Becky asked as they walked up.

"Yeah, we did a little shopping for tonight," Ryan said, "some beef jerky, crackers and bread. Doesn't that sound tasty?"

"Not really. When are you heading out?" Joe asked as he stood up.

"Well, I was thinking we should have a late lunch. The inn we walked by is still serving, I think. Then, we will walk with you back to the inn and Ryan and I can leave," Ken replied.

"Let's walk over there and see what the crowd is looking at," Becky said.

They walked across the street and toward the harbor. There was a crowd watching the British ships seem to weigh anchor where they had been re-assembled from the bombardment of Fort McHenry last week. They watched with the other spectators and then turned and went to the inn to eat. The food was good, but not very warm, as Joe commented while they walked back. Once at the inn, Ken went through to the back and asked the same young man he asked this morning to saddle up both of their horses. They were heading out. Then he went up the stairs and into his room. Joe, Ryan and Becky were sitting there. He got the guns out of the wardrobe and put one in his saddlebag and handed the other one to Ryan. Then they each stored some of the supplies in their bags. Ryan went to his room and got the knives, rope, and a bandana he had brought in case they had to gag Tom. He returned.

"You be careful," Becky said, looking worried at both Ken and Ryan.

"If one of you isn't back tomorrow morning, we'll come out there looking for you and then, if we can't find you, we're coming back here and waiting another day," Joe said solemnly.

"At least one of us will be back here tonight. If we catch him, I'm heading back with him tonight, but Ryan will be here with the horses so you can make your way back to our machine," Ken said. He grabbed a heavier jacket and a blanket, and he and Ryan left.

17

Ryan and Ken rode out of the back barn area of the inn toward the river Patapsco and its northern point. It was about four in the afternoon when they tied their horse up across the road in a wooded area where they found a little clearing in the middle of it. They walked back to the hiding place Ken had created earlier in the day and Ken laid out the blanket so they weren't sitting on the cold ground.

"After the sun sets, we'll try to see what's up around the area. I don't want to be walking around in daylight in case Tom is making his way here," Ken said as he tucked his saddle bag under a shrub.

"Sounds good. I'm thinking we should get these pistols ready in case we need them, though," Ryan answered as he took the pistol out of his saddlebag along with the box. He set to work loading powder and the ball into the barrel, then placing the flint cloth into the hammer spot. He gently returned the hammer to the cloth, to only be cocked when he needed to use it.

Ken did the same, and they sat quietly and listened. Just as the sun was setting, Ken tensed as he heard several horses approach. He looked through the brush and relaxed as he saw two men dismount and noted they were in military uniform. The one pulled a very long rifle out of the other side of his saddle, while the other rider pulled off what looked like a bedroll and some supplies. Ken and Ryan watched as they gathered up their supplies, tied up the horse near where Ken and Ryan hid and made their way up the ridge to where the stones were set. As they walked up, Ken and Ryan heard them, with one saying, "You set the rocks up yesterday, did you not, George?"

"Yes, Sir. I did just as you asked," the younger man responded.

"Good. We might have some time to wait, but I want to be set and ready when those British make their way around the river bend," said the man who was clearly the senior person and the one holding the long rifle.

After they had reached the top and were talking about their plans, Ken looked over at Ryan and whispered, "Well, players one and two in place. Now all we need is player three to show up."

"Where do you think he'll arrive from?" Ryan asked.

"My hunch is that he stayed out of town, but that's only based on what I would do. I mean, if I knew I was being pursued and I wanted to stay out of notice, I wouldn't go into Baltimore. I'd find a place out of town where I wouldn't be looked for. Of course, everything I thought Tom would do, he didn't, so who knows?" Ken explained.

"For a guy who doesn't know much about time travel, he sure has evaded us," Ryan added.

"Yeah, and that alone drives me nuts! All this other nonsense with him cutting you and getting away from us twice is just icing on that cake," Ken concluded.

They got quiet because the younger soldier came back down the rise to their horses and got a bag off of the other soldier's horse. Then he went back up and all was quiet for a while. During that time, Ken and Ryan ate some. The sun completely set, and everyone on the ridge got very tense. The younger soldier was holding a retractable eye glass, like sailors used, and the older one was lying on his stomach on a blanket, with the rifle between the two rocks. He kept looking down the barrel, checking for the British coming around the bend in the river. It was getting late when the one soldier leaned over and whispered loudly that he thought he saw the landing party. Ken and Ryan got ready in case Tom showed up at the last minute. The older soldier checked his rifle one last time and got into position.

"I think one of us should get closer," Ryan whispered.

"You get closer if you can. I'll stay here and watch for Tom. It would be better if we can get him before he gets close to the soldiers," Ken agreed.

Ryan moved tree to tree until he was at the end of the tree line near the top of the ridge. He could clearly see both soldiers and all areas of the top of the ridge.

"Sir, it has to be them. There's a third small craft coming around the bend now," the younger soldier said excitedly.

"Ok. I'm going to take out that lead man in the first boat. Keep watching," the soldier with the rifle said.

Just then there was a rustling of grass and Ryan saw Tom aiming a pistol at the sniper. Then he saw Ken coming up behind Tom. Tom fired, but Ken pushed his arm and he missed the sniper and the shot ricocheted off the rocks and hit the tree near where Ryan was hiding. The young soldier turned around just as the sniper got his shot off. There was screaming from the river, but no one was watching as they were concentrating on Tom with his gun and his struggle with Ken. Ryan, moving out from his location, took aim at Tom, who had pulled away from Ken and was standing off with him about ten feet away. The sniper yelled to the younger soldier to check the water. He turned back and looked through his eyeglass, and grinning, he said, "You got him. He was an officer; I can see his medals on the coat one of the British is holding. The other two boats are turning around!"

Ryan's shot missed Tom and Tom turned and ran down the hill, with Ken giving chase. The sniper stood and looked at Ryan. "Just who are you?"

"My apologies, Sargent," Ryan replied.

"I am a captain, young man. Again, identify yourself," the captain replied, as he took a step toward Ryan.

"I have traveled from Virginia with my friend and his brother and we stopped at an inn several days ago and heard that young man that was trying to stop you, discuss his plans. We didn't know who to contact, and we decided we should just come here and wait for his arrival and stop him. He said he was a spy for the British," Ryan explained.

"Well then, my thanks are required here as your friend kept that spy from murdering me," the captain replied.

"I should go after my friend and provide assistance," Ryan said as he turned to leave.

"Take Wilkenson with you. He can drag that spy back here after you have secured him," the captain said. The young soldier followed Ryan as he ran down the hill in the direction he saw Ken go.

When Ryan and the soldier reached the road, there was no one in sight. Ryan said, "They might have gone into those woods." As he crossed the road after pointing in that direction.

"We should split up and search these woods. I do not know how far they stretch. You take the southern side and I will take the northern," the soldier said as they reached the trees.

Ryan started making his way into the woods, which were now very dark. He stopped hearing something and then raced toward the clearing where they had tied their horses. No one was there, but he thought he heard someone running through the brush. Ryan took off toward the sound, further in and southward in the woods until he came to another small clearing just as the light disappeared from the other machine. He looked around and saw Ken lying on the ground. He rushed to him.

"Ken, are you alright?" Ryan asked.

Ken opened his eyes, looked around and said, "Why, why does that menace keep getting the best of us?"

"Our horses are gone," Ryan said.

"That's when I caught up to him. Just after he released the horses. I chased him in this direction and stopped by this tree to listen for him when I got hit on the back of the head," Ken said, sitting up and rubbing the back of his head.

"We can't look at it now. Are you bleeding?" Ryan asked.

"No."

"Can you walk?" Ryan asked.

"Yes, but if we can't find the horses, we have a really long night of walking ahead of us," Ken said as he stood up.

They began walking back toward the clearing where their horses were formerly tied up. Wilkenson came upon them there.

"Did you locate the spy?" Wilkenson asked.

"No, he turned our horses loose here and took off on his own. We could not catch him," Ken said.

"I found your horses. I tied them up close to the road where I came upon them. Did you happen to see those bright lights? What on earth could it have been from? Do you think it was the spy with some new-fangled device?" Wilkenson asked.

"Thank you, Sir, you have really saved us," Ryan said.

Ken said, covering for the machine, "We did not see any lights. I am not certain what you saw, but perhaps it was the moonlight peering through the trees?"

"I don't know, but we should return and report to Captain Jameson," Wilkenson said as he turned and headed toward the road.

They reached the ridge top where the captain had waited, and Wilkenson made his report. Captain Jameson turned to Ken and asked, "Can you describe this spy so we can send men out into the countryside to search him out?"

"He was approximately five feet, six inches tall. His hair was light brown, but I do not know the length, as he was wearing a hat. He had on simple clothing, such that a farmer would wear," Ken provided.

"In which direction did he go?" The captain asked.

"Southwest, Sir," Ryan answered.

"Very good. Again, thank you for assistance here. Your efforts helped prevent a British landing tonight. The Admiral at Fort McHenry will hear of your bravery and aid," the captain said as he turned to provide some instruction to the younger soldier. Ken thanked the soldier again for retrieving their horses as he and Ryan turned to walk down the hill. They gathered their things and mounted their horses for the ride back to Baltimore.

"You know, when I was talking to Mary, she said the reason we can't track this guy down is because he is evil. That his mind works differently than ours and that's how he can always get a jump on us. We have to figure out a way to get ahead of him," Ken said as they rode the fifteen miles back to Baltimore.

"I was thinking about that when we were sitting in the bushes waiting for Tom to show his hand tonight. Here's what I was thinking. I read in Kim and Deb's notes that the first time this general Richard Ewell sort of waffled on his response was his delay getting to Gettysburg because of correspondence from Lee saying to be between Cashtown and Gettysburg to be ready when needed. This made him delay a day getting to Gettysburg. That was on June 28. Then when he receives word that there was fighting near Gettysburg, that's when he moves and is helpful to the Confederates. It is just after that when he gets the second note that he delays and rests his soldiers and gives up Cemetery Hill. If we get there by June 28th, maybe one of us can provide some intel to this guy Ewell and get him to trust us, then, no matter what Tom does, he can't move Ewell on when that second note arrives," Ryan offered.

"Ok. But what do the rest of us do?" Ken asked.

"I think the rest get to an inn in Gettysburg and track Tom as he moves in the area," Ryan ponders.

"Ok. Let's check the notes back at the inn and go over it. I like the idea of being there days before. We need a more concerted effort to find him and the other machine," Ken said as they approached Baltimore.

While Ken and Ryan were having their adventure in the woods, with no success, Joe and Becky were trying to remain calm and entertained all afternoon. They decided shortly after Ken and Ryan left to go for a short walk. Ending up at the general store, they perused the goods and Joe picked up some candy, a deck of cards and both a newspaper and a periodical for reading. He came around a corner with all of this in his hands and Becky laughed, "And you say it's always the girls buying unnecessary things!"

Well, we need something to keep our minds off of what's going on outside of town," he said, sheepishly.

You are correct about that," she replied.

Joe paid for their purchase, and they returned to the inn. Becky sat down and read through the periodical which covered many important tips for gardening, flower planting, making use of all of a pig at harvest and how best to propagate chickens. She commented about the wealth of knowledge as she closed it and set it on the table. Joe looked up from the newspaper and said, "This paper, by contrast, has very little good information in it. I'm hungry. Is it time for dinner yet?"

"They refer to the evening meal as supper here, remember?"

"Ok, is it time for supper?" Joe said, while rolling his eyes.

"Yes. Let's go find some food for you," Becky said as she got up and retrieved her gloves and parasol.

They left and found a new inn on Second Street. This evening, they were having some sort of pork and potatoes. When they returned, they played a few hands of cards, but then Joe began pacing. When Ken and Ryan finally arrived, around ten that night, Joe jumped up after Becky had convinced him to sit.

"What happened?" Joe asked.

"Well, we kept Tom from wrecking the war of eighteen twelve, and stopped him from sabotaging the American soldiers from killing that British general. So, no history changes to worry about," Ryan said as he sat down hard in the chair and started to pull his boots off.

"And Tom?" Becky asked.

"He tried to shoot the sniper soldier with a modern pistol and I was able to get behind him and shove his arm so the shot missed," Ken started.

Ryan interrupted and said, "yeah, and it almost hit me!"

"Anyway, then he and I struggled for a minute and he got lose and we kind of faced off and then Tom thought better of that and took off running down the ridge. I chased after him. He must have been scouting out that territory for days. He knew where our horses were tied up in the woods across the road from the ridge and he let our horse go and then took off toward his machine. I was still chasing him and I stopped by this tree so I could listen for his movements and he snuck up on me and hit me in the back of the head. I think with his pistol," Ken finished.

"I showed up just as the machine disappeared and found Ken laying in the clearing the machine had been sitting in. We talked to the soldiers and one of them found our horses while we were dealing with Ken's injury, so we could get back," Ryan added.

"Now what?" Becky asked as she threw up her arms in frustration.

"Ryan has a plan, a good plan," Ken said as he too took off his boots. He sat up too quickly from this effort and fell back into the chair.

Becky quickly came over and said, "Let me check your head."

"It's ok. Just a good bump," Ken replied, but his eyes were closed.

Becky put her hand on his shoulder and pushed a bit. Ken sat forward, and she brushed the hair away to look at the raised lump on his head.

"Well, there's no cut on your head. You have a pretty good knot here, but that's it," Becky said, as she stepped back from Ken's head.

"What he needs is ice, but where are we going to find that?" Ryan asked.

"It's fine," Ken said.

"Ok, what is your plan, Ryan?" Joe asked.

Ryan explained his plan again, and they agreed it sounded like a better way to stop Tom. Then, they all agreed that Ryan was going to attach himself to the regiment of Ewell and Joe and Ken would look for Tom, the machine, and track behind this regiment and watch for Tom to make his move.

"We have just about everything packed up," Becky said. "When do you want to leave?"

"Tomorrow first thing. I will return the carriage and horses and ask for someone to take us back to the village we started in. Then we'll make our way to the machine and get out of here," Ken said.

"Good. I need a bath and some rest!" Ryan said.

With that, Becky went to her room, Ryan went to his room, and Joe and Ken sat up for hours, talking. They talked about what Mary had said, everyone's frustration, and how they really had to catch Tom this time.

18

Early the next morning, Ken got ready and went down to the desk. He informed the clerk that they would leave that day and asked that his accounts be prepared. The desk agent said he would prepare them immediately. Ken then asked, "I need to return the horse team and carriage as well."

"We can take care of that, Sir," the clerk replied.

"However, I need some conveyance out to Bristol. It is a small village west of Baltimore," Ken added.

"I believe you might hire a driver at that same holstry down the street," the clerk answered.

"That would be a gift. I will take the team down right now and settle my account with him and request this driver's service. Thank you, Sir," Ken said as he turned toward the barn. He turned back and said, "I will return shortly and will break our fast with my family and friends. Can you bring the room bill to the dining room?"

"Of course, Sir," the clerk answered.

Ken drove the team down and paid for the use of it for the few days they were in town. They had someone that needed to pick up a horse team from near the village so they could convey Ken and his friends to Bristol. Ken said they would be ready around ten that morning.

He returned to the inn and found everyone waiting in Joe and Ken's room. He told them what he'd been up to, and they all went down the stairs to the dining room for breakfast. While they ate, the clerk arrived with the statement of the charges. Ken retrieved the money from his jacket pocket and paid him. When they finished eating, they retrieved their belongings from the room, laid the keys on the counter for the clerk, just as a man came into the lobby and said he was to be their driver to Bristol.

They went out and climbed into the wagon with the driver and the road out of Baltimore. The driver asked if they had heard the news about the war with the British, and Ryan said they had not. He regaled them with the story heard at the harbor of the soldier that killed the British commander and the confusion going on in the harbor that morning with British ships nearly hitting one another in an effort to communicate. The man said the paper had a story with a headline of who is leading the British. The man thought that was extremely funny, and he laughed and laughed.

When they arrived in Bristol, Ken tried to pay the driver, but he insisted he had been instructed no payment was needed as they were going there anyway to get the new horses. He left them near the general store and took off on a northerly road, presumably to the farm where he was picking up the new horses.

Ken turned and said, "Well, let's get going. It's about a twenty-minute walk, isn't it?"

"Yes, that's how long it took us to get from the machine here," Becky answered.

They walked over and found the machine untouched. Joe prepared the coordinates and settings while Ryan and Ken helped Becky get one of the new dresses out and they left her in the machine to change. When she was ready, she waited outside for them all to change. By that time, the settings were ready and coordinates plotted. Each of them strapped into their chair and Joe started the machine up. Ken got up first when the machine's processes came to a stop. He looked out the window of the door and saw they were in another wooded area. He opened the door and stepped out of the machine. The others joined him and they walked eastward toward where the woods thinned and they could see a road. They expected the road to be Carlisle, that ran north and south into Gettysburg. Ken turned southward when they reached the road and, in fact, saw that they were just a short walk into town. They headed in that direction and right at the center of town where Carlisle Road intersected with both Mulmasburg and Harrisburg roads, there was an inn and public house where food was served. They went directly to the inn with their bags and asked for three rooms. Storing the gear, Joe and Becky went to the public house and waited for Ken and Ryan to go to the savings and loan down the street to exchange some of their gold for money.

After they ordered food at the public house, Ryan began talking about the plan. "I'm heading out first thing in the morning to get to Carlisle and join up with Ewell. I'll be with him until one of you finds me or I catch Tom."

"How will we communicate with you?" Becky asked.

"You won't be able to until I get closer to town. Ewell is going to come down from Carlisle and be north of town when he gets the communication from General Lee that he misunderstands. That's where Tom will be to change that notice or change his mind. If he does, Ewell will continue to push where he has made headway and take Cemetery Hill. If the confederates get that hill, it will change the outcome of the battle," Ryan continued. "I'm hoping to infiltrate and keep him on track for the way the battle plays out."

"While you're doing that for the next two days, Joe and I are going to look around for Tom and his machine. I'm sorry, Becky, it means you might have to stick close to the inn," Ken added.

"How do you think you'll be able to infiltrate?" Joe asked.

"Well, I was thinking while we were at the bank that bringing some supplies to them would be a good way to get an in with old Richard Ewell. I will say that I'm from Ireland, but family in North Carolina and I brought supplies to help them out and to locate my cousin," Ryan suggested.

"So, we got some extra money and talked to a farmer that was at the bank. We're heading out to his farm after this meal to get a bunch of eggs, chickens, and pork," Ken interjected.

"That should work. Those southerners are starved right about now," Becky said, smiling at their ingenuity.

"Yeah, I only have to convince him I'm needed, so he keeps me close," Ryan said, wiping his face with the cloth napkin.

"Hey, maybe you could give him a little intelligence," Joe said, a little excited. "We know where the union army is in his battle up there. If you get up there tonight, instead of tomorrow, you could warn him. That way we ensure his success there."

"That's a great idea, Joe!" Ken said.

"Maybe we have to be here for him to win that battle?" Becky suggested, "Does anybody remember if there was a spy or intelligence related impact of this guy's success in Carlisle?"

"We need Deb or Kim for this," Ryan said, smiling to himself.

"Ok, if we're going to get Ryan up there by nightfall, we have to get going," Ken said, standing up and heading to the front to pay for their meals.

Joe and Becky returned to the inn and sat in Joe's room, waiting for Ken to return. Ken and Ryan bought the wagon and horses and drove northwest to the farmer's house. He was thankful that someone was buying what he wanted to sell before the troops came into town and just took what he had. He accepted the money from Ken, and helped them load up the pails of eggs, the smoked pork and the twenty or so chickens he needed to sell.

"Get close to town, but not too close and I will hop out. You can then take those back roads we found on the map to get to where Ewell is up in Carlisle. Keep your eyes open for Tom and someone that might be a courier," Ken instructed.

"Got it," Ryan replied as he took a momentary diversion to avoid both Mulmasburg Road.

He dropped Ken off a little west of Carlisle Road, and then he drove the wagon north toward Carlisle. Ken walked into town and went directly to the inn. It was nearly four in the afternoon when he arrived back there. Joe and Becky were sitting in the room discussing the plan for tomorrow and where they thought they would look for Tom and his machine.

Becky turned when Ken entered the room, "Did Ryan get out of town ok?"

"Yeah. He's taking those back roads north to Carlisle. He said he might stop and carefully assess where the troops are when he gets close. I hope that works," Ken said, as he kicked off his boots and laid down on the bed.

"We were just going over the map and things to figure out where Tom might think to join the troops and where the machine might be," Joe said, looking over at Ken on the bed with his right arm covering his eyes.

"And?" Ken said, without moving.

"Well, Becky thought he would also want easier access to Ewell as he came south to town, so we were thinking of heading out Harrisburg Road early tomorrow. But we're just debating on how much lead time he might think he needs. I think he's going to want to get in here and intercept Ewell, so he won't arrive until June thirtieth. Becky thinks he might want more time, and she thinks he might show up on the twenty-ninth," Joe said.

"I like the location idea. I think we should scope things out north-east tomorrow anyway and try to figure out where he likely will have the machine. Maybe stake it out if we find a really good spot," Ken said.

"I think scoping it out is a good idea, but staking it out might be harder. There are so many more placed to hide a machine with so few people living near town. There are farms and woods and creeks and I just don't know how we can do that effectively," Joe said.

"Well, let's head out just after breakfast and see what we can see then," Ken said.

They sat quietly for quite a while and then Becky said, "I'm worried about Ryan."

"I am too. Tom is getting very violent and I don't like us all being split up like this," Ken said as he sat up. "I'm also worried about Mary and Kim back home, and Deb in the middle east. I want this to be over."

"Me too," Joe said.

"I know this has taken a toll on all of us, but we have to keep going and finish. Otherwise, the risk never goes away. Keep looking forward, that's what my father always says," Becky added, trying to get the guys out of the mood they seem to have fallen into.

"You're right, but I just wish we could get inside this guy's head and know what he's up to," Ken said as he stood up. "Let's get some sleep."

Becky went to her room and worried for quite a while if the boys would get some sleep. Joe did, Ken got very little.

While the discussion was going in the inn, Ryan was approaching Carlisle from the south. He encountered a young man walking along the road and asked him if he needed a ride. The young man hesitated, but Ryan caught sight of a leather pouch hidden inside his coat. He tried to entice the young man again by offering him some bread. This did the trick, as the young man was starving.

When he had settled onto the wagon seat, Ryan asked, "So, I'm Ryan McDonnell. What should I call you?"

"Colton," he replied after he chewed up some of the bread.

"Where are you headed, Colton?" Ryan asked after a few minutes when he had finished eating the bread.

"Just outside of Carlisle, Sir," he said, but then looked suspiciously at Ryan and asked, "You ain't with the Union Army, is you?"

"No, Colton, I actually hail from Virginia. I'm trying to get some supplies I have to General Ewell. I heard he was up here near Carlisle and I thought he could use some food. It isn't much, but I wanted to share what I had," Ryan answered.

"Much obliged, Sir. I'm sure those boys could use some food right about now. I know I can," Colton answered, smiling.

"Well, the issue for me is I am not completely certain where to find this general, and I certainly do not want to encounter his enemy while I am riding about at nightfall. Perhaps we could help each other. I can give you a little smoked pork if you can take me to General Ewell," Ryan offered.

"I certainly will. I have to deliver some correspondence to him, and I have the clearance code to get to him!" Colton cried.

"Shhhh. We do not want to alert any union men scattered around here," Ryan said as he put one finger up to his lips.

"Oh, yes, Sir," Colton said, smiling as Ryan handed him a long piece of smoked pork. The boy took it and devoured it.

"I haven't eaten in two days. I feel down right refreshed from this pork and bread, Sir. Thank you," Colton said as he smiled contentedly and rubbed his belly.

They rode along quietly for about twenty more minutes when Colton pointed to a dirt pathway and said, "Turn down that road."

Ryan turned the wagon onto the road that was really more like two ruts worn down in a field. After riding a few minutes, he could see the lights of fire rings in the distance on the ridge. When they rode about a quarter mile, Colton told Ryan to turn into the field to the left and move toward an area of trees. Ryan did as Colton directed, but when they had gone a very short way, three men appeared out of the brush with guns pointed at the wagon and its occupants. Another man stood up and walked toward the now stopped wagon.

"Halt. What are you about, mister?" the man asked.

Ryan looked at Colton to answer, and he did, saying, "Lieutenant Colton Rockway of the 53rd with correspondence from General Lee for General Ewell, access code four-eight-six-three."

The three men lowered their rifles and separated to provide a path for the wagon. The man in front moved to the side and said, "You are clear to proceed."

They moved on toward the trees, where Ryan tied up the team to a lower branch and followed Colton toward a large tent. A man that still had remnants of a confederate uniform on, with a jacket and some bars, but no uniform pants, just regular black, and a tattered uniform hat, opened the flap of the tent and motioned Colton and Ryan inside. There, in the middle of a room made by the tent, stood the confederate general, Richard Ewell. Ryan quickly looked around the tent for Tom and didn't see him. That didn't mean he wasn't there, just that he wasn't in that tent. Ryan relaxed a bit. They stood there for a moment while Ewell talked to several men over a map. Then one man turned and saw Colton holding the leather case rolled up. He touched the general's arm, and he turned, looked at Colton and said, "Is that my communication?"

"Yes, Sir. From General Lee," Colton replied, holding out the leather wrapped roll.

The general took it and then looked at Ryan, then looked back at Colton and said, "Have you brought the enemy into my tent?"

"No, no, Sir. This here is Ryan McDonnell from Virginia originally. He has brought some supplies," Colton said, shaking his arms with his hand up to better punctuate the no in his answer.

"Supplies, from where?" General Ewell said, now looking directly at Ryan.

"General, these are supplies I was hiding from the Yankees and felt with you now close to Gettysburg, it was safe to bring them to you. It isn't much, but there're loaves of bread, some chickens and four or five pails of eggs," Ryan answered.

"Oh, and smoked pork," Colton added, smiling at Ryan.

"Yes, indeed. There are two whole smoked pigs out there for you and your men. Being from Virginia, I support the cause and wanted to help," Ryan said.

"Why aren't you serving?" one of the other men asked Ryan.

"As much as I wanted to, I cannot. You see, I have an injury to my eye from my farming and my left eye is never clear. I likely could not shoot the broad side of a barn. As such, I am no benefit to you and your brave men in that regard, but I can still farm, and so I offer what I can," Ryan quickly thought up an answer they couldn't verify.

"Very good. Mr. McDonnell, we thank you for the supplies. You are correct, the men have barely had any food in days. It will be welcomed," General Ewell replied, satisfied with Ryan's answer.

"General, there are also blankets and some cotton bandages in a few pairs of boots I scared up," Ryan added, "And, might I add, that being from here, I can travel about the area without raising any concern. I could be of aid to you that way, Sir."

"This is a good idea, General. We were just trying to find a way to see what was going on down in town," one man said, leaning over to General Ewell.

"And he helped me get here nearly an hour ahead of schedule. His wagon can move all kinds of notices around, if you please, Sir," Colton added, thinking Ryan wanted to be of more help.

"You, Lieutenant, and you two," Ewell pointed to several men, standing in the tent, "go with Mr. McDonnell to unload that wagon. Get the bandages and blankets to the surgeon and the food to McIntyre, and be sure he sends some eggs and one of those chickens in here."

Then he looked at Ryan, saying, "Thank you for the support. Stick around, we might have use for you."

Ryan, Colton and the two officers that General Ewell pointed to left the tent and went to the wagon. Ryan climbed up and handed down first the supplies that the general said were to go to the surgeon. Colton took those. Then he began handing down the food. The two officers carried the bread in bags and the eggs in pails to the cook's tent. Then they wrangled the chickens down and took them to the cook's tent, along with the smoked pork. One officer giving the instruction that General Ewell was expecting at least one chicken and some eggs at his tent soon. They all walked back to the general's tent together, and the officers entered first.

"Mr. McDonnell, tomorrow morning, I would like you to take the Lieutenant back in the direction of Gettysburg. He is to rendezvous with another courier we expect in the morning. Simply trade communication and bring the Lieutenant back by way of Carlisle. I want intel on the union troops nearby," General Ewell said when he saw Ryan was with the officers.

"Yes, Sir," Ryan replied, "happy to help."

Colton pulled on Ryan's sleeve and the two exited the tent. As they walked toward the cook's tent, Colton said, "You can bed down in my tent tonight. We can head out at first light."

"Thanks," Ryan said.

"We be needing a fire and some food. You get some grub and I's goin' to get some wood for the fire," Colton said, as he left Ryan at the cook's tent and pointed to a tent that was at the end of the line of tents with troops everywhere.

Ryan stopped at the cook's tent and asked for a loaf of bread and some of the pork. The cook gave him a small bowl of scrambled eggs as well. Ryan took the food to the tent where Colton was now building up a fire. They sat quietly in front of the fire and ate. Colton got up at one point to fetch some water and they finished the food. As he got up, Colton said, "That must be the best I done ate in weeks! I can surely get them communicates back and forth speedy now."

"Well, that certainly is a good thing," Ryan said, smiling at Colton.

They went into the tent, and Colton handed Ryan a bedroll. Ryan rolled it out and went to sleep. Ryan didn't sleep all that well on the ground, but it seemed dawn came early. Colton touched Ryan's shoulder to wake him just before sunrise. He handed him another piece of pork and said they needed to go. Ryan got up, rolled up his bedroll, and went out to douse his hair in cold water to wake up. They went to the wagon and headed south. When they were approaching the western side of Gettysburg, Ryan thought he glimpsed the courier. He actually sat up suddenly when it looked like Tom. He quickly thought and said to Colton, "I think it might be best if I wait here. We have no knowledge of this guy, right? We also have no way to know if there are union troops around. If we have to go and do intel for the general, I think I should stay out of sight."

"Good idea. Stop here and I just walk down to 'im," Colton said as he climbed down from the wagon.

Colton walked over to Tom, who was cautiously approaching him. Tom looked around and didn't see anyone coming. He wanted to shove this poor fellow out of his way, but he really needed to get to General Ewell before tomorrow.

"General Ewell says we trade communicates right here. He wants you to go back with what I bring and I's to bring the one you have to the General," Colton said, as he got up to where Tom was.

"They instructed me to get this to General Ewell," Tom responded.

"Yeah, well, General Ewell sent me with instrucshons, and he wants us to trade communicates and return to where we come from," Colton answered, holding out his leather pouch.

"I think you should take yours on to General Longstreet, and I'll take mine to General Ewell, as I was instructed," Tom said, pulling his pouch back and getting closer to Colton to intimidate him.

"You listen here! I's doing what I was told," Colton responded, throwing his pouch to the ground and pulling out a pistol from his back and pointing it at Tom's chest.

"Ok, ok, we'll do this your way," Tom backed up, then leaned down and picked up the pouch Colton and brought and threw the one he had down on the ground.

Colton leaned down and picked the pouch up, and stood up. Tom had motioned like he was going for Colton's gun, but Colton stood too quickly. Colton waited a minute while Tom did not move, then said, "You git goin' now. I aint movin' till you do."

Tom turned and walked away. Colton waited until he was over the small rise, and then he turned and walked back to where Ryan was waiting.

"What happened?" Ryan asked. "I was just preparing to get out and back you up."

That guy thinks he's smarter 'an me and he's just plain wrong. I's been in this war a long time now, and I's know how to get by and who to obey and not," Colton said as he climbed up onto the wagon seat.

Ryan laughed and then said, "Well, the way it looked from here, that is for sure, Colton. You showed him!"

"Jus' cuz I's from the backwoods, don't make me no backwards," Colton kept complaining.

"You are correct in that statement. I wonder though. He seemed a little suspicious to me. Did he seem that way to you?" Ryan tried to plant a seed, so as to prevent Tom from getting more access to General Ewell.

"He sure did," Colton said.

Colton sat on the wagon seat, still mulish looking as they approached Carlisle from the south and intended to ride around the eastern side of town. They sat quietly, keeping a watchful eye for union troops. After a few minutes, Colton leaned over and whispered, "them's Yankees over there. We needs to swing wide of 'em."

Ryan turned the wagon further east to swing around the soldiers, making camp around the area. Then, as quickly as they could, they made their way back to the Confederate camp and went straight to the general's tent. The officer at the door announced them and they entered the tent. General Ewell was talking to several men, and they stood, waiting for him to finish. He turned slightly from the table they were all hunched over and saw Ryan. He stood and turned completely, saying, "What did you find, Mr. McDonnell?"

"I've got your communicate from the other guy," Colton offered, walking forward and handing the pouch to the general.

"Good, Lieutenant," the general said, taking the pouch.

"That guy seemed more 'an a little suspicis to me and Ryan, here. I'd be wonderin' if that there communicate is real," Colton added.

"Really? How did you assess that?" the general asked.

"He was none too ready to turn over his pouch when I 'splained' your instructions and he argued with me. Wouldn't give up his pouch for a bit," Colton explained.

The general looked at Ryan and Ryan added, "Yes, Sir, I noticed he looked suspicious as well. Colton and I were not sure what we were approaching, so I stayed hidden with the wagon while Colton approached him, but the man was not at all willing to hand over the communication. Colton handled it well, though."

"Lieutenant, if you believe this communication might be suspicious, leave right now, and go directly to Longstreet and confirm he sent that man. Take Lieutenant Smith with you," General Ewell said.

"Yes, Sir," they both said and turned to leave.

Ryan stayed and waited for General Ewell to confirm with the other men about what was in the communication and attempt to confirm if they could tell if it was true. The general turned back to Ryan and said, "What of Carlisle?"

"Sir, the Union Army is scattered in small groups all around the north-eastern end of the town. They are stretched right now about two miles along the eastern side of town," Ryan explained.

"Come here and show us on this map," the general said.

Ryan walked over and put his finger down on the farthest northern spot they had seen the troops. He then drew his finger down and around the area they had seen them.

"Thank you, Mr. McDonnell. You have been very helpful. If I could ask one more thing of you? Can you load up the cook's tent and supplies and swing around the western side of Carlisle and await us? I think a mile or so from town to the southwest should be good. The Surgeon will stay here to manage injured, and we will all, God willing, meet you later in the day tomorrow," the general asked Ryan.

"Yes, Sir. Do you want us to leave now?" Ryan asked.

"No, at first light," the general said, and then he turned away from Ryan to talk to the other men.

Ryan left the general's tent and saw Colton walking toward him from the cook's tent.

"Are you off?" Ryan said as he reached him, walking toward the rows of tents.

"Yep. Be back tomorrow, to be sure," he said, smiling, "maybe cartin' a prisoner with us!"

Colton walked off and Ryan went to confirm with the cook on whether they could load any supplies that night. Then, he moved the wagon and team closer to the cook's tent and the two of them moved some of his supplies into the wagon.

Tom stormed away from his interaction with the backwoods farmer steaming over his failure to get to Ewell. He was out of sight of the guy, so he swerved off the road into a little brush. He sat down on downed tree to think.

How did that little soldier that could barely put words together get the better of him? He should have been more forceful with that guy. Without the communication, he had to come up with a new way to get close to General Ewell. He didn't really want to get involved in the fighting, but was that his only way? Maybe if he just went with some intel. He wished he'd brought his notes. He couldn't remember exactly where Ewell's first battle was going to be. That would be the best way to get to him now. He needed intel.

Tom sat there for several more minutes and then he decided he would have to scout around and see what was going on. He headed back to Longstreet's encampment to find some food. Then he would head out to find some intel to take to Ewell. That was how he would get close.

19

While Ryan was having his adventures and at least spotting Tom, Ken and Joe left town just after breakfast with Becky. Leaving Becky at the inn, they walked out-of-town first to the southeast. After walking a few miles, they decided they were getting too far away from where the battle would be and they doubted Tom would have the machine this far away from where he was. Retracing their steps and then, after stopping at the inn to get Becky and then having lunch, they headed out again, this time to the northeast. They approached a wooded area about a mile out of town, and Ken suggested they search them. They split up just after entering the woods, with Ken taking south area and Joe taking the north.

"Go to where it thins out and then walk back toward me. Grid search though, so walk as far east and as far west as you can to stay in the woods," Ken said as he took off to the south to do the same. Ken was nearly done with his search and had not located the machine. He was getting frustrated when heard Joe yell, "Over here!"

Ken ran to where he heard Joe yelling from and there it was. The machine Tom had stolen. Joe was standing there, waiting for Ken. Ken arrived and grinned. Joe approached and opened the door. He looked in, and then turned back to Ken. "Geez, Tom's a pig!"

Ken walked up to the door and looked in. There were clothes, food and all kinds of notes all over. "What a slob," Ken said, as he stepped inside, adding, "I should take this machine back to Mr. Brewster's barn, or you should. I mean, I have to be here to help Ryan stop and catch this idiot."

"I think we should just move it, Ken. I mean, we might need we all three of us to capture and stop Tom. If we simply move it to near our machine, Tom won't be able to get out of here without us. If we haven't captured him yet, he'll have to come find us," Joe said, as he picked up a bunch of food containers and put them in a bag he found. He took it outside.

Ken followed shortly with a load of garbage. "You're right. But can we move this to the location of our machine and not cause some rift and meet ourselves?" Ken asked.

"Yeah, we tested that, remember? Way back when we were just barely using the machine, when the new programming was ready, we tested by taking it a few minutes forward and then brought it back to the exact time we left. We can do this. So long as I remember the coordinates of where our machine is," Joe said, looking up as he was thinking.

"I've got a note in my wallet of those coordinates, I think," Ken said, smiling and pulling his wallet out of his jacket pocket.

Ken handed the note to Joe, who turned and went into the machine. Ken piled the garbage up and went back to pile up all the notes. They might need those, so he simply put them together and set them on the seat. He watched as Joe programmed the machine and tested everything. Ken then shut the door and bolted it from the inside and the machine started up.

A few seconds later, Ken got up and looked out the window. He could see the other machine behind some brush. He and Joe got out, took the notes and then dragged some brush over to the machine they just recovered and headed back into town. They arrived at the inn and were joking, feeling better for the first time since this whole thing began. Upstairs, Becky could hear them coming up the stairs laughing. She opened the door just in time to see them smiling, Ken's arm around Joe as they came to the landing.

"You both look pleased!" Becky said, smiling at Joe. "How did it go?"

"Let's get inside and I'll tell you everything," Joe said, coming to her, kissing her on the cheek and steering her back into the room.

Ken shut the door and put the notes on the table. He went over to the bathroom and washed his face and hands. While he did that, Becky brought Joe a glass of water and they sat down on the loveseat.

"We found it, Becky. We found the machine Tom has been using!"

"That's fantastic! What did you do?" Becky asked.

"Well, we cleaned out a bunch of garbage first. Tom's kind of a slob. Then we moved the machine to near where ours is. We covered it as best we could with brush and came back here," Joe explained.

"Wow! That is so great," Becky exclaimed just as Ken returned to the main room.

"Yes," Ken said, "Now if Tom wants to leave Gettysburg, he has to find us. He'll have to know we have it. This will all be over soon."

"Finally!" Becky said, laying her head back against the back of the loveseat, and closing her eyes.

"I hope Ryan's having as good of luck as we've just had," Joe said, sitting up farther in the seat.

"Is there any way we can reach him?" Becky asked.

"Well, we know what's supposed to happen tomorrow. General Ewell is supposed to trounce the Yankees near Carlisle and then head down here toward Gettysburg. That's where he's supposed to go. We could head out that way later tomorrow and see if we can find him," Joe said.

"Let's do that. But right now, I want a good steak meal if there's one to be had in this town and then a shower and bed!" Ken said. "Well, I mean a bath, I guess."

Joe and Becky laughed, and it felt fantastic to have the upper hand. They went downstairs and asked the clerk at the desk where they might get such a meal, and he directed them to an inn two blocks away. Becky brought along the notes they found and she read over them while they waited for food and looked up every once in a while, as if she found something interesting to share.

"Hey, it looks like Tom's going to take a communication to Ewell and get in with him so he can convince him to push forward when Ewell gets that note from Lee. He says here he's going to start with General Longstreet that is closer here to Gettysburg and try to get to a point where he sends him with a communication," Becky said just before food arrived.

She put the notes under her in the chair when the food arrived, and they ate. Ken took a few bites and smiled. Then he looked up and said, "The good news is hopefully Ryan is already ingrained with Ewell and he can head off Tom when he gets there."

"I would have to think he is. He didn't return to town. He must be with the general," Ken said, smiling, "we've got this guy now!"

"It's really important we contact Ryan tomorrow if we can, so we can warn him and to see if there's anything we can do to help him ensure General Ewell is where he needs to be," Joe added between bites.

When they finished, the server brought both Ken and Joe glasses of sherry. She brought Becky tea. Becky got the notes back out and continued to look through them, but found nothing they didn't already know in them. When they finished eating, they went back to their inn, and Joe and Becky went up to the room. Ken decided he would go to the tavern and see what he could find out. He sat at the bar for an hour listening to the gossip of the townsmen of the battle that was quickly approaching them and how they felt it would be sport to go out and watch for a bit. As he was preparing to leave, he heard a couple of guys talking about the goings on in Carlisle and how the Yankees were spread across the countryside near town. Tomorrow morning there would be a battle there, they were sure.

As Ken, Joe, and Becky were enjoying their dinner outside of town and to the northwest, Colton and his companion reached General Longstreet's camp. Colton didn't see the guy he had the encounter with anywhere as they made their way to the general's tent. They approached and announced they had word from Ewell. They were granted access and reported that they needed to speak to Longstreet in private on the direction from General Ewell. General Longstreet dismissed everyone but the guards outside the tent. He turned to Colton and said, "What do you have from Ewell?" as he held out his hand.

Colton handed him a duplicate of the morning communication and as he did, he said, "General, Sir, this morning I was told to trade communicates with someone comin' from your camp and go back with what you'd sent. The guy that came to me said he wouldn't give up your communicate, and we had words."

General Longstreet looked concerned, as Colton continued, "Your communicate made it General Ewell, Sir, but I done looked for the guy as we come into camp and he ain't here. Least I didn' see him. I was suspicis like, and toll General Ewell that, so he sent me back here to tell you and to bring you the same communicate the guy was posed to be bringin' you earlier."

General Longstreet opened the pouch and began reading and then looked up and said, "No, I got nothing like this from General Ewell this morning."

"I done toll you!" Colton said as he looked at his companion.

The other officer said, "General Longstreet, do you have any reply for us to take back?"

"No, not tonight, but I likely will in the morning. You two find a place to bed down after you walk this camp and see if you see the man you saw this morning. I recall he was new to camp yesterday and offered to bring that notice along since he had to go check on his sisters at home. I believe that was his story."

The two turned and left the tent and did as they were bid, and walked through the entire camp. They walked by every tent, in all three rows of tents, then walked near the trees where men were laying out under cover of the trees. Not seeing the man Colton had words with that morning, they had no way of knowing that the man was retrieving his gear a mile or so away and preparing to make his way toward Carlisle in the morning.

Tom lay out under the stars near a small fire he had lit. He was so frustrated at that dumb southerner that stopped him from getting to Ewell today. It really didn't matter what the notice said that he was supposed to take to General Longstreet. It would have been so much easier to be the deliverer and see if he could make himself valuable with the information he knew about the battles to come in the next two days. Then he would be trusted when the word came from Lee that had Ewell resting instead of heading into Gettysburg to take up position on Cemetery Hill. He would convince Ewell to push forward. That would make the confederates the victors here and they would march on to Washington and they would win the war. It would change history. That would fix those darn Fitzgeralds. They would suffer from this, he was sure. Even if it didn't change their lives, they would be upset about what he'd done. They would have to find a way to fix what he did, and that would distract them. Then he would make his move back at home. He kept going over how he would swoop in back home and get all the glory that Joe had received. He would invent those small computers and he would get all the awards and fame in the news. Then he would move on to break up his sister and that hockey player that was always right there with her. It made him sick sometimes to watch them together at Choate. Man, he wished he had hurt him badly when he cut him. Maybe he had really hurt him? That would be perfect if he already had taken one of them out. Not knowing for sure, but he had seen none of them here. He laughed, thinking he had kept them from following him. He saw them in Baltimore, man. That didn't work as he planned. Again, those Fitzgerald's and their pals Becky and Ryan kept stopping him. He drifted off to sleep thinking this time, he would win and he would make sure he spent the next year messing with both Deb and Kim, that little pipsqueak that kept following Joe around. He'd almost forgotten about the littlest Fitzgerald. All those blond curls and sweet talk he heard from her when he walked close behind them to and from the cafeteria. He needed to get her, too.

The sun brought a battle cry from the confederates who had moved late yesterday and positioned themselves within striking distance of the Yankees that were outside of Carlisle. Ewell's troops quickly won the battle since the Yankees were just waking when the attack hit. They spent most of the day rooting out all the little pockets of Yankees that had spread out across the countryside and then circled back to the primary unit late in the day. By the time Ewell arrived back in camp, Ryan had moved the cook and his supplies back closer to camp and they had managed to get two pigs in the process that Ryan bought from some farmer. The cook had questioned him about the pigs, and Ryan had told him the southerners around Gettysburg were more than happy to sell supplied to the confederates rather than having the Yankees just take it from them. Luckily, Ryan had some money left, but it was running low now, so hopefully he would not need to use it again to seem so valuable to this bunch of southern soldiers.

Everyone was well fed and jovial as they shared stories of each of their conquests during the day. Ryan stayed close to the cook's tent during the day and learned how to butcher and roast a pig over an open fire. He thought to himself he might never use the skills he learned today, but it would be fun sharing it with Deb later. He sat down to eat when Colton and the officer that had traveled with him appeared.

"Whoee, somethin' sure smells good here!" Colton said as he approached Ryan.

"Grab some while there still is some to grab, Colton," Ryan said, smiling at him. "How was your trip to General Longstreet?"

"We got there jus fine. Had words with the General bout that man that tried to mess with me yesterday mornin', though."

"Did you find the guy?" Ryan asked, hopeful that Tom was well out of the way.

"Naw. We walked that whole camp and didn't see 'im at all. And that yeller lizard dun ran off with the communicate that General Ewell sent! General Longstreet had no idear there even was a communicate from Ewell!"

"It is a good thing you shared your concerns about that man and General Ewell sent you back there, then. You might have saved this battle, Colton. If something important was in that communication to Longstreet, anyway," Ryan said.

Colton smiled and puffed out his chest in pride at what Ryan had said. He was sure he'd appeared the savior of the battle. He nudged the officer that he'd spent the day with, saying, "Mayhap you should go on up to the general's tent and make sure he knows about this again, to be sure, that is."

"Did you bring back a communication?" Ryan asked as they two sat down to eat what they had received from the cook.

"We did, but General Ewell was not in his tent when we arrived back here and we hadn't eaten all day. We decided to eat and then go back and wait at the general's tent," the officer said.

They finished eating and talking about looking for the man. Ryan was sure Tom wouldn't be sticking around, but he suspected he was trying to get in with Ewell. He would have to keep his eye out today and maybe stay close to the general's tent. When they finished eating, all three of them walked back to the general's tent. Someone summoned inside them and the officer handed the general the notice from General Longstreet. After a few minutes, General Ewell looked up and said, "Lee will be here soon. We are to move south to Gettysburg. Looks like we are to take a position between Longstreet and Hill. As soon as everyone had eaten, tell them we will not fully make camp and will start a process to move south. Three battalions, a half a mile apart."

The three officers all said in unison, "Yes, Sir."

Ewell turned to Ryan. "Please continue to assist the cook with his supplies and movements. You might have the only wagon left in the confederacy at this point. We need you."

"Yes, Sir. I will go to him now," Ryan said as he turned to leave.

"Be sure to bring the wagon in close to my supply movements. You will travel just behind my officers and I, as we move south," Ewell said.

Ryan turned back, "Yes, Sir. I will tell the cook."

Everyone began packing up. The rank and file of the troops were not thrilled. They had to pack back up right away and leave, but they did as commanded. Slowly, the battalions made their way south to Gettysburg.

Tom woke to the sound of movement and was alarmed. He quickly gathered his things and kicked dirt on the fire and made his way into some brush. While he was searching for his pistol when a few wild turkeys squawked and made their way past where Tom was hiding. Releasing a heavy breath, he finished gathering his things into his pack and then made his way to where Ewell had been the night before. He swung wide to avoid the main roads and to ensure he didn't encounter any troops in the area. As he walked, he thought about a plan for today. He decided he would try to intercept the courier and take the notice from him. He would then carry it to Ewell and tell him that Lee had added instructions for him, that he didn't want written. That way, he could convince Ewell to march straight to Gettysburg and take up position on Cemetery Hill. He was satisfied with the plan. He arrived in the clearing the camp had been, only to find they were gone. Tom stomped the ground and then smacked his hand on the side of his head. Of course, he thought, there is a battle today and then Ewell starts toward Gettysburg. That might have been what was in the courier notice he was supposed to have taken back to Longstreet. Darn it! He left that in the brush back by the road he met that darn southerner on. The more he thought about what he read about the battle today, the more he remembered the courier from Lee found Ewell closer to Gettysburg. That's where the courier finds him, and because of all this movement today, Ewell rests his troops. Tom had inadvertently travelled north of Ewell without even knowing it. So much for swinging wide. He sat and had some water and calculated that it was late in the afternoon. He would have to move quicker to catch that courier now.

Becky, Joe and Ken were anxious all day. After they had breakfast, they walked the streets of Gettysburg and looked in the shops and had lunch. They returned to the inn simply because there were no more streets to walk. They sat down in the room Joe and Ken were occupying with heavy sighs.

"I know it's getting close, but what can we do to help Ryan at this point?" Becky lamented.

"We can't start roaming around. Troops are gathering and we might get caught up in something, pressed into service, or even worse," Joe said.

"But we have to find out what Ryan's been up to," Ken said, looking up at the ceiling, "I think I should try to find a horse and ride out where we expect Ewell to be getting to and see if I can find Ryan. Then at least we will know he's ok."

"I agree. One of us should find out where he is and what he's done. We should tell him about moving Tom's machine too," Joe added, resting his elbows on his knees and then his head into his hands, "but take a weapon with you."

"I was thinking the same thing," Ken said as he got up and went to the wardrobe and retrieved his gun.

"I'm going to leave this here and go see if I can find a horse to use for the afternoon. If I do, I'll tie up downstairs and come get this," Ken said as he put it in a leather bag and put his jacket back on. He left the room.

"I hope Ryan's ok. We don't have any idea if he was able to make contact or if he's ok. I mean, there was a battle yesterday. We have no idea," Becky said, standing up and pacing across the room.

"I'm sure he's fine. But doing this will get us some answers and get him some information and maybe we can work together now that he should be getting closer to town," Joe said, getting up and walking over to her. He reached out and hugged her for a minute. They sat back down and waited for Ken.

Ken went down the street to the blacksmith's and asked him if he knew anyone that would let him use a horse for the day. The blacksmith said he had a horse that Ken could use for the day, and Ken paid him.

He rode the horse back to the inn and tied it up to the hitching post in front of the inn. He bounded up the stairs and opened the door.

"Did you get a horse?" Joe asked as he jumped up.

"Yes. I'm heading out to see if I can find Ryan before nightfall," Ken said as he picked up the bag and started to the door again. He turned and asked, "Do you have some money? I don't want to leave you two without a way to eat dinner."

"Yeah, I've got some of the money we exchanged when we got here," Joe said.

"Ok, I'll see you soon," Ken said, and he left.

As Ewell and his entourage, and the cook with Ryan and the wagon, were slowing because of the setting sun, a man approached cautiously. Ryan saw him first and halted the horses and called out, "We see you. State your business!"

Ewell turned at that moment and the man hesitantly came out of the bushes and said, "I'm looking for a white rabbit."

Ryan was very perplexed by this statement, but an officer called out, "They are in the henhouse."

The man came fully into view at this point. Ryan surmised this must be some secret code that allows the couriers and troops to know which side they're on. The courier approached the general sitting on his horse and said, "I have a communication from General Lee."

An officer approached the man and took the pouch from him. He walked to Ewell and handed up the pouch. Ewell stopped him and dismounted his horse. He handed the reins to the officer and then took the pouch.

While the general read the note, Ryan heard another rustling in the bushes and looked over just in time to see Tom coming into view and then his shocked look as he recognized Ryan. Ryan went to call out and Tom took off back into the bushes. He was about to climb down and give chase, but he stopped as the general spoke.

"It seems Lee is preparing and wants us to support Hill and Longstreet in Gettysburg, but has given me leave to decide whether to rest tonight and carry on in the morning or push forward now after our resounding victory earlier today. He congratulates us all on that effort.”

“What will you do, Sir?” an officer asked him.

“The question is, what is best for the Confederacy?” General Ewell pondered.

“The men are exhausted. Perhaps stopping here for the night would put them all in a fresh position to fight again tomorrow,” the officer proposed.

“I can’t feed the men on the move, General. At least consider stopping for your supper. I’ve got to get the rest of the pork cooked or it will turn by tomorrow,” the cook offered. “We don’t want to lose all this good grub Mr. McDonnell has brought us, do we?”

General Ewell scowled at the cook for just blurting out his opinion. The strategy of the fight was not dependent on the cook, but he had a point. They procured the most food his men had had in weeks. He couldn’t spoil what might be for some of these men their last meal. And, he thought, Lee had given him the authority to decide, probably knowing Ewell’s men might be tired and need rest before another victory tomorrow. He rubbed his chin with his thumb and index finger as he thought.

“Yes, we will give the men a bit of rest. Send notice to the two flanks to pull in ranks and set up camp here,” Ewell said to the officers that had dismounted and gathered near him.

“Good decision,” the cook whispered to Ryan, and laughing.

Ryan climbed down at this point and began unloading the cook’s things from the wagon. By now, he knew where the cook liked to put his tent in relation to the food tent and where he liked his supplies. The cook joined him and they had the cook set up pretty quickly. Ryan said, “I will go look for some wood for you.”

“Good. I can get started on this pig then,” the cook said as he turned away from Ryan and started moving rocks into a circle and setting up his spit over them.

Ryan walked into the woods a bit and picked up wood as he went. He really went into the woods to look for Tom. He didn't see any trace of him and he had his hands full of wood, so he headed back to the cook's tents.

Ryan sat and tried to figure out what he should do now. He knew they had prevented Tom's plan at this point because Ewell had stopped for the night to rest his troops. They would miss the opportunity to take Cemetery Hill and the battle would go on as expected. Should Ryan sneak away and get back to Ken? Should he go after Tom, even though he had no way of knowing where he had taken off to? He rested his elbows on his knees and looked down at the dirt below him. As he was sitting there, a small rock hit the ground near his left boot. He turned quickly and saw Ken in the brush behind the wagon. Ryan smiled. He didn't have to come up with anything. Ken was here. Ryan stood, walked to the wagon and grabbed his gear, and then looked around. No one was looking his way. He made his way into the brush to Ken. They walked a few steps deeper into the woods and then Ken turned and said, "Man, have we been worried? I don't know about you, but I can't wait to get back to modern times when I can use a telephone again!"

"Yeah, it's been tough," Ryan said.

"You ok?" Ken asked, getting concerned.

"Oh, yeah. It's just that it's been eventful, and I was at a point when I didn't know what to do and there you were. You don't know how glad I am to see you," Ryan said, smiling, "And have I got a lot to tell you?"

"Yeah?" Ken questioned.

"First, I saw Tom yesterday morning. He was trying to get to Ewell and this backwoods southerner that I've befriended stood up to Tom and stopped him. Then today, when the note from Lee arrived, I saw him again. He took off into these woods about twenty minutes ago."

"No kidding. So, he was trying to do what you managed to do. Get in with Ewell. Finally, we got ahead of this idiot!" Ken said, slapping his leg with his hand.

"Yeah, I think he was trying to bring a notice yesterday, but Ewell had told Colton to just switch pouches and come back. Really, Colton was trying to follow orders, and it thwarted Tom," Ryan said, shaking his head.

"Who's Colton?" Ken asked.

"He's the southerner. I met him on the road when I first headed out to find Ewell. He helped me get into the general's tent and the food worked. I also had the only wagon around, so I got drafted to move food and notices around for the last day or two. I think Tom might have tried again today to get here and come up with a way to move Ewell along, but he decided to rest, like he was supposed to," Ryan explained.

"Let's head back to my horse. I've got news for you too," Ken said as he turned and started walking toward where he had tied his horse up.

"What's your news?" Ryan asked as he walked with Ken.

"We found the other machine!" Ken said, as they had reached the horse. Ken untied the reins from the tree branch and started leading the horse out of the woods.

"You found the machine Tom's been using?" Ryan asked, standing still from shock.

"Yes, Joe and I found it yesterday morning," Ken said as he mounted the horse.

"Finally!" Ryan said, smiling.

"Give me your hand. You can ride behind me and we can get back to town quicker," Ken said, holding out his hand.

"What about the wagon and everything?" Ryan asked, "Should I come up with a better way to exit?"

"No, just come with me. They can have the wagon. Maybe they'll think you got snagged by the Union out in these woods," Ken said, again holding out his hand.

Ryan reached up, and Ken pulled him up. Ryan sat behind Ken and held on to the back of the saddle. They rode in silence back into town. Ken rode directly to the blacksmith's and returned the horse. When they turned to walk up the street, Ken said, "So, Ewell is doing what he's supposed to, and we have Tom's machine. Now all we have to do is locate this crazy person who has been causing us so much grief and go home."

"What did you do with the machine?" Ryan asked as they entered the inn and headed for the stairs.

"We moved it to where our machine is," Ken said, grinning.

They were both laughing when they walked into the room where Joe and Becky were waiting for them.

"Oh, thank goodness, Ryan. We were so worried about you!" Becky exclaimed as she got up from the chair and walked over to him and hugged him.

"I wouldn't do that. I'm filthy and haven't bathed in days," he said, but he returned the hug, grateful to be back with them.

"We were thinking about finding some dinner. How about you go take a bath and we'll wait. You can tell us about your filthy couple of days over food," Joe said, laughing but holding his hand up to prevent the hug Ryan was walking toward him to give out.

"Ok. Be back soon," Ryan said and left the room.

About fifteen minutes later, Ryan returned, clean and in different clothing. They all laughed when Joe said he could already tell Ryan smelled better. They walked out of the inn and down the street. Finding a tavern still open, they went inside and sat down. Ken ordered them all some food and when it was brought to the table, Becky looked up at Ryan and said, "Tell us what happened."

Ryan began telling them of all the events since he left them two days ago. He talked of Colton and his language and loyalty. Then he talked of Ewell and how he seemed to be a thoughtful man and not one bent on annihilation, but wanted simple victory and turning the enemy back with the least casualties on both sides. He talked about the Irish cook and his funny ways of doing things and saying things. Then he talked of his encounters with Tom and how they guessed right about his motives and plans to impact this battle and the war. He did all this while shoveling food into his mouth, as he hadn't really eaten well the last two days. When he was finished, Joe told Ryan of the details of finding the machine and moving it and where it was located now.

They had all finished eating, with Ryan cleaning up everyone's plates since he was still hungry when he finished his plate of food. They walked back to the inn and went up to Joe and Ken's room. As they all sat down, Joe said, "Now, what do we do?"

"Couldn't we just take the two machines back?" Ryan asked.

"We can't just leave Tom here. He has no way to earn a living and his family will miss him and never understand what happened to him," Becky said, rejecting the idea of just leaving Tom in Gettysburg.

"Becky's right, we can't leave him here. We have to locate him," Joe added.

"We have no idea where he's been staying, no idea where he ran off to when he saw me and saw Ewell decide to wait," Ryan said.

"But we do where he's going to get out of here," Ken said, smiling at them all.

"That's right. At some point, he's going to find his machine to leave," Joe said.

"We're going to have to camp where he expects it to be. We do not know what his plans are now," Ryan said, not liking his suggestion even as he said it out loud.

"We'll check out tomorrow morning, gather what supplies we can and go to the area we found his machine and wait. We don't really have any other choice," Ken said.

"If that's the plan, I'm gonna get some sleep. I've been sleeping on the ground for two nights, and it was not fun and it was not good sleep," Ryan said as he got up and headed to the door.

"Let's meet downstairs and get some breakfast and then head out," Ken said to Ryan as he opened the door.

"Ok," Ryan said as he shut the door behind him.

"We better pack some things up now so we don't have so much to do in the morning," Becky said as she stood up.

"I'm going to throw my stuff in the bag in the morning, I think," Ken said, closing his eyes.

"Me, too," Joe said, looking up at Becky, who was standing in front of the chair Joe was sitting in.

"Well, I have to pack now. These dresses are a pain to put on, a pain to wear and a pain to pack up," Becky said, "I'm going to go do it and take a bath in case we don't get to for a day or so waiting for Tom."

Joe stood up and hugged her and then turned to Ken. "I'm going to get a bath too before bed."

Joe walked Becky to her door and made sure she was safe before he returned to bathe. By the time he got out of the bath, Ken was asleep. He laid his head down and went right to sleep, thinking they had finally gotten the upper hand.

20

Tom couldn't believe it! His miscalculations on where Ewell was cost him intercepting the courier. Then, to add insult to injury, Ryan was there, right in the thick of things. Now how was he going to get Ewell to move on to town? He thought for a minute and then he thought up a plan. He would fabricate a note from Lee and take it to Ewell, saying that he had to make haste to town as fighting had already begun and was to take up position on the hill. That was it! Now all he had to do was to draft a note. He went back to where he stored his gear and he tore a page out of the only notebook he brought with him. Having photocopied a letter from Lee, he tried to write like Lee and forged his name. Tom rolled the note up and tied it with some twine. He made his way back to the camp and saw that Ryan was no longer sitting on or near the wagon. He sat for a few minutes, watching. With no sight of Ryan, Tom stood and walked right up to the general's tent. He said to the officers standing guard that he had a notice from Lee for Ewell. They let him in. Tom looked around and he noticed the young man he encountered on the road that forced him to give up the notice they sent him to bring to Ewell yesterday. He scowled at him. They were talking, this courier and an officer and Ewell. Tom couldn't really hear what they were saying, even though he tried to take a step closer. The officer that admitted him reached out and held Tom's arm. He was looking back at this officer when one man at the table turned and said, "That's him!"

Ewell, the man who spoke, and another officer turned at this announcement to look at Tom. He pulled his arm free and said, "General,

I have an important notice from General Lee here and he gave me explicit instructions I was to bring it directly to you."

"That can't be, Sir. You asked yesterday for us to search for this man. General Longstreet wanted to question him after his actions with Colton here," the officer said.

"I'm afraid you've confused me with someone else, Sir. I was with Lee just a couple of hours ago. I've been one of his couriers for weeks now," Tom lied.

"Let me have this notice," Ewell said, holding out his hand.

Tom held it out, and Ewell unrolled it. He looked at it and then turned to the officer. "What kind of paper is this? And what ink is used here?"

Ewell handed the note to an officer that had been standing on the other side of the table. He looked the note over and then he said, "The fox has entered the henhouse."

They all looked at Tom and he looked at each of them, not under-standing what was going on. Then the officer standing nearest Tom said, "The code."

Tom didn't realize they were talking to him. He said, "General Ewell, are you going to do as General Lee instructed?"

"Do you have a code for us, young man?" was all Ewell said in reply.

It was then that Tom realized they exchanged a code to note the validity of courier, and he didn't know it. He knew he was in trouble now. Having no other option, he darted around the officer standing behind him and to his left. He ran out of the tent and past the guard-ing officers, and darted into the woods. Stopping only long enough to register the footsteps of someone following him, he tiptoed off to the left a few steps and crouched down behind a felled tee. When two men ran past him, he figured they were the only ones dispatched to capture him. He waited, listening. The two men stopped a few yards ahead and turned back and forth. They too listened, probably hoping to hear Tom in the woods. When they heard nothing, they started walking back. They walked past where Tom was hiding without saying a word. Tom waited for another fifteen or twenty minutes and then he stood and walked east out of the area he had been hiding. He intended to swing around where Ewell was camped and sort through what to do next. When Tom exited the woods, he realized the sun had gone down. He headed back to where his gear was hiding so that he could decide where to go. When he arrived where his gear was, he had decided he would indeed go east from where Ewell was camped, as there was no way now to contact him. He had failed again. Those stupid Fitzgerald's had stopped him again. With no other plan, Tom realized he would have to return home and start from scratch. Maybe what he needed to do was stop trying to distract the Fitzgeralds with historical events and start simply hurting them. He could go back to Choate before they arrived and turn Dave against Joe and then steal the plans for the computer and take it all away from them. He would hurt Ryan again and maybe hurt Mary, too. Oh, and Becky for sure was going to get something. That's what he would do! And he had that money. He hadn't put it all in the bank yet. He would finish that and plan his trips back to the time they were all at Choate. As he sat there, waiting for it to be clear for him to leave his hiding place, he smiled. He was done with this nonsense of trying to change history. He was just going to hurt the Fitzgeralds!

When the two officers returned to the general's tent, one entered while the other took up guard again.

"Sir, we lost him in the woods," the officer said.

"Just as well. It is getting dark now. We have no way to locate this spy in the dark. It will have to wait until morning," the general replied to the officer, "return to your post."

The officer went back outside. While inside, the conversation resumed, with Colton saying, "Sir, that man mus' be a traitor. He wanted to git me outta his way a day or so ago. Now he come in here wi' a note he says is from Lee?"

"The note is ordering us to make haste to Gettysburg, Sir. Do we do this?" the officer that had tried to get the code from Tom said.

"What kinda paper is that, anyways?" Colton asked, reaching out to feel the paper of the note Tom had brought into the tent.

"I do not know. It sure feels strange though," the officer said, then, "Well, General, are we following this strange note?"

"We do not. This could be a trap to get us to move in the dark. We could be separated and split and ambushed. We will stay here until day and then when we can see what is before us, we will make haste to Gettysburg," the general pronounced.

The general turned to Colton and the officer that had accompanied him and said, "Thank you both for your information and service. I will deliver commendations when this battle is over."

"Thank you, Sir," the officer said, and he turned to leave the tent, knowing that was a dismissal and a complement.

"Thank you kindly, Sir. I's hopin' to be of more service to the cause. Can I do more than this?" Colton said.

"I think you might be ready to be my personal courier. How about that?" the general replied.

"Oh, yes, Sir. That'll do me just fine!" Colton said as he turned and practically ran from the tent.

Tom made a small fire and sat before it. He couldn't believe how badly things had gone here again. Going over it all again, he hoped to find an answer. He couldn't help his great-grandfather. Darn if he didn't think that money thing through. Then, in Baltimore, he wasn't able to stop the sniper. Ken had stopped that. Now Ryan had stopped him. As he drifted off to sleep, he went over his ideas to hurt them all. First Joe, then Ryan, then Becky, then Kim, and then Mary. He would take the computer from Joe and leave him with nothing. That was pain enough. He would steal all his notes so he couldn't even protest and claim Tom had stolen it. He wouldn't be believed. Then he would start pecking off the others. Yes, this was a good plan. Enough of this sneaking around in times he didn't understand. He would go to where he knew how to manage things and get them.

Tom got his gear together just as the light was coming up the next morning. He put on his pack and made his way to where his machine was. Now, he had a plan and it would be better than anything he had tried so far. He was busy plotting and not really paying attention to where he was walking when someone called out, "Announce yourself!"

Tom turned back and forth, trying to see the person who had said that. He couldn't. He ducked his head and said, "I'm a local farmer. Well, worker and heading to do my daily work."

"So, you're a confederate?" the voice said.

"No, Sir," Tom said, trying to get out of this mess he suddenly found himself in.

Tom walked and the voice said, "Stop right there!"

Tom started to run. He knew he was in for it, and figured the best way out was to get as far from that voice as he could. Then, Tom heard the crack of a shot. He tried to dive off away from the road, but then his side hurt something fierce. He fell to the ground, fainting. Two men walked up to where Tom was lying on the side of the road. "You shouldn't have shot him, Robert. We can't get information from him now!"

"He ain't dead. I can see his chest rising and falling. We could drag him back and see what he can tell us when he wakes up," the other man said.

"No, we can't do that. It could be hours before he comes to and we ain't got that kind of time. Besides, he's bleeding pretty bad. He ain't gonna make it through the day."

The two turned and went back to where they were hiding with instructions from their captain to detain and question anyone on the road today.

Tom opened his eyes when the men had walked away and inched himself off the road and into some brush that lined it. He pulled himself upright and began a slow, arduous process to use the trees and strong brush to make his way to the machine. Looking around, he thought it was close, but after a few minutes, he realized it was much farther than he thought. Falling over, he began using the trees to hold on to and slowly make his way through the woods. Thinking he had to be close, he was sure this was where he had the machine. He stopped and opened his pack, looking for something to wrap around his middle to stop the bleeding. He found two shirts and rolled them. Then he wrapped his middle. It burned like crazy. He tried to stand again and fell flat on his face. He passed out again. When he woke, he didn't know how long he'd laid there. The sun was still filtering through the trees, so it must still be day. He tried to stand but couldn't. He had to get to the machine and get out of here. He began crawling.

Becky knocked on the door and Ryan opened it, revealing their bags on the bed and them ready to go. She smiled, "You guys are all ready, I see."

"Let's get some food and head out," Joe said, after he kissed her in greeting.

They carried their bags downstairs. Joe and Ryan and Becky waited while Ken returned their room keys and paid the clerk at the desk. They walked out and headed east down the road leading out of town. They were quiet as they made their way to where Tom's machine had been. When they got close, Ken whispered to the others, "We should walk off the road, so we don't make too much noise in case he's close."

They started into the woods at Joe's direction and were almost to the clearing where Tom had the machine before Ken and Joe found it when Becky dropped her bag and said, "Oh!" and pulled up her skirts and ran to the other edge of the clearing.

Joe called out, "Where are you going?"

Then he too saw what Becky had seen. There was Tom laying on the ground, holding his side, with his eyes closed. Becky fell to her knees near Tom and touched his shoulder, saying, "Tom, can you hear me?"

Tom opened his eyes just as Ryan, Ken, and Joe arrived. He groaned as he said, "Of course, it had to be you that found me."

Becky gingerly loosened the wrap that Tom had tried to do. The blood started pouring out of his side as soon as she got the wrap opened. She looked at Joe and said, "Get my bag. Get the first aid kit, quick!"

Joe ran back to where Becky had dropped her bag and opened it. Finding the kit, he ran back. He laid it beside Becky, saying, "What else do you need?"

"I'm going to need some fabric to wrap this. In my bag there is a petticoat, it's white. Bring it over here and start ripping it in strips," Becky said as she used the scissors in the first aid kit to cut away Tom's shirt.

"We should take him somewhere. We can't fix this here in the woods," Ryan said.

"We can't move him. If we try to lift him, he will probably bleed to death. He's probably lost a lot of blood already," Becky said.

"Just leave me. The last thing I want is you saving me," Tom hissed.

"Well, you heard him. Let's just get out of here then and let him fend for himself," Ryan said, shaking his head.

"We absolutely cannot leave him like this. He might die from this gunshot!" Becky said, turning her head to look up at Ryan.

"We aren't going to leave him, but we need to figure out how to help him right here. Do you think we need to get that shot out of his side? I'm thinking it might be lead and we have to take it out of there," Ken said, setting down on his haunches beside Becky.

"I agree. We have to get it out," Becky said, "but I'm not sure how to do that." Becky kept rambling. "We'll need something long and sterile and it would be great if it were tweezers or something like that."

"Let's dig through the first aid kit," Joe said, as he knelt down too and started taking everything out of the kit. After a few minutes of digging, he held up a pair of longer tweezers and asked, "Will this work?"

"It will have to. Now, I think we need to pour some alcohol on those and then we need to put some iodine on his side. Then we will need to probe in that hole for the shot and try to grab it and pull it out," Becky explained what she hoped was a process that would work.

"I'll light a fire. We're going to need light and probably some heat will help us all," Ryan said as he began picking up some larger stones he saw to make a fire circle. He had the ring ready and then he ventured off to get firewood. While Ryan did that, Joe looked at Ken and said, "We should probably move him closer to that fire, right?"

"Yeah, that's a good idea. We can't fix this with him propped up against a tree," Ken said as he stood up.

"Ryan, come help them, we need to keep his side stable as we carry him so you three should carry him as flat as you can," Becky said as she picked up all the items from the first aid kit and the strips of cloth Joe had ripped for her.

The three of them moved Tom and laid him close to where Ryan was setting up a firepit. Then, Ryan went to get wood for the fire and Joe finished ripping up a petticoat into strips. Meanwhile, Becky began preparing for this latest bit of doctoring by pouring a bit of alcohol they had in the first aid kit on the tweezers. Ken put some alcohol on a gauze pad and rubbed it on Tom's side.

"What is that? Are you trying to kill me?" Tom yelled.

"No, we're trying to save you, you idiot. If we don't clean you up first, an infection is going to start and that will do you in before we can get you home. We're in eighteen sixty-three you know, and most people on these battle fields died of infection, not wounds," Ken said, exasperated with him already, but at the same realizing he needed to be a better person than he had been toward Tom.

Ryan had a good fire going by the time they had prepared everything. Becky rubbed iodine around the gunshot hole in Tom's side and then she handed the tweezers to Ken, saying, "I don't think I can do this part."

"Great, it's not like I'm an expert at this. What should I be doing? Do you at least have some plan?" Ken asked as he took the tweezers from Becky, but did nothing with them.

"I think you should use these gloves," Ryan said, as he held out the latex gloves he found in the first aid kit.

Ken held out the tweezers and Becky took them by holding the bottom so she didn't touch where they had just cleaned them. Then Ken put on the latex gloves. He held out his hands like a doctor who had cleaned before a surgery. Becky smiled and then said, "I think you should stick your finger into that hole and see if you can feel the bullet or shot or whatever it is. That way, you can determine if the tweezers will reach it."

Joe made a face at this information and then said, "Ok, that's gross. Glad you're doing that Ken."

Ken looked over at him and made a face back. Then he turned back to Tom and put his index finger into the hole created by the shot Tom took. He probed down into Tom's side and came abruptly to a hard obstruction. He looked up, saying, "I think I found it."

"Great!" Becky said, smiling. "Can you feel the edges of it?"

"Not sure," Ken said.

"Try to see if you can feel the edges. That will give you something to grasp with the tweezers," Becky said.

Ken maneuvered his finger around in the hole in an attempt to feel the end of the bullet. He was doing this for a few seconds and then he withdrew his finger. He held out his hand for the tweezers, saying, "I think I can get it."

Becky handed him the tweezers and Ken put them into the hole. He grasped the bullet and pulled it out. Just as he pulled the bullet out of the hole, blood started seeping heavily out of that hole. Ken dropped the bullet just as Joe reached down and put a wad of cotton against the hole. The blood soaked the cotton that Joe had pressed to the wound quickly. He looked at Becky and said, "Is that normal? Should he be bleeding this much?"

"I don't know. I know absolutely nothing about gunshot wounds. All I'm going on is what my aunt told me about first aid and fixing wounds in the woods while camping from when I was a kid. I don't think it should bleed that much, but I'm not sure," Becky said, grabbing more of the ripped cotton petticoat and pressing it on the wound.

"Maybe we should cauterize it?" Ryan said, looking over Ken and Becky's shoulders at Tom.

"How would we do that?" Ken asked, turning to look up at Ryan.

"More importantly, why would we do that?" Joe asked as he handed more cotton to Becky.

"You do that to sort of close off the exposed, open veins and arteries that are impacted by this wound. It's how they stopped bleeding like this in this time period, actually," Ryan said.

"Ok, it's as good an idea as any," Becky said, pulling a shirt out of one of the guys' bags to use as they were running out of petticoat strips. "How do we do it?"

"Well, we'd need something more substantial than the tweezers. We would heat them up to as hot as we can in the fire then put it just inside the hole and it would cauterize the wound and hopefully stop the bleeding," Ryan explained the process as his grandfather had explained to him when he was younger.

"We don't know where the bleeding is coming from. He wasn't bleeding like this until I pulled the bullet out. Is it possible the bullet was holding back a damaged organ or something and when I pulled it out, I opened a bigger hole into something important?" Ken pondered.

"Is it pulsing out?" Joe asked.

"Why does that matter?" Ryan countered.

"Well, if it's pulsing, it means you opened something that is getting blood flow from the heart and it pulses because of that pumping action. Then we would know it was an organ or something important, I think," Joe explained.

Becky withdrew the cotton padding, and they watched. The blood didn't pulse out of the hole left by the shot. It just oozed out. She commented, "Well, it's not pulsing out, and it seems to slow down after the pressure we had on it. I think that means it isn't an organ."

"My vote then is to cauterize and then stitch him up," Ken said.

"I agree," Ryan said.

"Ok, what can we use?" Joe asked.

"I know!" Becky exclaimed as she got up off the ground and went to her bag. She came back with an iron rod that she purchased to curl her hair and wanted to bring back and show Deb and Kim. She brought it back near the fire and Ryan put it into the fire. After a few minutes, he used a leather bag he opened to grab up the rod and brought it to Ken. Holding it out to him, he said, "You do the honors, since you dug out the bullet."

Ken took the rod via the leather bag to protect his hands from the heat and pushed it into the hole. Tom woke up and screeched. Becky tried to hush him, but he passed out before she could accomplish the task. After Ken pulled the rod out, Becky leaned in and began stitching his skin with the needle and thread from the first aid kit. She put some antibiotic ointment on it and then a bandage. She then wrapped his whole waist first with cotton and then with an ace bandage from the first aid kit.

"Now we have to just hope he doesn't get a terrible infection," Becky said.

"We cleaned everything, didn't we?" Ryan asked as he stoked the fire with more wood.

"We did, but we did all this in the woods, and we don't know what he did before we found him. He could have dragged himself through the mud picking up who knows what," Becky responded.

"Let's get him to the machines and get out of here," Joe proposed.

"We can't do that. We don't have a wagon to take him and he certainly can't walk," Ken said, standing up and going to the creek nearby to wash his hands.

When he came back, he said, "We'll have to stay here and try to keep him safe until we can walk him out of here, or we can find a wagon."

"The battle starts in earnest tomorrow. We aren't going to be able to find a wagon. All the horses and men are going to be engaged in battle and moving wounded out of the way," Becky said. "We'll be lucky if they don't come here and press you three into service."

"Ok, we know we can't walk out of here tonight. Let's plan for a night in the woods. Do we have anything to make any shelters?" Joe said, grabbing all their bags and bringing them close to the fire.

"We knew we'd have to do this, remember? I gathered up several blankets," Becky said.

"I had two tarps from when I was with Ewell that I brought back with me. They're in my bags," Ryan said as he reached for his bag.

They searched through their things, and then Joe spied another bag. He ran a bit into the woods and came back with the bag he saw.

"What do you have?" Ken asked.

"I think it might be Tom's bag. It was laying over there in the woods and it has some blood on it," Joe said as he sat down on a felled tree limb near the fire. He opened it and looked up and smiled. He pulled out a large sheet of canvas and then another one. Then he pulled out a bedroll and two blankets.

"Great! We can use the three canvas tarps for tents and these blankets and what Becky brought for bedrolls!" Ryan said, "I'll search for some tree limbs we can use as poles to hold the canvas up."

"I'll go with you," Joe said.

The two returned a few minutes later, holding four evenly lengthened tree limbs. While they were away, Ken cleared some of the ground brush away and searched for some more firewood. When they all returned, they set up three tents. They set each so one end opened toward the fire. Ken announced, "Becky, you get this one. Will put Tom in one, and we will take shifts watching over Tom and the two that aren't watching will try to sleep in this other tent. I think it's best to keep Tom close to the fire, though."

"I agree. He needs to stay warm or he might catch a fever," Becky said, "But I can take a shift watching him."

"No, you've done enough," Ken announced in a manner that did not allow debate.

"Now all we need is some food," Ryan declared. "I've got some smoked beef, but not a lot."

"I have some bread. I took it from the inn at breakfast, thinking we might need some," Joe said, smiling.

They all sat around the fire eating the meat and bread. It was enough to sustain them, but not a substantial meal, as Ryan pointed out.

"I could go for a cheeseburger and fries about now," Ryan said.

"I could go for my warm bed," Joe added, and they all laughed.

Just as they were cleaning up, three men appeared out of the woods and stalked toward their fire.

"State your names!" one man said menacingly.

Ken stood up and squared off with the men, saying, "How about you state your names and your business running up on us like this?"

"You with union or confederates?" another of the men asked.

"Neither. We're from out west. We've returned to fetch our cousin, but we were too late. He got tangled in some gun fire. He's here, and we're trying to keep him alive. So, state your business and be gone!" Ken said, a bit more angrily.

"What side he with?" the first man said.

"Neither. He's a farmer from here. Just got caught by a skirmish on his farm," Ken said.

"Got any food? We're really hungry," the third man said.

"Sorry, we have nothing left. We just finished the last of our food," Ryan said, standing to join Ken.

"Mind if we check in your things? Perhaps we don't believe you," the second man said, starting to walk around Ken.

Ken grabbed his arm to stop him and pulled him back. "Yeah, I do mind. I'm thinking at this point that you three probably shot my cousin. I think I'll just run you into the sheriff in town."

"We ain't shot nobody today. We're just starving," the first man said.

"We don't have any food. So, move along," Ryan said, as he took a step closer to the other two men.

"Ok, ok, we're leaving," the third man said as he turned and pulled the other two back into the woods.

After the men disappeared into the woods, Becky whispered, "Can we be sure they won't come back?"

"I don't think they'll be back. They were starving and looking for food. I don't think they really want to hurt anybody. They just wanted to bully someone into giving them some food," Ken said, trying to reassure her.

"They were southerners, weren't they?" Joe asked.

"Yeah, one of them had on a blue army jacket. They were confederates. Probably scouting around," Ryan said. "General Ewell did that with a lot of his troops once they settled somewhere. So, I imagine the other generals did it too. And none of them have eaten much lately."

Becky knelt down and checked on Tom's bandages and was happy the blood hadn't seeped through. She stood and said, "I'm going to rest. This has been a long day."

"Good idea. You two should rest, too. I'll take the first watch once we move Tom. Ryan and Joe, give me a hand," Ken said, moving to take a position at Tom's right side. Ryan took the left side and Joe took his feet and they moved him to the largest tent that was positioned closest to the fire. Then Ken sat down on the felled tree limb near Tom.

Ryan and Joe said goodnight and to wake them for their watch and crawled into the tent. Joe called over to Becky goodnight and told her to wake him if she needed anything. Then it got quiet, and the night left Ken with his thoughts.

21

Ken put another few pieces of wood on the fire and poked it. As he sat down, he heard the sound of footsteps. He stood back up and circled around, looking to see if anyone was coming. As he turned back to the fire, two men approached him around Becky's tent. Ken tensed and asked, "Who are you?"

"Are you with the union?" one man asked.

"I ask the questions here, declare yourselves!" Ken responded, while taking a step toward the men.

"We are with the union and we got turned around. We are not here to harm you," the other man said, and pointed to the felled limb by the fire, in a request to sit.

Ken motioned it was ok to sit, lowered his stance and sat as well, saying, "What are two of you doing out here alone at night?"

"We are part of a scouting party that got split up when we heard some confederates yelling in the brush. Our commander is down in town waiting for our assessment of the confederate troops," the second man said.

"What are your names?" Ken asked.

"I'm lieutenant David Greenbriar and this is Ben Fitzsimmons. And you are?" the lieutenant said.

"My name is Ken Fitzgerald," Ken answered.

"How did your man here get injured?" the lieutenant asked.

"We were on our way back to territory out west, above Missouri. We had to come and retrieve my younger brother and his fiancé from

Gettysburg. My parents want him away from this fighting. This here is my brother's friend that was traveling with us. He went out to hunt for some supper and got caught in the crossfire of some fighting today. We patched him up and hopefully we can move on in the morning," Ken explained.

"So, you are not attached to any regiment?" the lieutenant asked, looking at Ken a little skeptically.

"No, I have stayed out of this battle between the states, Sir. I do not condone slavery, but I also do not condone brother fighting brother, and I have seen that very thing in my travels," Ken replied.

"It has been a strange war and stranger still why we keep at it. It is true," the lieutenant replied.

"Have you been into Gettysburg?" Ben asked.

"Yes, we have, but not today. I have no details to provide you with any troop movements today. I am aware of confederate movement coming south from Carlisle, however," Ken answered.

"How about directions?" the lieutenant asked.

"Into town?" Ken questioned their destination.

"Well, perhaps around the outskirts of town, on the eastern side," the lieutenant provided.

"If you go out of our encampment here to the south, and go about forty or fifty yards, then turn west. At some point, you will reach the road that leads into town. You will see the woods across the road, so if you want to continue on with some cover, cross the road and stay in the brush. That wooded area runs nearly the whole eastern side of town," Ken said.

"How about some food? Got any of that you can spare?" Ben asked.

"I have a bit of smoked beef here," Ken said, as he stood and walked toward the tent Joe and Ryan were sleeping in. Just outside was a saddlebag. Ken reached into it and came out with two pieces of the smoked meat that Ryan had brought from the camp. Ken walked back and handed a piece to Ben and a piece to the lieutenant.

"Thank you for the food!" Ben said, as he hungrily bit into the beef.

"Here," the lieutenant said, as he too stood and pulled a small paper folded up out of his bag and offered it to Ken, "Mix this powder with some water, it will help fight the fever your man here is likely to wake up with. That's what you need to worry about out here in the field. The infections and the fever."

Ken took the small folded up paper and said, "Thank you."

Ben stood, still eating the beef, and the two started in the direction Ken had provided to them. They both turned back as they reached the edge of the clearing and said, "Thank you for the food and the directions."

"You are welcome. Good luck to you both. May you both make it home from this," Ken replied as he watched them disappear into the dark woods.

Ken sat back down by the fire and again poked the logs and wood there to ensure the flame did not go out. He tossed another log on it and then went to where Tom was laying and hunched down to check him out. The bleeding must have stopped, as the bandage was no longer seeping through with blood. Hopefully, Ken thought, this was a good sign. He undid the binding and checked the wound. It looked better, but it was hard to tell by firelight. Ken went back over and sat down. He started thinking of the two groups of men he had encountered tonight. He wondered if they would even see their homes again. The battle of Gettysburg had the largest casualty count of the war. It was a little creepy that he met men that would go into the battle starting tomorrow and not make it off the fields.

Shaking his head, he really should focus on a plan to get them all out of here, without getting too close to the battles that would start come morning. He figured they could skirt around the encroaching troops to get to the machines, but how were they going to do that with Tom? They had been here five days as of tomorrow. He couldn't remember what Becky had said in terms of days progressing at home. He was going to have to ask that. At some point, they were going to run up on something one of them couldn't miss and it was going to be a problem for them still being here. These thoughts rumbled around in his mind as he watched the fire. He missed Mary, and he worried about Deb way off in the middle east. Ok, he knew Kim was safe, but how was she dealing with not hearing from them? He was very thankful they had control of both machines now, but what if Tom died here? How would they explain this to his parents? Would they explain it to them? Or would Tom just become one of the hundreds of missing young people in the country? The questions swirled as the hours passed. The fire burned down and the sun trickled into the clearing. Ken looked up when he heard someone in the tents waking up. The first to emerge was Joe. He stood, looked around and looked right at Ken when he said, "Why didn't you wake us up? Have you been sitting there all night?"

"I was thinking, and we had other visitors after you all went to bed, and I didn't want one of you to have to deal with that if anyone else showed up. Plus, I needed the time to sort this all out," Ken responded as he stood and stretched, "but man, sitting on that log, didn't do me any favors!"

Ryan emerged from the tent, and then Becky stood up. She stumbled a bit, and Joe turned to help her up.

"What were you deep in thought about?" Ryan asked.

"Oh, the people we've met during this trip and how some of them aren't making it past the third of July alive. How to deal with getting us back in the middle of the biggest battle of the Civil War, and what to do with Tom if he dies here? Oh, and what to do when we get him back and he still needs medical care? Just a few things," Ken responded as he walked around the clearing.

Becky had knelt down by Tom and was checking him when Ken finished. She said, "Tom has a fever. A high one, I think."

"The union army lieutenant that showed up here last night gave me some powder, he said, fights fever. We should give this to Tom right away," Ken said as he reached down to the bag. He had put the powder in. He handed it to Becky, telling her to be careful opening it up. Joe poured some water from a canteen into a cup and brought it to Becky, along with a spoon. He got down on his knees beside her.

"Here, mix the powder in this," Joe said, handing Becky the cup full of water.

"How much should I use?" Becky asked to no one in particular.

"Maybe not all of it. We don't know what this powder is, do we? Plus, if it doesn't work right away, we might want to give him another dose later," Ryan said, looking over the process.

"I agree. Use about a third of it, Becky. That way we'll have two more chances to reduce his fever. I'm heading out to find us some food. Ryan, can you gather some more wood?" Ken said as he headed toward the eastern side of the clearing carrying a fishing pole he had fashioned during the night with a long stick and some string he found in the first aid kit, and a rifle he found near Tom's things.

"Are you planning to hunt while you fish or fish while you hunt?" Ryan asked, smiling at the picture of Ken with both tools.

"I'm going to hunt while I fish, I think," Ken called, laughing as he disappeared into the woods.

Becky used the spoon to gather about a third of the powder and placed it into the cup. She carefully closed the paper back around the rest of the powder and put it into the pocket of her skirt. She then turned and stirred up the powder into the water. When she finished mixing it up, she looked at Joe and said, "We have to wake him and sit him up some so he can drink this, I think."

Joe pulled the bedroll out of his tent and rolled it up, and placed it near Tom's head. Then he asked Ryan to help him and they pulled Tom up so that they leaned him on the bedroll. This put Tom into nearly a sitting position. He groaned when they let go of him and opened his eyes. He looked at Joe and scowled, "what are you doing here?"

"We're saving you, despite all that you've done. That's what I'm doing here," Joe said, as he helped Becky get closer to Tom to administer the medicine.

"You have to drink this, Tom," Becky said, putting the cup near his face.

"I don't want to. My head hurts and my side hurts," Tom answered, closing his eyes.

"You hurt because they shot you, and your head hurts because you have a terrible fever and this will help. There's some medicine in this water. It will ease the fever," Becky said, trying to coax Tom.

"You're probably trying to poison me," Tom said as he opened his eyes and looked at Becky.

"No, we're trying to help you, and we need you to get better so we can all go home," Becky said, trying to remain patient.

"What medicine and how did you get it?" Tom remained belligerent.

"A union army lieutenant gave it to Ken last night when Ken was watching over you. This lieutenant saw you and knew you would develop a fever. He was trying to help too," Becky tried to explain.

"I said I don't want it!" Tom yelled.

"Keep your voice down, you idiot! The battle starts today and we don't want to draw any attention to ourselves. Just drink the darn water!" Ryan said, leaning over where Tom was sitting in as menacing a manner as he could manage.

"Alright, alright, give me the cup! If you're trying to poison me, might as well get to it," Tom said as he reached for the cup.

Becky helped him take drinks until it was almost all gone. She put her hand to his forehead and said, "It seems worse than when I first checked him."

"Give it a little time, Becky," Joe said as he emerged from the tent, having rolled up the other bedroll and putting on a clean shirt and socks, "Let me watch over him while you do whatever to clean up. There's a bowl full of water over there, but it's freezing. I left the towel I used hanging there on that bush."

Joe sat down near Tom after he helped Becky stand up. She went into her tent and changed her dress and put on clean stockings. Then she went to the bowl with a smaller towel and a bar of soap and her toothbrush. She yelped a bit when she doused her face with water. Joe called out, "I told you it was cold."

When she had finished, she took the toothbrush back to her tent and put it in the bag she had. She rolled up her bedroll and folded the blankets she used. She came out, saying, "I left the soap and rags over there in case you or Ken or Ryan want to clean up a little."

A bit later, Ryan returned carrying a bunch of kindling size wood he had roped up in a bundle and several larger logs he found. He set them down near the fire and started stirring the fire and getting it warmed up.

"I'm going to look around for a way to cook some food, just in case Ken gets lucky," Joe said, standing up and walking into the woods.

"Were you warm enough last night, Becky?" Ryan asked.

"Yes, you all really shouldn't have given me all the blankets. Were you and Joe, ok?" Becky asked.

"Yeah, we ended up sleeping pretty close together, but it was ok," Ryan said, laughing.

Joe returned carrying three long sticks. Two had a "y" like branch near the ends and the other was a long, nearly straight stick. He broke off some ends of the "y". Ryan stood, saying, "Good plan. Let me get that little shovel from the saddlebag and help."

Ryan went to the tent and pulled the little shovel out of the bag and came back to the firepit. He dug a little on each side of the fire and Joe pushed the "y" branches down into the holes. Ryan packed dirt around the sticks to stabilize them and then Joe put the big straight stick next to the fire hoping Ken came back with some food to eat.

"Wow, you made a spit to turn food on. Look at you two, so resourceful!" Becky exclaimed.

The three of them sat down and Ryan said, "Well, we better start thinking about how we get us all to the machines and back home. Do we have any idea how much time has elapsed back there?"

"I think we can figure it out," Becky said as she got up and went to her tent. She returned with a notebook and pencil. She sat down near

Joe and turned to a clean page in the notebook and started calculating. Joe watched over her shoulder.

At some point, he pointed to a place on the page and said, "The calculation wouldn't be the same for the first part of the trip to eighteen thirteen, would it?"

"Oh, you're right. We should probably calculate these two sets of trips separately, but how do we combine them? This is very different from the trip to Philadelphia," Becky answered as she erased a bunch of the work she had just done.

"Let's see what it looks like when we calculate the two trips separately and then talk over how to combine," Joe said and he turned back to Ryan, saying, "We also have to figure out what to do with Tom when we get him back. He really needs a hospital, but how do we explain an eighteen sixty-three gunshot to an emergency room doctor?"

"I know, I've been thinking about that too," Ryan added, shaking his head.

"Ken was considering it too last night. He said," Joe added, putting his head down in his hands.

"I think I have the two trips figured out. Trip one to eighteen thirteen, one day and about nine hours probably elapsed. This trip to Gettysburg so far, three days roughly, have elapsed," Becky said.

"If we simply string those together, like we went and came back from eighteen thirteen and then came here, it would be four days and nine hours. I think we should go with that. If not completely accurate, it will be close," Joe said.

"We left on Saturday, so that means, back at home, today it's Tuesday, right?" Ryan asked.

"I think it might be late in the day on Tuesday, yes," Becky said.

"Ok, so we have three days at home until we start to have problems, right?" Joe asked.

"I'm good through the weekend. My parents left on a vacation," Ryan said.

"I'm good for this entire week. Remember Joe, you were taking me to see Diana, and I was going to be there the whole week," Becky said.

"I'm supposed to be at MIT, so no one would bother me all week. The only outstanding issue would be Ken and work," Joe concluded.

"So how many days does it mean we can stay here, then?" Ryan asked.

"We have a little over five days before we run too far into the weekend back home," Becky concluded.

"Ok, good," Ryan said as he got up to pace around the clearing. "Now all we have to do is figure out Tom and get out of here within five days."

"Doesn't this depend on what kind of shape he's in when we get back home?" Becky asked.

"Well, in part. I mean, we can't just take him to an emergency room and we can't take him home. Either place, we would have too much explaining to do. But I was thinking more along the lines of fixing it so he can't do this nonsense anymore," Ryan pondered as he paced.

"Don't you think he will decide he's learned his lesson from this?" Becky asked.

"I don't think so," Ryan answered, "If the way he's talked to all of us since we found him last night is any sign, the gunshot, or his dire state haven't taught him anything."

Just then, Ken emerged from the woods, carrying a turkey by the neck, with the rifle slung over his shoulder and a couple of fish dangling from the fishing pole.

Joe stood up, saying, "Our hero! You've brought food!"

"Food that needs to be prepped before we can even cook it," Becky said, turning up her nose at the growing smell as Ken got close.

Ken, laughing, "Hey, I know they smell, but imagine this turkey once it's cooked."

"It sure will, but can you clean it and prepare it over there?" Becky asked, pointing to the edge of the clearing.

Joe came to her and hugged her. He whispered to her, "That's actually a suitable spot. There's that big, flat rock over there. It can be the table."

Joe went and got his knife and Ryan got his and they went to the big rock and sat on the ground. The three of them started working. Ryan took the fish, cause he had cleaned fish with his grandfather and knew just what to do. First, he cut off the fish's head and then began using his knife to separate the fish into two pieces and pull out the bones. He finished pretty quickly, and he brought it over to the fire. Then he said as he set it down, "I've got just the thing to cook this!" He dashed into his tent and came out with a small metal basket. He put the fish filets into the basket and hung the straight stick over the fire. He then hung the basket on the stick.

"Great job, Ryan! Where in the world did you get that?" Becky exclaimed as she already smelled the cooking fish.

The cook from Ewell's troops gave me that when we were working on the cooking the other day. He said it was the best way to cook a fish over a fire and he wanted me to have it for helping him," Ryan replied as he stood from helping Becky hang the basket over the fire.

"How fortunate for us he gave that to you! Now we can eat! I'll monitor this. Go help Ken and Joe."

Ryan returned to the rock to find Ken and Joe trying to de-feather the turkey. Ryan looked down and said, "Maybe we can cut off his feet and head, and cut an opening between his legs to gut him."

"Don't we have to get all these feathers off first?" Ken asked.

"Yeah, but maybe pull on them the other way and don't pull the small stuff out. We can cut that off and skin him a little," Ryan said.

Joe stood up, saying, "How about you get in there? I don't know the first thing about preparing game for cooking."

Ryan got down on the ground and he and Ken pulled the larger feathers out in the direction they grew in. When they had most of them out, Ken cut the head off close to the bottom of the neck and Ryan cut both the feet off, leaving the legs. Then Ryan cut a hole between the legs and began pulling the insides out. Joe had brought a small pot they had close to the rock they were working at, and Ryan put the insides of the turkey in the pot. When it was full, Joe took it out into the woods, a good way from the clearing, and dumped it. They had to do that several times to finish the job, and then Ryan pronounced he was ready to cook. Ken carried it over to the fire. Ryan pulled the basket with the almost done fish off the stick and then pulled the stick off the "y" brackets. They ran the turkey through with the stick and Joe produced some twine they tied him up to the stick so he wouldn't fall off into the fire. Together, Ryan and Ken hung the stick back over the fire and then Ryan put the basket back to finish cooking the fish.

When the fish was done, Ken pulled the basket down, and they carefully removed the fish. They thankfully had several plates in their packs and Ken portioned it out. Silence fell onto the clearing as they ate. Joe took all four canteens and left the clearing to go get more water. He returned with four full canteens and handed them around to Ken, Ryan, and Becky. They each drank the cold water and smiled. Ken set his canteen down first, and looked around at all of them and said, "Ok, we have to have a plan."

"I know," Ryan agreed.

"We have to consider first how we can get Tom out of here. He can't walk out. We can't carry him all the way back to the machines," Joe added.

"So, we either wait until Tom can walk, or we have to go in the middle of a tremendous battle and find some horses and a wagon," Ken said, thinking out loud.

"I think we should wait. We figured out we have five more days here until it impacts us back home in terms of the time elapsed. That should be more than enough time for Tom to get better enough for us to walk him out of here. Plus, the battle is going to be all around us for the next day or so. We likely will be safer here than trying to make our way around it. We can't nurse anybody else here," Becky said, expressing her fears. "If something happens to one of us, I don't think we can manage it."

"I think waiting, at least until the battles are over, is probably a good idea. Hopefully, during that time, Tom gets better enough that we don't have to go find horses and a wagon. We will run low on money soon if we have to keep buying horses," Joe added, somewhat to support Becky's fears and somewhat because it was probably the best plan.

"Ok, so we wait here for at least two more days. We might need some supplies, so I suggest Ken and I make our way into town and see what we can find at the general store," Ryan said.

Ken was quiet for a minute and then he said what he had been thinking since the middle of the night, "Or, you three could go now, to the machines and take one and return home. That way, you are all safe. I can stay here and watch over Tom and get him to a point where I can get him to the other machine and bring him home when we can."

Joe stood up. "No. We're not leaving you here by yourself. We would have no way of knowing you're safe and you can't do this alone!"

"I'm with Joe on this. Ken, you can't take this on by yourself. If something happened to you, we'd have no way of knowing and no way to help," Ryan added, but he didn't stand up. He merely looked at Ken.

They all looked at each other for a few minutes, and then Becky said, "Ken, I know you feel you need to protect us all, just like you have always felt the need to protect Joe, Deb and Kim. I don't have brothers or sisters, but if I did, I'd want an older brother just like you. I like the feeling that you are watching out for all of us. It's probably a big part of the reason we've always felt confident to do this time traveling. You're always keeping us safe. But you have to remember, we have a role to play, too. We all do. None of us is capable enough to do this alone. Even you. It is just not a good idea for you to stay here alone."

"She said it better than we did, I think," Ryan said, smiling at Ken.

"I would like to point one more thing out. Remember that summer we promised no more trying to save our parents and never again would anyone go alone in the time machine? We never said, unless we have two machines and we need to keep as many of safe as we can," Joe said, sitting down but still looking just at Ken.

"Yes, Becky has a point, and yes, you do too, Joe," Ken said, looking down. When he looked up, he said, "Ok, we stay together. Ryan and I will go see about some more supplies and check on the status of things in town. Becky and Joe, you stay here and watch over the turkey and Tom."

Ken stood up and motioned for Ryan to join him. He put his knife in his pocket, grabbed his pistol from his bag near the fire, and waited for Ryan to be ready. Ryan asked if there was anything in particular Becky needed and she grabbed the notebook and pulled a page out. She jotted down a few things and handed it to Ryan. He looked it over and put it in his pocket. The two headed south through the woods.

Joe turned to Becky after they left and said, "Thank you. I don't think I could have convinced him by myself. You really got through to him."

"I know he feels a strong desire to protect everyone. It's strange how I understand it, but I don't. I don't have an older brother, but I get how an older brother would feel that way. You're lucky to have him," Becky said, holding Joe's hand.

"I've never really seen him as anything other than the overbearing older brother. Well, that's not true. Before Choate, that's how I saw him. I think it just rears up for him when we're in these kinds of situations. He feels this overwhelming urge to protect. Sometimes, though, his act of protecting us puts him in a dangerous situation. That's what he doesn't see easily," Joe said, looking down at their entwined hands.

"I think he probably sees his protection as causing him less harm than not protecting you. I think he just takes that in stride and treats it like a cost of his responsibility," Becky said.

"Maybe. I'm really glad you got through to him, anyway," Joe said, smiling at her and leaning over to give her a kiss.

Just then, Tom moaned and fell over from leaning on the bed-roll. The two jumped up and went to him. Joe got Tom into a better position laying down and Becky felt his forehead. "He's warmer than he was before," she said, looking up at Joe.

"We need to get some more water into him. We probably should have been doing that the whole time," Joe said, again pulling Tom up onto the bedroll. He grabbed the cup they had administered the medicine with and washed it out a little from one of the canteens. Then he filled it with fresh water and held it up to Tom's lips.

"Drink Tom. You have to drink this water," Joe pleaded with Tom.

Tom opened his lips a little and Joe tipped up the glass. He stopped when it dribbled over the rim of the cup onto Tom's shirt. He waited a few minutes and did it again. Joe repeated this process until he got most of the water from the cup into Tom. Joe then looked up at Becky and asked, "Do you think we can give him some more of that medicine?"

"It's been a few hours. I think it might be alright," Becky said, slightly uncertainly. She pulled the powder packet out of her pocket and picked up the cup for Joe to fill it back up. He got the spoon and Becky gathered up a spoonful and poured it into the cup. She refolded the packet around the last dose of the medicine and put it back into her pocket. Then she turned to Tom and tried to coax him to wake enough to take the medicine. He opened his eyes, but they were very bloodshot and he seemed unable to focus on her face. She told him he needed to take more medicine, and he feebly complied. Joe held him up and Becky got him to drink the cup full of water mixed with the powder. Then they laid him back down to rest.

Joe periodically checked the turkey as they sat and talked about the people they had met on the trips they had made, and their impression of the war, now that they had seen it more up close. They again tried to get more water into Tom and Joe left for a short time to refill all the canteens before it got dark. The afternoon was nearly gone when they heard gunfire and cannons. Becky stayed close to Joe and worried about Ken and Ryan. She again tried to get Tom to take some water, but she couldn't wake him up. Just then, Ken and Ryan could be heard talking coming toward the clearing. Becky stood up. They entered the clearing, and she visibly relaxed. "I'm so glad you're back. Did you hear the guns and cannons?"

"Yes, we saw them from a distance. They are moving down that road that runs into town. It will get fainter as the night goes on, so long as they get to where they are headed. They're the union army moving into town," Ken said.

"Did you get the supplies?" Joe asked.

Ken and Ryan set the bags down near the fire. Ryan said, "We got everything you asked for and a few other things."

"We got some more cotton to rip up for bandages, and a lot of salt. The store owner asked if we were nursing a wound and when we said yes, he threw in a thing that looks like a turkey baster. He gave us a lot more salt and said we might need to flush the wound with salt water," Ken added.

"Tom isn't getting better. We gave him another dose of medicine," Becky explained.

"We probably should open the bandages up and see what the wound looks like," Ken said, "before it gets totally dark, anyway."

Joe sat down and started cutting the cotton at the edge and then tearing long strips of it to use as bandages. Ryan got down with Ken and Becky to help. When they got the bandages off, it was clear there was an infection. Red lines radiated out from the wound.

"Geeze, that looks bad," Ryan said, what they were all thinking.

Joe walked over to look over their shoulders and said, "We have to flush that out or he will go into septic shock."

"Ok, let's get a lot of water, and we should probably get a towel or something to soak up the liquid. We need to take his shirt off to do this," Ken said.

"Get the baster and the salt, Joe, out of the bag we brought back here. I'll go fill this big pot we bought with water," Ryan said as he stood up and left the clearing carrying a pot.

Ken pulled out his pocketknife and went to the fire and held the blade in the fire to clean it off. When Ryan came back with water, they dumped about half of the salt into the pot and Becky stirred it up. Joe and Ryan worked Tom's shirt off and hung it up on the bush. Becky got the towel under and near the side they were about to flush. Ken leaned down and cut the stitches Becky had put in and pried open the healing skin. It smelled bad right away. He looked up and said, "That's the infection that smells."

Ken put the baster into the salt water and then started forcing it into the wound. Tom reared up and Ryan got behind him and held him down. Tom screamed for them to stop. Ken kept flushing the salt water into the wound. It started to bleed profusely. Eventually, Tom passed out from the pain of having salt water poured into an open wound. When they finished, the streaks seemed to dissipate. They wrapped him back up. Ken held him up while Joe and Ryan got his shirt back on. They picked him up and moved him to a dry spot onto the bedroll that Becky rolled out. They all sat quietly for a few minutes.

"If that doesn't clear the infection, there's going to be no saving him," Joe said.

"All we can do is watch and see," Ken said.

"I think the turkey is done," Ryan said. "I don't mean to sound callous, but I'm starved, and this thing smells amazing."

Ken laughed at that and said, "Well, let's take him off the fire then."

Ken and Ryan took position on both sides of the fire and pulled the straight stick off the fire and over to a makeshift table they had made of a fallen tree and a big flat rock. They cut the turkey up. Ryan pulled a loaf of bread out of one bag they returned with and they sat and ate turkey and bread. They all smiled when Ryan said, "This may not be the ritz, but a turkey over a fire is pretty close to perfect."

After they ate, Ryan again filled the big pot with water and they cleaned the dishes and utensils. Then he filled the pot again with clean water and they put the scraps of turkey into the pot and some vegetables they bought from a farmer they passed on their way back from town.

"We'll have soup tomorrow!" Becky exclaimed when she finished cutting the potatoes, carrots and beans they brought back.

Ken and Joe hung the straight stick back over the fire and they hung the pot over the edge of the fire so it would simmer. Becky checked Tom again and said she was exhausted. She crawled into her tent and went to sleep almost immediately.

The three sat around the fire for a while not saying anything, each with his thoughts, then Joe said, "You should sleep, Ken. Crawl in there and sleep for a few hours at least."

"Yeah, you go to sleep and I'll sit up with Joe," Ryan said.

"You get me if anything happens, and I mean it. There is fighting all around now, so don't take any chances. Wake me," Ken said as he crawled into the tent.

Joe and Ryan talked and kept the fire going. It became quiet. The fighting had stopped for the night. Joe suggested Ryan go try to get some sleep. He was refusing until Joe stopped him from falling over into the fire when he nodded off. After Ryan went to bed, Joe went over and sat near Tom. He checked his forehead. He was not as hot as he had been, but he was still hot. Joe filled the cup with some water and tried to get Tom to drink. He opened his eyes and tried to focus on Joe's face. After a minute, he shook his head a little and looked again.

"What are you doing here?" Tom said in a weak voice.

"I'm here with Ken, Ryan and Becky and we're taking care of you," Joe said, again trying to get Tom to drink.

"Why don't you just leave me alone!" Tom said, after sputtering from the water that Joe was trying to pour down his throat.

"Well, two reasons. First, they shot you. Second, even though you started all of this, we want to help you. See, we aren't as bad as you thought," Joe said, trying to reason with Tom, who clearly was in the midst of a high fever.

"I wish you'd never come to Choate. You ruined everything, you and your family. If you would just go away, everything would be fine," Tom said as he drifted back to sleep.

Joe sat there, thinking about what he had said. If they hadn't come to Choate. Sure, Tom might be ok, but would he and his siblings be ok?

What if Aunt Alicia hadn't shipped them off to Choate? In New York, they might have still become very close, but Ken wouldn't have met Mary, Deb wouldn't have met Ryan, and he himself wouldn't have met Becky. Would Kim be the artist she was now, or so fantastic at navigation? Come to think of it, Joe thought, would they be close if it weren't for the time travel? All these thoughts sifted through his mind as he sat and watched the fire burn. It must have been an hour or more when Joe finally came out of his reverie and notice the fire needed more wood. He got up and walked to where they had been piling wood and pulled several logs out and put them on the fire. Just as he was sitting back down, Tom started tossing and turning. Joe got down on his knees and felt Tom's forehead. He was burning up. Joe tried to keep him from rolling around more, but as soon as Tom lay still, he started mumbling in sleep. He talked of his father and how they fought all the time. How his father always thought the world owed him something and how he took it out on Tom and his mother. He mentioned his father disappearing. Then he started talking about Choate and Joe taking away his best friend. The mumbling took a sinister turn as Tom vocalized his desire to hurt all the Fitzgeralds, not just Joe. He was talking about really physically hurting them. About how glad he was that he cut Ryan. Then he talked about how he was going to go back since his plans didn't work and expose the time traveling and blame Joe and the others for all kinds of events in history that were not even places and times that they had traveled to. All this to hurt them. Joe tried to wake Tom at this point, either to confront him or to stop him from revealing all of this. He didn't know, but the effort failed. Tom would not wake up. Thankfully, Tom finally settled back down and was quiet.

Joe returned to his log seat and stared at the fire some more as he thought about what Tom had said in his fevered, fitful state. How could they stop him? Yes, they had the machine back in their control, but if Tom had made copies of the notes, he took from the barn, he could use that to go public, and then things would really get complicated. Joe pulled one blanket that had been drying over a bush off and rolled it up. He put it behind his head and leaned back against the log farthest from the fire and closer to Tom. He closed his eyes for a minute. As Joe finally nodded off, he realized what they had to do.

22

Back in New York, the day Ken, Joe, Ryan and Becky left, Kim and Mary and several of Mary's friends, along with Mary's mother and Aunt Alicia, all met at the bridal store. As they went inside, Kim said, "I'm so excited about this! Aunt Alicia, you need to make sure the dresses will work for both Deb and me."

"I'm hopeful that Mary and her mother will take some guidance from me, but we shall see. Anyway, we will work with a dear friend of mine, so perhaps I can provide some direction through her," Aunt Alicia replied as they entered the main salon. Mary caught sight of them and came over.

"I'm so glad you're here!" Mary said as she hugged Kim and then Aunt Alicia.

"I'm so happy to be here and so pleased that you included me," Aunt Alicia said as they separated from their hug.

"Include you? My goodness, we desperately need your expertise!" Mary's mother said as she walked up and overheard what Aunt Alicia said.

"Mother, this is Ken's aunt, Alicia Reynolds," Mary said, introducing them, "Mrs. Reynolds, this is my mother, Francis Rollins."

"Please, call me Alicia," Aunt Alicia said as she held out her hand to Mary's mother. They shook hands as Mary's mother said, "You should probably call me Fran."

Aunt Alicia smiled and then turned to Mary and said, "And enough of this, Mrs. Reynolds' business. You should really call me Alicia as well, dear."

"This is Ken's youngest sister, Mom. Her name is Kim," Mary said, introducing Kim to her mother.

"It's a pleasure to meet you, Ma'am," Kim said, holding out her hand.

Mrs. Rollins smiled and shook Kim's hand, saying, "My goodness, you have such pleasant manners, Kim. It's a pleasure to meet you as well."

Just then, the store owner walked up to Alicia and greeted her. She turned and smiled at Mary. "This is our bride?"

"Hello. My name is Mary," Mary said, "and this is my mother, Mrs. Rollins."

They greeted one another and the store owner said, "You can all call me Donatella. Welcome to my salon. What shall we start with today? The bride or the attendants?"

"Let's start with the bride, shall we? Unless you found something on your other shopping trips?" Aunt Alicia took charge.

"No, I couldn't find anything that felt right on our last trip. But it wasn't nearly as nice a place as this, and I didn't have all these experts around to help me," Mary said.

"Mary, is there anything you are particularly interested in or, more importantly, particularly wanting to avoid?" Donatella asked.

"I want something sleek, with long sleeves and maybe a dip in the back," Mary said.

"Of course, I would prefer something more like Princess Diana. The bell sleeves and the volume skirt and long train," Mary's mother said.

"How about we find both, and you can at least see the difference?" Donatella said, trying to give them both a chance to change to their minds.

Thus began three hours of trying on dresses and discussing the unique features and getting to the point of decision. Mary shifted her opinion and so did her mother and then ended up with a fitted top with lace long sleeves and an A-line skirt that fanned out some. Then they moved on to the bridesmaid dresses and that was harder because of the girls' different sizes and shapes. Finally, Aunt Alicia suggested that they have all the same color dresses, but have each girl in a more flattering style for her body type. Mary loved this idea. They left with the orders for everyone's dress, including Deb's, because Aunt Alicia knew just what she would like and would work for her.

After all the dress shopping, they went to lunch and talked about all the plans and parties and such for the wedding. It was a wonderful day, but Kim commented as they returned home that it was exhausting shopping that much. They were laughing as they entered the house and Uncle Darrick came to greet them, asking what was so funny. They shared the day's events with him and he commented he was glad all the men just needed to get fitted for tuxedos.

The next day, Kim spent the morning with Uncle Darrick and Aunt Alicia, again shopping, but this time it was for a birthday gift. This year, with Kim turning sixteen, they had decided they would let her pick out what she wanted. She decided on an extravagant trip to the art supply store. When they got home from all the shopping and dinner, Deb called to talk to Kim. They spent an hour on the phone and finally Deb asked if Kim was alone. When she said she was, Deb said, "I don't suppose you've heard anything from Ken, Joe or Ryan, have you?"

"No, they left two days ago. I don't suspect I'll hear from them for another day or so. Hopefully, it doesn't take them long to locate Tom and get this over with," Kim replied.

"After what happened on the last chase for Tom, with Ryan getting hurt, I'm really nervous about this. I hate being so far away," Deb said, in a frustrated tone of voice.

"I'm sure Ken is looking out for him. Plus, they had more supplies on this trip," Kim said.

"That's what I'm afraid of. It was bad enough when Tom was armed. Now they're all armed," Deb lamented.

"Well, not Becky," Kim said, trying to console her.

Just then, Uncle Darrick walked in and Kim said her goodbyes to Deb. She went to her room and organized all her art supplies.

The next day, Jake came over and they played board games because of the weather. As the afternoon started winding down, Jake asked about Ken and Joe. Kim told him she had heard nothing. Jake suggested she call Mr. Brewster, so they went to the office and she dialed his home number.

"Hello?" Mr. Brewster said.

"Hi, Mr. Brewster, it's Kim."

"Hi Kim, how was your birthday celebration?"

"It was really nice, thank you. I got all kinds of art supplies."

"I can't wait to see what you create next."

"Mr. Brewster, have you heard anything from Ken, Joe, Ryan, and Becky?"

"No, nothing new in the barn and no word, of course."

"Ok. Be sure to call me as soon you hear, ok?"

"Of course. Enjoy your summer."

"Bye Mr. Brewster."

"Goodbye Kim."

"So, nothing yet?" Jake asked.

"Nothing. I guess we can't do anything but wait. There're no phones where they're going," Kim said.

They went back to the board games until Uncle Darrick came home. Aunt Alicia would be out that evening, so Uncle Darrick suggested they go for pizza. The kids thought that was a great idea. The next day, Kim left with Uncle Darrick in the morning to meet her friends from school at the train station. They all left on the train to spend a week visiting one of the girls' grandparents in Boston.

All that week, Kim thought about Ken, Joe, Ryan and Becky. She called Mr. Brewster, but still no word. She called Jake, and he tried to calm her down. He said he would check in with Mr. Brewster the next day, as that was the travel day for Kim. Jake said he would meet her at the train station and take her home.

23

Ken crawled out of the tent, and Ryan followed a moment later. Ken sat down and nudged Joe awake. "You didn't get either of us up for our watch, Joe."

"Sorry, I was thinking a lot and thought you could use some sleep, and didn't expect to nod off," Joe responded as he stood up and stretched. "Man, I can't wait to sleep in a bed again!"

"When did you nod off?" Ryan asked after he had gone off in the woods to go to the bathroom and returned to put wood on the fire.

"Not sure, but it had to be after two in the morning," Joe said as he left to go to the bathroom.

"Tom seems to be sleeping," Ken said to Ryan as he finished putting wood on the fire.

Ryan went over to check on Tom and looked up suddenly at Ken, saying, "He's not sleeping. I think he's dead."

"What?" Ken asked, getting up to come to where Tom lay on the ground.

They both checked for his pulse and couldn't find one. Joe returned and asked what they were doing.

"Tom's dead, Joe," Ken said, looking up at Joe.

"Great. Let's make things a little more complicated," Joe said, sitting down at the fire and putting the soup Becky had made on the hanger over it.

"What happened last night?" Ryan asked.

"He was very feverish. I tried to get him to drink. He started talking in his sleep about how he was going to hurt me and all of you and about his father and Choate. It was terrible to listen to. He talked to me for a minute earlier in the evening and, of course, he wasn't happy to see me. But then he settled down, and that's when I started thinking. He said it would have been better if we never came to Choate. I was thinking about that, and what that would mean for all of us, and then I was trying to figure out how to keep Tom from releasing the information about the time travel and the machine. That's what he was talking about in his sleep," Joe explained.

"Well, we don't have to worry about him telling anyone about the machine now," Ryan commented.

Becky came out of her tent just then and asked, "Why don't we have to worry about Tom telling anyone about the machine?"

"He died last night at some point," Ken stated as calmly as possible.

"Oh, my gosh. Now what do we do?" Becky said, sitting down close to Joe.

Joe wrapped his arm around Becky, and they all sat in silence for a few minutes. Then Ken said, "Well, without a wagon or something, we can't take him to where the machines are. We can't carry that dead weight."

"This might seem like a really dumb question, but what do you think will happen when we put a dead person into the machine? Will he stay as he is right now, or will he decompose before our eyes?" Ryan asked.

"We don't change in the machine. Why would a dead person change that much?" Becky asked.

"I don't know. We never talked about it, never postulated over it or discussed it on any level. I don't think he'll decompose before our eyes by moving back to nineteen eighty-one, but he will decompose here pretty quickly," Joe answered.

"What do we do with him when we get back home, though?" Ryan asked.

"What do you mean?" Becky asked.

"I mean, if we bring him back to Mr. Brewster's barn, and he's decomposing, what do we do at that point?" Ryan continued.

"Well, we can't take him to any hospital. They'll want to know what happened to him. We don't have any explanation for the eighteen sixties wound he suffered or why we didn't take him to the hospital sooner," Ken said as he got up to dish out the soup.

As they ate, Joe said, "We can't just take him home to his parents, either. We have no better way to explain to them than we do to a hospital."

"This is terrible. If we leave him here, they will probably consider him an unknown soldier of this battle, and his parents will never know what happened to him," Becky said, putting her face down into her hands and starting to cry.

"Don't cry, Becky, we'll figure something out," Joe said as he rubbed her back and tried to get her to calm down.

"I'm sorry," she said after a few minutes, sitting up and looking around, "this is really getting to me. I guess I always figured there was a possibility that we would see Tom end in this way, but the implications are just too much."

"I know. If we leave him, his parents will never know, and he may lie here for days. If we try to take him, we have a whole lot of explaining to do. I don't know what the right answer is," Ken said, getting up and pacing around the clearing.

"We need to decide today. If we don't, he's going to decompose to the point we can't move him. I know this is terrible, but we have to all take the emotions we've been wrestling with and put them aside. We have to figure this out and then deal with what it means later," Ryan said.

"Ok, first, if we decide to take him with us, we have to figure out how to get a wagon or something. The battle should be over now. We might have a chance of scaring up a wagon at this point. If we aren't taking him back, we should probably get him nearer to the battleground so we can get him buried. That is the right thing to do," Ken succinctly stated the choices.

"How about if you and I go have a look around town and see what we can find?" Ryan said.

"Yes, Joe, you stay here with Becky and make sure she's ok. We'll go see what we can find," Ken said.

Ken and Ryan left the clearing, and Joe held Becky for a long time. She finally sat up and said, "We should probably move him out of the sun. Don't you think?"

"Ok, but we'll have to drag him back into the tent," Joe said as he stood up.

"What did he say to you last night?" Becky asked, "You seem strange today."

"He went on about how he wished we never came to Choate. Then he started talking in his sleep about how he was glad he cut Ryan and how we wished he could cut us all. He went on about how he was going to expose us and make our lives miserable. It all just shook me up. I started thinking about what would have happened to all of us if we hadn't come to Choate and what would happen to Ken and the business and everyone if he exposed the time travel," Joe explained as he went to Tom's head and picked him up by the shoulders, "you grab his feet to help move him. I'll hunch over and pull him inside the tent."

They dragged Tom into the tent. Becky asked what they would do when it was time to move him, and Joe said they would pull the tent down first. Then they went back to sit by the fire.

Meanwhile, Ken and Ryan walked the two miles into Gettysburg. It was so quiet they were worried and kept looking around to see if anyone was in any of the buildings and businesses lining the main street. No one was around. Every once in a while, they looked through some windows and saw no one. They tried the door to the general store, but it was locked. They went around the corner and there was an older man there. Ken said, "Excuse me, Sir. Might we have a word with you?"

"You aren't southerners, are you?" The man questioned.

"No, Sir. We're from up North. It seems like the fighting stopped and we were trying to find out what happened here. We were caring for several injured men and only today came out of hiding to see if we could find a wagon to move our wounded," Ken said.

"I have a wagon. Only one horse left, though," the man said.

"Would you be willing to sell them or loan them to us?" Ken asked.

"I can't see selling my last horse. How long will you need them?" the man asked.

"For most of the day today. We have one man who didn't make it through last night. We need to see about burying him. Then we'd need to move the others to where our unit has moved to so they can get with the doctors. We could have it back in a few hours," Ken said.

"The wagon's in the barn. The horse is in the stall. Come on, you can use them," the man said as he turned toward the barn that was behind the building. He brought out the horse from the stall and harnessed him up to the wagon. Ken pulled out all the money he had left and handed it to the man.

"I cannot take all of this. It is too much," the man protested as Ken tried to give him the money.

"Sir, we are truly in your debt. You must take it," Ken said, offering the money again.

The man took it and said, "You are going to return the wagon and horse, right?"

"Of course. You have helped us more than I can express gratitude for, so take the money and take care of your family and friends," Ken said as he climbed into the wagon.

They exited town slowly, looking around as they went. Ryan said, "It's so strange. It's like the whole town was in the fight."

"Yeah, the battle eventually spilled out into the town and everyone made a hasty retreat out. I'm sure they're still waiting to see what will happen today," Ken said.

They drove the wagon through the brush and got nearly to the clearing before the trees and growth prevented their advance. Ryan hopped down and tied the reins to a tree branch. They walked the rest of the way to the clearing.

"We got a wagon. Where's Tom?" Ken said as they entered the clearing.

"We moved him. He was lying in a sunny spot and we didn't want to speed up his decomposition. That will start soon," Joe said, standing up.

"That was probably a good idea," Ryan said, getting his canteen and drinking some water as he sat down. "So, did we decide? Are we taking him home with us or what?"

"I don't see how we can take him home. I hate it, but we will be all embroiled in so much mess if we take him. We can't explain what happened without exposing the time travel and we just can't do that. If nothing else, this has taught me at least that we can't let the time travel be public. It will make a total mess of history and the future. We can't even do something we think is helpful without changing history. We can't let this get out," Becky said as she came out of her tent with a new dress on.

"I agree. We can't take him home. It will cause issues with his parents, probably the police, not to mention all our parents and their businesses. Joe, it would impact your studies at MIT and as much as that sounds selfish of us all, Tom started this and we didn't shoot him. We tried to save him. I think we have to leave him here," Ken said, pacing around the fire.

"We can't just leave him in this clearing. We have to bury him," Joe said. "I know he hated us, me most of all, but we have to take him close to the battlefield where the burials are probably starting, and bury him," Joe said, putting his head down in his hands.

"Ok. I agree, let's bury him, but let's get going then and then make our way to the machines and get out of here," Ryan said.

"Yeah, we need a plan," Joe said.

They all sat down around the fire with this new focus on a plan and welcomed it from the overwhelming weight of the discussion about Tom.

"I think we should load everything up and take him in the wagon to a burial area around the battlefield. Then we can get everyone to the machines, and I can bring the wagon back and go back and get into the machine that's left and come home," Ken said.

"I don't like you traveling alone. If something happens, you'd be here alone," Joe said.

"I can go with Ken. We both saw the guy about the wagon this morning. We can return it together. Joe, you and Becky go in one machine and Ken and I can go in the other after we get the wagon returned," Ryan suggested.

"I like that idea," Becky added.

"I think I should go alone. I want everyone out of here as quickly as possible," Ken protested.

"Listen, Ken. Didn't we talk about this last night? Just let Ryan go with you," Becky said in what she hoped was an encouraging voice.

"Ok, ok. I just want this over with. I don't think I have any fight left at this point. Ryan stays with me. Let's get everything packed up," Ken said, standing.

They each went and packed up their things, and then Ken and Ryan began dismantling the tents. Joe and Becky took the bags to the wagon and came back to get the bedrolls and tents. Then Ryan and Ken spread out the fire and put dirt on it to put it out. They lifted Tom from the shoulders and feet and carried him to the wagon. Then Ken drove the wagon out of the woods and onto the road. It took them a few minutes to spot a group of men and women burying the soldiers that had died in the battle. They drove the wagon close and told an officer that was overseeing the process they had a man that had died that needed burying. The officer allowed them to move down the line of burials, in the direction that they would be given shovels, but they would have to bury him.

For the next hour, Ken, Joe and Ryan took turns digging a deep hole to put Tom in. Then they laid him out with the few belongings he had with him. They filled in the hole and Becky placed the white cross that a preacher had brought her into the ground at his head. A woman came over carrying a small bucket with paint on it. She asked the name of the soldier buried and then painted Tom's name on the cross. The four of them stood there for a few minutes in silence. Then Joe said, "Lord, we place this young man in your hands. May he be forgiven for the hatred he felt for me and my family, and may he rest in peace."

"That was nice, Joe," Becky said, taking his hand.

They walked back to the wagon, and all got in. Ken drove them out of the burial field and onto the road. No one said anything until they reached the area the machines were in hiding in the wooded area. As they got out of the wagon, Becky said, "It's been strange being here. There's so much open area. Woods and fields where no one had ever been, or had built anything."

"Yeah, it's strange. But I sure will be glad to get home and have a burger and sleep in a bed," Ryan said as he handed down some of the gear.

"I know I probably shouldn't feel this way, because Tom died, but I'm relieved this is over," Joe said as they walked into the brush toward the machines.

"I'm relieved too. I know this isn't the outcome we may have wanted, but honestly, would Tom have ever stopped trying to cause trouble? Maybe this is the only way this could have ended," Ken said as they arrived at the machines.

Joe went into the first machine and entered the information to get them back home. Then he went and set the same information into the other machine. While he did that, Ken and Ryan, and Becky loaded all the gear. When they were done, they stood there, looking at each other.

"Well, Joe, you and Becky get going. Ryan and I will be right behind you," Ken said as he touched Ryan's sleeve to turn to go.

"Be careful and get back here as quick as you can," Becky said.

With that, Joe and Becky got into one machine and Joe started it up. With a flash of light and wind stirring up the brush, one machine was gone. Ken and Ryan had already exited the wooded area and were climbing into the wagon when the light flashed. They rode back into town and found the man they had borrowed the wagon and horse from. They returned the equipment to the barn and thanked him.

"Joe seemed a little shaken up today," Ryan said as they walked out of town toward the other machine.

"Yeah. I think this might be the first time in his whole life he's had to encounter and deal with someone that really had evil intentions. And it was singularly focused on Joe. That's a new thing for him," Ken said reflectively.

"I'm not sorry he died. Is that terrible?" Ryan asked.

"No, I don't think it's terrible. I've been thinking the same thing all day. I really didn't think this could end well, no matter what we did. Either something like this was going to happen or we would have gone back and always been on edge about him trying something else or exposing the time travel. That wouldn't have been good. I'm not happy Tom died, but you know, he took the risks he did. His hatred for Joe and all of us made him make some poor decisions. I'm really glad no one else got hurt, like you did," Ken said, trying to reassure them both.

"I've also been thinking about what I did here. I mean, I interacted with all kinds of people here. This might sound strange, but I was wondering as we were digging the grave if maybe we had to be here. Does that sound weird? Would General Ewell have done what he did if I hadn't been here? If there was no interaction between Tom and Colton, would it have turned out as it was supposed to? If you think about the possibilities of this time travel, you really get going in circles," Ryan said.

"Remember when we went to Dallas, and you all went to Vegas? There were little footnotes in history books about what we did. I wonder if, like you said, we had to be here for things to turn out the way they were supposed to. What if all the time we were studying the Civil War, the footnote that didn't get to the books was what you did with Ewell and Colton and all that?" Ken pondered. Then he added, "I just wish it could have all happened without you getting knifed."

"Yeah, I can't wait until I have to show off this scar and try to explain how I got it," Ryan said, smiling.

"I think the thing to appreciate here is that it wasn't worse and you can always come up with some dramatic story to explain it," Ken said, smiling back at Ryan.

"You mean one more dramatic than a crazy guy charging at me with a knife when we tried to get his time machine back?" Ryan asked, trying to be serious, but ending up laughing.

"Yes, a different story than that one," Ken said when they finished laughing.

It took them nearly two hours to walk back to where the machine was. Once they got to the wooded area, Ryan looked both ways down the road to be sure no one was within eyesight. After being passed by several wagons and a family walking back toward town, they didn't want anyone to see them enter the woods and perhaps follow them and see the machine or their exit. With no one in sight, they darted into the woods and made their way to the machine. Ryan started things up and they strapped into the seats and, with the flash of lights, they were gone from Gettysburg.

24

Joe powered down the machine and opened the door. He saw the barn was dark, meaning no lights were on and Mr. Brewster was not in the barn. He climbed out and helped Becky out. She stretched and said, "I'm getting back into my regular clothes right now!"

Joe laughed as she went behind the partial wall and changed clothes. He said, "I'm going to go see if Mr. Brewster is home. I'll be right back."

Joe went to the door and knocked. Mr. Brewster came to the door and smiled when he saw Joe. "You're back!"

He opened the door for Joe, but Joe said, "I left Becky in the barn. Can we go back over there?"

"Sure, let's go," Mr. Brewster said as he exited the house. As they walked back, he asked, "Is everybody back?"

"No, Ken and Ryan are coming back soon in the other machine. We had to return a wagon and horse he borrowed earlier today," Joe said as they arrived at the barn.

They entered the barn and Becky jumped down from the stool she was sitting on and went to give Mr. Brewster a hug. He greeted her and said, "I guess we should sit down and wait for Ken and Ryan. Do either of you need something to eat?"

"I'm starved, but you don't need to feed us, Mr. Brewster," Joe said.

"It's no bother. How about we go make some sandwiches, Joe, you and I? Becky, if you want to stay here in case the others get back. Then you can tell me what happened when you're all together," Mr. Brewster said, as he turned to return to the house.

"Is that ok with you?" Joe said as he turned to Becky.

"Sure," she said, and she climbed back onto the stool.

They returned a short time later with a basket full of sandwiches and a bucket full of bottles of soda. They all got situated at the table and started eating. Mr. Brewster was eager to hear what had happened, but thought it best to wait. When they finished, he suggested Joe go and call Kim.

"Is she back home from her week away?" Joe asked.

"I believe so. She called this morning and said she was on Long Island with Jake and your uncle," Mr. Brewster explained.

"Is it ok if I go inside and use your phone?" Joe asked.

"Of course," Mr. Brewster said. "You don't have to ask, Joe."

"Maybe take your regular clothes with you and change, huh?" Becky asked.

Joe laughed and picked up the pile that was his clothing. He left to go call Kim. After he changed in the bathroom, he went to the kitchen. He dropped his rather dirty clothes from the traveling on the floor and called the house on Long Island.

"Hello?" Uncle Darrick said, answering the call.

"Hi, Uncle Darrick, it's Joe."

"Hi Joe, how are things at MIT?"

"They're great, but I'm ready for a break, I think. If we get finished today, I probably will come home tomorrow."

"Good. We've missed you, here. Kim especially."

"Yeah? Is she around? Can I talk to her?"

"Of course. Let me see if I can pry her away from Jake."

Joe waited a few minutes, and then he could hear Kim running. She picked up the receiver and said, "Joe, you're back. Is everyone back? Everyone ok?"

"Becky and I are here at Mr. Brewster's. Ken and Ryan should arrive soon in the other machine," Joe said.

"You didn't all come together? Oh, you got the other machine. Good. So, you stopped Tom?"

"It's a long story. We should be out there tomorrow. I can fill you in then. Is that ok?"

"I guess. It probably will be better then, anyway. I'm nervous that Uncle Darrick will catch on that we were back to time traveling if he hears me talking to you," she said a little breathlessly, "but I'm glad you called. Is everyone ok?"

"Yes. We're all fine. I will call later to let you know when to expect us, ok?"

"Yeah, sure. I can't wait to see you all!"

"Bye, Kim."

"Bye."

Joe returned to the barn. Just as he entered the barn, the wind blew, and the light flashed and the other machine appeared. Joe was relieved when both Ken and Ryan stepped out of the machine.

"Welcome home, you two!" Mr. Brewster said as he walked up to Ken and shook his hand.

"Thanks, Mr. Brewster. It's certainly good to be home!" Ken said, smiling.

"Is that food? I'm starving!" Ryan said, as he, too, shook Mr. Brewster's hand.

"Yes, it is. Sit down and eat," Mr. Brewster said as he went back to his seat.

"First, we need to make some calls, I think," Ken said.

"I called Kim. She knows we're back, and I told her that at least some of us would go to Long Island tomorrow," Joe said.

"Did you call Mary?" Ken asked.

"No, I figured you would want to do that," Joe answered.

"Mr. Brewster, may I use your phone?" Ken asked.

"Of course, you all know my home is your home. You don't need to ask," Mr. Brewster said.

"Thank you. I'm going to call her. I'll be right back," Ken said, turning to leave the barn.

"Hey, take your real clothes with you and change," Joe said. "As Becky has pointed out, we kind of have a smell about us!"

"Good idea," Ken said as he turned and retrieved his bag from the machine and headed out of the barn.

Ryan sat down and started to eat and drink and said, "I'll go in when Ken gets back and change, everybody."

"Should we wait until Ken returns for you to give me the details?" Mr. Brewster asked.

"I think Ken would appreciate us waiting, if that's ok with you?" Becky responded while the boys continued to eat.

"That's fine, we can wait," Mr. Brewster returned to his stool. "I can't believe we have both machines here."

"Hey, Mr. Brewster, where's the car you were working on?" Ryan asked as he realized that one machine was now occupying the space the car used to have.

"It's in town at the garage. I'm having it painted and new tires put on it," Mr. Brewster commented.

"Wow, so it's drivable now?" Becky asked.

"It is. It's a birthday gift for Kim," Mr. Brewster replied.

"Does she know?" Joe asked.

"She does, and more importantly, so do your aunt and uncle," Mr. Brewster answered.

A few minutes later, Ken returned. He sat and opened a soda bottle and drank it down. He set the bottle down and said, "So, I guess the important issue for us to discuss is what happened to Tom."

"What happened?" Mr. Brewster asked.

"Well. We were in Gettysburg; Ryan had ingratiated himself with General Ewell and stopped Tom from interfering in the battle's progression. While he did that, Joe and I located the machine that Tom stole and we moved it. We were gathering finally as the battle had really started and were finding a safe place to sit and figure out how to locate Tom when we came across him. He was crawling through the brush. A scouting party or something had shot him. The truth is we never really found out what happened to him. Anyway, we removed the bullet, or musket ball, or whatever it was, but it did a bunch of damage to Tom's insides. He got a terrible fever and well, there's no polite way to say this. He died yesterday," Ken explained.

"Oh, my goodness," Mr. Brewster said, "Are you all ok, though?"

"Yes, we're all fine," Joe reassured him.

"What have you done with Tom?" Mr. Brewster asked.

"Well, we talked about this for a few hours, and I'm pretty sure we all thought about it all day. We weren't sure how much the time travel back here would impact his decomposition, plus we didn't know how to explain everything to his parents, or anyone else, so we buried him there," Joe said.

"Do you think we did the right thing, Mr. Brewster?" Becky asked, anxiously.

"You're correct, there would be no way to explain this if you brought back a dead body. How could you explain his injuries to the authorities and if you had brought him, you would have to take him to some authority? That would be the only way they could issue a death certificate and you need that in this time to bury a person. Then they would discover the injuries and likely surmise the antique weaponry and yes, then the questions would start. So, I suppose it was the right thing to do," Mr. Brewster thought through the issues, just as they had earlier today.

"The thing that I'm still having issues with is that his parents will never know what happened to him. There's no way to explain this to his parents. They would likely not believe us anyway," Becky said tearfully.

"It's a shame you couldn't get Tom to see the error of his ways. Then you could have all just come back here," Mr. Brewster thought out loud.

"He never would have seen the error of his ways. I don't think, anyway. He was delirious last night from the fever and he talked about his hatred of me and how he was happy he hurt Ryan and he would hurt us all worse once he got back here. He was so obsessed with his hatred, he didn't see anything he was doing as wrong on any level," Joe said.

"Well, that's certainly a shame," Mr. Brewster said, looking around at all of them. "you four shouldn't feel guilty about what happened. He made choices to do the things he did, and the consequences are his alone."

"I know this will sound insensitive of me, but I don't care. Tom put us through a few weeks of agony. We had to be careful about what we were doing and what he was doing. His ignorance of all the lessons we have learned from time traveling made this much harder. Besides, he was bent on causing us harm. Plus, we again had to make up stories about what we were up to and lie to people that are important to us. I for one, am not overly sorry he got caught in a battle he didn't fully understand. And, I'm really ready for all of us to get back to our lives," Ken said vehemently.

"I agree. I'm having a hard time feeling sorry for Tom," Ryan added.

"Not to change the subject, but what did Mary have to say?" Becky asked.

"She said she was going to head out to Long Island as soon as church was over tomorrow morning to meet us there. She's glad we are all back safe and beyond that, I didn't explain much about what happened," Ken said.

"Where did you bury him?" Mr. Brewster asked.

"We took him back to where the soldiers and townspeople were burying the dead from the battle and we buried him there," Joe answered.

"I wonder if that marker is still there?" Becky asked no one in particular.

"Maybe at some point we could go there and look," Joe said, as he reached out to hold Becky's hand.

"So, what's next for you four?" Mr. Brewster asked.

"A shower, a good meal and then some decent sleep, I'm thinking," Ken said.

"I meant for the two machines here," Mr. Brewster said, smiling at Ken's answer.

"Can the barn be locked, Mr. Brewster? I think we need to protect them for a short period of time, while we figure that out. But I'm thinking we should dismantle both of them," Joe offered.

"Yes, I can lock the barn," Mr. Brewster responded, "but are you sure you want to dismantle both machines?"

"After all the trouble they have caused, I'm thinking it's the right thing," Joe said, looking directly at Ken.

"I think it should end as it started. We should all decide together," Ken answered directly back to Joe.

"I think that's a good idea, Ken," Ryan agreed.

"Let's clean up then," Becky said, climbing down from the stool.

They all got up and started cleaning up. Joe and Ryan and Ken emptied the machines of all the gear and bags. They stored the gear on the shelves behind the table and then Joe powered down everything. While that was going on, Becky helped Mr. Brewster gather and carry inside all the leftover sandwiches and soda and all the garbage they created.

As they gathered near the cars, Mr. Brewster smiled, but was a little sad that they were leaving as he said, "You keep in touch, all of you."

"I will call you soon, Mr. Brewster," Joe said as he hugged him.

The rest of them said their goodbyes, and Ken said they should stay in town tonight. They went to the hotel and Ken got three rooms. After they had showered and cleaned up, they went to a pizza place and ate. While they ate, they talked about what everyone was going to do to resume their summer plans and if anyone had got Kim a birthday gift. It was a lighthearted conversation, but they were all still a little saddened by what had happened and when they were done eating, everyone said they just wanted to sleep.

Ken struggled to sleep. What had happened weighed heavily on his mind. Mr. Brewster had agreed they had done the only thing they could have done under the circumstances, but man, it was a hard thing to contemplate. They had buried someone they went to school with in the nineteen seventies in a field outside of Gettysburg, in the eighteen sixties. The idea blew his mind. While Ken was pondering this, Joe was also having trouble sleeping. He faced away from Ken's bed in the room they shared, but he couldn't sleep either. He was back to contemplating the core of the problem, having the ability to travel through time. If they hadn't found that formula, if they hadn't built the machine, or gone anywhere, none of what had happened in the last nine days would have happened. This was the circular argument with time travel. Their ability to time travel was like a ripple in a lake that hadn't stopped yet. Joe knew it was time to put an end to the trouble the machines had caused, even while he understood he couldn't do that alone, that everyone had to have a hand in what happened next. They had started this together; they needed to end it together.

Both Ken and Joe were up with the sun the next morning. Ken came out of the bathroom to find Joe sitting up in his bed. He said, "Didn't sleep?"

"Not really. You?" Joe said.

"Not really. I don't know what it is about this time we went time traveling. Well, yes, I know what it is. We buried Tom in the past. But I find myself right back at the beginning when we were first considering this. All the reasons I questioned it seemed to have come true," Ken tried to explain all he had been mulling over.

"Yeah. I know what you mean. I think we really need a big pow wow to sort this out," Joe said as he stood up.

"I agree," Ken said as he went to his bag and started putting his things in it. "I'd really like a change of clothes, too!"

"You don't like the half Gettysburg, half nineteen eighty-one look?" Joe asked as he turned around wearing his jeans and a shirt. He thought was the cleanest of the costumes they took along with them.

"Oh, yeah, sure!" Ken said.

Ken and Joe went downstairs and found Ryan and Becky waiting for them. They were also dressed in a bit of hodge podge of clothing. They all laughed when Ken and Joe walked up. Ken went and checked them out of the hotel and they left. Joe took Becky home and then went to his apartment near MIT to grab some things. Then he began the journey to Long Island. Ken took Ryan to his parent's place in New York city, then he too went to the apartment to grab some clothes. He stopped at the office to get some things, then he left for Long Island.

Joe pulled up in front of the house and hopped out of the car. He ran up the steps and opened the door. It was so good to be home, he thought, in a moment before he heard Kim yelling from the back of the house, "Joe, Ken, is that you?"

Joe waited until she reached the foyer before he broke into a big smile and said, "Only me, for now. Ken took Ryan home and stopped at the city apartment, but he's probably right behind me."

Kim ran to him and wrapped her arms around him. Then she whispered, "Wait till he gets here then. It's so good to have you back here."

"That's probably a good idea," Joe said, as she let go of him.

"You really ought to change your clothes. This mix of costume and regular is a little weird and Uncle Darrick will probably ask questions," Kim said as she looked at him more closely.

"Yeah, I brought clothes," Joe said, as he bent down to pick up his bag, "I'll go up and unpack this and get changed."

"Oh, hey, Deb's on her way home!" Kim said.

"She is? I thought she didn't come back until next week?" Joe asked, turning on the stairs.

"She was, but they got done early cause they didn't find what they were looking for, so she gets to come home," Kim said.

"Ryan will be happy. When does she arrive?" Joe asked.

"Tonight. Uncle Darrick is going to the airport to get her and then bringing her here," Kim said. "I left a message for Ryan at his parent's house. He should know now. Uncle Darrick said to invite him out here. Jake's coming back tonight too."

"Good. We all need to talk," Joe said, as he turned back and went up the stairs.

Just then, the door opened again, and Ken and Ryan walked in. Kim smiled and jumped at Ken, but looked at Ryan as she said, "I guess you got my message?"

"I did. Managed to get Ken before he headed out here and hitched a ride," Ryan said, smiling at the reunion going on in front of him.

"I'm glad you're back," Kim said to Ken.

"I'm glad too," Ken said, putting her down.

"Are you hungry?" Kim asked.

"Definitely!" Ryan answered.

The three of them went into the kitchen and found some leftover fried chicken. Joe came down while they were eating and helped them finish the fried chicken and a bag of chips. The doorbell rang and Kim turned, but Ken put a hand on her arm as he stood and said, "That will be Mary. I invited her out too."

Ken left to get the door. The rest of them cleaned up and went out on the back terrace. Ken opened the door, and Mary smiled up at him. He reached for her and pulled her inside. He held her for a long time. Finally, muffled against his chest, she said, "Are you ok?"

"Yeah, it's been a long ten days and I'm really glad to see you," Ken said as he let her go finally.

"I missed you too. And it's not been ten days here, remember? But that's not what I mean," Mary said, taking his hand and walking back toward the kitchen.

When they realized the rest of the group was not in the kitchen anymore, they turned and heard Kim laughing about something and they walked toward the terrace. Mary pulled him up to a stop just before they walked out and reached for his other hand, and looked up expectantly.

"It was just hard. Tom died. I know you'll have all kinds of questions, but so does Kim and so will Deb and we should wait until everyone is together," Ken tried to explain the big issue for him, but warn her off of some more questions.

"Ok, I have lots of questions, but I'll hold my questions until we're all together," Mary said, as she turned toward the doors to the terrace.

They walked outside, and Mary greeted everyone. They all talked about remaining summer plans and watched the sun start to fade. As the conversations dwindled out, the phone rang. Kim jumped up and ran inside to answer it. She returned a few minutes later and announced, "That was Uncle Darrick. He said he was leaving to go get Deb from the airport. I told him Ryan was here already, and he said that would be a nice surprise for Deb that he's also home early. He didn't expect they would be back here until after seven, and he suggested that we all go ahead and eat."

"What about Aunt Alicia?" Joe asked.

"Uncle Darrick said that she was staying in town tonight to go to some fashion party," Kim relayed.

"When are we going out for your birthday, then?" Ken asked.

"Tomorrow. Hopefully, you can all stay," Kim said.

"Of course, we can," Mary said. "I brought clothes for the entire weekend. I was hoping we could hang at the beach tomorrow!"

"Is Jake staying too?" Ken asked.

"Yeah, he's supposed to be here any minute. Can we wait to deal with dinner plans until he arrives?" Kim asked.

Ken was about to say sure when the doorbell rang again. Kim again rose and ran for the house. She returned ten or fifteen minutes later with Jake.

"Hi everybody!" Jake said, looking around.

"Hi back. Hey, the door isn't that far from this terrace. What took you two so long?" Joe asked, smiling at Kim.

"Nothing!" Kim responded as she took Jake's hand.

Jake looked down at the floor and blushed. Joe laughed and Ken turned from Mary and said, "Now, Jake, I know we were busy this summer with Tom's nonsense, but maybe you and I should have a little talk."

"Leave him alone!" Mary said as she fake punched him in the arm.

"Sorry, Jake, I didn't mean to start something with Ken, but Kim here. She teased me something awful when I started dating Becky, so I figured I owed it to her. I don't owe it to you though," Joe said, walking over to Ken, "I'll calm Ken down by saying that Kim here has really counted on Jake to help her the last few weeks while we were busy, and that should count for something, right Ken?"

Ken nodded in agreement and stood, holding out his hand to Jake. Jake smiled and shook Ken's hand. Everyone laughed a bit, then Joe asked what they were doing for dinner. They decided they would walk into town and go to the Italian place that had opened that spring. As they walked away from the house, Mary asked Joe if Becky was coming out, and he said her parents were dropping her off on their way to see friends down in Martha's Vineyard tomorrow morning.

They ate and laughed and had a lot of fun, sometimes getting a little loud in the restaurant before Mary or Ken settled them back down. When they were done eating, they prepared to go, but then Mary suggested they bring back some food for Deb and their uncle. Ken ordered some to-go food and he and Mary and Ryan waited for it while Joe, Jake and Kim went and got ice cream. They ambled back to the house and when they got up the driveway; they saw Uncle Darrick's car parked in front of the house. Kim ran up the drive and got to the car just as Deb came out to get the rest of her things from the trunk. Kim screamed and ran up the stairs and wrapped her arms around Deb, who was now laughing at her sprint up the stairs. They hugged and whispered to each other for a few minutes while the rest of the group walked the rest of the way up the driveway.

"Well, you found a really great tan, anyway," Ken said as he hugged Deb. Then he turned to uncle Darrick, who had heard the commotion, and came out the front door. "Hi, Darrick. Thanks for all the taxi driving to get our Deb back here!"

"That's what I do. I taxi you all everywhere! It's all about to be over, so I guess I should enjoy it," he replied, then he added, "Where were you all?"

"We went to get some dinner. We brought you something too!" Kim said.

"Thank goodness, I'm starved!" Deb said, turning from greeting Mary and Joe. "What did you bring?"

"Me!" Ryan said as he walked up.

"We brought pasta!" Joe said.

Deb walked down the stairs and wrapped her arms around Ryan's neck. He smiled and gave her a kiss, but didn't let her go for several minutes.

They carried the rest of Deb's things inside and then Mary directed Kim and Jake to carry the bags upstairs while she got Deb and Uncle Darrick situated with food. They ate on the terrace, so they all went out and sat while the late arrivals ate some dinner. When they finished, Uncle Darrick got up and collected the plates, as he said, "Thanks for the food, you guys."

"I can help with these," Deb protested his taking all the dishes, but he said, no, he would do it.

Then he added, "You kids all look like you're not ready, but I'm beat and I'm headed up to bed."

"When is Aunt Alicia coming home?" Kim asked.

"She is staying in town tonight and will be out tomorrow. We have a bit of a surprise for tomorrow night. Something about a birthday?" Uncle Darrick said, laughing.

"You know I've had to wait and wait for everyone to be here. Don't tease me, Uncle Darrick!" Kim said with a pouty face.

"I know. Getting this bigger and bigger family together is harder and harder each year. With the businessman, computer wiz, archeologist, and all the rest of you going in a million directions, it's hard to plan," Uncle Darrick said, more seriously.

"What about artist? You forgot artist!" Kim said, stamping her foot.

"I didn't forget. I have the announcement of the show in August hanging by my desk. You are remarkable too. I didn't include you in the list, as it's your birthday," Uncle Darrick, knowing how sensitive Kim was to her younger status, said to soothe her.

"Kim, you are the best of all of us," Ken said, wrapping his arm around her shoulder, "you know that. We've told you that for years."

Kim smiled at that, as Uncle Darrick said goodnight and left with their dishes. Then Jake asked, "What is the plan for tonight?"

"I've brought you all things. Can I go get them and bring them down?" Deb asked.

"That sounds great. Then you can regale us with tales of your latest digging adventures," Ken said, "unless Ryan here doesn't want to share you tonight?"

"I knew that coming out here meant I would have to share her tonight. I'm ok with this. I can always steal her away tomorrow for a bit before the big birthday celebration," Ryan conceded. "How about if I help you bring your horde of gifts down?"

Ryan and Deb went into the house and the rest of them decided they would go into the family room. Deb handed out the gifts to everyone. Mary got a beautiful scarf that Deb found in a little market, Ken got a chessboard made of stones from the region, Joe got an intricate abacus that was created in the middle east as the first calculator for his desk. Kim got a fancy robe, Jake got a small statue of an ancient man holding a spear, which she said was the meaning of the name Jacob, the supplicant. She looked at Ryan and then said, "I got you this."

Deb handed Ryan a small bag with a drawstring. He opened it and turned it over. In his hand was a chain with an oval cylinder on it. On one side of the cylinder were Hebrew letters. He looked up at Deb and she said, "It's Hebrew for love. It opens up."

Deb showed Ryan where the lock was, and he opened it. Inside, on one side, was a picture of Deb standing in the desert. Ryan looked up and smiled at her. He leaned over and gave her a kiss, then said, "Thank you."

"I got something for Becky and Aunt Alicia and Uncle Darrick, but I left them upstairs," Deb said as she looked around.

"Thank you, Deb. These gifts are so thoughtful. Something meaningful for everyone," Kim said, giving Deb a little hug.

"Ok, enough of this mushy stuff. Tell us about the dig," Ken said.

Deb launched into telling them about the new dig site. How it was in caves near valleys outside of Jerusalem. She described the desert and how you could stand on a rise and look out over miles and miles of desert. How even in the dry, arid climate there was life and plants and beauty. Then she described the dig and how they painstakingly brushed away thousands of years of dirt and dust to find evidence of life and where the Hebrew people hid and went when the Romans came to take Jerusalem. Everyone asked all kinds of questions. Joe asked if there were scorpions and snakes and bugs. Kim asked about the people Deb met. Jake asked how they decided on where to dig and who else was there. Deb answered each round of questions, yes there were scorpions and the snakes were asps that were very dangerous. Deb described the local people and how friendly they were. How she and her bunk mate were invited into someone's home for a dinner. They dug in an area that was suspected by years of study of old documents to be where some of the rebel Jews had gone to regroup, but when Ken asked what they found, Deb said they had not found much of anything. They determined they had miscalculated the cave location. The professor was planning to spend the rest of the summer poring over more documents and in more musty libraries to find more information.

"So, does that mean you start again when he figures out a new location to dig?" Kim asked.

"Well, he wants to. What I have found is that although interesting, I don't really want to spend all my time digging in the dirt. I've found that I really like the document digging much better. I don't know, that's how I feel now anyway," Deb explained.

"I bet you're glad she doesn't like the dirt, huh, Ryan?" Joe said, nudging Ryan in the arm.

"Well, if I'm honest, I'd rather not have her halfway around the world all the time," Ryan said, pulling Deb over toward him.

"Wow, will you look at the time?" Ken said, standing up.

"It is getting kind of late, and I'm exhausted from the travel," Deb said. "I think I'm heading up."

They all got up at that point and agreed that sleep was a good idea. Soon, all the upstairs doors were closed and everyone was settling in for the night.

25

Kim was the first one up the next morning, followed by Uncle Darrick. As he entered the kitchen, he found Kim busy cooking.

"What are you up to?" Uncle Darrick asked her, smiling.

"I'm making breakfast. I thought everyone would be starving, and I was up, so I decided why not," she answered as she bent over in front of the oven and pulled out a muffin tray with blueberry muffins, just finishing up.

"Wow, those smell delicious. Is there anything I can do to help?" he asked.

"Maybe you could set the table and then go do the honors and wake everyone up. The eggs are done, the sausage is done, and now the muffins are done," she announced as she pulled the muffins out and put them in a basket and then covered them with a clean dishtowel.

Uncle Darrick took the stack of plates and silverware off the counter and went into the dining room and set the table. Then he headed up the stairs and began knocking on doors to tell everyone that Kim had made breakfast.

Joe and Ken came down pretty quick. The rest of them trickled down to the table and sat. Kim smiled at everyone and said good morning, and then Joe pulled the covers off the food. It was pretty quiet in the dining room for a bit as everyone ate. As they were finishing up, Uncle Darrick said, "I better get going. I'm heading into town to get your aunt."

"When will you be back, do you think?" Deb asked as she began gathering up the dishes that held what they left of the food.

"We should be back around two or three this afternoon. I guess we have a party to prepare for?" he asked, reaching down to hug Kim as she sat in her chair.

Kim smiled up at him, while the others made a show of how they didn't have any idea whose birthday it was. They all laughed and Uncle Darrick left to go get their aunt. The rest of them cleared the table and stored the left-over muffins and washed the dishes. When they had finished, Kim said, "Does everybody want to go to the beach today?"

"I certainly do!" Mary said.

Just then, the doorbell rang. Kim ran and came back with Becky. Her parents had dropped her off. Becky hugged Deb and then hugged Joe, while he pouted and said he felt he didn't rate. She just smiled at him. Then Kim reminded them about the beach and they all went up to get in swimsuits. Deb and Ryan were back in the kitchen when the rest of them trickled down, making sandwiches and packing a cooler with drinks.

"Do you have towels and things yet?" Ken asked as he and Mary came into the kitchen.

"No, not yet," Deb answered.

Ken and Mary went and gathered up towels, two big beach umbrellas, some toys and a kite. They loaded it all up into two beach bags. Then they packed some pretzels and cookies into a bag and the rest into the cooler. Everyone was ready and then carried all their supplies down to the beach. After they set everything up, Jake and Kim headed for the water, and Ryan took Deb's hand and suggested a walk. Joe laid down on a towel and said he was still very beat. Becky agreed with him and said this trip was the most exhausting one they had ever done.

"Well, you were gone for a long time," Mary suggested as she put sunscreen on Ken's shoulders.

"Actually, when we were in Philadelphia, were gone for a longer amount of time. This one was grueling because we hopped all over and what happened in the end," Joe explained.

"I think we should wait until we're all sitting here. That way, we don't have to do this more than once. How about we throw the frisbee or try to fly that kite you got, Joe?" Ken suggested.

Becky and Mary let them go off with the kite and they both laid down. Becky, with her eyes still closed to the sun, asked Mary how her wedding plans were coming. Mary explained what was going on with the dresses, which Becky was going to need to get to the dress shop to pick her style out, and then the other decisions that had been made in terms of the church, the reception and all the pieces of the wedding plan. Becky assured her she would get to the dress shop this next week and said she would be sure to bring Deb with her. Then they heard Kim squeal. They both sat up and shielded their eyes to see what was going on. Kim was fine. She was just excited about the kite that Joe had made with his MIT friends that he and Ken had just got launched into the air. After Joe got the kite really high up there, he brought the string over to the blankets and umbrellas and tied the kite to one of the umbrella poles. They all went swimming for a short time and then came back to dry off for lunch.

Ryan and Deb had walked about a half a mile from where the others were set up when he turned and put his arms around her. He held her for a long time without saying anything, then he whispered in her ear, "I missed you so much! I can't tell you how hard these past two weeks have been without you."

"I'm so sorry. I thought about you every single minute I was digging and dusting things off, and every night while I lay in my cot in a hot room. It's all I did," she whispered back.

"I don't want to stop you from doing what you want, but I hate it when you're gone, even when we aren't chasing a maniac through time," he said as he pulled out of the hug so he could look at her face.

"I learned on this trip that I don't want to be gone like that anymore, either. I talked a long time to a professor from NYU. She was there, providing the research that Professor Reinhardt needed. Anyway, she does her archeology in libraries and with old manuscripts and papyrus and church records and things. It was so interesting and I really thought the research side was really more my thing," she tried to explain what she had been thinking about for the whole time she had been gone.

"You aren't just finding a way to be happy without the dirt, are you?" he asked, worried that he was swaying her decision.

"No, it's not that. Here's the truth," she said, looking down at her feet in the sand, "I don't really like digging in the dirt."

Ryan laughed out loud. She kept looking at the sand, and he put his finger under her chin and pulled her face up to look at him, as he said, "I'm sorry. I didn't mean to laugh at you. I'm just really glad there is a chance you'll be on this continent from now on."

She smiled back at him. He leaned down and kissed her. They turned then and started walking back to where the others were playing in the water. As they walked, Ryan asked, "Does this mean you have to change your major or do anything different at school?"

"No, I'm in pretty good shape to shift the focus of my specialization. I think I can do it. I plan to talk to my advisor next week and make sure, but I think it'll be ok," she answered as they sat in the sand.

After a few minutes, she looked over at Ryan and put her hand on his shoulder. "Are you ok? You seem sort of off somewhere."

"I know we're supposed to wait until we're all together and ready, but man, I can't keep anything from you. This trip was really hard."

"Do you want to tell me?"

"Tom died."

"Oh, my gosh. What happened?"

"We don't know for sure. Ken and Joe found the machine he stole and moved it. We think he was trying to make his way to that machine when he was shot by some scouting party or the beginnings of the Gettysburg battle."

"You found him dead?"

"No, he was alive when we found him. He died during the second night when we were trying to keep him alive and get better enough to get him to the machines."

"I can't believe it. I mean, I think we all thought something like this might happen on these trips, but I still can't believe it. Where is his body?"

"We buried him in the beginnings of a burial area of the battle."

"Oh Ryan. I'm so sorry. I wish I had been with you."

"No, I'm glad you weren't there. It really wasn't safe. We were in the middle of the largest battle in US history."

"But it's really affected you."

"Yeah. Well, it's a lot of things. The risks we took by traveling to these wars. That Tom was so bent on hurting all of us. That we buried a guy from the nineteen eighties in a field of Gettysburg soldiers. All of it. It just feels weird."

"What can I do?"

Ryan looked over at her, and he wrapped his arms around her. "Just having you with me is enough." They sat like that for a few more minutes and then Deb looked down the beach and everyone was back on their blankets. She suggested they head back and Ryan stood, pulling her up. They walked back and sat on the blankets.

"Who's hungry?" Joe asked as they sat down.

"Are you always hungry?" Becky asked him, as she went to open the cooler.

"He's still a growing boy," Ken said, laughing at his brother's appetite.

"I'm not a boy anymore!" Joe pouted.

"No, probably not, but you are still filling out, Joe," Mary added, trying to soften the blow.

"You have grown some," Deb added. "Who knows? You might get bigger than Ken."

"Not likely!" Ken said, shoving Joe down on the blanket and wrestling a bit.

"Stop it, you two. We're getting the food out," Becky admonished them, but laughing.

Becky and Deb passed around the sandwiches, and Mary, and Ken passed around drinks and chips. They all ate and talked about how nice the day was, the kite building, and the water. They laughed and enjoyed this growing group of close friends. As they finished up and Mary was collecting trash and things, Ken finally said, "Well, we're all together. It's probably time to go over what's happened."

They all situated themselves in a circle on the blankets and expectantly looked around at each other. Kim was the first to speak up, saying, "How about Ken? You give us the timeline. I'm sure everyone has something to add, but at least start there."

Ken began. He explained the trip to Baltimore, where they were, how they stopped Tom from changing the course of the war of eighteen twelve. Then he talked about helping the sniper that killed the British general coming ashore after they couldn't bombard the fort enough and they attempted to make land and circle around the back of the fort. Still going, he explained how Tom tried to stop the sniper, but he and Ryan had made camp there to watch for and stop Tom. He told them how Tom got away in the fray of the shots and soldiers. That, of course, led to their having to go to Gettysburg. Ken explained how they changed things by shifting their focus to getting in front of Tom. They did that by inserting Ryan into the troops Tom was going to target. He talked about how Becky had done such excellent research that they knew exactly where to find the general Tom was going to target. This general, who misinterpreted a note from Lee and delayed his troops, was instrumental for the Union army to flank and take the confederate army. Then he got to the harder part. He talked of them finding Tom's machine while Ryan was busy, and about how Joe and he moved it. Then, when they were sure they had kept Tom from disrupting history, they started searching around for him, figuring he would make his way back to the machine he had stolen and getting out of there. That was when they found him injured. Ken detailed Becky's efforts to nurse Tom. How they had removed the bullet that had wounded him, but then he got a fever. He likely had an infection from the wound, and they tried to flush it. Then he stopped talking. He looked at Joe.

"My turn, I guess?" Joe asked.

"I think so, since you were with him that last night," Ken offered.

"Well, he was delirious for most of the night. Although, he was awake some, but it's hard to know if what he was saying was something he really meant or not. He talked about how much he hated me. Surprisingly, he even refused water when I offered it out of hatred. He then rambled on about how he hated all of us. I'm sure you all got lumped in out of association with me. Anyway, it started with my taking over his best friend at Choate, but then it grew. Grew as we all did things and as he watched us being so happy and so close. He didn't have any brothers or sisters and apparently that was our fault as well," Joe haltingly explained.

"It's hard to imagine someone so angry at you Joe, you wouldn't hurt a flea," Kim said, reaching for his hand.

"I think he must have been so blinded by that hate that he couldn't think straight," Becky added.

"Did he say anything else, Joe?" Deb asked.

"He did. Tom went on about how he had hoped to make himself rich and famous by changing his family's fate with the money and his great-grandfather, but we had interfered. He said he wished we'd never come to Choate, and he was going to go back in his machine and do everything he could to stop us. Then he rattled off who and what he was going to do," Joe said forlornly.

"Who was he going after, Joe?" Jake asked.

"All of us. He wanted to mess up Ken in the business and stop his wedding to Mary and he wanted to hurt Ryan and make Deb cry and he was going to slash all of Kim's artwork and mess up the show he knew was coming this fall. It was hard to listen to. But it also made me think a lot that night," Joe went on, "It made me think about what would have happened if we hadn't come to Choate, if we hadn't found the formula and built the machine and if we had met none of you."

Joe looked around at those that were now a big part of who he considered his family. Even Jake was now clearly a part of it. They all sat quietly, each with their own thoughts, until Deb spoke up, "Listen, we can go over what Tom had to say and think about the 'what-if' for all time but that doesn't change the primary issue here. We went to Choate, we found the formula, we built a time machine. I know when this started it was all about trying to change the path of our parents' lives to stop that accident, but I think we need to recognize that we have what we have today, this," she waved her arms around indicating all of them and where they were, "because of what happened to our parents. I, for one, am so very glad that we're sitting here today, together. And nothing that some angry person says or does should change this."

"I don't want to change what we have now. I'm sad still that we couldn't have all this and have our parents, but the thought that night that we might not have met Mary, Ryan, Becky and Jake, or the fact that we wouldn't be planning a family wedding or going to art shows or digging in the middle east makes me really sick to my stomach. My conclusion, sitting by the fire as Tom died, was that it had to be this way. We can't have all this and not have the summer we chased Tom through time," Joe concluded his thoughts.

"Well said," Mary smiled at Joe.

"Anyone else?" Ken asked.

"I'm still really mad at Tom," Becky whispered.

They all quieted down and looked at Becky, waiting for her to continue.

"I mean, he made us lose all this time together this summer. It makes me mad. It makes me mad that Ryan now carries a horrible scar from Tom attacking him, and we all missed Kim's birthday, and Ken wasn't around to help with wedding plans. It just makes me mad. But I'm also very confused about leaving him there."

"What do you mean?" Kim asked.

"Well, we weren't sure what to do that morning. He was dead from injuries we didn't cause, but in fact were caused by Tom's own actions and poor decisions all the way back to when he found the machine and stole it. But he died. And we had to decide whether to bring him back here or leave him there." Becky tried hard to express what she had been thinking since that morning.

"Could you have brought him back? I mean, what would happen if you time traveled forward with a guy that had died in the past?" Jake asked.

"That question came up that morning," Joe said, smiling at Jake, "but we reasoned through the logic of it and decided that nothing really would happen to Tom's body if we brought him back. We travel and do not age at all, well so far, anyway, so there was no reason to expect Tom to suddenly disintegrate before our eyes or something."

"But the questions that would be asked when you got him back here. I mean, how would you explain his injuries and he would decompose wouldn't he, during the time you got him to the machine and once you got him back here and were transporting him to his parents or whatever?" Mary thought out loud.

"That was the big thing for us, too. We didn't know how to address the questions. You can't simply show up at an emergency room with a dead person and expect the hospital to not ask questions. I don't even know if they would issue a death certificate in that situation. We also thought about bringing him to parent's house, but yes, the travel and all that would start his decomposition, and, again, how would we explain it to his parents," Ken explained.

"So where is he?" Deb asked, even though she already knew this answer from what Ryan told her.

"We buried him in the area that the other dead from the battle were being buried," Joe said solemnly.

"Do you think there's still a marker for him?" Kim asked.

"Possibly. I know that at some point, all the burials from the battle of Gettysburg were formerly marked with whatever information was on the stones or wood markers from the time period," Deb said.

"I wonder what his mother is going to think?" Becky asked out loud, her biggest fear.

"What do you mean?" Jake asked. "How does she know what happened?"

"She doesn't know. That's the issue. She'll never know what happened to her son. It will be like he disappeared one day and she'll never see him again," Becky said, crying.

"We can't tell her. As much as you'd like to tell her, that would start a flurry of investigation. I mean, I'm sure she'd think we were nuts and call the police," Deb said, reaching out to hold Becky's other hand.

"I know, it's just that for all we've done when we time traveled and all we had to contemplate, this just wasn't one of the things. Maybe it should have been. Maybe if we considered the possibility that someone from our time would die in the past, we would have done everything differently," Becky said.

"I thought a lot about how close we've come to disasters in the past, since we got back," Ryan said, "like when Joe went back to talk to his father, what if he had gotten closer to his other self? That would have been a disaster. And when Deb and I went to stop him and we all got hurt, Deb most of all."

"What about when Joe was in jail? That could have ended badly too," Kim said.

"We probably should have considered all this, way back when the talk first started about going back to save your parents, but we didn't. Fortunately, no one got hurt worse," Mary added.

"Not that I think anyone deserves what happened to Tom, but the fact of the matter is that he was driven by this hatred and he actively was looking for ways to hurt all of us. None of this would have happened if he would have just left the machine alone. Let's keep that in mind," Ken said, trying to stop them from feeling sorry for Tom.

"That's right, he stole and sought trouble," Joe came around.

"But he had no idea what he was getting into. I mean, he didn't think any of it through. Time travel is a big deal, and he didn't even think through what money he could spend where," Deb said, remembering the trip earlier.

"True, he messed with science and logic with little thought, but that's what evil does. It rushes headlong toward destruction," Mary added.

"And hatred is evil," Jake put his two cents in.

"Ok, enough dwelling on what happened to Tom. It's his fault we had to go through all this. I think there are some other big questions we have to answer here." Joe tried to steer the conversation toward his current thoughts.

"What do you mean, Joe?" Kim asked.

"Well, we just presumed the machine was safe in Mr. Brewster's barn, but that clearly is not the case. And now we have two machines there. I've been thinking, especially since things went so bad this summer, that we should take them both apart," Joe put his plan out there.

"Forever?" Kim asked.

"Why not? Haven't we learned how bad time travel can be?" Joe asked her.

"Well, we did also help people, remember? We helped Mr. Brewster and Mary, although that didn't seem like help for a while, and we helped those fugitive slaves. I don't think we just discount that some good happened too," Kim implored them all.

"Ok, Kim, you've got a point, but for the foreseeable future, we don't want anyone else steeling the machines," Ken replied.

"How about if we take them apart and store the parts all over?" Jake asked.

"If we're going to disassemble them, do we need to keep all the parts? I mean, the seats, and all that stuff?" Ryan asked.

"I think this idea has merit. But I agree with Ryan, we probably don't need to keep all the parts. What if we kept the critical parts and computer parts and maybe even left them together and stored them in different places?" Joe thought out loud.

"What about all the documentation?" Becky asked.

"That should probably be a third place," Ken added. "We recently bought some warehouse space, Joe, and there is a large locked closet in there. I have the only key right now. The facility manager suggested it a month ago, that I keep it for more secret invention documentation and materials. I think this qualifies as the first installment to that closet."

"Is it big enough to handle the computer and magnetic field parts?" Joe asked, getting more excited about the plan.

"Yeah, but I think we should crate them all up," Ken answered.

"Ok, so site one for the critical machine parts. Where is the next one going?" Ryan asked.

"We have a barn behind the house. If it's crated up, I think I could ask my father if we can store a big box up in the barn's loft," Becky suggested.

"I'm going to put all the documentation in a box and store it in the closet of this place. I think there's very little chance they will sell this house," Joe said.

"Ok, that takes care of the plan for the machine. No more time travel," Ken concluded.

"Well, no more unless something happens and we need to use it, right?" Kim said, hopefully.

"Let's decide right here that if one of us feels the need to use the machines, we have to all gather and decide as a group. That way, it will tempt no one to just use it," Deb suggested.

"Good idea. Now, it's getting a little late and we have to all get ready," Ken said, as he stood up and gathered up the things they had brought down to the beach.

"When are we going to dismantle the machines?" Ryan asked.

"Don't we have to check with Mr. Brewster?" Kim asked before anyone answered.

"I can't do any of this next weekend. I owe my fiancé here a whole weekend to help with planning. It would have to be two weeks from now for me," Ken said after he had pulled down and wrapped up the two umbrellas.

"Aunt Alicia wants to take us shopping next weekend, Deb," Kim added.

"Well, it looks like two weeks from now, if that's ok with the rest of you not getting married and not going shopping," Joe said, smiling.

"Sounds good to me," Jake said.

"Me, too," Becky said.

They finished packing everything up and trooped up the stairs to the backyard area of the house. They walked up to the terrace and found both Aunt Alicia and Uncle Darrick sitting on the terrace.

"I was just going to come down and get you all," Uncle Darrick said as he stood up when they walked up.

"We knew it was getting kind of late. We're sorry," Deb said.

Aunt Alicia got up and walked up to Deb with her arms outstretched. Deb cautioned her, "Aunt Alicia, I've missed you so, but I'm covered in sunscreen and sand. You probably should wait to hug me."

"I don't care. Come here," she said, smiling.

They hugged while the others headed in to unpack the gear. Uncle Darrick conspiratorially pulled Deb down on the lounge chair. "Good, Kim is gone. We have to fill you in on some plans."

"What plans?" Deb asked.

"First, Mr. Brewster is here in town. He drove down with that car he had been working on for years. He's giving it to Kim," he said.

"Wow, that's a great gift!" she said.

"Hopefully, none of the rest of you are angry about his giving it to her. I think he feels very protective of our little Kim now that the rest of you are gone from Choate," Aunt Alicia said.

"I'm not mad. I doubt Ken or Joe are going to be either. Plus, I like the fact that she's getting this. She's always so sensitive to our doing things she can't yet and this will give her something really special," Deb said.

"Good, I'm glad you feel that way. Now, we have closed off the dining room and the kitchen. Ken knows, so whatever you needed to return to the kitchen he should be handling. We have a cook here making dinner and we decorated the dining room. That's the second thing. Third thing is we brought in her friends and they are all due here in an hour. We had Michael going around and collecting them all day today," Uncle Darrick continued.

"Oh, my gosh! She'll be so happy," Deb exclaimed.

"We hope so," Aunt Alicia added.

"I need you to first confirm she is in her room and you and Becky keep her up there. I've already enlisted Ken and Joe and Jake to help us come down and decorate the terrace. We're setting up some music and we'll do cake and presents out here after dinner. So, we need you to keep her out of the dining room and off the terrace," he explained.

"Ok. I better go make sure she's in her room and shower quick then. I'll check with Becky too," Deb said as she stood up. "I'll send the boys down as soon as I know her status."

Deb went upstairs and knocked first on Kim's door. She opened it when Kim didn't answer and heard her in the shower. She knocked on that door and announced herself and suggested that Kim come to Deb's room when she was ready and bring Becky. Kim agreed. Deb then went to Becky's room and caught her about getting in the shower and told her the plan. Ryan appeared in the hall just as Deb turned from Becky's room.

"Get the guys and go help Uncle Darrick and Aunt Alicia to decorate the terrace. They're waiting and Becky and I are going to entertain Kim until it's time to go down," she explained.

Ryan smiled at her, hugged her quickly, and then turned to go back down the stairs. Deb went and showered and got ready in a speed only rivaled by her quick morning routine on the dig. Just after she finished putting her hair up, there was a knock on the door. Kim and Becky came in and sat on the bed.

"Where's Mary?" Kim asked.

"Oh, I totally forgot to ask her to come here. My gosh, hang on while I go get her," Deb said as she went out into the hall. She knocked on Mary's door and Mary opened it, wearing her robe.

"I can't decide what to wear," Mary said forlornly.

"Come down here, you can pick something from my closet!" Deb said to her and turned back to her room.

They returned to Deb's room and Mary exclaimed, "I'm so excited! I get to pick something designer!"

She opened Deb's closet and started rifling through the clothes there while the other three laughed. Mary turned and looked at them and said, "Oh goodness, I need this. You're all in dresses and I didn't bring a single dress."

Deb got up and helped her find something. She went into Deb's bathroom and changed. She came out, and they all said she looked perfect. They sat down and Deb announced she had two gifts for Kim that she wanted to give her with only the girls around. She went into her dresser and pulled out two small gifts. She handed them to Kim, sitting at the head of Deb's bed. They all turned to her, and she opened the first gift. Kim reached into the first box and pulled out two chains with some kind of charm on them. Deb explained, "These are an ancient family tradition in Israel. The two interlocking circles signify the bond we have as sisters. They come apart like this," Deb said as she took the two chains from Kim and showed her the way to twist them to take them apart. She handed one chain back to Kim as she said, "They signify our bond eternal as sisters and how we will always be closely tied whenever we are together."

Kim was crying when she reached out to hug Deb. Then Mary offered to help Deb put her chain on and Becky helped Kim. They all sat down and sniffled. Then Kim picked up the second box. Again, she carefully opened the box and this time she gasped when she saw what lay inside. She looked up at Deb and said, "Mom left this to you."

"She left all kinds of things to me simply because she did not know what you would want. I know you used to love that necklace and bracelet set and it's right that you should have it," Deb quietly said.

"Kim, they perfectly match your dress!" Becky said when Kim picked up the bracelet from the box.

"You should wear those tonight," Mary said reverently.

Kim got up, holding the box, and stood in front of the mirror on Deb's dresser. She turned slightly and pulled on Deb's hand, pulling her up to a standing position. She handed the box to Deb and said, "Help me, please."

Deb smiled and set the box on the dresser, and took out the necklace. She fastened it around Kim's neck and then she picked up the bracelet and clasped that on Kim's right wrist. The necklace sparkled with diamonds and rubies in the light. Kim had tears running down her cheeks, and Deb wrapped her arms around her from behind. Kim whispered, "Thank you."

"I know Mom would love seeing you nearly all grown up wearing this," Deb said. "It's perfect."

"Splendid gifts, Deb!" Mary said.

"I've been dying to give these to you since I left the first time on the dig. I could barely stand it last night when I got home. I wanted to rush in here and get them," Deb admitted.

"I'm glad you waited. This was really special," Kim said.

Just then, there was a knock on the door. Deb let go of Kim and went to open the door. Ken was standing there, smiling.

"Are you four going to hide in this room all night?" Ken asked, looking at them all, "Why are you crying?"

"Deb gave me the most wonderful gifts, Kenny!" Kim said as she walked up to him and wrapped her arms around his neck, "She gave me Mom's necklace and bracelet that I always loved and a special necklace she had made when she was gone."

"Let me see," Ken said as she pulled away.

She showed him the two necklaces and bracelet and he smiled over her head at Deb. Suddenly, Kim looked up, "What was that?"

"What?" Ken asked, trying to be innocent.

"Who's down there?" Kim said.

"Oh, a few people you know came over to help us celebrate," Ken said, as he looked up, trying to seem like he had no part of the planning.

Kim snuck past him and headed down the stairs. Ken turned back and held out his hand to Mary, who had stood up and the rest of them went down the stairs to the sound of Kim squealing.

Uncle Darrick and Aunt Alicia came out from the office when the noise started and smiled at the kids crowding the foyer. At some point, Ken, Mary, Deb, Ryan, Joe, and Becky retreated to the dining room. Aunt Alicia tried to get the kids' attention to no avail. Uncle Darrick whistled, and that stopped the chatter. He announced that dinner was ready and then directed them to the dining room. Kim got the head of the table, and she smiled when she saw Mr. Brewster there with Ken and Mary. They all sat and a team of servers began bringing in the food. There were several courses, all containing Kim's favorite foods. Everyone enjoyed the meal and then Aunt Alicia stood and announced that cake and presents were on the terrace. Mr. Brewster stood at that point and said, "Well, all but one present is on the terrace. I couldn't get my gift out there for some reason."

Kim got up and went to him. He took her hand and walked out of the dining room, when he turned and asked, "Is this ok that I go first?"

"Of course, but all the gifts will now pale by comparison," Uncle Darrick said as everyone got up to follow them.

They walked out to the front steps, and Mr. Brewster waited to see if Kim would notice the car at the bottom of the steps. When she did, she looked at him, and smiled the biggest smile she had ever had. He reached into his pocket and produced a key chain. He held it out and waited for her to hold out her hand. Then he dropped the keys into her hand.

"It's for me? Mr. Brewster, it's so nice! I love the color," Kim asked.

"It's for you. You the youngest, who has waited all this time to be grown up," he said.

"Thank you, Mr. Brewster, for everything!" Kim said as she turned to see Jake approaching.

"Not sure I'm gonna like my girlfriend having a cooler car than I do," he said as he smiled at Kim.

"You'll have to get used to it, because I'm not giving you up," Kim said, grabbing his hand.

"Does that mean you're giving up the car?" he joked.

"Not on your life!" she said.

After a few minutes of everyone admiring the car, Jake suggested she go in and open the rest of her gifts and go for a ride later. Kim liked that idea. She took a moment to thank Mr. Brewster and say goodbye as he was leaving. Then they all went in and were led out to the terrace where Kim jumped at the site of all the lights and decoration. She sat and opened gifts for nearly an hour, but then they had cake and Joe started the music. Uncle Darrick and Aunt Alicia left the party in Ken's hands and went to bed.

A few hours later, the guests, all worn out, slept all over the place. The next morning, the cook made a huge breakfast and Michael took all the guest's home. Joe left to take Becky and Jake home, while Ken left with Mary so they could be in town for work the next day. Kim spent the rest of the day painting on the terrace while Ryan and Deb walked into town.

26

After the shopping on Saturday, Deb suggested they all take a drive out to Gettysburg to see if they could find Tom's grave. Ryan had still been struggling, and she thought this might help. Becky thought this was a great idea, so along with Kim, they piled into Ryan's car and drove out of the city. It took most of the rest of the day to arrive in Gettsyburg, so they stayed in a hotel that Deb had arranged for and had dinner at a little pizza place in town. Then, Sunday, they found a church to attend services at and drove out to the burial field of Gettsyburg. Joe and Becky veered off from Ryan and Deb and Kim for a moment alone, but after twenty minutes, Kim came running up to tell them Deb had found Tom's marker. Joe and Becky followed Kim back to where Deb and Ryan were standing.

"I'm surprised we found him," Becky said as she stood in front of the white cross.

"It doesn't have a birth year on it, like some others," Kim said, "but there are a bunch of markers that don't have birth years. I guess Tom wasn't the only one here where they didn't know when the person was born."

"Some soldiers here had traveled and fought for months and even years before this battle," Deb said. "I'm surprised all these markers have names on them, actually."

"Some don't. Where Becky and I were, there were a bunch that were just noted with union or confederate on the stone and the date of this battle," Joe added solemnly.

They all stood there quietly for a long time. Each pondering their own thoughts about being where Tom had been buried over a hundred years ago. Finally, Ryan said, "It seems strange. We know who he is, but all the tourists and all the people that pass through here have no idea. They stand here and just think, 'oh, another soldier that died that day'. They do not know who he was."

They stood silent for some time and then Deb suggested they leave so they could make it back early in the evening.

Two weeks later, after wedding plans continued to be made, shopping was done, the Gettysburg visit complete, and everyone gearing up for a return to school, the group made their return to Mr. Brewster's. Joe brought Becky, Ryan and Deb brought Kim and Jake and Ken brought Mary. They all assembled at the worn table they spent so many hours discussing, planning and digesting the time travel they had done for years. Joe explained their plan to disassemble the machines and store the parts they intended to keep. Mr. Brewster agreed his barn was no longer a safe place, and he agreed they should dismantle them for now.

So, the work began. While the group started to take apart the magnetic field parts and the computer parts from inside both machines, Ken and Mr. Brewster went and picked up all kinds of boards, and then Jake and Ryan built two large crates. By the time they built the crates, the parts were ready to pack away. They stopped for the day at that point and sat again at the table. Joe looked around the table at each of them. Mr. Brewster smiled and said, "So, we have come to the end."

"Not the end, Mr. Brewster. In some ways, it's the beginning," Joe said. "Remember when we started? We were a mess. After being dropped here when we lost our parents, we didn't really know how to deal with each other, let alone this big secret. But you all had faith in me. Thank you."

"Given this year, I'm surprised we weren't more scared, but honestly, what we were doing didn't seem all that scary back then. It seemed like we were deciding to work together to save them," Deb reflected.

"The scary came later. When you all tried to take matters into your own hands. When Joe went on a solo mission, and then you and Ryan went to stop his mission, and everyone got hurt," Ken added, "but there was some good, wasn't there?"

"We helped Mr. Brewster!" Kim exclaimed.

"Then my foolish trip," Mary said, "And all the pain that came from that."

"Yeah, I'd rather forget that trip," Ken said, reaching for Mary's hand.

"Then Joe went to jail, and we almost got caught," Becky said. "That was a big year."

"It sure was. We had to reveal our secret that year. Uncle Darrick helped us, but then we had to help him," Deb added.

"And then this. When someone who hated us so much found out our secret and took the machine," Joe said.

"This could have been so much worse than it was, Joe. I mean, it took a while to catch him, but remember, we kept him from changing history. What, three times?" Deb protested.

"It was four, counting the Civil War attempt. I know we stopped him, but it took a sizeable chunk out of all our lives, and we ended up with this even bigger secret. Tom's death," Joe continued.

"But, Joe, like Deb said, you stopped him from transforming history. After all the times we had tiny minor changes, we had to fix. Can you imagine the nightmare of fixing his messes?" Ryan offered in support for Deb.

"True. I just wish it could have ended differently," Joe lamented.

"I think, Joe, there was no other way for this to end with Tom. He was filled with rage and misguided in his aim. I also believe he wouldn't have stopped. If you hadn't located the machine he took, he would have kept at it. As you pointed out, you lost a big part of this summer. Imagine if he got away from Gettysburg. You would still be at it," Mr. Brewster suggested. "No one should die like that, but keep in mind, there are good people in this world and there are those bent on evil and misdeeds. Tom was the latter."

"I guess," Joe concluded.

"What are you doing with all the metal?" Jake asked.

"I don't know," Joe replied.

"My suggestion is the scrap yard," Mr. Brewster said. "If you decide you need to resurrect the machines, you can always go back to the scrap yard and start afresh."

"I think that's a good idea," Ken said, getting up, "but we should do that tomorrow morning before we head out."

They all got up and went into town. Ken got them all rooms at the hotel and they went out for dinner and then went to the bowling alley. The next morning, they returned to Mr. Brewster's and made two trips, taking the metal parts of the machines to the scrap yard. Then they bid Mr. Brewster goodbye and started on their way back home.

Two weeks later, Ken went out to Long Island on a Saturday morning to see Deb, Joe, and Kim. It was their last weekend before Deb and Joe returned to college, and three weeks before Kim headed back to Choate. Ken pondered how far they'd come as he drove down the driveway. He parked near the blue mustang that was now Kim's car. He smiled as he headed inside. They spent the day at the beach again. The kite was out, and the water was warm. They lay there and played and had a great day. Ken suggested they have a barbeque on the beach and he and Joe went and gathered the wood while Kim and Deb went and got food. After they cooked and ate, they sat there looking at the water. Even though the sun was setting behind them, the light was reflecting on the ocean and making it pink. Ken looked at his siblings and said, "I wouldn't have our lives any other way, you guys. When Mom and Dad died, all I could think is that I wanted my old life back. Now, I know this is how it should be. This was always the plan. I am the person I am because of you three."

"We belong like this," Deb said, smiling and laying back to look at the stars beginning to appear in the darkening sky.

"I'm so thankful you guys trusted me and stood by me," Joe added.

"I love how you all have taken care of me. And let me help on things," Kim said, then added, "Do you think Mom and Dad can see us now?"

"I hope so," Ken said.

"I believe they are watching us all the time. I hope they're proud of what we've done," Deb whispered.

"I think about that all the time. Wishing they were seeing what we've done, how we are. I like to think they're proud of all of us," Joe added quietly.

"We need to come back here often," Deb added.

"This feels like home now, doesn't it?" Ken pondered.

They laid there, all silent with their thoughts, until the sun totally set and it was dark around them. Ken stood and gathered their things by the light of a nearly full moon. As they finished cleaning up, they began walking to the stairs to take them to the backyard.

"Will we ever time travel again?" Kim asked.

Ken smiled. He knew Kim was always going to look for ways to help others, and he liked that about her. He replied as he took her hand, "You never know what the future will bring."

They put their beach things away and headed up the stairs. As Ken laid his head down that night, he said a little prayer. He thanked his parents for all the preparation they gave him and he fell asleep with a smile for all his siblings.

27

AUTHOR'S NOTES

As with any work of fiction, authors take some license to use factual information to help tell the story. I am guilty of this as well. However, I would like to take this moment to give credit where credit is because of those people, dates, accomplishments, and events.

Choate Rosemary Hall is an actual boarding preparatory school located in Wallingford, Connecticut. It was founded as Rosemary Hall for girls in 1890 by Mary Atwater Choate. Later, a boys' school was added, the girls' school relocated and then returned to the original location. It became a Co-Ed School in the 1970s. President John F. Kennedy, and many other famous people, attended throughout its history. Several of the buildings named here are actual buildings at Choate. However, the inclusion of younger children Kim's age and various aspects of the schedule, buildings, and activities are my creation. You can learn more about this wonderful school at: www.choate.edu.

Time travel is theoretical. The theory of bending time has been in academia for many years. The idea that time is not a linear concept, but a plane that can be bent with magnetic fields and energy, is widely recognized as a valid theory. What is known about two people being in the same space and time continuum and what one would know if you jumped forward in time are also mainstream academic theories. In this installment of Time Benders, the siblings and their friends travel again to the past. The idea that one can make a simple change in the past and have it trickle through many lives and events is also a big part of time travel theories. I have used this information to make assumptions and create the possibility that time travel can be accomplished, but to date, no machine has ever been created and no actual live tests have been documented of time travel.

Vogue magazine has been in production since 1892. It became the premier fashion magazine later in the 1960s. Grace Mirabella was, in fact, the editor of Vogue during the time period of this story. Several of the people and places mentioned related to Vogue are factual. However, Aunt Alicia being employed there and her activities are fictional.

The Wharton Brook State Park is an actual park near Wallingford, CT. This park opened August 1, 1919, and was the precursor to modern highway rest stops. It has evolved over the years and offers fishing, picnicking, swimming, and several footpaths. Unfortunately, in 2018, a small tornado transitioned into a microburst and caused extensive damage to the park, causing it to close for the rest of the year. It re-opened in January 2019.

The stock market crash of 1929 that led to the great depression actually began with great expansion of the stock markets. In fact, in the early part of 1929 the stock prices soared. People had become very accustomed to buying stocks and bonds from the war bonds sold during World War I. In addition, a new concept, buying stock on margin had grown in use. This allowed for stock purchases with little to no money. All of this buying increased both the volume and prices on the exchanges. By the summer of 1929 the Dow Jones average had moved to its highest point, 381 and nearly 300 million shares were carried on margin. Then in late September and into October, the prices began to fall. This created panic as all those shares bought on margin lost their value. The first big sell off began on October 18. The real start of the panic began on October 24, known as Black Thursday. It didn't stop there, as there was a Black Monday and a Black Tuesday. By the time the dust settled, the market had gone from 381 to below 30. The stock market did not rise above 200 again for twenty years. While it is true the crash made many lose all they had, if you had seen all of this coming, or perhaps had a time machine, you could have used this information to buy and sell at the right times and made a lot of money even in this crash. Not many did, however.

The early 1900's saw great invention and innovation. One of these inventions was the combustion engine. The first patent for a combustion engine was filed by George B. Seldon in 1897. However, there other players in this industry and a patent battle ensued. This created the Association of Licensed Automobile Manufacturers. This organization then charged every car company a fee for the use of the parts created by these patents. Henry Ford at some point decided he was done paying this fee and in 1903 a patent infringement suite was filed against him. Over the next 8 years, Henry Ford battled George Seldon and although the first trial upheld the patent, the appeals court ruled that the ford engine was four-cylinder combustion and the Seldon engine was two-cylinders so they were not in conflict. Henry Ford won, and George Seldon was sent into obscurity. Tom Thornton is a fictional character, and so is his great-grandfather, Reginald.

The War of 1812 was a war began to teach the fledgling United States some lessons. The British made quick headway in this attack but could not breach Fort McHenry located in the Baltimore Bay. As was the practice during this time, prisoners were often held on ships off the coast and negotiations were frequently undertaken to win the release of these prisoners. Francis Scott Key was an attorney from Baltimore that was engaged in such negotiations during the attack of the fort. He was on a ship in the bay. Because he was there, the British would not allow him to leave while they were preparing for and beginning their attack for fear, he would reveal information to the American troops. Therefore, he watched the battle from the deck of a British ship. It was during that time that he wrote a poem that was originally titled The Defense of Fort McHenry. It was printed in papers and put to a popular tune of that time and became a battle cry of the American forces and supporters. After the attempt to attack the fort from the water, the British determined a land entry would be successful due to the weak defenses on that side of the fort. A British commander led a small group for a landing to infiltrate the fort and somehow the Americans found out this plan. A sniper was placed high on ridge on the river Patapsco. This sniper managed to hit the commander and repel the attempt to land. Ultimately, this caused confusion with the ships in the harbor and they abandoned their efforts to take Fort McHenry.

Gettysburg was the greatest battle of the Civil War. More Americans lost their lives in this several days of fighting than in any other war where Americans were involved. Over several days, from late June until July 3rd, battles occurred all around Gettysburg and Carlisle. One of the confederate Generals involved was Richard Ewell. General Ewell was trained at West Point, where he graduated 13th in his class of 1840. He began his military career in the Mexican-American War. In early 1861 he resigned his commission with the US Army and joined Virginia Army when the Civil War began. He was known for some level of indecisiveness and was frequently chastised in the news for his lack of drive against the Union troops. In Gettysburg, he had much success in the battles around Carlisle, but again, he chose to rest his troops rather than push on to Gettysburg, which allowed the Union Army to fortify its position and take up critical position on Cemetery Hill. Many war strategists have theorized that if Ewell had pushed on to Gettysburg, the Confederates likely would have won the battle and pushed on to Washington D.C.

Other references to movies, dates, events in the book are occasionally adapted for use in the story and do not represent actual release dates or actual dates when certain events took place.

JB Yanni, author of the Time Benders time traveling adventure science fiction series, ready with a smile at any time, and beach-lover. Surrounded by a boisterous but loving family, she began writing during her teens on newspapers and her high school yearbook. Always searching for creative outlets, JB painted, drew and created her whole life, but found writing novels later in life. A great collector of books, JB believes that a book can change you, move you and become a lifelong friend. Her favorite quote, "Reading is the sole means by which we slip, involuntarily, often helplessly, into another's skin, another's voice, another's soul," Joyce Carol Oates.

JB can usually be found with a book or her Kindle in her hands, reading, when she is not writing. Her motto - "In my utopia, books are free, and reading makes you thin!"

You can contact JB via Facebook - jb_yanni; twitter - @jb_yanni; email - jb@jbyanni.com

www.ingramcontent.com/pod-product-compliance
Lightning Source LLC
Chambersburg PA
CBHW072040150726
47996CB00014B/104